Enduring Promise

CAN LOVE WITHSTAND THE TRIALS OF FIDELITY?

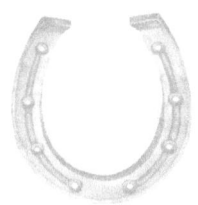

Enduring Promise

CAN LOVE WITHSTAND THE TRIALS OF FIDELITY?

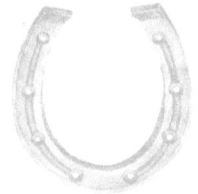

SUSANNA LANE

WESTERN WRITERS OF AMERICA SPUR AWARD WINNER

HAT CREEK

HAT CREEK

An Imprint of Roan & Weatherford Publishing Associates, LLC
Bentonville, Arkansas
www.roanweatherford.com

Library of Congress Cataloging-in-Publication Data
Names: Lane, Susanna, author
Title: Enduring Promise/Susanna Lane | Promises #2
Description: First Edition. | Bentonville: Hat Creek, 2024.
Identifiers: LCCN: 2024943241 | ISBN: 978-1-63373-979-6 (trade paperback) |
ISBN: 978-1-63373-980-2 (eBook)
Subjects: | BISAC: FICTION/Romance/Western | FICTION/Western | FICTION/Women
LC record available at: https://lccn.loc.gov/2024943241

Hat Creek trade paperback edition October, 2024

Cover & Interior Design by Casey W. Cowan
Editing by Staci Troilo & Rachel Santino

To my supporters, I cannot thank you enough. You are my listeners, advisors, and truth-tellers . . . honest opinions that so many shy from but I embrace.

I am grateful and thankful for my dear friend and fellow writer, Deborah Swenson, who is the perfect listener and guide. Her spirit and kindness mean more than she can ever know.

K.S. Jones is fearless, brilliant, and charitable of heart. When I need a friend, she's there with her wisdom.

Finally, I'd like to hope my deceased parents are smiling down at my following my heart with bravery and determination. They taught me to embrace my talent whether found in my heart or head; or both. And that's what I've done. Love you always.

PREFACE

WITH REGARD TO *Enduring Promise,* please note, as in all my works, the characters are fictitious, having been placed in the context of the story scenes. Any of the characters' names are strictly part of my imagination, and any similarities to real life are coincidental. I stay true to research for setting and backdrop, using accurate details unless it is necessary to embellish them in terms of storyline or events. A few geographical locations are nonexistent or altered in description to accommodate the storyline.

As to the writing of a story, there are some key features I adhere to. First, I always write from research and outline. I never begin a story without first having an eye on historical background, if for no other reasons than plotting and realism.

One of my chief tasks is to flesh out characters so that they are believable. Along with that, every character is flawed or has had a problematic background, thus promoting emotion and drama while keeping the pages turning.

Writing dialogue that is real, especially within the setting and time period, is certainly one of the most important things for an author to achieve. And I'm a stickler for crisp POV and use third person so that there is freedom to invite DPOV into character development.

Where do my ideas come from? That is a question often asked and most authors cannot tell you. Why? Because much of an author's personal experience is already built before the story reaches the writing stage. Also, an author is able to step outside of the box and solve problems. In real life, we have little or no control over the endings.

In terms of historical western writing, survival, bravery, and determination are universal themes. In the case of my "Promise" series, each backstory revolves around a core theme with several common themes.

In *Imperfect Promise,* courage, sacrifice, and honor are at the forefront. In *Enduring Promise,* courage, fidelity, and determination illuminate the main characters. *Lasting* portrays the characters as brave but sacrifice and jealousy loom large. And in *Distance Between Stars,* courage, sacrifice, and final surrender are overriding themes.

ONE

FORBIDDEN PROMISE

May 1878
Ogallala, Nebraska

"WHO DID YOU say you was lookin' for?"

Bryce kept his eyes on the bartender's hands as they drifted out of sight. It had been a simple question, and he sure wasn't thinking he'd meet a shotgun for his trouble. Damn. Bryce Cairn Enders hadn't gotten off at this Ogallala train stop to wind up shot. All he wanted was a couple of whiskeys and be on his way. Instead, it seemed he might have stumbled onto what he'd been looking for.

"Said I was wonderin' if there was an Enders around these parts?" Bryce lowered his whiskey but kept his eyes on the broad, beefy man. Just in case things went wrong, he dropped his gun hand to his holster as slick as he could manage.

"Who needs to know?" The barkeep raised one bushy eyebrow, but the man's hands were still hidden. A fair enough warning. The loud voices quieted, and a piano tune drowned the hushed mutters. The man sure seemed prickly at the mention of the Enders name. If he had to hazard a guess, it would have something to do with newspaper articles about his infamous brother.

No sense in beating around the bush. "I'm his brother. Name's Bryce. Been looking for him. Just about gave up till now."

Bryce flattened both of his palms against the scarred wood and waited, signaling he didn't want any trouble. The bartender's bunched shoulders relaxed, and his hands returned to wiping down a spill. "Well, now. Didn't know Cort had a brother. Never said. You come to the right place. Everbody knows Cort and his family around here. You should've just come out with it."

Bryce unclenched his teeth and ran a hand over the ache in his jaw. He figured no sense in arguing the point now that he'd escaped a dangerous situation. He just accepted his good fortune. The next question only Cort could answer. Whether his brother wanted to set eyes on him after all these years. He'd left his little brother behind and gone off to war. Trouble was, Cort followed him into that bloody mess and neither his sister nor brother were anywhere to be found once he'd made it back to Virginia. His parents lay buried in the back of their run-down house.

"Can you tell me how to find him?"

"The Double E land starts about ten miles outta town to the southwest. But it takes almost two days to get out to the house. Gotta big spread. Used to be the Harris place. Far as I know, he set up a nice little halfway place. Sure he won't mind you stayin' there for the night."

"Thanks. Just might do that, after I pick up my horse and gear. By the way, you gotta name?"

"Jim."

Bryce lifted his hat from the bar and turned, pausing midstep at Jim's gravelly voice.

"Surely is a surprise he has anybody exceptin' his wife and baby. You best keep watch. His men are a mite twitchy about uninvited guests on Enders's land."

Grinning, Bryce swiped a hand across his beard. The thought never occurred that his own brother wouldn't recognize him. But, in point of fact, he might even get his head blown off before they said a word between them. He hadn't come all this way to turn tail and besides, they had things to settle between them. Without looking over his shoulder, he called out, "Much obliged."

TWO

GUNFIRE WELCOME

THE MORNING SUN burned across the sky in an explosion of yellow streaks as Bryce nudged his buckskin, Hunter, alongside what appeared to be a wagon trail. This had to be the ranch supply route. Couldn't hurt to follow it awhile, then take to the ridges for a better view. From time to time he came across some rangy-looking Herefords mixed in with longhorns. The grass spread out in endless green waves, giving way to rock outcroppings. An occasional stand of cottonwoods and willows dotted the banks of the river where he'd camped last night. No doubt, he'd be discovered before long. That fact and Jim's warning necessitated keeping his rifle handy and his eyes open.

Leaving the worn wagon trail, he nudged his horse into a climb to reach the top of a windswept rise, his boots raking through tall switch grass. Once there, his gaze searched the expanse of grassland. The Double E land soothed his soul like smooth bourbon, and he understood why his brother had settled on this land. The how and why of it niggled and momentarily struck him with more than a little envy.

Just as he stood in the stirrups and stretched his weary muscles, a shot rang out and his horse jerked at the bit. Reining his mount, he scanned the horizon, looking for signs of the shooter. Then a second shot cut the air. Bryce nudged his horse down slope and headed in the direction of the shots, hoping to set eyes on the culprit. Good cowhands didn't fire shots unless there was trouble. Bawling and rumbling let him know he was too late to stop a stampede.

Skirting the dust stirred by about a hundred running cattle, he squinted to locate the shooter. Following the wagon trail, he looked skyward at the buzzards circling against the blue sky. Nudging his horse forward, he came upon a cow laying in its own blood, the animal's long tongue hanging from its mouth... blood dripping onto the grass, the bloodstained hide twitching. Bryce dismounted and eyed the gouged flesh that had been hastily hacked away, leaving the rest of the carcass to rot. Who would kill one cow and leave the rest of the meat?

At the sound of pounding hooves coming his way, he looked across his shoulder. A string of scowling men rode toward him, and he was clearly their target. In the opposite direction, a rider disappeared into a gully and then out of view. Watchful, Bryce eased back into his saddle and gripped his rifle. The chance he might be able to cut off the sona-fabitch who'd put him in this position was now lost. And judging from the glares approaching him, guns drawn, they most likely weren't of a mind to hear him out. He wouldn't outrun them. Besides, he'd get a hole in his back if he tried.

They encircled him, their faces shadowed beneath broad brimmed hats. With their guns aimed, Bryce had to admit he looked as guilty as hell with his rifle gripped in his hand. Facing ten furious cowhands, he didn't think they'd give him time to defend himself before either hanging him or dragging him to death. The scarcity of trees determined his fate.

"You drop that rifle, mister," shouted an older man with a scruffy white beard.

Pegging him as the leader in a foul mood, Bryce leaned to the side and lowered his rifle to the ground. "Mind if I step down?"

"Soon as you drop that gun belt beside that fine rifle."

Nodding, he unbuckled his belt and dropped it to the ground beside his rifle. Now that he was unarmed, he figured it best to start explaining. But just as he thought it, a high-pitched singing cut the air, then a painful thud struck him with enough force to send his horse rearing. Unseated, he slammed onto the ground, the impact knocking the breath from his lungs. It took him a minute to blink clear his vision and suck in air, only to realize he'd been roped. Being dragged into a bloody pulp was the verdict he'd wanted to escape.

The rope jerked him flat onto his belly. He grasped the taut end and lifted his head, hoping death would hit him quick. Pain shot through his ribs and gut as he was hauled over rocks and tough switch grass, all the while trying to keep his head from slamming into the hard dirt. He heard the sound of a horse skidding from nearby. That's when his body stilled and the rope fell slack, giving him time to suck in air and spit out grit. From one corner of his eye, he saw the legs of the armed men surrounding him. Lifting his head, he saw their eyes were focused on someone out of his view.

"What the hell is goin' on here?" shouted a man with a hoarse voice.

Whoever it was had given him a reprieve, and he used the time to try and twist his body over to get a look at the man who was obviously in charge.

"We caught the damned cow killer, boss," someone hollered.

The sound of jangling spurs closed in beside him. He blinked away some of the dust in his eyes and managed to ease onto his side, wincing with pain. His eyes trailed upward, following the length of blue pants and dusty boots, until settling on the man standing over him. The sun from above the stranger's hat blinded him. Tensing his gut, he hoped a kick to his midsection wouldn't break a rib or worse. Expecting a strike, he gritted his teeth. Instead, the man asked a question that the others hadn't.

"That true? You killed my cow and all the others?"

Bryce coughed and spit. "Nope. Just riding through when I heard shots. Found the dead cow."

"That so? Looks like you had a rifle out."

Bryce cleared his throat. "Check it. Shells still in it. I saw the killer and was about to go after him. Until these men roped me."

Saddle leather creaked. After a moment, one of the men said, "He's right. Nothing fired from his rifle. Might be tellin' the truth, Cort."

Cort. Christ. My brother. Bryce wrenched against the rope and tried to get to his feet. Strong hands gripped his arms and lifted him to his knees and then the lasso was yanked free. From behind, someone helped him stand, steadying him while he scowled at each one of the riders.

"Take it easy. Sure am sorry about this, mister. The least I owe you is a hot meal and maybe a bandage or two. My men were a bit too anxious to find the cow killer we've been tracking," Cort said.

Bryce straightened and shrugged from the gloved hands still clutching his arms. His long-lost brother stood in front of him, taking him in. Swiping his face with his torn sleeve, he studied the piercing gray eyes looking back. Cort was shorter but he'd filled out into a rangy, broad-shouldered man. The intent, pursed mouth, and hardness of his study were marks of a man who didn't hold much trust in those he didn't know. That might've come from experience that wasn't all good. His stubble looked to be about two days' growth, telling him that his brother worked as hard as his men and just as long. The creases around his eyes suggested he'd spent a fair share of time in the sun. The newspaper articles about his exploits were most likely true, judging from the look of him.

"Looks like you got a cut on that cheek. And maybe a few more above your belt. We'll get you tended to," Cort said.

There was a penetrating stare without recognition, as far as he could tell. "I've had worse. A few scratches won't kill me. Just glad you got here when you did."

"Like I said. I'm sorry and I'll try to make up for it."

"Hey, boss. You want us to go see if we can track that rider that took off? Like *he* said?" Tangle asked. Cort turned toward the men as though he'd almost forgotten they were still there.

"You and Damon see if you can figure out where that killer got to. One other thing, Tangle. Don't do any crowding of whoever it is. Take some men out again tomorrow. At least we know he can't be far. And probably be back."

"Here's your rifle, son."

Bryce snatched the gun from the white-haired old man's hands. There was an amused twinkle in his blue eyes, though he couldn't figure what the man found mirthful about this situation. The more he thought about almost being dragged to death, the angrier he got.

"Thanks." Bryce spat on the ground. "My gunbelt."

A second man handed it to him and backed away. Bryce strapped it on and then looked toward the men sitting their horses, his jaw hard. There was nothing he wanted to say to them. He had the right to be pissed off.

"Surely am sorry, fella. Your horse is settled. Best leave you and Cort here to discuss this situation. Name's Zeke if you need me. Guess we'll be seein' you back at the ranch house. The meal Lark puts together will heal a spirit faster than whiskey."

Without a last backward glance, Zeke mounted and kicked his horse into an easy lope, waving his hat in farewell, his snow-white hair blowing behind him. The others followed, leaving him and Cort alone.

For now, it was time to focus his attention on his brother and all the changes since the war. All he remembered was the skinny kid with a dirty face, begging to go along. Apparently, the same recollection still hadn't dawned for Cort. He stood beside his brother, both watching the men riding into the distance, giving them space to hash out the matter at hand. There was more to this *situation* than any of those cowhands could imagine.

"That cowboy, Zeke? Called this a situation. What do you call it?" Bryce asked.

"I'd call it a case of mistaken identity. And like I said, I'd like to make it up to you."

"If you want to make up for this, I'll gladly take that hot meal. And a job, if you got one." *Christ.* How did he come up with *that* idea? He hadn't herded cattle in years. What did a gold miner turned train guard know about working a ranch? Sure, he'd chased a few cows in Texas. But that had been a lot of years ago.

Cort peeled off his work glove and extended his open hand. With a firm shake, they watched one another. His brother's strong grip reminded him that out here, a man's handshake counted as a deal—guess he'd just been hired.

"That I can do. Maybe we can start with exchanging names. This is the Double E Ranch you're standing on. I'm Cort Enders, the owner. And what might your name be?"

"No might about it. Name's Bryce Enders. Though didn't expect our reunion to be quite this momentous. Maybe you got a shirt you can spare, while you're at it. Looks like one of yours will fit since we're still about the same size."

Cort's eyes widened at that revelation, then his jaw dropped. He looked as though he'd seen a ghost and was more than rattled by it. Their gazes locked. Disbelief flickered across his brother's eyes before they squeezed closed and opened again. A quick grin told Bryce it had sunk in. Throwing back his head, Cort laughed.

"I can't believe what I'm seein'."

"Good to see you again, little brother," Bryce finally managed to squeeze out of his raw throat. "The years changed us both."

Cort swallowed. "Jesus Christ! What the hell? Why didn't you tell me right off? I ought to...."

Whatever his brother was about to say died before spoken. "And spoil the shocked look on your handsome face? Ma always did say you were the better looking, depending on what trouble we were in that day."

There were no words left for either of them. Cort's Adam's apple bobbed in his throat. In spite of their age, the two brothers embraced. Looking across his brother's shoulder, Bryce saw the row of mounted cowmen, keeping watch. Seemingly satisfied, they turned and disappeared from sight.

After a time, he and Cort mounted their horses and they walked their mounts in the direction of the main house, this time firing question after question at each other. There were too many subjects between them that gave way to even more. But now they had time to sort out the years.

———————

LARK BUSIED HERSELF, heaping platters with potatoes and beef in celebration of the Enders family reunion. She listened to snatches of Cort's conversation with his brother while little Bryce Wade wriggled on his proud papa's lap.

"Looks like he keeps you pretty busy," Bryce said between bites. "Good-lookin' boy. He has the Enders eyes and our dark hair. When you have a little girl, she'll be a beauty like her mother, little brother."

"Guess I'll have to fight off the wild bunch working my cows," Cort replied between chews while he forked meat into his mouth. "You gotta learn how to eat and hold a baby at the same time around here."

Little Bryce squirmed and stretched his chubby arms toward his uncle, who set his coffee down and leaned back in the chair. Cort handed the baby to Bryce. She couldn't help but notice how Bryce appeared to tense until his bundle curled against him and sucked his thumb.

Bryce looked toward Lark. "Don't know how you do it. House, cooking, baby."

"You'll meet Theresa and Nita. That's how. In fact, it's almost bedtime for the baby and Theresa will be in to put little Bryce down for the night. Don't know what we'd do without their help."

"I can see where you need the help."

Cort cleared his throat. "They work alongside my wife. We think of them as family. Zeke, Theresa, and Nita... they've been here longer than we have. You'll get to know them. They're in and out of the kitchen most of the day. Or down at the cookhouse."

"I'll make a point of learning who everyone is," Bryce said. "Introduce myself when I see them."

"Word travels fast among the men. They're already gabbing about Bryce Enders." Cort looked over his brother's head and winked in her direction. The discomfiture in her brother-in-law's eyes gradually faded. She was a bit more confident he'd settle into his role as an uncle. Listening to their conversations gave her time to draw comparisons between the two men. It was easy to see the same gray-blue eyes hid most of what they were thinking.

Bryce was broader in the shoulders and slightly taller. His sun-browned skin suggested he'd worked outdoors, yet Cort mentioned he hadn't worked as a rancher. What had brought him to their doorstep? That thought niggled. Why now? What had he been doing all this time?

"Well. What do you think, Lark? My brother seems to be able to put our son right off to sleep. Might come in handy."

Lark smiled at her husband's rare grin that always melted her like hot butter. "Depends on how long he plans to stay around. We could sure use help with little Bryce and everything else."

"Already asked him to stay on. He's got a job as long as he wants it."

"And what did he say?" Lark joined the teasing while she watched Bryce's eyes fasten on their little boy, pressing a slobbery thumb against his uncle's shirt.

Bryce looked up. "After I give thought to it. Leaning to stay on for the short term."

They'd given him little time to clean up, let alone form decisions, before Cort whisked his brother into the office for a private conversation. Lark had sent her husband a disapproving scowl when she'd seen how roughed up Bryce looked when he arrived. Cort allowed her a nod and whispered, "Later." Well, she'd darn well find out how those cuts and torn shirt had happened. Even if she had to go down to the cookhouse to get in on the men's gossip.

Theresa walked into the kitchen and lifted the sleeping bundle away from Bryce's lap and Lark smiled at how his shoulders relaxed, like a relieved man who'd faced down an Indian attack and chased them off. "Thank you, Theresa."

"Time for him to be in bed." Holding the baby, Theresa added with a pointed look in Bryce's direction, "I'll see you here for supper, tomorrow. Heard you was staying on. Nothing fancy around here. Anything special you need to eat, you came to the wrong place."

The door to the big kitchen closed, leaving a stunned expression on Bryce's face and the distinct sound of the woman's throaty chuckle from the hallway. Lark hadn't taken the time to warn Bryce about Theresa's directness. Three adults were left seated around the table with a silence as thick as churned milk.

"You'll get used to Theresa," Lark said.

"Sure will. I guess."

Lark looked from one to the other. Where did anyone start? There were so many questions, Lark could hardly imagine where her husband would begin. In fact, he'd probably already shot off a number of questions on the way back from wherever the incident had occurred. And they'd holed up in Cort's office a while.

Bryce spoke first. "In answer to your question, Lark. Yes. I'll be staying on for right now. But as I told Cort, I don't plan to take up space in your house. I'll bunk down with the other cowhands and earn my keep."

"Cort? You agreed to that?" Lark turned her attention to her husband. He set down his coffee before it got as far as his mouth.

"He's a grown man. He can decide what he wants to do."

Bryce swiped his mouth, seeming to consider his answer.

"I appreciate the offer, Lark. So you understand. I'm not about to start living in this big house. Just not used to having folks wait on me. In fact, I'm not used to anything this fine."

"Fair enough. As long as you come up to this *big* house, as you put it, to have a meal and get to know us all. Whenever you want. You're family," Lark reminded him.

"Sure. I can do that. Especially if you put out that apple pie. Best I've ever had."

"I can't take all the credit for that. Theresa is far better at baking."

"I'll have to say I haven't eaten this well in a long time."

In that moment, his eyes skimmed over her scar and settled there for a moment, leaving a familiar sting of shame she'd managed to hide... time and time again, over the years. To his credit, he hadn't asked outright about her disfigurement, but she wasn't fool enough to think he wouldn't eventually find out. Very few openly mentioned it. When it happened, Cort was quick to set folks straight about minding their own business, in words that made her blush.

"Guess you need to have some questions answered," Bryce said, breaking into her inward musings. His attention returned to the mug of coffee that she was refilling as he spoke. "Cort and I haven't seen each other since the war started. He told me he followed after me when I left.

Sure as hell didn't know he had. Our pa was shot right off. I was near him. Said he would make it home to die."

He pinched the bridge of his nose before continuing. "By the time the conflict was all over, I headed back to the homestead in Virginia, thinking my brother, sister, and mother were probably down to the last bit of food they'd scrounged up. I'd been shot up and lay in a field hospital for weeks. Thankfully, I got some *good* nursing."

He paused and winced at something crossing his mind. Recognizing pain in his expression, whatever happened... it had been life-changing.

"Thought I'd find my little brother and we'd head off together. Take him along to Texas. Turns out, Cort wasn't there. My mother was buried out back beside my father. Our sister, Nora, was gone. One of the old ladies from the local church said she'd married a wanderer and they didn't know anything more. So, I sold the land to the squatters and made my own way to Texas. Didn't know what else to do. Didn't know how to find Cort to give him his share of the four hundred dollars I got for the place. Figured I might be able to work some land in Texas. Build something."

"How did you finally find me here?" Cort asked.

"Stopped in Ogallala and asked the bartender if he'd ever heard of you. Jim was mighty protective."

"Christ. He'd know me, for sure. Anybody in Ogallala would have heard of me."

"Farther out than that. You got quite a reputation. The Enders name was all over the newspapers. Read about you in a crumpled paper I picked up in Virginia City. How you killed Will Cardin and came up against his gang. Wish I could've seen you and that gun in action, brother. Came upon Cardin's gang myself and lucky to be still breathing."

Cort's eyes widened. "How did that happen?"

"I wandered into Texas and worked a small ranch for a while. That's another story I don't want to get into. When I left there... well let's just say I was full of fight about everything. I decided to cure all my problems by getting rich. Found out staking a gold claim was only half the trouble. Keeping jumpers and robbers out of my camp became a full-time job."

"Finally, I took what gold I found and banked it. Decided working as a guard on the Santa Fe line and Union Pacific was safer and less backbreaking. Until I ran into robbers like Cardin, Jack Davis, and Bill Miner. Along with a host of others craving what the big miners wanted to keep. Then I had a sudden change of heart because what I'd hoped for in Texas wasn't going to happen. Gave up that fool dream. That's when I traced you to Nebraska after reading about my notorious brother. Here I am."

She tensed at her husbands reddened face. He never considered himself a hero. Far from it. Simply put, he'd put her ahead of his own life.

"I'd always thought you might've been killed during the war, Bryce. Went back and found somebody living in our old house. Figured our sister sold out, but no one would say. The new owner told me to git while I faced the business end of a shotgun."

"Been carryin' guilt about leaving you and Nora behind. The damnable war broke up a lot of families. Glad I finally found you, at least. With a beautiful wife and babe. You were always a lucky son of a bitch, even as a kid." Darting a glance to where she sat, he added, "Pardon. Gold camp language."

Lark reached across the table and touched his hand at the sheepish look on his face. "You'll find I'm not prissy. Cort was hard as nails when I met him. In fact, it took a while before we finally got around to marrying. It'll all settle in for you after a while."

"You been married over the years, Bryce?" Cort asked.

Bryce darted a glance toward the ceiling and then back to her. She managed a sympathetic smile.

"Nope. Never married."

Cort cleared his throat. "Like we said. You'll settle in here. Could use a good cowhand and a man who can use a gun."

"Got no problem using a gun when needed. Have a lot to learn about chasin' cows. As long as we're asking questions, I have one for you. This is quite a spread. Be interesting to hear how you came to own a place like this."

Cort darted a glance in Lark's direction. Even though it was time to let Bryce in on their past, she couldn't bring herself to speak of it. Instead, she busied herself with cleaning up the dishes, leaving Cort to explaining. Shutting out whatever they were about to say wasn't possible. The memory of it was written on her scarred face. This was one of those times when she'd prefer closing off the hearing part of the story.

"I was married before I met Lark. A widow lady owned this place. And she pretty much owned me."

The warmth of the reunion chilled like a winter storm. There was a scrape of chairs and when she turned to look, both men had left the room. Pain-filled secrets would be spilled in Cort's office. It was time for it. But she worried at how much he'd reveal to his brother.

THREE

THE LADY OF ROCKY CREEK

A FEW DAYS later, they cantered away from the homestead, side by side. Cort couldn't help but notice how much Bryce had settled in, even winning over Zeke and the others. Clean-shaven and wearing fresh clothes, he began to see beyond just how much they looked alike. They were both secretive and equally ambitious. They both wore their guns low and like him, their eyes were ever watchful. Deep down, he'd do whatever was needed to keep his brother at the ranch. Somehow, he'd convince him this was a place worth building a life on.

"Where are we headin'?" Bryce called out as they walked their horses up and over a slope toward Blue River.

"Thought I'd give you the lay of the land."

"How big a spread you got?"

"Just about twenty thousand acres. Inherited the place from my first wife."

"There's a story. You want to tell me about it? You told me about Lark and Cardin. But owning this much land. That doesn't just happen."

"Nope. Not yet," Cort said, gritting his teeth. "One day, I'll let you in on the price I paid."

"I won't bring it up again. Unless you want to talk."

"Appreciate if you'd give me time on that. Best tell you over a bour-bon. I'm still raw about how it came about. Don't bring it up in front of Lark." Cort pointed in the direction of Hannah's place. "For right now, thought we'd head over to Rocky Creek Ranch. It sits on the opposite side of the main river where there's a creek. Small place of about two thousand acres, give or take. Been tryin' to buy it from the owner. A thorn in my side."

"That why we're goin' there? So you can change their minds?"

"Yep. I stop in occasionally to check on *Missus* Van Stadt. She's a friend of Lark. Not many women out here for company. They hit it off. Course, that hasn't swayed the woman into an agreement to sell. I'm too stubborn to give up."

A sidelong glance convinced Cort that his brother was letting the topic of his first wife drop. Now all he had to do is find Hannah in an amenable frame of mind. She could be cantankerous but sooner or lat-er, she'd have to sell.

———————

AS THEY NEARED the river, Bryce smelled cook smoke and just as he gave it thought, a woman's scream and a gunshot brought them both up short. Yanking their rifles from their boots, they kicked their horses into a ground-eating run in the direction of the woman in peril. Water splashed around them as they crossed. When they reached the opposite bank, they climbed to the top of a slope and pulled up.

A lady wearing a gray skirt and blue blouse, wielding a big rifle, centered his attention. From here, she looked mighty pretty but in a fine temper. Cort waved his hat and Bryce shoved his rifle back into his scabbard. "This must be Missus Van Stadt?" Bryce quipped, not hiding his grin.

"Yep. Come on. I'll introduce you to the strong-willed woman with no quit. Hannah has a stubborn mind of her own."

With a hand shielding the sun from her eyes, she wore a frown like she'd swallowed sour milk. Bryce studied the run-down log cabin, smoke pluming from the stone chimney. The smell of fresh baked bread drifted in the air. Three range cows stood inside of a broken fence, grazing on what appeared to be grapevines. Carrots draped from their chewing mouths, seeming to consider the rest of the garden and ignoring the angry woman. While a chuckle threatened to erupt, the woman's furious scowl had him swallow it before he got into trouble with this gun-wielding woman. She glanced in his direction with a stay-out-of-it look before shifting her anger toward Cort.

"Cort. Those cows of yours broke my fence and trampled my vegetables, as you can plainly see. Just what are you going to do about it?" she snapped.

Bryce gave serious attention to the lady. Her brown hair was shot full of gold strands and fell loose from her long braid. Not young but not old, she couldn't be more than twenty-five. Slender, tall, and womanly curves beneath that long shirt sent thoughts of how long he'd been without a woman, making a mental note to do something about that in Ogallala.

Drawn to her remarkable face, he acknowledged to himself that his open stare was rude. But he was captivated by her clear blue eyes. Just as he thought it, those eyes flicked over his face then looked away. Cort dismounted and commenced checking the fence while Bryce glanced at her, amused at how she perused him from his boots to his head while they waited. When he raised an eyebrow, her cheeks turned crimson and she looked away, but not before her rosy lips quirked into a hint of a grin. Her kissable mouth begged for a man's attention. He'd seen more beautiful women... but this woman had courage. She was pretty with a grace in the way she walked.

"Are you sure they're my cows, Hannah?" Cort asked, the corners of his mouth lifting.

"They wear the Double E brand—as anybody can see."

Cort removed his hat and swiped the sweat from his forehead. Bryce swallowed a burst of laughter while his brother appeared to study the brands. Even he could read the brands from here and wondered why Cort was being contrary. Or he was just amusing himself by being ornery.

"Huh. Surely are. I'll send someone back to fix your fence, and in the meantime, Bryce can chase those cows toward the other side of the river."

Without waiting, Bryce unhooked the coil of rope at his saddle and rode toward the cows, slapping their hides and hazing them from the woman's garden. Of course, he figured he'd done a fair job of crushing even more vegetables. Once he'd sent them running in the direction of the river, he circled back. Unlike Cort, he kept his hat on his head and his eyes in shadows. Maybe she wouldn't notice his study of her delicate face, like some schoolboy wanting more than a few peeks. Keeping in mind that there must be a husband somewhere around, he tried averting his glances. He wanted no trouble from the woman's husband.

"Hannah. This is my brother, Bryce. He'll be staying on for a while, I hope."

"Pleased to meet you, Mister Enders. Had no idea Cort had any kin around. Don't blame you for this. They're Cort's cows... just as stubborn. Only one took off when I fired into the sky. Those three didn't want to leave."

"Like some others I know," Cort muttered.

She walked to the side of his horse with a graceful, gliding gait, seeming to dismiss his brother's glib remark. When her hand reached up, he realized she meant to shake his. Hesitating, at first, he proffered his rough palm. That sweet smile had him gulping. Words escaped him at the feel of her small hand against his calloused skin.

"Thanks for getting those cows out of my garden. I expect they'll stay where they belong. At least I'm counting on that." She slanted a pointed glare in Cort's direction where he'd already mounted his horse.

"You know I can't promise that, Hannah. Cows tend to move where they want. Got no fence."

Now her attention returned to Bryce as she dismissed his brother. "Still. I thank you for chasing them off, Mister Enders. After all, they are Cort's responsibility. While you're not to blame, I hope you'll remind him that I don't want my garden eaten up again."

"I can hear you quite well, Hannah. I'm right here," Cort remarked.

Bryce laughed. "It's Bryce, Missus Van Stadt. And no thanks needed. Glad to help getting it fixed. Have to come back with more posts, wire, and tools. That should keep the cows out. Sorry if I did some additional damage."

She lifted one corner of her mouth as she inspected the torn vegetables. He reminded himself she was *Missus* Van Stadt. He'd already been stupid once. Best to keep to the kind you paid. Removing his hat, he then swiped his forehead before looking toward her again.

"That'd be fine," she said. When she promptly frowned in Cort's direction, Bryce couldn't help but be amused. "Appreciate it." The question lingered in his head as to this perversity between them. Yet, they were friends.

"Unless you got a husband around. Maybe he'd rather take care of it."

"My husband is away, Mister Enders."

Cort cleared his throat as he mounted and turned his horse, calling, "Don't have time to gab all day, Bryce."

That was interesting. Where was the husband? "Again. Call me Bryce." Tipping his hat he added, "In that case, I'll be back to repair the fence. Unless Cort has another job for me." Bryce looked toward Cort through narrowed eyes. His brother's brow furrowed.

"Not at the moment. We'll drive the cows to the other side, Hannah, and I'll send Bryce back soon as I know I can spare him. Have to get home to Lark before one of my hands reports he heard a gunshot. Next thing we know, my wife and men will be out looking for us."

"You give Lark my best. Tell her I'll be coming by with those gingham dresses she ordered. Get there in a few days."

Cort nodded. When he turned his horse, he said, "Don't forget my offer still stands. I'll pay you top dollar for Rocky Creek. My herd is getting too big for the Blue to handle. Besides, the money could set you up with your own business in town."

"We already talked about this. The ranch belongs to my husband. He has to decide."

"If you say so."

Bryce didn't miss the sarcasm in the retort. The edginess between Cort and Hannah had him wonder about Cort's persistent offer. They rode alongside each other, but he couldn't resist a last look over his shoulder to where the comely woman stood alone beside the broken fence, her rifle still gripped in her hand.

"I saw how you looked at Hannah. Maybe you better hear this from me again. In case your hearing is bad. She's *married,* Bryce. She just told you. Unless I miss my guess, you've had woman trouble before. This could only get you into real trouble."

"Don't have to tell me twice. I'll still fix the damned fence and be on my way. Still. Couldn't help but notice she's a fine-looking woman. That doesn't mean I'd step onto another man's property like I was a thief. Where is her damned husband, anyhow?"

"Placer mining. Thinks he'll strike it rich. If you ask her, she'll tell you she's not sure where he is, except that he went north. Only got one letter from him. Let me tell you this. I've known Lars since I first came here. He's one mean son of a bitch and built like a barn door. You'd never win a punching match with him."

He gave thought to his brother's warning. It gnawed that she could've ever married someone like that. "I don't intend to let it get that far. Don't plan to make the same mistake twice."

He couldn't resist looking over his shoulder one last time. Seeing her standing back in the shadows of her porch, he clenched his teeth. She looked right back. Jerking his head back around, his brother barked a command.

"Get that woman out of your head. Lars might be back here any day."

"Jesus Christ, Cort. He abandoned his wife for gold? A pretty wife, at that. I've been crazy enough to try my hand at mining. At least I had sense enough to stay out of Sioux and Cheyenne territory. If that's where he headed. There are still bands on the loose that'll lift his scalp."

"Well, I'm hoping to convince her he isn't coming back and that she'd be best to sell out to me. She has a deep sense of right, wrong, and loyalty to a man who plumb doesn't deserve it."

Bryce nudged his horse into a faster pace to keep up with his brother, but the vision of the woman was still in his head. The last time he'd been with a forbidden woman had nearly gotten him killed. Even if it was for the right reasons, he sure wasn't looking for another fight. No, indeed. Missus Van Stadt was not going to stay in his head and send him to a hell he'd already visited.

THE FOLLOWING DAY, Hannah adjusted her sunbonnet and brandished her rake with a vengeance. Once she had the torn-up vegetable patch cleared, she still needed to saddle her horse and look for unbranded cattle on her land. Anything not branded on this side of the river belonged to the Rocky Creek Ranch. Cort and she had worked out a deal. The Double E cowhands rounded up her cows and either branded them or put them into Ender's count.

In return for that service, she patterned and sewed dresses for the women and shirts for the men at the Double E. Sewing was a talent she used to put some food on the table. She'd never thought she'd ever be a rancher's wife. Worse, a lonely rancher's wife. When would Lars come home? Was he alive? Should she sell out to Cort? If she agreed, and Lars returned, he'd kill her. Deep inside, she'd be glad if he never came back. Especially recalling how she'd felt when he bedded her. Or the times he'd been blind drunk and in a rage. She wanted no parts of men.

Biting her lip, she gave thought to the money. Just like Cort said. She'd set herself up in town. Maybe a dress shop or bakery. She'd survive this ugly life. The ranch was a pretty piece of land, but winters were hard. Marrying Lars had been a very big mistake. But she'd said her sacred vows and was obliged to keep them, in God's eyes.

Setting the rake aside, she figured the patch was about as good as she could hope for. Brushing her hands, she marched to the corral where her bay gelding stood, swishing his tail and nuzzling the fence. His ears twitched and perked straight up when she approached. She'd come to figure he recognized her denim pants and that meant he'd be saddled.

Sidestepping, the animal shook his head. She smoothed her hand over his soft hide, feeling the muscles bunch. "Pie. Just you and me. We gotta figure out what we're going to do. What do you think?" The horse nickered and she rested her head against the warmth of the animal's neck and closed her eyes. At the sound of approaching horses, she lifted her head. Blinking into the sunlight, she saw a stone-faced Bryce, leading a packhorse.

Bryce had kept his promise and returned. Once he pulled up, he sat atop that buckskin horse as lean and handsome a man as she'd ever seen. *Hannah, you have no right to such thoughts.* He leaned forward in his saddle and rested his forearm across the pommel. His horse pawed the dirt and then with a touch of his hand, the animal settled. Wearing blue pants and a sweat-stained gray shirt, he doffed his hat and offered her a quick grin. She felt the blood rush to her face and hoped he didn't notice. Shame washed through her at the thought of looking at another man like a silly schoolgirl.

So captivated by him, she hadn't devoted attention to the packhorse behind him until she looked around him. The animal was strapped with a shovel, posts, and sundry tools. For a moment, Bryce's eyes held hers when she lifted her face to study his. Now that he'd removed his hat, she took notice of the bruises and scabs on his chin and one on his jaw. Of course, they were none of her business. Still, she'd dearly like to know the story behind them. Yesterday, they hadn't been as prominent beneath the shadows of his hat.

Wearing pants, she suddenly felt self-conscious, wondering what he thought of a woman in such unladylike garb. She never thought of herself as particularly womanly in the way Lark was. But surely wearing pants made her look like a hoyden. Sometime after she married Lars, she'd concluded there was little time for dresses and fine bone china. Besides, she had no desire to entice her husband with frills nor anything else.

She waited, taking in his broad back while he walked his horse up to the corral gate, leaned, and shoved it open. He tugged the short-legged packhorse behind him. So fascinated with the man, she'd found her boots pinned to the dirt instead of opening the gate for him. Dismounting, he slapped his hat over the saddle horn and went to work tying the mounts to a fence post before dropping the shovel and wire to the ground. Intent on the job, he didn't look in her direction.

For a moment, she thought he wasn't going to speak at all. As she was about to leave him to his work, he said, "Won't take long to fix the fence." Yanking on his gloves, he loosened the hammer from the tool bag slung over the packhorse. "Didn't bring a wagon. Wasn't sure if it might bog down in the river."

While she watched, he ignored her.

"Thanks," she managed to murmur. He'd taken a snappish tone, and she was at a loss for anything else to say. He sure didn't seem happy to be here. Being alone with him made her nervous for reasons she didn't want to think about. For one, if Lars were to show up, there'd be big trouble over this man's presence and that notion set her teeth on edge. For another, she hardly knew him or what he'd been before. Still, she was grateful to get that garden closed against the varmints. Then he'd be on his way, probably not seeing each other again.

"Be out of here by the afternoon. If you got something to do, you don't have to stay here." After that quick glance over his shoulder, he returned to the posts. "Looks like you were getting ready to ride out somewhere." He jutted his chin toward her waiting horse. "Best get to it."

"I raked up the mess those cows left behind yesterday. Figured it was time to look for unbranded strays. I have a corral down by the creek where I chase them."

"That's man's work," he said while he loosened the cinches on his saddle, still avoiding looking in her direction.

When he finally turned to face her, his eyes raked her from head to boots before returning to his work. She puzzled over his cold assessment. Yesterday his eyes had stayed on hers. Today, there was censure and disdain. Of all the conceit. Seething, she lifted her chin while her mind searched for a response.

"Man's work? I've got no man to do the work. How else would it get done?"

"After you round up these cattle and chase them to that corral, just how do you plan to brand them? Besides that. Those penned cows need hay," he called out. "Need to get them to water or they'll bust down the corral."

"Cort's men brand them and haul a wagon of hay over from time to time. Then head the penned animals across the river. They count them in on their ledger. When your brother runs his herd to market, he takes mine along and pays me whatever he gets by that count. Takes a fair cut for his trouble. Not that it's your concern."

His eyes narrowed. He stopped what he was doing and moved a few steps toward her, close enough for her to admire his muscled arms beneath rolled up sleeves. The bruises he bore meant trouble. From now on, she planned to discourage his visits.

"Why not sell out? Your husband might not ever be back, Missus Van Stadt. Or do you plan to do this forever?"

She didn't miss the gibe and she didn't need to be reminded, by him, of Cort's offers. Nonetheless, he had no place telling her what she should or shouldn't do. "I'm legally married and I won't do such a thing behind his back. Besides, it isn't mine to sell so long as he is my husband. The ranch is in his name."

He shrugged. "Tell you what. If you can fix me some supper, I'll finish this fence and see if I can find a few cows before dark."

"That'd be late to ride back to the Double E, Mister Enders. By the time you do all that work, it'll be getting dark."

"I'm used to riding after dark. I might just sleep in your barn, if you don't mind? All I need is a bed of hay. One other thing. Stop calling me Mister Enders. It's Bryce."

"I suppose that would be all right, *Bryce*. I'll see you have a hearty supper for your time. And as long as we're at it, you may call me Hannah."

"All right. A deal."

"If you're close enough, you'll hear the clanging bell... a call to supper. Except that I can't invite you inside the house. I'll set it out on the porch."

"Does it include that bread I smell?"

"Surely does. I got a cured ham and potatoes to go with it."

WHY DID SHE have a damned husband? Bryce shook his head when

Hannah pivoted on her bootheels and sashayed in those pants toward the log and stone cabin. His eyes stayed on her until she was gone from view and then he turned his attention to the fence. All the while, he couldn't help but grin at her prim manner. Looking was as far as he'd allow it to go. But she was a pleasant view.

Hannah.

The name was easy on the tongue and warm where it shouldn't be. Sweet as honey. The fact of the existence of her husband drummed inside his head. Just spending the night in her barn was asking for trouble. Especially if her husband chose tonight to make his return. Worse, Cort might get the wrong idea and keep him so busy he'd be in the saddle for the next two weeks if he stepped across a line. Hard work might not be such a bad idea.

To think he and Hannah could be friends was as precipitous as riding a ridge in an ice storm. Maybe he'd never had a woman friend, but it was all he had to hope for, and he was willing to try it out. For now, he thought how her nervous fingers had twisted at the waistband of her pants, making him wonder what she might look like in a fancy dress.

Sweat trickled over Bryce's face and dripped from his chest beneath a warm mid-May sun. Pounding the last post into the ground, he stepped back and used his arm to swipe beads from his brow. Bending to retrieve the last section of wire between gloved hands, he sensed her presence behind him. Twisting around, he blinked once and then again. *Was this the same woman?*

Standing there in a green dress, her hair brushed into a neat braid with her blue eyes fastened on his bared chest, his breath caught. She looked so young, innocent, and sweet he couldn't drag his eyes away. Common sense warned him to ride out of here as fast as he could load his gear. Something inside itched to yank free of these work gloves and pull her flush against him. He'd give up a lot to touch his mouth to hers.

He imagined the silky touch of her gold strands between his fingers. She made him feel alive and needed. He wanted the right to be here. In truth, he had no right. The silence between them stretched until he found his voice. "I didn't hear the bell."

"No. I just thought you'd like to take some cool water in the shade. Looks like you're about done here."

"I'll be up to the porch for that drink as soon as I finish this. Might as well dump some over my head while I'm at it. Then I'll chase what cows I find. Just leave a water bucket by the steps."

"I'm sorry I agreed to that. The cows, I mean."

"Why is that?" Maybe she was as nervous as he was. Or maybe she was trying to convince him to leave. All it would take is one word and he'd be gone. But he wanted it to come from her pretty mouth.

"You're working much too hard for a supper. Besides, you must have chores over at the Double E."

"I admit I need to get back to work. And I won't be able to do more than round up a few cows. Leaving at first light before my brother has time to send men looking for me."

"You don't have to stay. I'll go out tomorrow myself. I'm used to doing a man's work, as you put it."

Damn but the woman intrigued him. While he was sorry he'd said anything about her doing man's work, he'd meant it. Stubborn, defiant, and too brave for her own good, he wanted to shake her and kiss her at the same time. Bryce took two long strides to close the distance between them, stopping short when the length of her tensed. She bit her lip. Clearly, he'd frightened her when he closed the distance. Now, why was that?

He sighed. "Look, Hannah. You shouldn't be here alone. You shouldn't be doing men's work. A ranch is tough and rough. What will you do if your cows all die off this winter or if your well runs dry? What if you get stomped on by that horse of yours? You've got to sell and do it before that husband comes back. Go back home. Wherever that is."

Her pert chin lifted. "This is the only home I have. I can't go back. For reasons I won't go into with you."

When she started to back away, he was quicker. Grasping her arm, he held her in place. "I won't hurt you. *Ever.* Stop looking at me like you think I will."

He followed her gaze to his gloved hand wrapped around her slender arm, and he felt her flesh tremble. He released his hold as though he'd been burned. Wanting more than to touch her was an ache he'd have to deal with. Wanting to protect her smoldered inside like a banked fire. Nothing good could come out of this.

"Why don't you go inside out of the heat while I take care of the cows," he said, keeping his voice level. "Won't be so far off that I'll miss supper. I'll get that water in a few minutes after I string the last two posts. Shouldn't take more than a few hours before I head back."

His eyes followed her graceful stride. The feel of her quaking beneath his touch would stay with him tonight. What had made her so afraid of being near him? He'd bet her no-account husband was at the root of her wariness. If he found out for sure, there would be no way he'd set it aside.

Two hours had turned into almost three, with only five cows he'd hazed out of the brush. After he'd just finished looping the wire gate closed, the clang of the bell from the cabin rang out. He thought about ignoring it and leaving, taking his good intentions with him. Tomorrow, he'd send some of the Double E men over to drive these animals across the river. Instead, he decided to camp out here instead of in the barn, mostly to keep the predators from getting to them. But it wouldn't hurt to keep his distance from Mrs. Van Stadt.

After stripping down and dunking himself into the creek, washing away both his sweat and his meanderings, he reconsidered supper. After all, he was obliged to accept the invitation out of pure politeness and she'd already gone to the trouble. Still, he had to set his mind on anything and that was going to be an impossible task. Somehow, he'd make sure he resisted coming here for the rest of the days he was in Nebraska. For now, he'd enjoy a supper with a pretty lady. *Just as a friend.*

Leaving his horse in the corral beside the packhorse, Bryce walked to the porch to find a table already set with a platter of ham, potatoes, and a long loaf of fresh baked bread. His mouth watered at the sight. A tall honey jar held two stalks of wilted blue lupines. The screen door squeaked open, and she stepped outside with a pot of coffee in one hand and a pitcher in the other. She smiled her rare but sunny bright smile of hers that had him lick his lips. Which forced him to focus his attention on the vittles.

Taking his seat on a worn oak chair, he kept his eyes on her as she sat across from him and poured coffee from a speckled blue pot. There was no platter in front of her. He raised an eyebrow.

"Aren't you eating?" he asked. Damned if he felt right eating alone while she stared. Nor did he want to eat her meager food supply.

"Oh, no. I already ate. Lars liked to eat alone. My job was to make sure his plate was kept filled... so I always ate before he did."

"I'm *not* Lars." *Sonofabitch.* The man was manipulating his wife, even when he wasn't here. Right now, he wished her husband were here so he'd have the pleasure of putting his fist in the man's mouth.

She waved her hand dismissively. "I guess the habit is hard to break. I'm always alone, anyway. No matter."

"Well. If it comes down to eating with me again, you best have a platter in front of you. Getting mighty tired of my own company. Not often I get to sit with a pretty gal over supper."

"Or what?"

"Pardon?"

"You said I best have a platter in front of me. Or what?"

"Or I'll likely not eat. I'll wait you out."

Her hands folded on the table in front of her. Wishing he had the right to hold them between his own, it was prudent to keep his mind on the meal. Jabbing his fork into the meat and potatoes, he was glad he changed his mind about sleeping in the barn. With his eyes on those cows, he wouldn't have his eyes on her house. As he chewed, he looked up to see her daintily sipping coffee. Her mouth curved into a faint smile. And he was a fool. It sure was becoming a bad habit... of enjoying the sight of her.

Focused again on the food, he felt her eyes watching him with every bite. Sweat drizzled beneath his collar. He hoped she hadn't noticed his tight grip on the fork. The food was delicious, and he'd walk barefoot through a desert for that bread. Except for his brother's wife, he hadn't relished a gentlewoman's company in a long time. Damn. He'd give everything he owned to have Hannah in his bed tonight... or *any* night. With Hannah, he wouldn't even remember the woman he'd lost in Texas.

When he finished, he leaned back in his chair and lifted the coffee mug to his lips while her fingers fidgeted with the flowers in the jar sitting between them. Deciding to dig a little deeper into her husband's whereabouts, he asked, "How long you been married, Hannah?"

"Two years. He's been away more than a year."

"Why'd you marry a man like that?"

"Like that? I imagine there's worse. After all, I'm the one who came to the ribbon dance, and he found me. He offered. That is why women attend. He just wasn't what I expected."

Jesus. Cort had described how he'd met Lark at that dance. Still, Lark had been far luckier. "Do you want children?"

"Babies? Lars doesn't. I'm not sure what kind of father Lars would make, in any case."

"You didn't answer my question."

"I'd hoped I'd have children. I'm accepting it won't happen."

"Lars is no good as a husband or he'd be here. And he'd make no better a father."

"You don't even know him, Bryce. You are presumptuous to express an opinion."

"Lars isn't here, Hannah. He should be. Besides, are you sure you should stay with him?" *Damn his hide.* He was sticking his nose in where it didn't belong, and he knew better. The logical part of his mind questioned his motives while his head and heart denied each one.

"I said my vows. Promised fidelity. He's my husband."

She looked away. Snorting, he stood. Taking the few steps separating them, he waited beside her, wanting to touch her. She stared at some distant point. He kept his hands at his sides, not daring to move them, knowing how easy she startled. When he saw her hand trembling at her throat, Bryce said, "Vows. A husband wouldn't leave his wife to fend for herself if those vows mattered to him. How can you think of him without being spitting mad?"

Her eyes closed. "I can't go back on my word. My sacred promise. None of this should matter to you."

In the silent tension arcing between them, he stared at her until she tucked her chin and her eyes opened. He chomped back the word he had in mind to describe her so-called loyalty. He hadn't meant to be blunt. *Blunt, hell.* He'd been downright *rude.* But anyone could tell she didn't love the man. It was conceivable that Lars was already dead. In point of fact, he knew how rough those camps were and how often men were shot for their gold.

Her face lifted and her eyes flitted across his. Her lips were pursed. He'd said enough about Lars. Tonight, the thought of her husband would churn over and over, keeping him awake.

He sighed. "You're right. I should've kept my opinion to myself. I won't need the barn. I'll keep watch near those cows of yours till morning and send men back for them. Thanks for the supper. Best I've had in a long time, Hannah."

He pivoted, not waiting to hear what she might say in return. Taking the porch steps, he marched to the corral, slipped onto his saddle and led his packhorse toward camp, without a backward glance. *Bryce, the fool.* He was glad he'd gotten away before he'd done anything stupid... like showing her how a real man could kiss away her hardheaded notions.

FOUR

THE LONG WAIT

O VER THE NEXT few weeks, every muscle in his body ached. Blisters on his feet and fly bites on his neck reminded him of the backbreaking days in the mine camp. If it wasn't for his work gloves, he wouldn't be able to hold the reins. Getting to understand ranching and staying in the saddle for most of the day was almost as hard as picking and sluicing.

Sitting down at a real table and eating with his brother and family became more comfortable, if and when he got in from the range early enough. Still, he preferred playing cards with cowhands and wranglers in the bunkhouse rather than feeling out of place in the main house. Besides, interrupting Cort's personal life didn't sit well with him.

Family or not, when husband and wife exchanged longing glances, he was an interloper whether he meant to be or not. But Lark wouldn't hear of him spending all his time down at the bunkhouse or in the chow line. His brother was right. You didn't want to get on Lark's wrong side because she'd win the argument.

"You look like you've been in a saddle for two weeks, Bryce," Lark said from the door, while he stomped his boots.

Her voice drew his eyes to hers where she stood on the other side of the screen. What she really meant was he looked beaten up and needed a shave, haircut, and bath. At least he'd taken time to dunk in the river before he'd returned from chasing cows.

"I'll tend to cleaning up before I come up to the house again."

She waved her hand. "We don't mind. The men around here work hard. Goodness, Bryce, beards and long hair go with that. That's not what I intended to mean. Cort says you stay out longer than any of the others. You've proven your mettle."

Cort appeared behind her with his squirming son in his arms. "Lark's right. You comin' inside or staying out there?"

In answer, Bryce opened the door and stepped inside to the scent of buttered potatoes and tangy beef. After he'd taken his seat, Cort used his free hand to pour black coffee into the mugs. He watched as his brother set his boy into a basket where the baby promptly curled into a ball and contentedly sucked his thumb.

"Best listen to my wife. And me. You're a top hand. You need to ease up on yourself. Maybe go to town the next time you get time off. You haven't taken any. Time is yours whenever you need it. Got to have some fun once in a while."

Lark turned and her mouth drew into a frown just as he was giving serious thought to a visit to the saloon. When she cocked her head, he wondered if she'd read his mind. Best to think about something else.

"You missed supper. Got plenty left, though. Just take me a minute to put it out."

He held up a hand. "I already ate at the cookshack. I'll pass, this time. Coffee is fine. Maybe pie to go with it."

She nodded. "I'll be taking Little Bryce up to bed soon. He'll be crying for attention before too long." He sat back as she set a heaping slice of pie in front of him, sending his thoughts back to the supper with Hannah.

"He's no trouble. I'm getting used to my nephew. When I'm not so trail dirty, next time I'll pick him up. He smells like soap and milk." The kinds of things he'd missed out on, like a wife and family, started to make him feel like an old man. Like Zeke.

While he sipped the coffee, Theresa came into the room and fluttered around the table, picking up forks and plates. But his eyes were on

Lark's willowy figure and her straight back. It occurred to him that he was comparing her with Hannah.

Lark's clothes weren't prim, but they were proper. He admired her grit and her wholesome sweetness. Her beautiful gold hair looked spun with red sunset. Biting down on his back teeth at the sight of the scar along her jaw, his curiosity piqued once again about the details that Cort hadn't revealed. Except for the fact he wouldn't tolerate Lark's scar mentioned, he still didn't know who'd done that to her.

Cort always managed to confine his conversations to the ranch, careful to keep Lark from discussion. Not since that night after he'd first arrived had Cort brought up much of his past. But whenever his brother's attention strayed to his wife, Cort's usual hard expression softened. He envied their abiding love.

Bryce had heard stories of his brother's gunfighting days from some of the hands. A newspaper article filled in some of the rest. His men considered Cort a hero. Not many men would have lived to tell the tale after a gunfight with Cardin.

Lark turned from the dishwater pan and smiled in his direction. "You seem to be settling in just fine. And little Bryce has gotten to know you."

"Yeah. Well. Lived too long on my own. But I still remember how I used to sit at a proper table. Course that was years ago when Cort was still a young boy."

"I seem to remember you kicking me under the table," Cort said on a grin.

"Maybe I did." Swallowing the last of his coffee, his eyes followed his brother as he lifted the baby and handed the bundle into Lark's waiting arms.

"It's time to get this little fellow up to his bed. Give you two some time to talk," Lark said.

"Good night, Lark."

"Bryce. Don't forget to take some time off."

He watched as both Theresa and Lark started toward the hallway, remembering to stand. Once they left, he turned the chair around and straddled it. Cort was opening a cabinet door where he procured a bottle and set it on the table beside two glasses.

"Join me?" Cort asked.

"Thanks. Could use it."

Except for the snapping embers and ticking clock, there was yawning quiet between them while they sipped their drinks. Both seemed to want to keep their thoughts to themselves, and for his part, Bryce was just as glad.

Cort cleared his throat. "So. Do you remember much of life back in Virginia?"

Bryce studied his brother's serious expression. "Like what?"

Cort shrugged. "How our mother used to sing. How pretty she was and liked us to mind our manners. How we had to hide the cows if the Billies came near. Sneaking off to fish in the river and catching hell from Pa. Just things."

"Yeah. I remember. Can't say I've met many ladies like our ma until I got here."

"Lark. She's not uppity. She doesn't expect you to stand for her each time she leaves the room."

"Huh. Well, I'll still make sure I stand. If I forget, you get to kick me under the table like you used to."

"Suit yourself. By the way, speaking of working. The men hold you in high regard."

Bryce leaned back in his seat and swallowed the bourbon. Darting a glance at his brother's intense scrutiny, it seemed like a good time to say what was on his mind. "Thanks, Cort. For taking me in. Being here is what I needed. You've got good men working here."

"You're hiding a bunch of worries. Care to share some of it?" Cort prodded. "Nothing like this bourbon to loosen a man's tongue. If you need to unload whatever it is that brought you here."

"In due time. Nothing can be changed, anyhow."

"We all come to that conclusion many times over in our lives, Bryce."

"You're a lucky man. She's a real beauty and a good mother."

"That she is. Think it's about time to tell you some of it. Already talked to Lark about letting you in on what happened. We had rough times. You do a good job of skittering over that scar of hers without staring. You should know what happened. From me. Don't want to go over it a second time."

"How 'bout we go to your office to talk. More private. Don't mind hearing the story so long as Lark doesn't think I'm a nosy brother-in-law."

"She won't think that. But I'd expect this to stay between us. Some of it I won't tell. Because I can't."

"You should know me better."

"I'm beginning to."

Not for the first time, Bryce was impressed with the books lining the shelves on either side of the stone fireplace as they took seats. Cort's big mahogany desk took up one side of the room, facing the tall windows fronting the big house. Bryce sat on a cowhide chair while his brother settled on his leather chair behind his desk. He wondered at the piles of documents and maps spread out between them. When did Cort have time to read it all?

"Remember, brother. I'll answer your questions and that's the end of it."

"All right. I'm listening."

Bryce wasn't sure he wanted to hear Lark's story. Once his brother started, his stomach coiled at the images he painted. All the kinds of ways she'd been hurt and yet she rose above it all. Downing another bourbon, he leaned back and listened. His brother scrubbed his palms over his face and continued the story while he took in the twisted tale of survival, manipulation, and justice.

"Lark was cut by Will Cardin. He paid with his life. I saw to it. The reasons? First, Will was infatuated with her. But like all women he fixated on, he had no idea how to treat any of them. Branding them with a knife. Making them property. In short, he was insane. Putting him out of his misery did the world a service and I'd do it again. Lark has had to live with stares, questions, and even derision from small-minded folks. Most around here have accepted her as she is. They had better not cross me where she is concerned."

"She seems confident and poised, despite what Cardin did."

"Outside, yes. Inside... she'll never forget. I've seen her wake at night, her eyes filled with terror."

"Christ. I'm sorry. So, how did you come by this place? You mentioned a wife before Lark."

"That's another long story. One of the reasons I got the bourbon out."

"We getting drunk together?"

Cort laughed. "Lark might take offense to my liquored breath. But in short, yes."

Tipping back his head, he swallowed his laugh at the sight of Cort's taut expression. Bryce sucked in a long breath, set his glass down, and settled deeper into the chair with his hands folded across his stomach.

"I'm warning you. It's still a pretty sore spot for both of us. Especially her. Living in this house is a reminder of the Harris name. Sometimes wish I'd burned it down."

LATER THAT NIGHT, the stars winked maddingly against a black sky when Bryce staggered to the bunkhouse. The Double E had a long and tragic past. Grim yet nostalgic. Hard yet kind. Were the Harrises laughing at the twists of fate or had they calmly moved on to quiet peace? All of it reminded him of Gabriella. Damn. Once again, another woman had stolen his soul and she was out of reach. He'd have to accept that and stay away from Hannah.

Damn his brother. He gave orders and meant them. Tomorrow he'd be out in her pasture, chasing whatever cows he could find. Even if only a slim chance of encountering Mrs. Van Stadt, he was determined to look the other way. Maybe Cort was testing him.

Worse, he'd been given the task of driving her wagon back here at the end of the week. Something about the women canning and sewing. What was his brother up to? Sending him into temptation, that's what. He'd already admitted to his brother that he'd fallen from God's grace when he'd gotten involved with a married woman down in Texas. A mistake he'd come to regret with every waking moment. Gabriella wouldn't leave her brutal husband, leaving him no choice but to let her go. Yes, indeed. Bourbon loosened his tongue tonight. Contrary to his brother's suggestion, he didn't feel one bit better. He was raw inside.

Long, backbreaking days in the goldfields gave him little time to visit his past mistakes. Whores left him cold. Drowning in whiskey had never helped. Now, his brother's stern warnings about Hannah and Lars rang in his head like the tolling bells of Hell.

Tripping over the porch step, he stumbled up to the door and shoved it open, finding his bunk in the dim lantern light. Ignoring the snores, grunts, and stink of unwashed men, he staggered to the mattress and unsteadily sank down.

An opportunity rolled around in his dull head. Cort offered him a cut of the land for a reasonable price. Too reasonable. That led to the discussion of buying out Hannah. How his brother might convince her to take the deal escaped him. After all, it was in her best interest. But pushing her didn't sit well.

Bryce grabbed at his boots and missed twice. Finally, he managed to tug them free. When he finally lay back and closed his eyes, he imagined blue eyes and strands of golden-brown hair beside him.

Flustered at the sounds of coughing and farts, he recollected base suggestions he'd overheard about Hannah. Dropping his arm across his eyes, he ground his teeth. Something to do with who'd bed her first.

After all, she was pretty and tempting. Groaning, he rolled to his side and squeezed his eyes closed. "Over my dead body," he muttered. Any man who touched her better be ready to have a fist for supper. She wasn't *that* kind of woman. He'd take that matter in hand.

FIVE

STUBBORN WOMAN

HOOVES POUNDED TO his right, stirring dust from dirt that was dry as old bones. Looking across his shoulder, he saw a single rider just on the other side of the rain-starved creek. Yanking his rifle from his scabbard, he leaned forward and kicked his horse into a lope, wondering if there was a trespasser on Rocky Creek land.

Splashing through the low water, he reached the short rise overlooking the cabin below. He squinted against the sun, searching the pasture for the rider. What he found were twelve cows, by his count, scattering in different directions. That's when he set eyes on Hannah, her braid over her shoulder and a black-brimmed hat shadowing her face. With a coiled rope in one hand, she was right in the thick of the cattle, swatting at them, when they decided to turn direction. She shouted over their bawling and cut her horse out and around them, clearly trying to head them back. They weren't cooperating.

Thinking to watch her to see how she managed this feat, he shoved his rifle back into the boot and rested his forearms across his pommel, admiring her grit and her curvy frame in those britches. When her horse balked and reared, his heart lurched and he straightened in his saddle, watching to find out how she'd handle her mount. Her hat flew to the ground as she hauled back on the reins. That was all he needed to see.

Sending his horse into a gallop, he closed in on the turmoil. So much for keeping his distance. Twisting in her saddle, he saw her eyes widen at his approach. Her hair was a swirl of sunlight and her figure filled out her blouse. With a shake of his head, he focused on the situation before she was hurt. By the time he closed the distance, she'd managed to head the cattle and turn them. Easing back, he watched her with new admiration at how she moved with her horse.

Joining her, he used his horse to cut the rest of the cows into a new direction and then circled back beside her. Just as he thought things were under control, a stray cow charged in their direction, surprising her horse, setting the animal into a whirl. When she slid sideways, the reins were jerked from her hands but not before he leaned in and caught her around her waist, setting her backside snug between his thighs. His well-trained horse moved easily alongside the stream of cantankerous cows.

Once they were all heading in the right direction, he pulled up. Hannah's quivering body leaned against him. His own body shook at how close she'd come to falling beneath her horse's hooves. With his heart pounding in his chest, she looked across her shoulder, her lips puckered. Was it fear or anger?

"Thank you. I'm not usually so careless. I'll need to find my horse."

"You're welcome, *Missus* Van Stadt. I'll go round up your horse and those cows after I see you back to your cabin. You're shaking like a leaf in the wind. Damn, you could've been killed if you'd dropped beneath the hooves. I told you this is no place for a woman."

When her lips twitched and her eyes flashed, he figured it was the latter. She was mad. The blue of her eyes deepened.

"Like I said. I can take care of myself. I have no other choice. I've taken falls before and survived all of them. I'll thank you to take me to my horse so I can get back to work. They're my responsibility."

His back straightened and he swallowed against his tight throat. Her priggish response was about to engage them in a battle of wills. From his standpoint, she had no business riding with cattle until she learned more about cattle. Few women had enough horse sense or experience for this kind of work. If she had to learn the hard way, it could mean being killed. Though, he couldn't deny her worthy mettle.

He imagined she'd spent most of her life riding in a wagon or carriage back East. He wasn't about to sit by and watch her fall to her death because of her foolish, independent notions. The darned woman was asking for trouble. Someone needed to get it into her head, and it might as well be him.

"Well?" she snapped. "Will you help me find my horse? Or sit here all day?"

With every movement, her bottom rubbed against his groin. Gulping, he clamped down on his back teeth at her saucy demand. If he knew anything about women, he knew she was about to throw a hissy fit depending on his answer. He planned to hold his ground.

"You were about to find yourself stomped. Small or large herd, it doesn't matter. Dead is still dead. Thought I'd better intervene. And no, I'm not taking you to that horse of yours. I'll finish up the job, then find your mount… if he isn't already back at your barn."

"I can handle my horse. I'll thank you to keep to whatever you're here for and I'll do what I have to do. What are you doing on this side of the creek?"

Caught between a laugh at her high handedness and her flushed face, he gnashed his teeth hard enough to break walnuts. "I'll be sure to keep to myself from now on. The next time, I'll watch your horse dump you on your fine ass."

"Let me down. *Immediately.*"

That cute little smirk of hers prickled. When she wriggled, he grasped her around the waist with one arm. Clutching her snuggly, he dropped her like a sack of potatoes onto the ground. That's where she sprawled, resting against her elbows, very close to a pile of fresh cow shit and wearing a killing glare. Standing, she brushed off her boy's pants.

Fists at her sides and a pout on her lower lip, he wanted to answer an urge snaking through him. An inclination to step down and kiss her silly was capped by how he'd regret that decision. Swiping his mouth with his sleeve, he tipped his hat and rode away from her. But not before he suggested she pick up her crushed hat and watch where she stepped.

In his agitated state of mind, he left her standing there because he was in no frame of mind to be too near until he cooled down. For the moment, he'd take his time finding her horse. Although, spanking her held some appeal, if only he didn't want to hold her in his arms and pretend she belonged to him. He'd be damned if he'd let himself get sucked into an affair with a married woman. Shit. Sooner or later, he'd either pack up and leave or settle the matter of her husband.

THEY HADN'T SPOKEN in two days. Somehow it bothered her more and more. Why was she counting? He'd led her horse back and handed her the reins. She'd turned on her heels and stomped away, surely signaling he wasn't welcome. The truth of it—Hannah May was a married woman, and she didn't want to be.

Kicking dirt with the toe of her boot, she gave thought to her mother's life of drudgery beside a husband she hated. Neither she nor her mother had had the courage to walk away from their no-account husbands. Their church wouldn't have tolerated any such thing. But the thought of life with Lars was too dismal to contemplate. She'd never been so miserable. At least Lars wasn't here to inflict his husbandly demands. But she was still tied to him.

Hannah knew where Bryce usually camped when he was near here. In fact, Tangle and Damon happened by, looking for him. When she told them where they'd find him, Tangle's raised eyebrow sent heat through her face. What had he thought about her having this man nearby? If she knew anything, she knew there was talk about them in the bunkhouse.

To quell any gossip, she invited the two men to partake in coffee and a smoke on the porch, thereby changing the subject to any news from the Enders' ranch. Once they'd gone, she slipped the bread dough into her Excelsior National oven—the one gift Lars had ever given her, ensuring his hearty meals.

Turning her attention to peeling potatoes, slicing carrots, and cutting dried beef, she'd soon have a fine stew. The question of whether Bryce would stop by niggled. Worse, she hated that she cared. Dropping the knife to the table, she plunked onto the chair and buried her face in her palms. Loneliness tore at her, piece by piece. She'd been abandoned except for a man who'd shown her kindness, while at the same time, he'd opened her eyes to the way she'd been treated. Why did Bryce have to be right and what difference did it make? She was still married to a man she'd come to loathe.

In three days, he'd be by to drive her wagon to the Double E. Working on sewing and gossiping with her friend always cheered her up. Twisting her fingers together, she shook her head. Her heart raced in anticipation of both a visit and the sight of Bryce Enders... a handsome man who'd awakened her to feelings she'd buried.

Shoving a loose strand of hair behind her ear, a surge of envy of Lark forced her to consider her situation—a woman with a husband who had not one bit of care for her. She stood, then dumped the vegetables into the scalding pot while steam curled around her face. It was time to stop wallowing in self-pity. Nothing could change who she was and dreaming about it was too painful.

Lifting her head, she listened. There was a steady *thwack, thwack* of hammering from somewhere in front of the house. How long had that been going on without her noticing? Slipping her Colt .45 into her hand, she walked to the front doorway. The hammering paused and then began again. Clutching the grip, she stepped out into full sunlight.

The pounding stopped once again. She tilted her head and waited. A horse stomped and whinnied. Squinting in the direction of the far end of the corral, a familiar buckskin stood slack-legged and still saddled. Sucking in a breath, she lowered the gun to her side.

Thwack. Thwack. Thwack. Pacing closer, she cupped her hands over her eyes, then lifted her face. Her eyes settled on the far end of the barn where she found a shirtless Bryce, kneeling precariously at the edge of the roof. Her eyes fixed on his rippling muscles and glistening browned skin. She couldn't move. If he knew she was there, he gave no immediate indication. Shameful as a hoyden, she walked nearer, trying to gain a better vantage. The thought occurred that sneaking up on him might send him falling from the roof. Her heart raced at the thought.

A rough ladder leaned against the wall of the barn. The soles of his boots rested over the edge. Hunched over the shingles, he lifted the hammer and it stilled in midair. She hadn't moved a twitch, but his head jerked up and he glanced across his shoulder. His hard stare sent her stepping backward. Swiping his face against his arm, he set the hammer down, saying nothing, yet his perturbed expression was there.

"What are you doing, Bryce?" *What a stupid question.*

"Finished chasing those cattle over the river and decided to see if anything else needed tending before I head back to the ranch. I'm branding tomorrow. No telling how long before I can get back. Damon and Tangle took fifteen more I'd rounded up. Some wore the Double E. Remembered seeing a hole in the roof. Decided to fix it before I left."

Biting her tongue, she thought better of reminding him of their agreement. "Thank you, Mister Enders."

"Back to *Mister Enders.* Why you do that... confounds me."

From the tic in his jaw and his angry response, she knew she'd irked him. She cleared her throat. "Still. You didn't have to go to this trouble. You've done quite enough. You could easily fall."

"Yep. Break every bone. It needed fixing so I fixed it. Like I said, I noticed daylight over the feed bin inside the barn last time I was here. Figured I could find a few boards to do a temporary fix. You'll need a new roof one of these days. As to falling. That would be my problem."

"Are you about finished?"

He returned his head to the job at hand. "Just a few more nails and I'll be down and on my way," he shouted as he picked up the hammer.

"How about having supper? The least I can offer you for your kindness. Which you don't need to do." As soon as the invitation left her foolish mouth, she regretted it.

He stopped but didn't turn to look in her direction. From her vantage, she thought she caught a slight grin. Instead, she heard him mutter something.

"Don't think I could turn down an offer of that bread and some fresh coffee. You're a good cook. But we did have an agreement."

"I remember. Still, I feel obliged after all that work. And it'll include pie. I make a respectable apple pie," she added. "Stew tonight. Nothing fancy. Got plenty."

"In that case, I accept. I'll wash up before I come up to the porch. Maybe you'll think about putting away that Peacemaker you're toting. Don't want to ruin my reputation at being shot by a lady."

"Oh!" Shoving it into the holster at her hip, she whirled and her long strides took her back to her house. All the while, she tried to think how she'd make day-old pie taste good. Turning to look over her shoulder, she found him smiling from ear to ear and knew her face must be red as a sunset.

The darned man was both teasing and maddening. At this point, she wasn't sure she liked it one little bit. Running her hand through her hair, she nearly tripped over the stair. The sound of his laughter peeved her even more. Once inside, she pressed her hand to her heart. This was a very bad idea and playing a dangerous game.

BRYCE SPLASHED WATER over his head and shoulders. Running his fingers through his wet hair, he pulled on a clean shirt he'd brought along. For the hundredth time, a voice inside called him mule-headed. Stomping his heels against the wood step, he brushed his pants with a swipe of his hand. Just as he started toward a chair on one end of the porch, he took note of the rotting railings and the holes in the floorboards. The place was in real need of repairs only a man could handle. If she refused to sell to his brother, she'd be a fool.

The sound of her humming some song he didn't recognize from somewhere on the other side of the screen door captured his interest. Darned woman didn't know the effect she had on men. That's the moment it occurred to him that there were no plates setting on the porch table. Had she forgotten that he'd been invited to supper?

"Hannah. Do you need help with anything?" he called from his side of the door.

A few moments later, she appeared, pushing open the door and holding it in invitation. His heart tripped at the sight of her in that pretty green dress with little pink flowers at the collar. He stood dumbly, trying to think of something to say. Slack-mouthed, he gave himself a shake. Curving breasts and slender hips filled out her dress. Hannah May was transformed into veritable loveliness, and she could send a man to Hell with a smile. He had no business being alone out here with her. He should've paid heed to his brother's orders.

"Come in. It's too hot to eat out here on the porch. You look to be in deep thought. Is something wrong?" she asked.

He nodded at the understatement. Probably just as hot inside as outside, in his opinion. He followed her to the back kitchen and took the proffered seat across from her. Tearing his eyes from her, he focused on the bowls of stew and steaming bread, both smelling like heaven. Despite the tempting food, he wanted to run like a coward. Scant courage held him nailed to the seat. And now he didn't know how to start a simple conversation.

"You look mighty grim. I hope you didn't overdo yourself in that sun," she said.

"No. No. I'm just not used to home-cooked meals across from a pretty lady. I haven't had much in the way of polite society in years. Until Cort and Lark."

"A meal is the least I can do. Nothing fancy. I wasn't expecting you to fix my roof."

Lady, if only you knew what other things I'd like to do, you'd run for the hills. I have to draw a line, knowing you're a married woman.

Scooping his fork into the thick meaty stew, he sopped up the juice with his bread, leaving any further talk to her. When he did look in her direction, she stirred her food around the plate. It was clear she felt as awkward as he did.

As much as he fought it, this was an attraction that went beyond common friendship. And neither of them would be able to do a thing about their feelings until Lars was out of her life. He hated a man he'd never met.

After he finished, he eased into companionable conversation about little, everyday things. Cattle. Repairs needed on the house. How she made a living with a mixture of sewing, cattle, and vegetables in trade. When she alluded to some improper suggestions from some of the cowhands in exchange for favors, rage vibrated inside him, but he had no choice but to tamp it down until later.

"Will you be coming by to escort me to the ranch?"

"That was the plan. But nope. Cort needs me for branding and then we'll be on a buying trip. Be away for a few weeks. Tangle is coming out to get you."

"That's fine."

"Is it?"

Her frown was answer enough. She looked away and he watched her fingers where they were laced together against the table. She tilted her head up and looked toward him.

"Bryce."

There was silence. Whatever she'd meant to say died on her lips. The clock ticked and she pinned him with a look he couldn't identify. Was it pleading or was it question? Or both. Clearing his throat, he stood before he probed for more information about her husband, a marriage he had no business questioning. Lars wasn't his business. "Thanks for the supper. I'll be at the camp tonight, minding the cows. Be gone come dawn."

When she rose, they were close. Too close. His body tingled, wanting her touch. When her fingers reached for his hand, he slipped from her reach.

"I'm sorry. I was too forward," she whispered.

"No. Don't say it. Don't think it. I'm trying to be the gentleman and keep to my promise to stay away and not make this hard for both of us. But it is hard. This playacting between us is putting me on edge. Worse, I think it's hard for you."

"Bryce. Please. I...."

"Shh. Don't say it." Placing one hand on each of her shoulders, against his better judgement, he watched as her mouth trembled. His fingers drifted upward, tracing her neck. Then he cupped her face and lowered his mouth, grazing her lips with a light touch. Her mouth was soft, warm, and delicate—sending him to perdition. He was falling. Not from any roof. But from the promise he'd made to himself.

Unless he left now. Warning bells sent him tripping backward, and without a word, he went out of the door. He didn't remember anything until he sat astride his horse, his camp gear on the ground beside him. Without recollection of thought between here and there, he stepped down from his saddle at the camp beside a corral. Smoothing a hand across his horse's neck, the animal's hide twitched beneath his hand. Drawing a breath, he was obliged to make a decision. Even if it meant leaving a place where he'd found home. Lighting a cigarette, his hands shook while he gazed toward the setting sun.

SIX

BREWING STORM

THE NEXT MORNING, Bryce nudged his horse across the river onto Enders land. Once on the opposite side, he set out to the east where there was a penning corral. Today he was pitching in with branding. But while he rode, he thought about his brother's generous offer to Hannah. If her ranch failed, Cort would have more leverage in forcing a sale. Except for Hannah's sweet nature and her trading goods and services, there were few business advantages for Cort. The motivation behind this deal was two sides of a coin for his brother. Thinking about that kiss, he hoped she'd sell out soon. If she didn't, he'd be forced into leaving rather than risk what was left of his dignity. One misstep and he'd have no option but to get his gear together and move on.

"Hey! 'Bout time you showed up!"

Zeke's gravelly voice snapped him out of his musings. His horse trotted up beside the white-haired foreman who lazily sat atop his white horse like a wizard from an ancient kingdom. The old man was more likable now that he'd come to understand that his gruffness was just the nature of a man who'd seen more than he could imagine. A fixture on this ranch, Zeke was as wise a man as he'd ever met. A man who'd seen a long life. Now his enemy was the arthritis that plagued him with pain.

The ache was written on his wrinkled face, but Zeke wasn't the kind to whine. Cort often spoke of the man's ranching skills, learned beside the legendary Wade Harris.

"Yeah. Well. I'm here, Zeke. What do ya need me to do?"

"For starters, you can help roping the cows and draggin' them over to the brandin'. Then you better get down and start learnin' the trade closeup. Once you get used to the smell of burnt hide, you'll do fine. I figure you'll be stickin' around in the ranchin' business."

"What makes you sure about that? Hadn't thought that far."

"You better start. Cort's over by the main corral, hazing cows to the pen. He might want to see you doin' something besides jawing. 'Sides that, I remember Cort his own self, some years back, sayin' the same damn thing about leavin' here. He's still here."

"Everybody has opinions. I'll just keep to my own."

"Far as I can tell, you got the makings of a cowboy. Best prove it if you have a notion to be one."

Bryce tipped his hat and kicked his horse toward the corral, uncoiling his rope as he rode. The old man was genuine cowman—prickly jokes and sharp wit. But there was no disagreeing with Zeke. Keeping his head on the work was the best way to stay out of trouble.

After roping and dodging irritated, balky cows well into the afternoon, sweat dripped from his face. The heat was enough to burn your boots. At the two o'clock break, he and the rest of the men gathered near the water wagon where everyone guzzled their fill before chomping down dried beef and biscuits. The saddle horses were turned loose in an empty corral to drink from a trough, slapping against each other.

He joined the other hands in stripping off his shirt and dumping water over his head. Some men headed into the trees nearest the river to attend to personal needs then plunged into the river. Just as he decided to mount up and get back to work, Cort joined him.

"You want to try branding some tomorrow?" Cort asked.

Bryce tugged on his shirt. "Sure. Think I got the hang of it. Course, don't know if I'll ever get used to that stink. It's something mighty hard to forget."

"You better manage it. The men took bets that you'd puke. Guess we'll find out, big brother."

"Got money on me, huh? That include you?"

"Maybe. Better bet that you saw Hannah. Even against my repeated warning."

Poking his tongue into the pocket of his cheek, he darted an annoyed glance at his brother. Ignoring the scoff, he walked toward his horse and shoved his knee into the animal's side, flipped the stirrup over the saddle and tightened the cinch. Cort followed, leading his horse up beside him. He didn't need to look across his shoulder to know his brother waited for an answer. He never figured Cort to be such a busybody.

"Yeah. Saw her. Rounded up six head. Three ours. Tangle and Damon found more and moved them out while I patched up a hole in her barn roof. Anything else you want to know? I swear, never thought you'd be the one to get into my business."

"From where I stand, the lady has gotten to you. I warned you once. Figure I should keep warning you. You're playing with dynamite if Lars ever finds out. He could break you in half with one hand."

"I'm a grown man. Don't see what's wrong in helping out a woman in need of help. No harm in that." He ran a hand over his horse's neck and turned to face Cort's hard stare, sensing the lecture wasn't over. Maybe.

"If you think that's all you see in her, I'm disappointed in you. That aside, her place needs more than a roof. You already know I've tried to convince her to sell but she has it in her head that Lars will be back... spitting mad at her if she dared to sell out. I'm betting the grass is waving over him."

"She gave me supper." He said it flatly, keeping his expression blank. "*Ohh*."

That long, drawn-out *oh* riled him. "No *ohh* about it. Just supper. Heard enough times she's married. I fixed a roof, ate, and left."

"I'm thinking you're telling yourself one thing then thinking about doing another. Don't get yourself involved unless we figure her husband is gone for good. What you need is time in Ogallala. Hear tell they got some interesting gals at the saloon. Not that I could swear to it."

Swinging into his saddle, Bryce wrapped the reins around the pommel and buttoned his shirt. Squinting beyond Cort's shoulder to the southwest, the black-and-purple sky gradually shut out the sun, foretelling a storm. A gust of wind picked up dirt and sprayed it against the horses, sending them sidestepping. The branded cattle stood in the meadow, yanking up grass, while a few raised their heads and sniffed the air. There was a moment when all was calm until it wasn't.

"Looks like we got something brewing, Cort," Bryce shouted, pointing toward the sky.

After mounting, Cort twisted in his saddle and stared into the distance. "Christ. Been hot enough to melt iron. Look at those ugly clouds rolling in. Mean enough to be twister clouds. Let's get to low ground and signal the others to do the same."

Like Cort, Bryce tugged his neckerchief from his pocket then tied it around his nose and mouth. His brother waved his arm at his men who'd already gathered their horses and were heading out in all directions.

Bryce nodded and pointed in the direction of a gully. Large drops of rain pelted them while some of the men were grasping the reins of skittish horses, leading them into the trees. Others were already riding for the gulch. His horse turned rump to the wind and he hunched his shoulders, waiting for Cort, who took a last look at his bawling cattle, running across the pasture and down into a hollow.

"Come on! Let's take cover in the ravine over that next ridge where Tangle and Zeke just headed," Cort yelled over the wind.

Looking skyward in the direction of Hannah's cabin, the bruised sky swirled. In that moment, he knew what he would do. Decision made, he pointed in front of him and didn't bother to listen to his brother's mumbled response, lost to the wind. He set his horse into a full-out run. Reaching the river and creek beyond, he found the water whipped into a fury. Not hesitating, he kneed his horse, plunging the animal across the river. Once at the creek, he slowed, giving his horse time to pick his way across the shallower, rock-strewn water. By the time his horse scrambled up the embankment, hail bounced off his hat. A mixture of ice and rain struck his back and his face. He took the time to lower his hat to shield his eyes while loping across the pasture toward her cabin.

The hail stopped as suddenly as it started while the sky grew as dark as night. The wind stilled. The abrupt quiet eerie. Hunter's ears flicked. Something bad was about to happen. He urged his mount nearer to the cabin but by the time he rode up to her barn, the wind grew fierce, bending the younger trees. With his jaw set and panic knifing through him, he found her rounding the barn behind the flapping-winged chickens. The sight of her chasing them lost all of its amusement at the sight of the swirling sky behind her.

Without noticing him, she used her dress to try to rush the uncooperative birds toward the makeshift henhouse. The problem was, they weren't obliging. Instead, they were flapping and running in all directions. She made quite a sight with her skirt held up, shooing them. Taking matters in his own hands, he rode up behind her and shouted. Turning, he saw the fear in her eyes, along with her stunned expression.

"What the hell do you think you're doing?" Bryce called out as he dropped from his nervous horse. Grappling his wild-eyed horse, he managed to yank his rifle from the scabbard, before turning him loose.

Wild gusts of wind swallowed her words. "The storm! I'm trying to get the chickens into the henhouse. They're not budging."

"Let them go. They got more sense than you. We gotta find shelter," he yelled.

Whatever her retort had been, her pinched mouth summed it up. Her hands were on her hips and the wind lifted her hair, twisting it wildly. With her skirt wrapped around her legs, she stood defiant. Until she saw what he'd seen. Her mouth dropped open and her eyes widened with the same fear he'd held in check.

Amid the battle of wills, the air fell silent again. The chickens scampered to the barn, strangely gathered and quiet. While his mouth gaped open at the whirling cloud bearing down on them, the silver powder horn against an ink black sky sounded like the roar of a locomotive engine heading for where they stood frozen. Her ashen face looked toward him with disbelief.

Grabbing her by her arms, her entire body shook beneath his clasp. He followed her eyes to where they riveted on the sky-monster. Latching onto her, he lifted her into his arms, gripping his rifle in one hand. And he ran for their lives.

"Where's the root cellar?" he hollered.

"Right side."

When he reached the heavy wood door, he set her down and yanked. The hinges balked then finally broke loose, yet another thing he vowed to fix—if there was a house still standing. Grabbing her hand, he tugged her toward the cavernous dark below.

"You got a lantern and matches down there?"

"No. In the house."

"Get down in there. I'll be back."

He handed off his rifle and with a last look in her direction, he ran toward the front of the house, cussing the fates and everything else.

NOW IT WAS Hannah's turn to be frantic. He'd shoved her toward the darkness before turning on his heel, running for the upstairs of the house and leaving her to scramble to the bottom of the ladder. Once into the depths of the cellar, her skin prickled. The storm above was bad enough, but she felt trapped in the dank hole where crawly things hung in webs. Whenever she'd been down here to store canned goods, she'd left shaking. Her routine had been to bring a lantern and avoid the den of spiders. Never did she think she'd need to keep a lantern here, mostly because she avoided this place. Looking above at the opening, she prayed for the sky to clear. The blackness above her head sent shivers through her. Maybe it would pass them by.

Petrified, she crossed her arms. Worry about Bryce and the storm sent her body into shivers. Gusts of wind picked up dirt and sprayed it above her head. She held her hand against her nose while she watched, wanting to look away but desperate to see his face. Waiting. How many minutes had he been gone? Putting one foot against the bottom rail, she kept her face skyward as rain fell hard. Swiping the water from her eyes, she whispered, "Bryce, where are you?"

Rain pelted her face and hair. She'd seen plenty of storms around here. But this was the first time she'd witnessed a twister. Now one was about to destroy her only refuge as well as this kind man who'd become so dear to her that she would go crazy if he were killed. *Lars should be here. He should be the one to take care of things. Someone tell me what to do.*

Without warning, he appeared above her, wet hair matted to his head, his shirt and pants soaked through, sticking to his body like another skin. Handing down a lantern and matches, he tossed a potato sack and canteen to the dirt floor. Climbing part way down the ladder, he twisted his body and yanked the oak door closed with a bang. He brushed his hands and turned, leaping the distance to the floor.

Both now stood motionless in the dark, with only the faintest streak of light from wormholes in the door. She barely made out his profile, but the rasp of his breathing told her he was near. Her eyes riveted on the last barrier between them and the whirling devil outside. Neither said anything. A gust of wind rattled the door, threatening to suck it from the hinges. Then the howling wind began in earnest, leaving only each other and the sound of ruination above.

Bryce was the first to move, snatching the lantern from her tightly clenched fist. It took a moment for her eyes to adjust to his movements. Striking a match, he touched the flame to the wick, adjusting the glow. Blinking, she searched the low-ceilinged space for the cobwebs and snakes she feared. The cellar held crates, barrels, and even whiskey bottles along the stone walls. Funny how she hadn't stayed long enough to take inventory before now. What Lars had stored down here were his, with the exception of some jarred vegetables and her medicinal herbs.

Setting the lantern on top of a barrel, he turned to face her. Spine-chilling shadows formed in the dim light. Looking beyond his shoulder, her eyes fixed on the store of jarred pickles and carrots. Biting her lip, she hoped he didn't notice her quivering mouth. With the sound of the shrieking wind outside, she pressed a hand against her throat.

BRYCE STUDIED THE emotions playing over her shadowed face. He couldn't decide whether to offer her his touch of reassurance. He had to tread easy, not wanting to alarm her more than she already was. Above them, the house moaned and creaked. She caught her lower lip between her teeth, fastening her wide eyes on the door.

Taking her cold hands between his palms, he squeezed them, hoping to warm them. If he took her into his arms… he'd seal his fate. How would he ever be able to return her to Lars? Right now, the prudent thing would be to distract her, thereby distracting himself.

His eyes trailed over the rough walls. Suspended from wood rafters were nets filled with potatoes and onions. Long stalks of sunflowers and milkweed protruded from a burlap sack near his head, and he released one of her hands long enough to touch them. He wondered what they were used for. Knowing her efficient nature, she made use of everything. He raised an eyebrow.

"I make medicines with them. For different folks."

"I see you keep this pretty well stocked, down here."

"I have no choice. I'd starve, otherwise. Come winter."

He dropped both hands to his sides. She moved closer beside him, and he took the initiative and settled his arm around her shoulders.

"What do you think is happening out there?" she asked.

"It's either coming toward us or moving away from us. Not sure."

She stepped from his arm and sat down against the hard packed dirt floor, then leaned her back against the wall. With her knees hugged to her chest, she looked like a scared child. After a moment, he took a seat beside her, and with his legs outstretched, he rested his head against the stone wall.

"I'm scared," she murmured.

"Seems natural."

He wouldn't admit that he was scared, mostly for what they'd find once it was over. Confirmation of that thought proved true at the sound of splintering wood and shattering glass above. She pressed a hand against her mouth. He reckoned she had stifled a scream. Deciding to keep her talking, he asked, "What possessed you to be out there with the damned chickens when the wind picked up?"

"Why... I have to hang on to whatever I can. What would I do if I lost everything?"

"Sell out. Not because he's my brother and it would benefit him. That's all true. But he is offering you a fair deal. Besides, you could use the money to start a new life someplace else." Away from here. *Away from me. Away from your husband.*

"Lars owns this ranch. I have no authority to sell. Already told you."

He wished he had bitten his tongue. Instead, he huffed out a breath and continued. "Hannah, face the facts. Lars abandoned you. Fool that he is. Still, he's likely dead. The goldfields are rough. Fevers, shootings, robbers, diseases. You can't go on living like this."

As though he hadn't spoken, she whispered, "Bryce. It's awful quiet out there."

She'd effectively avoided the topic. But she'd made a good observance. It *was* silent outside. "Uh-huh."

His experience with tornadoes was limited. Still, he knew what the silence meant. He draped an arm around her quivering shoulders and tucked her head against his neck, a closeness that ran against his sworn good intentions. What he did know was that this storm might do exactly what she feared—take everything. Without thinking about her marriage for once, she relaxed against his side, sending his heart beating into his throat. Slowly, her fingers moved against his skin where his shirt still lay partly open.

"I'm scared," she whispered. Her soft breath touched his skin then she shivered.

"You're chilled. Wish I'd have grabbed dry clothes for you."

When she didn't answer, he sighed and whispered across the top of her head. "We'll be fine. I won't let anything happen to you." And he meant it.

RELIEVED AT THE confidence in his voice, Hannah lifted her head. His intense gaze was both reassuring and frightening. Especially because she needed and depended on this man. His eyes sparkled in the flickering lantern light and his arms tightened around her. For the first time she could remember, she felt both cherished and protected. His mouth lowered, ever so slowly toward hers. Hovering just a breath from her lips, he gently touched her mouth with his.

She tasted tobacco and salt. Her world, as she knew it, faded. Prickles of something she'd never experienced and was uncertain of, poured through her like warm honey. For a long time, she'd given up on ever knowing tenderness. Now it grew from the depths of her soul, and she didn't want to lose it. But it couldn't last, except for this moment, and then it would be forever lost.

Unkindly, she wished Lars would never return. Was it God's reprisal, sending this storm? Could she turn her back on the sacred words she'd spoken, pledging her fidelity, while now coveting another man? Yesterday and tomorrow blurred.

Jerking from each other at the crack of thunder and flash of light piercing the darkness, their eyes centered on the door above them. Wind tugged at the oak slab, demanding it open. The Devil was here, trying to force his way into their secret place. Something slammed hard against the house, then the wood floor and beams above their heads shook and bowed, heaved, and dropped with a shudder. She jerked at the thought the floor was about to collapse on top of them.

Her ears hurt and she curled against him while he wrapped her within his arms. Squeals and squawks of birds were drowned in the howl of the wind. Furniture slid across the floor above their heads, followed by crashing and splintering. Her teeth chattered as his fingers drifted through her hair. The sounds of destruction continued for what seemed like hours, until a last boom from all directions caused her to stiffen in his arms, then closing her eyes against what would happen next, she focused on his breathing beside her. Bryce held her protectively between both of his arms until she somehow found herself seated across his lap, not remembering how she'd gotten there.

Reaching, he grasped an empty potato sack and tucked it around her head. Her hand dropped to her rain-damp dress and she slumped like a rag doll, numbed with terror. His hand stroked her back and he kissed her head. She whimpered, nuzzling the crook of his neck beneath his chin.

"Shh. It'll be over soon. Then we'll face whatever we have to face."

"The chickens?" she squeaked. His chest rumbled beneath her cheek.

"Leave it to you to think about chickens. And how about the horses? Or the milk cow?"

"Do you think they'll be safe?"

"Yep. They're smart enough to run off to a hollow and sit it out. All of them."

"Bryce?"

"Hmm?"

"Were you married before you came here?"

When her question was met with silence, she leaned away from him. His face flushed and his jaw taut, he lowered his arms and hands to his sides. The wind outside of their sanctuary eased and quieted but the tension of a storm grew inside. Leaning his head forward, he scrubbed a hand across his stubble and his eyes closed. She'd stirred some guarded, painful secret, now wishing she could call back her question. Maybe it was thoughtless. But she'd needed his voice. Had he been married and his wife had met with some terrible fate? There was a pain-filled quiet between them. When he finally spoke, he said, "No wife."

His voice was hoarse. *No wife.* Why did that give her satisfaction? It shouldn't matter to her. But it did. There was no doubt there had been someone.

"I usually don't pry into people's business. I just thought...."

His finger crossed her lips. "Because you thought kissing a married man might hurt your tender sensibilities? Your sense of Christian values? Propriety."

His retort hurt. "Of course. Only a trollop would be alone like this, allowing a man she hardly knew to kiss her. Lars would be furious. Kissing you back was unforgiveable." She drew a breath. "I needed to know."

Now that the spell was broken, she tried to slide farther from him, but his hand snaked out and caught her. He looked toward her, his eyes cold and his jaw set.

"That wasn't fair for me to say. I'm sorry. But you keep strict rules and live by every one of them. You've lived up to your bargain. From where I'm sitting, you got nothing in return. Still, I have no right. You didn't deserve my taunt. I'm sorry."

He didn't touch her now, but she watched his fingers clench and unclench at his sides. A part of her wished to have him hold her again.

He sighed. "Furthermore, you're every bit a lady. I respect that. You are *not* a trollop. Do you know what that is?"

"A loose and sinful woman who does things with men. Any men."

"How do you figure you could be that? Have you been with other men?" He lifted her chin with a finger and held her gaze when she couldn't think how to answer. He waited, his mouth a firm line.

"You haven't answered me," he said.

"Of course not. I'm married. I made a pledge to be faithful. Until I know he's dead."

"That's what I figured. I'm trying hard to understand your thinking. Knowing your sense of honor, I don't want to have your ruin on my conscience. But I don't agree with anything about this situation. After our kiss, I think you can figure out how I feel. And I suspect you feel the same. Knowing you, it will be best to keep my distance because I'll want more. Sometime when you come to your senses, if and when you decide what you'll do about Lars."

"Fine, *Mister Enders,*" she snapped. "You do that. Keep away from now on. I can surely get help from plenty of the men over at the Double E. We don't need to see each other. No sense in us crossing paths. I have no need for—"

"What kind of help from the men who work for my brother?" he asked sharply.

———————————

SHE SCOOTED FROM his lap. He drew up his knees and draped his arms over them. Just what did she mean? He felt like he'd just been punched in the gut. Whether she realized it or not, she'd just struck a jealous nerve.

"Agreed. I'll make sure I stay away. But I still have another question while we're at it. Have Mason, Tangle, Billy, or any of my brother's hands ever approached you in a rude way with demands?"

"Nothing I can't handle. Sometimes we trade work for laundering and sewing. Not that some don't make improper offers. None have ever tried to hurt me. Besides, it's not your concern."

He'd bet she *tried* to set them straight. But just so it didn't happen again, he would have a talk with each of them. Hearing she was off-limits from him would leave no doubt. Still confounded by her thorny response, he decided it wise to end this discussion until another time. And he'd make it his concern.

"Bryce. Is it safe to go up the ladder?"

While he'd mulled the storm of emotions in his head, he'd forgotten about the storm outside. "You wait here while I go out and check things over. I'll call you out when I figure it's safe."

After they'd scrambled to the surface, they stood side by side in stunned muteness. Most of the windows were broken, glass shards scattered everywhere. The barn door was ripped away and rested against the front porch where a post had given way. The porch roof, strewn with tree branches, lay flattened against the ground. The front door wasn't visible beneath the rubble. The corral fence was split into kindling. Chickens were nowhere to be seen. Nor were the horses. The house stood, though it had suffered roof damage. The barn roof was half gone. Both structures needed drastic repairs that would take time he didn't have right now, even if he had help. Even if he were welcomed. Right now, that was questionable.

"Best we get your wagon loaded with whatever you want to take to the Enders Ranch, if I find the wagon is usable. I'll go look for the horses while you set some personal things out in front. Go see if you can get in the back way while I scout around."

"I don't know if I'll be able to fix most of this," she murmured.

When he tore his eyes from the devastation, he found her unblinking eyes fastened on the barn. With one fist pressed against her mouth, her eyes were dull with shock. The distress in her face tore into his gut, especially at the sound of her hollow voice.

"I'll see that it gets done. In the meantime, let's just get you packed up since you were planning to head out tomorrow anyway. I'll bet Lark is worried sick about you by now."

She nodded. "Bryce?"

"Yep?" He had no idea what he could say to ease her worry. Tragedy and loss he'd learned to live with. How did he comfort someone else's shattered life when he'd learned to blunt his emotions to such things? Looking forlorn in her damp gray skirt and blue blouse with her tangled mass of hair draped over one shoulder, he figured she could ask anything of him, and he'd move the moon to get it done.

"If you weren't married. Did you love someone?"

Christ. Where had *that* question come from? And why was it important to her? Everything in her world was in ruin and she'd turned back to his past. "I question why you're circling back to my past?" This woman had dug deeper than anyone else had ever done. With her chin tilted up, he studied her eyes and still couldn't read what lay beneath her study. Hope he couldn't offer. Truth about himself was raw.

"All I know is I'm surrounded by destruction. I don't want to lose anymore. Expect it has something to do with that. I'm not sure where my mind is. I need someone to hold onto."

Using his finger, he lifted her face. Her eyes were blue pools of despair. "I loved her."

Her heart-stopping blue eyes stayed on his. She neither smiled nor frowned. But she was broken inside. She'd touched a sacred part of his life. Still, having kissed this very kissable woman, he questioned whether he'd ever loved Gabriella. Or had he just been too young to know the difference between obsession and love?

He was thirty-one years old now. Not that same boy who'd followed his nurse back to Texas and stayed on, hoping her wayward husband never returned. But the war had ended. And Luis finally drifted home. Just as Lars would rise from the dead and find a way to ruin whatever had begun to grow between him and this woman.

As he thought it, she averted her face and he was forced to lower his hand.

"Hannah. I question whether she ever really existed, now that I've met you." Maybe that was the only hope he could give this woman.

SEVEN

TORN APART

TANGLE REGALED HER with tall tales of his varied adventures during the wagon ride, likely intended to amuse and distract her. Even when she was able to concentrate on his stories, they were so farfetched that she had to laugh, thus relieving her mountain of troubles.

Facing the reality that her cabin and barn were uninhabitable, she accepted the hospitality of Lark and Cort until such time that repairs could be made. Most worrisome, much of her vegetable garden had been pummeled with ice or ripped apart in the wind. With the exception of the carrots and potatoes, her food was so meager she worried she might not have enough to see her through the winter.

Admittedly, she longed to have Bryce beside her on this wagon seat. At the same time, she was thankful that he was gone. Far more questions and doubts plagued her whenever he was near. Yearning to know more about the vexing, taciturn man confounded her. All the while her conscience warned her that he was not her business. It was hard for her to admit she was jealous of the woman he'd loved when she had no right to be.

Tangle explained that Cort, Bryce, and the others had left to check the damage to stock and fencing after the storm roared through. Mortification set in at the thought of gossip once everyone knew where Bryce had been during the storm. Even cowhands blathered about such things. If Lars returned and found out, she would suffer the consequences, leaving Bryce to face her husband's wrath. Maybe if she left, Lars would never find her.

She cleared her throat and offered a sidelong glance, finding Tangle's eyes centered on the horses. She needed to set things right, starting now. "Tangle. I just want you to know that I take my marriage to Lars seriously."

Tangle leaned over the side of the rattling wagon and spit a wad of tobacco, a custom she found appalling... yet she'd grown familiar with his bad habit. His eyes stayed fastened to the road as though she hadn't spoken.

"I surely do know that, ma'am. A woman needs a man's help from time to time. Nobody thinks nothin' of Bryce helping you out."

Slapping the reins harder, the horses picked up the pace and the two of them fell into a companionable silence. Drawing a breath, she felt a small sense of relief. When the ranch house was in view, Lark stepped down from the wide porch in greeting. Alonzo and Adoeete ambled from the barn to help with unloading the few bags of clothes she'd packed.

After a brief hug between the two of them, Hannah followed Lark into the big house, all the while listening to the myriads of questions her friend had on her mind. She hardly had a chance to respond to most. *How badly was your house damaged? Are you all right? Did you find your milk cow? You won't stay out there alone until we get time to fix the place, and no arguments, do you hear?*

"My heavens. That storm scared us all to death the way it blew in. Ripped up a lot of fences and chased our cattle from here to Kansas, I expect. Cort rode in here like a madman, gave orders and left with most of the men. Said he'd meet up with Bryce. That was when he sent Tangle to get you. Now sit while I put out some cold tea," Lark ordered.

"I appreciate your invitation. Just don't know what I'll do about Rocky Creek."

"Never mind your ranch, for now." Lark looked over her shoulder to where she sat at the long, scarred oak table. "Something is different about you. I see it in your eyes. And don't tell me it's just that house you're worried about. That can be put back together," Lark said.

"I'll figure things out one way or another. I'm just tired."

Avoiding Lark's intense glare and the looming topic of Bryce, she picked up the baby and held him against her shoulder.

"He's getting so big," she said.

"Yes. You deserve to have a family of your own," Lark said as she poured tea into each of two cups.

"Not as long as Lars is my husband. I've always wanted my own babies. Can't deny that."

Lark sat and stared at her. "Bryce is a good man. He's had his share of sorrows. From what Cort said, he'd run his horse as fast as a cut cat in the direction of Rocky Creek when he saw that twister heading your way. Sounds like he cares for you."

"I know he's a good man, Lark. I'm trying to be a loyal wife. Besides. I'm married and that's that. My first job is to make the house livable."

"We're all hoping you get that problem resolved. The sooner the better. And I don't mean the house."

Hannah switched the subject before she couldn't hold in an urge to cry. She was without a place to live, and her husband was gone. And the one man she cared about was out of her reach. And here she sat with a woman she could confide in. But the words wouldn't come.

"Little Bryce looks so much like Bryce and Cort." Hannah brushed her finger over his soft hair.

"That he does. I'll let you in on a secret. There will be another one come late winter or early spring. Haven't told Cort yet. Theresa and Nita know and are sworn to secrecy. When things calm down, I'll tell him."

"Oh, Lark! That's wonderful news. I'll be glad to help out in any way. I'll keep your secret. Don't keep this news to yourself for too long. Cort will be wildly happy."

"I'm counting on you to be here when my time comes. That is, if you still think you'll be here. I'm worried Cort'll become overprotective."

"Don't have much choice but to stay. At least until I know if Lars is still breathing."

"If it sets your mind at ease, I'll see that Cort doesn't press you on selling. In the meantime, I'll hope you reconsider. You'd be best to find a new life. If not here, then somewhere far away. I'm hoping you'll settle in town." Lark rapped her fingers against the table. "Nothing like keeping busy when we've got things on our mind. Once we repair some damage here, we'll all pitch in at your place. For now, we have clothes to sew and food to cook."

The baby touched her mouth with his little fingers, and she couldn't resist kissing him on his sweet cheek. "Lark. You're so lucky to have a wonderful husband and beautiful baby. And now another one on the way."

"About that, there's been hardships. Nothing has been easy. How about I take this one upstairs for his nap, then we'll finish this conversation. It might help you to know things weren't always so good around here."

When Lark left the room, her thoughts turned to her miserable, untenable situation. She didn't see how talking could possibly help.

TWISTING HER CUP between her hands, Lark didn't know where to start. She wasn't about to reveal everything. But this woman staring across the table at her folded hands didn't deserve to be bound to a contemptable husband like Lars van Stadt.

She cleared her throat. "It was a hard start for us when we met. Our story is different but similar. I almost lost Cort. If it wasn't for his tenacity, my life would have taken a very dangerous turn. I don't want the same thing to happen to you. The one thing you need to do is to find out the whereabouts of your husband so you can get on with your life."

"I've written a few letters of inquiry. I'm just waiting for a response."

"How long will you wait? What if he's dead and no one knows anything about him?"

Hannah's face lifted and her lips pinched. There was that subtle twitch that Lark recognized as worry.

"I don't know. I'd like to have the right answers, but I don't."

Lark reached across the space between them and patted Hannah's folded hands.

"I wish I had the right answer to give you. I guess it all comes down to how long you think you want to gamble on your future. Don't wait too long, Hannah."

She stood and tended the stew pot, her back to her sorrowful-looking friend. When she heard a brief sniffle, she could hardly bear her friend's anguish. Hannah would have to come to terms with her situation and she only hoped it didn't go on for much longer.

"How long do you think before the men get back?" Hannah asked.

Lark darted a glance over her shoulder at the question. Not for the first time, she knew that this strange quiet in Hannah was more about Bryce. Even usually stoic Cort had noticed something in Bryce.

"Cort said he'll be back in a week. Bryce along with him, if that's what you're wanting to know."

"I'm sure that Bryce can take care of himself. I've got no right to ask about him."

Lark set the long wooden spoon on the worktable beside the bubbling pot and turned to face the frowning woman. With her hands on her hips, she gave thought to all that her friend had endured. One thing was certain. Hannah had fallen in love with her brooding brother-in-law.

"Is that so? We're both women. I've seen how he looks at you. And you look at him the same way. Anyone with eyes can see how you need each other. From what my husband tells me, Bryce is miserable."

Lark watched as Hannah dropped her face into her hands. This woman was twisted up inside and until the matter of Lars was settled, nothing would be right.

"I thought I could hide it. My feelings. They don't belong there."

"Can't hide them from me. And they belong there. Sometimes we can't do anything else but accept our feelings."

Looking up, Hannah said, "Staying away from him is what I should do. Somehow, we're thrown together. For Bryce, the answer is simple, forget about Lars. *It isn't simple.* Besides, he has his own secrets."

"That he does. Cort knows more than I do. Those brothers are close-mouthed about most of it. Seems he manages whatever it is. And you have a chance to change everything. All you need to do is trust him."

"Do you know much about where he's been since the war?"

"Only snatches of things he says. All I know is that he left the Virginia homestead to follow his father into battle. Cort is younger by three years. Still, they both headed into war. They never did catch up with each other. Neither knows where their sister got to.

Seems Bryce was shot up and taken to a field hospital in Mississippi. That was where he got mixed up with a nurse from Texas. After the war, he returned to the Virginia home before he headed to Texas, trailing the nurse. Cort said she was married. Guess they both figured her husband might've been killed. But her husband drifted back. Bryce ends the story there. All he admitted to was heading for the goldfields and putting Texas behind him. Neither of us knows what happened in Texas… between *them.*"

"It's not my business."

At the sight of her drawn face, Lark's heart ached. "No. It's none of our business. But whatever happened carved out the man he is now. From the look of you, why don't you go upstairs and rest. I'll come get you in a bit?"

Hannah stood and started toward the hallway. Lark stopped her. "You know, Hannah. Things have a way of sorting themselves out. Tomorrow, we have canning and sewing to do. These wranglers could use some fixed-up pants and shirts. Besides, you and I could use a dress or two. Theresa and Nita can't wait to have something pretty to wear out of that calico and gingham."

"I'd appreciate keeping my hands busy. Thank you for having me."

"No thanks needed. Things will work out." Lark didn't miss Hannah's ramrod straight back as she walked into the shadows of the hallway. A shiver ran through Lark's body on a wave of melancholy. A

long road was ahead for Bryce and Hannah. One that reminded her
of her and Cort.

———————————

ALMOST TWO WEEKS later, four women were sitting in the parlor
amid shears, needles, and thread. Rolls of blue, gray, and green gingham lay across the dining table alongside spools of lace. Heads bent
over cloth, they measured, cut, and stitched. And gossiped. Their voices
stopped at the sound of riders. Their heads lifted in unison then listened to the beat of hooves growing louder then slowing.

Shouts and whoops drew the four women to the front of the house
where they crowded in front of the parlor window. A rangy, dirty pair
of lead riders ahead of ten scruffy, dirt-caked wranglers rode past, coming to a halt in a swirling cloud of dust beside the corral. Alonzo and
Adoeete waved their hats in greeting, helping take the horses into the
enclosure for much needed attention.

Hannah's eyes riveted on Bryce's broad frame sitting straight in the
saddle, not offering so much as a glance in the direction of the house.
His beard was full, and his clothes were sweat soaked and peppered
with dust. Cort didn't look any better. Their boots and stirrups held
clods of Nebraska dirt. One of the hands opened the gate, allowing
them all inside.

Each of the men set to work untying bedrolls and slickers from behind cantles. In the distance, a chuckwagon rattled up behind the men's
cookhouse where Alonzo headed to help unload gear and trail food. Damon and Adoeete shuffled from the corral and lent an additional hand.

Hannah followed Lark onto the porch to wait as Cort and Bryce dismounted, shucking from their chaps then handing them off. The smell
of horse, leather, and cows drifted on a soft wind. Hannah's sidelong
glance found Lark's eyes fastened on her husband where he marched
with purpose in his wife's direction, his eyes holding hers. When she
ran down the steps, he dropped his gear and lifted her into his arms,
neither concerned about the filthy clothes between them.

Wrapping her arms around her middle, she imagined how it would feel to be so loved. She was envious, watching them kiss, seeming without notice of anyone around them. The feeling of being alone had never been more jarring. An emptiness crept through her, forcing her to avert her eyes, not wanting to be a spectator to something so personal and sweet. For a moment, she wished for Bryce's touch and his kiss. The taste of it never left her.

Glancing up, she hoped to see Bryce and her wish was answered when he strode from behind the couple, offering her a brief glance without acknowledgment. With a rifle in hand, he changed course, striding around the house where she expected he intended to wash up at the back pump. Hannah turned and walked into the coolness of the big house then straight into the kitchen where Nita was rolling out dough. Against her better judgment, she was drawn to the squeak of the pump, finding herself standing behind the screened doorway, shamelessly watching.

While he splashed water over his face, she found herself fascinated at the drops clinging to his thick, dark beard. Unbuttoning his shirt, he shrugged out of it then draped it over the pump. Cupping his hands in the water pail, he splashed his bared chest. Her eyes followed the arrow of his chest hair to where it disappeared beneath his belt. Gulping, she brazenly watched, her eyes riveted on his rippling muscles, sun-dark skin, and firm stomach.

His gun belt, still fastened low on his hips, reminded her of his dangerous side. Still, he was the most handsome, sinewy man she'd ever seen. His head jerked up. She caught sight of his quick grin before it disappeared. Their eyes held a moment before he blinked away the drops running across them. Grabbing up his shirt, he seemed satisfied with her long perusal. Using his shirt, he dabbed at his face, and then with a quick smile he said, "Hannah."

She swallowed and couldn't think of a word to say. Neither could she look away.

"Did you miss me?" he teased.

Her face flamed and his eyes held hers hostage. Of all the audacity, he winked. She bit her tongue against a blistering retort, thinking better of it. In fact, not able to think at all. After all, she'd been the one caught gaping. When she averted her stare, he moved closer to the door where she stood. The blasted man waited and watched until she looked toward him. He peered into the shadows of the kitchen, and she lifted her chin.

"Huh. Cat got your tongue? I apologize. Didn't mean to goad you. I'll flat out admit that I missed seeing you."

"I guess seeing cattle all day gives you a new perspective on things."

"Perspective? Interesting word."

"It means—"

"I know what it means, Hannah. I'm just goading you because then your eyes sparkle. You're easy to tease. Have to learn to mind my tongue around you. Seems my brother wants me to come back up to the house once I get the smell of cows off me. Dinner at the big table tonight."

She nodded, searching for something to explain away her bold stare and came up dry. Instead, she said, "I better get busy helping with the food, in that case."

"I'll count on you being there. You know we can't keep avoiding each other. No matter how hard we try. Best get straight out with that. As long as we're both here, we're bound to run into each other."

"I don't know what you mean."

"Yes, you do. I spent long nights on my bedroll thinking about you. I'm betting you gave me some thought. Someday, you'll admit it."

With that, the inscrutable, perturbing man turned away, and strode toward the bunkhouse. But not before he called over his shoulder. "Best not drop open your mouth for long or you might catch a fly."

His laughter trailed off, leaving her to mull over how she should deal with Mr. Enders.

BRYCE STEPPED INTO the front hall to the sounds of familiar voices and laughter drifting from the dining room. In fact, he preferred the homey kitchen over the more pretentious dining table. Running his fingers through his damp hair, he strode in the direction of all the chatter, pausing long enough to glance at his reflection in the hall mirror.

Not much he could do about his beard. Wouldn't matter much to the cows he'd be herding to the Omaha cattle cars. Damn. Once again, he'd be staring at the stars and wondering if she gave any thought to him. More to the point, what would he do about her? Sure as hell, sooner or later he had to either take her or leave her. Leaving her was a bitter thought. If Lars returned, he wouldn't be able to live nearby, knowing she was sharing another man's bed. That man had to be dealt with. Sooner rather than later.

Stepping into the light from the massive chandelier, his jaw dropped. The platters in the center of the table were heaped with ham and beef. From a large pot on the sideboard, the smell of stew wafted through the air. There was enough food to feed the twelve men down at the bunkhouse. His mouth watered at the aroma of fresh bread. When he was able to tear his eyes away from the food and to the silent table, he was met with stares. Just what were they all looking at? Had he forgotten to button his pants?

"Take a seat, Bryce. You're late. We were waiting for you," Cort admonished.

"Sorry. Took longer for me to get cleaned up than I thought." He sat beside Zeke on his left while Hannah was seated across the table from him.

With his usual dry humor, Zeke said, "Glad you finally got here. I woulda volunteered to come lookin' for you. Except appears Mason and Tangle got invited and they look starved to death. Might be nothin' left when I got back."

Zeke's kidding lightened the mood, and the banter began in earnest while Lark smiled and began passing the plates around the table. Hannah drilled him with a sweet-as-butter smile. Her sparkling hair was pulled into a neat bun, her golden tendrils framing her delicate, sun-kissed skin. In fact, he noted a fair sprinkling of freckles across her nose. She wore a blue dress with little white flowers, lining a low-enough neckline to tempt a man. He ground his teeth at the thought of other men looking her way. Forcing his eyes back to her face, his throat tightened. If he had to describe her, he'd have to say both angelic, regal, and so tempting.

She passed a platter across the space between them and he nearly dropped it, prompting him to look away from her little grin. Shaking his head, he turned his attention to the food before he made a complete fool of himself.

Tangle, Mason, and Zeke conveyed tales about the herd and the weather. Zeke chimed in with guffaws and reflections about the storms he'd lived through over his many years. The twisters that he'd seen in his lifetime made the one that just came through seem puny, according to him. He'd learned that Zeke liked to embellish, more for his own entertainment than anyone else's.

Mason related his own stories of roundups and rustlers. In fact, he mentioned nearly becoming a rustler with the Cardin gang. No sooner had that name left his tongue, he lifted one corner of his mouth and winced. The table grew suddenly silent. Cort cleared his throat and Mason's face took on the color of a sunset.

The late afternoon wore on while everyone forked food into their mouths, dismissing Mason's mention. The women fussed with platters and scurried around the table, refilling coffee mugs. Theresa handed the baby off to Cort who sat the boy on his lap, handing him small chunks of bread to chew on, much to Lark's obvious pleasure. But his eyes kept drifting back to the woman sitting across from him. Convinced that Lark must've arranged the seating to torture him, with his brother's warnings ringing in his head he didn't know where to avert his eyes. They returned to her more than he wanted.

"You've been pretty quiet, Bryce," Mason chided.

"I guess I'm not in a talkative mood."

"You talked to them cows. If it wasn't for the rest of us, we'd hear daylight," Tangle quipped. "If you'd go to town once in a while, them gals would get you talkin'."

Bryce ran his finger around the collar of his fresh washed shirt, having had enough of the teasing. He was already uncomfortable at being in a fine dining room and eating food from china dishes. Making it worse, Hannah was gazing in his direction after that crude suggestion, seeming to wait on his response. Damn, those two men were making things worse with their quips, and he felt his face flame. They knew he was nervous as hell. Anyone could see that.

He vowed to get even at the first opportunity. All he wanted to do was eat and make excuses to return to the bunkhouse. Next thing he'd know, one of these men would bring up his snoring or his cussing, just to embarrass him more.

With a raised eyebrow, Cort said, "Tangle, remember we've got polite women here. Besides, my brother's face is red under that beard. Might bust a blood vessel."

Thankfully, Cort stifled the joking by coming to his rescue, though half-heartedly. If not, he'd considered leaving but her smile kept him fastened to the seat. Damned if Tangle didn't look contrite as he sipped his coffee. That was a first.

"Sorry," Tangle muttered under his breath over the rim of the cup. Bryce offered a quick nod.

"How about if you men go do your smoking out on the porch while we set out the pie and clear the supper?" Lark suggested.

When she stood, the men followed suit. Bryce blessed his sister-in-law for easing the tension and finding a way to relieve him of his embarrassment. If he were anywhere else, he'd be inclined to even the score with language not fit for the ladies.

"Sounds good," Cort replied, handing little Bryce off to Theresa who carried the boy into the kitchen behind the women.

The men left and found places to sit on the long, broad porch. Zeke took his usual perch on a rocking chair while Tangle headed down the steps toward the bunkhouse. Before he got to the bottom step, he turned toward Bryce.

"You want to join us in a game, boss?"

"I think I'll have that pie."

"Thought so. G'night."

Bryce squinted, watching as Tangle moseyed away on his bowed legs. Then he said to no one in particular, "Poker. Haven't played much of that since I left the gold camp." He rolled a cigarette and struck a match. He happened to look up when the silence felt heavy. His brother's eyebrow was raised.

"You don't like poker, little brother. I take it?"

"No. Not anymore. I'll take it unkindly if you mention poker in front of Lark."

Bryce wondered why. One of these days, he might hear that part of the story. Though he couldn't imagine how anything could've been worse than being sliced by that heartless outlaw. Still, he wondered how poker had played any part in it. Or even if it had. In the meantime, he took a seat on the bottom stair and lit the cigarette he'd been thinking about smoking since supper. Being outside settled his ruffled nerves, breathing in the scent of prairie sage.

"Hey. Ain't that strange?" Everyone followed Mason's pointed finger. "Looks like we got company coming. Kinda late in the day."

"Who the hell would be coming for a visit?" Cort queried.

Bryce's eyes had already centered on the approaching buckboard, drawn by two roan horses. His skin prickled. Something about the man and woman looked familiar. As they drew closer, he refused to believe what he was seeing—ghosts from his past. Sitting between them was a little boy with dark hair. The boy held on to the stern-faced woman's arm as though he were scared to death. Standing very slowly, he strained to make sure he wasn't mistaken. With his back ramrod straight, he tried to comprehend the unbelievable vision.

The boy's face paled in the afternoon light while his eyes searched the porch. As they drew close, Bryce tossed his cigarette then stepped down and crushed it beneath his boot. His brother followed behind and took a place at his side. Only Cort wore his holster and he wished he'd kept his on.

The door squeaked. There was the familiar clomp of Zeke's worn boots behind him. Glancing over his shoulder, he saw Mason and Zeke holding rifles clutched at their sides. Few folks came this way without a good reason, unless they were lost or looking for trouble. Bryce smelled trouble. In fact, he was certain of it. Especially since he knew this woman and man. They were older but he'd never forget them. They'd never been friends nor had they been particularly foes.

The wagon rattled and the horses snorted when the man brought the wagon to a stop several yards from the porch. Bryce stood shoulder to shoulder beside his brother, neither speaking. Without looking, he sensed that Lark and Hannah had joined the welcoming committee on the porch. Turning his full attention to the three people seated on the wagon, his heart lurched in his chest with such force... he feared he might drop to his knees.

At first, he staggered a step backward as though he'd been slugged by an invisible fist. Drawing a breath, he lifted his face. He had to be mistaken at what he saw. The three sets of unwavering eyes stared back at him with equal intensity and surprise. Sure as hell. These were people he never expected to see again. Salina and Ernesto Montez. With a little boy. Trouble was, they had no children. And this boy's hair. His eyes....

They were *his* eyes.

When he took a tentative step closer to the wagon, Cort stayed beside him. Bryce darted a quick glance at his brother. "Stay here. I need to take care of this alone."

"You know them?"

"I know them. Let me find out what they want. Alone."

"Play it your way. We'll watch them. I'm not out of earshot or gunshot range."

EIGHT

PAINFUL REVELATION

BRYCE REACHED UP and clasped Ernesto's proffered handshake. Salina sat stiffly, her eyes taking in the big house, doing her best to ignore him. The boy leaned against Salina, gripping her arm and avoiding the sight of the stranger standing near him. He appeared to be… maybe ten. But he wasn't around kids to know the difference.

"You've changed," Ernesto said with his familiar Spanish accent.

"Got older. Why are you here, Ernesto? It's a long way from Texas. How did you find me?"

"You have many questions. I have little time to answer. We are going to settle in Oregon."

"Sold your ranch?"

"*Sí.* Tired of watching my cattle die. We read of Cortland Enders and his magnificent gun and killing of Will Cardin. Gabriella told us of your brother before she died. Did you know she died?"

Drawing in a long breath against the punch to his gut, he slowly shook his head and closed his eyes momentarily. *Hell, no.* How would he know? His beautiful lover… dead. The news sliced through him then tumbled into an abyss of simmering anger mixed with heart-wrenching pain. Why hadn't someone told him? Somehow, he managed to return his focus on the man who'd delivered the blow. "How? When?"

"A fever. She had broken bones when we found her. The doctor thinks it was infection. Before she died, she left a letter with us. But we did not know we would find you here. We thought it would be only your brother. Now it is for you to read so you know we do not lie."

Salina pulled a folded letter from the reticule on her lap and handed it toward him. With eyes filled with unshed tears, he didn't miss how her hand shook at their touch. "She explains in her note," Salina said on a near whisper. The boy's mouth trembled, and Bryce figured the kid was doing a fair job of holding back an outright sob.

With quaking hands, Bryce unfolded the delicate missive and held it to the light. His eyes took in the ragged handwriting of someone almost too sick to hold the ink pen. The scrawled phantom words washed through him and filled him with regrets and recollections too painful to think about. Lowering the letter, his body jerked. Swallowing a gasp, his throat closed with grief.

With a sidelong glance toward his brother, Cort stepped closer. Bryce handed over the letter, and no one spoke. Cort's face grimaced as he read the words, then he offered him a hard stare before handing it back.

Clearing his throat, Bryce turned his full attention to the boy. Dark haired with blue-gray eyes like his own, the kid fidgeted on the seat. The boy's eyes returned again and again to the man and woman on either side of him. Traces of red glistened in the boy's hair, reminding him of Gabriella's tresses. This can't be real. He must be having a nightmare.

Face beaded with sweat, he turned it skyward and swiped the wetness from his eyes before he could bring himself to look at the boy again. That he was still standing upright when he wanted to sink to his knees was only by sheer determined will. And he quietly damned the fates.

"Are you sure he's my son?" Bryce asked. He heard his brother's long intake of breath at the question.

"Sí. Can you not see his face? He is *yours*. We found this place to return your son to his rightful family. It is good we found you here. Now he will have his father when we thought to deliver him to his uncle," Ernesto explained.

Bryce started to speak but his voice cracked. Words he wanted to say

lodged in his throat. What should he ask? Mindful that these folks waited, his shock emptied his mind of any reason. Anything he might say
might be construed offensive, especially if he questioned their honesty.

Cort stepped closer to Salina. "Ma'am. How old is the boy?"

"He is eleven years old. He was born in July 1868. Soon, he is twelve."

Bryce jerked his head up and calculated. The date fit. He'd left by then.

"He's *not* my pa! Ernesto is my father now. I want to stay with him.
I won't stay here."

The boy's outburst jolted Bryce from his numbness. *His* son sat stiff-
backed, his eyes dark with seething fury. Scowling in his direction with
his teeth and fists clenched, Bryce didn't doubt the boy would put up a
fight—like he would do in the same situation.

He glared at the unruly boy with both pride and dread. This boy
was his son and he owed Gabriella to see to his care. Now that it sank
in, how did a father deal with a defiant kid? Damned if he'd let Ernesto
leave with his flesh and blood. There was no doubt that this boy looking back at him with the same eyes… was *his* son. *Cort must see it, too.* His
brother's hand squeezed his shoulder. This scared boy was an Enders.
Gabriella had never let him know nor tried to find him. *Damn her for
that. Damn Luis.*

"What does Luis say about this?" Not that he'd give a damn.

"He left the boy with us after Gabriella died. That was about two
years ago. We gladly took in my brother's son. But now we have new
plans and cannot take him along. You are his father," Ernesto replied.

At that moment, the boy yanked his hand from the stoic woman's
arm and punched the seat with his balled fist. "I'm not going to stay. You
can't make me. I don't want to stay with him. I don't know who he is.
He's not my father!"

"You will stay with this man. He is your real papa. Your mother told
you of him before she died. Do you think she lied?" Ernesto argued.

"I won't stay. If you leave me, I'll run away. You don't want me. My
ma is dead. And Luis left me. I can find work. I'm almost a man."

Bryce stepped close beside the seat. Face upraised, he studied the
boy's hard jaw. "No. You won't. You *will* stay here, son."

The yawning years had fallen into his lap and right now, he had no idea how to deal with them. Except that he had no choice but to take this intractable kid in hand and figure something out.

"I'll run away. I'll stay long enough to steal a horse and you won't find me."

Bryce's first inclination was to wrench the boy down from the seat. Instead, he watched as Cort crossed his arms over his chest and addressed the recalcitrant boy, using a different tack. "Stealing a horse, even from me... your uncle Cort... is a hanging offense. At the least, I'd have you caught and while I might not hang you, I'd change your mind so you'd remember. I'm not about to let you steal a horse."

The boy's eyes widened and then became an icy stare. Dammit. What was wrong with Cort, scaring his son with threats? It was time to try a different approach.

"What's your name?"

The boy straightened his hunched shoulders. "My name is Reyes Morgan Montez."

"Nope. Afraid not. From now on, you will be my son. That means your name is Reyes Morgan Enders. And don't you forget it."

"I won't use your name unless I get something for it."

Now the boy sounded more like Luis. A thief and a calculator.

"What did you say?" If blood boiled, Bryce's was about to bust from his veins. What he'd like to do is turn him over his knee.

"I want a horse. Then I'll stay."

"If you meet *my* demands."

"What are they?"

"You'll find out after you step down from the wagon and face me man-to-man." While he waited for an answer, Lark's soft voice broke through the crackling air.

"For heaven's sake! Reyes, is it? Shall I call you Rey?" Lark asked while Hannah stood beside her. Bryce and Cort were both taken by surprise that the women had been in the background listening. Their sudden interference didn't sit right, but they sure looked formidable.

Reyes trailed his eyes rudely over the two women from their heads to their boots. Bryce watched the boy's brazen inspection, knowing Luis had played a role in this learned behavior. The women waited. Unless Bryce missed his guess, Reyes's quaking lower lip meant he'd reached his limit of control. The boy turned to Salina. She shook her head. "Go."

When he didn't move, Salina's husky voice said, "Go. Get down. This is your papa. Your mama would want you to be with him. Remember her. Remember she asked you to go to him." Salina whispered the last, averting her face from the boy as though the subject were closed.

The wagon seat tilted as Ernesto stepped down. Reyes followed, jumping to the ground and taking strides to stand in front of his uncle. Bryce noted the boy's flushed face and recognized festering resentment growing by the minute. How could he cool down a kid? This would take time to figure out. Time he didn't have much of these days.

Lean and tall for eleven years old, Bryce turned and offered his hand, figuring that would be a start. Instead, the boy stepped back, leaving Bryce to drop his hand. Now he added rebellion and ill manners to the list of problems.

Stiffening his back, Bryce cleared his throat. "I'll do right by you, son. You'll have me to count on from now on."

"I don't want *you*."

Flummoxed, Bryce looked to his brother who'd turned his attention to the men waiting along the porch. Apparently, Cort didn't know what else to say and left it to him. Bryce pressed his hand to the back of his neck, not knowing who would break the electrified air without a full-out storm.

Hannah spoke just as he had decided to grab hold of the boy's arm. "I'll bet you're hungry. We happen to have quite a feast on the table. Besides, while you eat, maybe Bryce... your father... will discuss what job they will offer you on this big ranch. I'm sure you will need the work."

The boy nodded agreeably. Damn. Hannah knew exactly how to frame the situation and turn the kid around. For the moment, at least. With a last glance at Ernesto and Salina, Reyes turned and followed the women toward the house, all the while chattering about the ranch.

Hannah's arm rested around Reyes's shoulders just as the three of them disappeared inside of the house. Not once did his son look back at the wagon. Grinning, a new admiration welled inside him for Hannah May. She'd accomplished a truce, whereas he and Cort fell short. Yelling wouldn't have worked. The boy warmed to the women, especially Hannah. If only he could make her part of his life, not just for the sake of Reyes. When he returned his attention to Ernesto's pinched mouth, Cort was standing beside the wagon, gripping a carpetbag.

"Is this all he has?" Cort asked, his voice hoarse.

"All he needs. We have little room in our wagon."

Bryce faced Ernesto. "Cort. Can you leave us a moment?" he said, not taking his eyes from Ernesto.

Cort nodded and ambled away a short distance then waited.

"Luis. Where is he?" Bryce asked. "Still in Texas?"

"Luis is not in Texas. We wanted to warn Cortland Enders that Luis fled north in a rage. He did not know where you had gone or how to find you. Instead, he talked of revenge for Gabriella. And the famous Cortland Enders became a fire inside. So, I say this. He is my brother. His head is not right since he was dishonored. I warn you that he may be nearby. If he finds you…." Ernesto swiped his hand across his neck in the sign of death. "This is all I will say."

From the corner of his eye, Bryce saw Cort's chin lift sharply at what he overheard. And his response was quick and to the point.

"Thanks for warning us. We'll look out for our own. If your brother comes here wanting trouble, he'll be met with more than he bargained for. I'd offer you food and hospitality, but under the circumstances, there's no use in stirring up the boy. I thank you for bringing Reyes to us. He will want for nothing."

"I am sure he will eat well. Your ranch is a good ranch."

"I speak for my brother," Bryce interceded. "On the way along this road you'll come to a large line shack. It is quite comfortable. If you get going, you might make it there by dark. Follow the wagon trail," Bryce offered.

"We will not see each other again. I will take you up on that offer of the little shack we saw."

"Bryce." Salina's soft voice surprised him. Her dark eyes softened for the briefest moment. "She loved you. But she was as foolish as you. If only you both had never met."

His heart hammered in his throat and his stomach clenched at her harsh words. "Salina, I guess I'll never know for sure if she loved me or if we were just too young to know what that means. Passion gave us Reyes. He's a fine gift."

He waited while Ernesto seated himself and then slapped the reins, sending the wagon into a turn toward the rough road. Neither of them looked back. Finally, the wagon disappeared over the rise and beyond the hillsides dotted with cattle. He couldn't bring himself to look toward his brother, though he was most likely still churned by what happened. Same as him. Too many things bristled between them—not the least of which, how he'd brought trouble to his brother's doorstep.

"Luis Montez is out there, Cort," Bryce blurted.

"You figure he's dangerous. I can see it in your face."

"Crazy and very dangerous."

Neither of them needed to say more. They headed up onto the porch. Five wranglers lined the stairs and porch, their rifles at their sides. Zeke sat in his usual chair, his rifle resting across his lap.

"Thanks for keeping watch, boys," Cort said. "Think we can call it a day now."

"Anything you need from us, Cort?" Mason called out.

"Tangle. Damon. Mount up and follow them a few miles to make sure they keep moving. Let us know if you see anyone else out there. From now on, we need all eyes on trespassers. We may have figured out the name of the cow killer. A man all the way from Texas with a mean bone to pick."

————————

THE HOUSE WAS dark. A few horses trotted around the corral situated near Zeke's house. Stars filled the sky like a million snowflakes cast skyward. The moon was full and bright—a hunter's moon. Hannah turned away from the window and finished wiping down the kitchen table. Setting clean plates out for breakfast, she couldn't help but smile to herself, recalling Reyes gobbling down everything on his plate.

She guessed that he hadn't had many good meals lately. She felt his anguish all the way to her bones. The sadness of missing his mother was in his eyes. Losing a mother wasn't easy for a youngster. To be left with strangers added to the list of betrayals. She was no stranger to such loss.

Looking around the dimly lit room, she couldn't help but miss her own little cabin. The place had become her sanctuary... more since Lars had left. No more raging, drunken insults and demands that reminded her of her own stupidity in marrying a man so brutal. To find a home, a place she'd feel safe—how foolish a hope. She'd become his wife as a girl and a woman in his vile bed. A woman afraid of each night when he might hurt her. Or drink himself into a stupor out in the barn, forgetting her existence.

She started toward the staircase at the end of the long hallway. Moonlight filtered through the sidelights of the massive front door. A creaking from the porch caught her attention. Taking a step closer, she recognized the scrape of a man's boots. Leaning near the glass, she peered out through the shadows of the porch. What she saw was the outline of a familiar man. Long, outstretched legs and tilted head, he looked toward the distant hills and sky, likely in deep thought. *Bryce.*

She stood fixated, taking in his broad shoulders and imagined both his sadness and overwhelming shock. Should she disturb him or leave him to his private meanderings? Did he need or want anyone's company?

After Cort, Lark, and she were able to settle the children in bed upstairs, the air in the house felt morbidly still, life seemingly sucked from the rooms. They'd sipped coffee and whiskey with few words exchanged. Disbelief settled over everyone. Reyes was a scared little boy while Bryce had missed his son's years as a babe... and the chance to learn how to be a father. Reunited, father and son were certainly strangers. They had to find a way to trust.

Decision made. Pulling her shawl from the wall peg, she snugged it around her. Closing the door softly behind her, she walked toward his silhouette in the shadows to where he sat on the top stair of the porch. He was still. There was no acknowledgment of her presence. Moonlight glinted from the bottle in his hand. He lifted it to his mouth and gulped.

"Mind if I sit with you?"

"Why would you want to?"

Slurred words didn't deter her. She wondered how long he'd been drinking. Men could become dangerous when drunk. It would be wiser to turn and leave him be. But she couldn't. He wasn't like Lars. Or her father. Bryce deserved a listening ear. That is, if he was willing to talk.

"Because you need me."

He snorted. "Suit yourself. I'm not fit company tonight."

"You've had quite an upset."

He chuckled and swigged another gulp before setting the bottle beside him. He still hadn't looked toward her. Wearing his buckskin jacket and gun belt, she wondered if he planned to go somewhere. Maybe Ogallala where saloons took care of men's urges and buried their tribulations. At first, she gave thought to turning away but was stopped at his indrawn breath.

"*Upset.* Now that's an understatement if I ever heard one. Not a fit father. Don't know the first thing about it. Except my father was a good man before he lit out for the Southern cause. Me followin' on his heels."

"If you want to be a good father, you'll find a way. You've had good upbringing. You have a family. Cort is a good example, and you share the same blood. All good starts."

Now he turned his head and looked up, his eyes searching her face. Her heart ached at his drawn, haggard expression. She could only imagine what it must be like to find a son he didn't know about. When he turned his steady gaze at the hills, she figured he was done talking. Then he surprised her.

"I don't have a wife. A house. Except for my brother's ranch, no place to go. How do I raise a boy like that, Hannah? I've been a drover, wrangler, gold miner, and train guard. I've spent more time wandering from one thing to another, never staying in one place. I'm too old to start fathering a son. Besides, he hates me."

"He hates that his mother died and left him. He's just a scared little boy who needs someone to show him that he's safe and things will be fine from now on. That this is his home for good. That's going to have to start with you. If he learns to trust you, things will work out."

"Huh. You're pretty smart, Hannah May. Have to admire how you and Lark handled him when he was dumped here. If I'd been him, I would have kept to my threat and stolen a horse. I wouldn't put it past him."

"I don't believe that. Think how you would feel if you were given up to some family you never saw before. And a father you never met. He's had a lot go wrong for his age."

The back of Bryce's head rested against the support post. He darted a glance up to where she stood. "Sounds like you're talking from experience. Being left alone with strangers."

She shivered at how close to the truth he'd come. With a sigh, she took a seat beside him, giving thought to her approach. She tucked her skirt around her knees. "Yes. My mother died when I was young. That's a long story and part of why I'm here. Married to Lars."

"*Leave* him."

"I can't. At least not till it's done legal." She thought she heard him mumble something akin to a cuss word beneath his breath.

He looked skyward. "Stars are pretty tonight."

Drawing in a breath, she was thankful he'd decided to change the direction of this conversation. She had no wish to argue, even if she could find a logical argument. Deep down, she knew he was right. Things had to change. At least she began to think along those lines.

"Yes. They are. Do you want to talk about what happened?"

"Happened?"

"Rey's mother? You obviously loved her. I don't mind if you need to talk about her."

Bryce bolted to his feet as though she'd poked him with a pitchfork. Walking a distance along the length of the porch, he paused with his back to her. Back straight, he looked as though he were giving thought to bounding over the rail to leave her. She'd touched a tender spot and wished she hadn't. Just as she thought about retreating, he scrubbed a hand across the back of his neck and returned to the seat beside her, training his eyes on the moonlit hills.

"She was a beautiful woman. Streaks of red in a mass of dark brown hair. She called it auburn. To me, it was like a sunset. I met her in a field hospital in Mississippi near the end of the war. Caught two Yankee bullets. One in my leg, the other in my shoulder. I killed the Yank before he got off a third shot at a little place called Brice's Crossroads during a hot June day. Kinda ironic name.

"Since I was handy with guns, I'd been assigned as a sniper. Once the skirmish was over, my fellow soldiers got me on a horse they'd scrounged up. There was a Reb field hospital in a farmhouse about an hour away. The Morgan Farm."

Dragging in a breath, he swiped his face and tucked his chin. Something seemed to cross his vision that she could only half imagine. She leaned closer and touched his arm. "Go on," she prodded.

"Gabriella Morgan worked as a nurse on her father's farm. They'd taken in so many wounded Rebs, the floors were bloodstained and the groans and cries were enough to shake the most hardened soldiers. Corpses were piled outside. Her father was a good doctor, but my fever raged. When I heard talk of cutting off my leg, I begged my angel nurse with soft brown eyes… not to let them. She promised."

He paused and darted her a glance. "Sure you want to hear more?"

"Yes."

"After what must have been days of delirium, I started to come around. She stayed by my side, reading to me. Telling me stories about a ranch in Texas. So many things. Until one day, I loved her. As much as a seventeen-year-old knew about love."

Hannah wanted to cry. Cry for him and herself. If only she could be loved by this man. She had no right to allow that. "What happened then?" she whispered.

"After I was well enough, the end of the war was near. We all knew it. They'd whipped us. Both sides were tired and just wanted it to end. Going back to Virginia to find my younger brother, Cort, was first thing on my mind. Figured my sister, Nora, would be alone and wondering if we were alive. But I also didn't want to leave Gabby. Besides, if I didn't return to the lost fight, I'd be considered a deserter.

"Just before I left to find what was left of my unit, I took her arm and limped beside her to the peach grove near the farmhouse. That was when I proposed. Told her I loved her. Her astounded expression should have put me off. When I took her into my arms and kissed her good and proper, she shoved away. Her hands covered her quivering lips as though I'd done something very wrong. Turns out... I had.

"Jesus, Hannah. Tears streamed from her eyes. I thought... what the hell had I done wrong? She admitted loving me. Then she plunged an emotional knife into my heart and I nearly retched. *Married.* Someone named Luis Montez of Texas. I don't know that I heard much more while my fury flooded through my veins. Snatches of her words are all I remember of that moment. *Gabriella Morgan Montez.* And she was bound to return to her husband, or he'd kill her. Yet, I still wanted her."

She watched the raw emotion in his face. He pressed his thumbs against his closed eyes before continuing. "I was ordered to join twelve ragtag Rebs the next day, moving out toward the Mississippi River. My legs felt like dead sticks. Walked for days, my body riddled with rage. All I wanted to do was kill some Yanks to make me feel better. When the war was over, I made my way to our Virginia home to find it occupied by another family, our parents buried out back. My sister, Nora, gone. Was told my younger brother, Cort, followed after our pa and me. Had no idea where he was. Maybe killed.

"So I sold the land to the vultures who'd squatted. Took off for Texas and Gabriella. Stupid and foolish. I hoped that she might be a widow. That *he'd* be dead, and we could start a life together. Then find out where my brother and sister got to."

"And was he?" she asked.

"Dead? No. But neither had he returned. Neither of us could be sure he'd come back. I stayed on, helping her get the ranch back together. We tried to keep our distance, as painful as that was. Temptation got the better of us. I wronged her husband."

"He came back," Hannah said.

She saw his almost imperceptible nod. Her fingers ached to touch him, but she dared not.

"Luis wasn't stupid. He figured out what was going on between us. Any man would figure it out just by how we looked at each other. I had already decided to leave. I tried to reason with him. He wouldn't agree to a divorce. He called her a lot of unthinkable, degrading names. Until she finally pleaded for me to leave so that she could mend things. Get back to her life."

"That was when you left for the goldfields to make your fortune."

A sad smile curved his mouth. He stared fixedly on her eyes. "I left because I finally understood she didn't love me enough to fight for us. Luis was crazed even before the war, from what she told me. I knew after I left, he'd go back to hurting her. And there wasn't a damned thing I could do. Except kill him and then hang for it. I only hoped that Salina and Ernesto would intercede to keep her safe. My staying nearby would only make things worse. Ernesto knew of his brother's temper. They promised to send me a letter to Virginia City if I was ever needed."

"No letters came?"

"None. We'd made a baby. No one told me."

"I see."

His eyes smoldered with a fury that was frightening.

Tucking her chin, her sense of jealousy warred with her sympathy at this tragic affair. Emotions so thick inside, she wanted to scream out the unfairness of it all. God help her. She hated the woman who had stolen his heart and then sent him away, trampling it. Yes, Bryce had been young and foolish. Now she, too, was faced with her own mistakes, much like Gabriella, she was clinging to a hopeless situation. Listening to the lonely wind brushing the grass, she bit her lip against the cry lodged in her throat.

He reached for her and enfolded her in his arms, holding her against him. With her head tucked in the crook of his neck, the pungent smell of whiskey reminded her of his deep pain. She chanced a look into his agonized, drawn face, his eyes narrowed. Averting her face, she wondered if he'd seen the pity she felt.

"You don't see, Hannah. Whatever love I held for her died when she turned me away, even if it was the honorable thing left to do. He'd returned and our time was ended. No matter what youthful infatuation between us, it never should've happened. You are the first woman I've known in all this time who filled my emptiness. Not just with your kind words and your sweet touch. You make me feel worthy.

"I'm scared out of my mind because like then, another man stands between us. I'm bound by decency to give up the woman I care deeply about because she belongs to another. I'm not sure how to fight for you. Unless you're willing to give me the chance. And the reason."

She broke from his hold and stood. "I'm married, Bryce. I admit I don't love him. I made a mistake. But I've always lived by rules. If I start breaking them, it will destroy the dignity in both of us. If I break my vows, it will eat me alive. In the end, we'll hate each other."

His eyes pierced hers from where he sat. With his face raised, he asked, "Should I take Reyes and leave here? Is that the answer?"

"No. You need this place. That boy needs a home, and this is a perfect place for him to grow up. Surrounded with family. You have a responsibility to that boy, and you know it."

"How can I stay? Watching you with another man would kill me inch by inch. When will you accept that he might never come back? Are you willing to pay that price in years?"

"You're drunk. Whiskey makes men say things."

"A little drunk. But I'm not talking with the whiskey. I know what I feel every time I'm near you. Even though I should know better, drunk or sober."

"We're hopeless. The *situation* is hopeless. Maybe I should take your brother up on that offer and sell out. Leave Nebraska."

"If you do, I'll probably go out of my mind wondering where you got to. Hannah, give it a little more time to figure out where your husband went. If you get a letter from him, we can make a decision."

"There is no *we*. I'm a married woman and neither of us can wish it away. Sometimes we just learn to live with choices we make. This is one of those times, Bryce."

"Not if your husband isn't coming back. Don't you think it's time to figure this out?"

Not waiting for her answer, he picked up the bottle, stood, and wobbled before stepping down the steps. She watched him as he strode unsteadily to the bunkhouse. Biting her lip, she gave thought to writing more letters of inquiry. Just maybe someone knew where Lars had gone. "And then?" she whispered into the lonely night.

She had to find a way to freedom.

NINE

THE COW KILLER

CORT YANKED A bandanna over his mouth and nose at the sickening smell of death. Swinging his leg over the saddle, he stepped down, sparing a glance toward Bryce and Tangle where they walked their horses in ever widening circles, searching the ground. A dead cow, rotting in the bright sun. Vultures hopped along the ground, angry at the interruption. Yanking his gun from his holster, he fired a shot and sent the ugly birds skyward so he could have a closer look.

Kneeling, he studied the large brown holes in the steer's head. Shot multiple times and left to rot. No one had cut out a chunk of meat this time... at least none that he could tell. Most likely the animal had been shot about three days ago. *Dammit.* He'd thought the cow killer had moved on. What did this troublemaker hope to get out of this, besides costing the Double E money? Worse, his men had reported wolf tracks. An even worse menace for his cattle.

This killer knew what he was doing. Drawing wolves could easily cripple his entire business. The shooter's tracks always managed to disappear amid rocks, washes, and the river. The son of a bitch stayed out of sight, and no one had found where he camped—if he camped. At the sound of Bryce and Tangle riding up beside him, he lifted his head. They yanked their bandannas over their noses.

"Any trail we can follow?" Cort stood and kicked dirt onto the fly infested meat as he spoke from beneath the cloth.

Bryce shook his head. "Nope. Saw tracks but they disappeared in the grass where cattle already trampled any sign of a trail. Following them would lead us into that rock-strewn draw. Which I'm betting is where he went. He's been gone from here for several days, judging by the carcass."

Cort nodded and mounted his waiting horse. "Tangle. Why don't you go back to camp and take some of the boys out looking? Make sure you trench this animal to discourage the wolves and other varmints."

"Will do, boss." Tangle tugged his scarf to his chin and spit tobacco before turning his chestnut gelding into an ambling trot, leaving the two men alone. Cort turned his attention to his brother who leaned forward and stood in the stirrups to stretch.

"What do you think, big brother?" Cort asked.

"Luis is behind this. He's crazy enough. You heard what Ernesto said. Christ. I'm damned sorry I brought trouble down on you."

"Whether you were here or not, he'd be bringing trouble as long as this ranch carries the Enders name. Now we have to find him and put an end to the bastard. I'm not just worried about my cows. More worried about my family and my men."

"He won't be easy to find. Luis spent a long while rustling cattle back in Texas. Brought them up from Mexico. Besides, it's between him and me. Hope to God Reyes isn't spotted by Luis."

Looking across the grassland following his brother's gaze, Cort read his brother's thoughts just by his demeanor. The anger was palpable. But he was wrong on one point. It was now his fight, too. "He's made it a family problem, Bryce. We'll take care of Luis together. He'll make a mistake and we'll be on him like flies on dung."

"I want to be the one to kill him."

"I've learned patience. Before long he'll figure you're here. That'll be a kick in his sorry ass. He'll make a big mistake because fools always do. If it comes down to it, you get first crack at him. But if he's in my sights first, I'll put him down."

"Yeah. I'll take great pleasure in ridding the world of Luis Montez."

"Let's agree not to mention this to the women. They're best not knowing. Lark already went through a lot, and we've got a new baby coming. Hannah has her own problems and no use in worrying Reyes. From now on, we're hunting for pesky wolves and coyotes."

"Agreed. Hate to have to say this. My own son could betray us. He is most likely more loyal to Luis than to me. Don't exactly blame him but I don't know a lot of how he feels. Loyalty isn't in him at the moment. He's been tossed around. Until I catch Luis, we can't trust Reyes."

"Christ. He's just a kid. Give him time to get used to you, brother. It'll happen. In the meantime, let's get the hell out of here before I puke my guts up."

BRYCE GUIDED HIS buckskin into the coolness of the barn. Tying him off, he started to unsaddle the animal when he heard a muffled sound from the other end of the cavernous stable.

"Anybody there?" he called.

When no one answered, he walked in the direction of shuffling feet. Passing the empty stalls mounded with tack, coils of fence wire, and racks of saddle blankets, a horse nickered. When someone sneezed, he drew his gun. Slowly, he crept to the far end of the barn.

A movement to his left caught his attention. He turned and faced his son, standing in the shadows. Lowering his gun, he could hardly swallow at how close he'd come to hurting his own boy. He poked his Stetson back and studied the scared, dirty-faced kid. He looked like he hadn't been handy with a bar of lye soap in a while.

"What're you doing sneakin' around in here?" Bryce barked as he angrily shoved his revolver into his holster.

"I work here."

"Huh. Well, you could've answered me when I called out."

"Didn't want to."

"I could've shot you. Don't like it when somebody hides."

"I just told you. I work here. Cort gave me a job. I don't want to talk to you."

Narrowing his eyes, Bryce did his damnedest to recall Hannah's advice about how to handle the boy. *Reyes.* A name that irked him because it was a reminder of Gabriella and Luis, a Spanish name. Folding his arms across his chest, he mulled over what he should do about the animosity that still stuck each of them like briars every time they came near each other.

"Well... I want to talk to you."

"I don't have to listen."

When the boy started to shove past him, Bryce grasped his shoulder and brought him around. Reyes looked up, his chin jutted in defiance. The boy's smirk so irritating, Bryce tightened his grip, forgetting how thin the boy's flesh was. Reyes shrugged from his grasp and Bryce was quite sure that if this kid held a gun, he'd be a dead man right now.

Before he had time to march away, Bryce stopped him. "If we don't talk now, it'll be at supper in front of your uncle, aunt, and Hannah. Don't care if they hear what I say. You might, though."

Reyes pivoted, his eyes hard as nails. Nostrils flared, his clenched fists pressed against his hips, he nearly snarled his response. "Go on and talk. I don't have to do anything you want me to do."

Bryce lifted his hat and slapped it against his leg before tossing it to the top of a barrel. "All right. I am your father. That's first. While I wasn't around to raise you till now, that wasn't entirely my fault, either. I can't change anything. I can only promise to try to do right by you and not ever leave you again. No matter whether I go or stay, you'll be with me. I'm hoping I can stay here, mainly because I like it here and I think you do, too."

"Why did you leave my mother?"

Breath rushed from his lungs as he thought how to answer his son. "She asked me to go." That wasn't quite true. Begging was more like it. "She was married to Luis, and I knew it. But I hoped that if I helped her on her ranch and waited with her, Luis might not return from the war. Maybe a prisoner. Maybe sick somewhere. Maybe killed."

"You had no right to be with my mother if she was married. Even Aunt Salina said that."

"I know. Your ma knew that. We fell in love back in a field hospital in Mississippi near the end of the war. Yes. I was very wrong to follow her, but when we're young, sometimes we make mistakes. That doesn't change the fact that we loved each other. Despite the wrong of it."

"But you left her with *him*. You left *me*."

"I didn't know about you until your uncle Ernesto and aunt Salina showed up here. Else I wouldn't have gone so far away. I would've stayed close to see you grow up. See that you were taken care of."

Open hostility was evident in Rey's glower. Raw temper darkened his eyes that were now glazed with unshed tears. His boy's eyes stayed on his as piercing as bullets.

"I still hate you. My mother told me Luis wasn't my real father, and for a time I hated her, too. Luis was mean to her and me. She cried a lot and when he hit her and I tried to stop him, he'd beat me."

Bryce flinched while his fists clenched at his sides, feeling every hurt Luis inflicted like a punch to his gut. Feeling like horse manure wasn't exactly new to him, but this was different. He'd failed the woman he thought he loved. They'd both failed their son. What fools they'd both been. If one of them had to be blamed, it was him.

"Well, he won't ever touch you again," Bryce seethed. Any minute, he expected his back teeth to break as he clenched his jaw, thinking about how Gabriella had suffered. And his son had been caught in the middle.

Reyes looked toward him, swiping at tears with his shirtsleeve and sniffling. The boy's hands relaxed at his sides leaving Bryce at a loss as to what to do next. He sensed that a boy of eleven years wouldn't much care to have his father hug him and let him cry. Or would he?

Bryce spread his arms out from his sides, welcoming his son. Holding his breath he waited. Reyes walked closer until they were toe to toe. Bryce's arms closed around him and held his son firmly against his chest. His heart ripped apart at the sound of sobs against his shirt. Oddly, in that moment, he took measure of how tall he was while his emotions welled inside.

Running his fingers over his soft dark hair, he allowed Reyes to cry out the cruelties of his young life. When the cries subsided, Reyes leaned away and stepped back. He swiped his sleeve over his red, snotty nose and drew in a shuddering breath. For a moment, Bryce recalled himself at the same age thinking that if he ever cried, it was buried deep in memory.

"Will you tell?"

"Tell what?"

"That I cried like a baby."

"Nope. That's between you and me."

"Will you stay? I told everybody I'd leave here. But I don't want to."

"I think we can stay on. Especially if that's what you want."

Reyes nodded and snuffed again. "Good. I like Cort and Lark. I like Hannah. She started teaching me more about reading stuff."

"There looks to be lots of books in the main house."

"Cort told me to help myself."

"*Uncle* Cort."

"He's really your brother?"

"Yep. Younger by three years. We've got a sister, too. Wish I knew where she got to."

"I got no brothers or sisters."

"You got a cousin and family right here. That's all that's important."

Reyes looked down as though studying his boot toes. Bryce gave him the time to think about what they'd talked about. Then he decided to press this break in the ice a bit further.

"Reyes. Is that what your mother called you?"

The boy's head jerked up. "Rey. She liked to call me Rey."

"That's what I want to call you, then. Unless you have a different name you'd like to be called?"

"Rey is fine. I'd like to sound Anglo."

Bryce felt a surge of pride at this breakthrough. They'd connected and somehow he'd keep trying to give his son the security he deserved. That would start by killing Luis. Then they'd see what was next. For now, Rey was his son, and his mission would be to keep him safe.

"R-e-y. Rey Morgan Enders from now on," Bryce declared.

"If that's what you want."

"It's what I want and a plain fact. In case you didn't notice, we have similar hair and the same eyes. No getting away from it. Do you still plan on stealing a horse and leaving?"

"Maybe. Depends."

"On?"

"On if I think you mean everything. And if I think you lied."

"I'm not ever lying to you."

"That's what Hannah says. I think she's sweet on you."

"How do you know that?"

"She gets all happy-looking when she talks about how you and I need to talk and get along. Sort of like what Ma told me before she died. She wanted me to go to you."

Bryce gulped hard and tucked his tongue into the side of his mouth. Hugging his son with one arm, he couldn't find enough voice to choke out a single word. If he did, he expected it would be *Hallelujah*. Eleven... almost twelve years lost.

Every time he thought of Gabriella, her face interposed with that of Hannah. Punching the wall wouldn't solve his problems but mending his son would be a good start. Except for the problem of the forbidden woman he couldn't get out of his head, things were looking up. Tucking his son against his side, they walked side by side into the daylight, accepting that indeed, they had a long way to go.

LARK PASSED THE bowl of boiled potatoes down the table and followed it with the roast pork. She enjoyed the pleasurable chatter between Zeke and Cort while Tangle laughed at something Hannah said. Bryce sat beside Rey. She couldn't miss the way Bryce's attention wandered to the woman sitting across from him when no one was watching. Except for her. Yes, indeed. These two were meant to be together. This was interesting, though Cort seemed dismissive of this budding attraction.

If only Lars weren't between them. Father and son prattled about horses, gold, and ranch life. Something was heartwarmingly changed since the two of them had come through the door. Rey appeared glued to every word from his father's mouth.

A glance in Cort's direction at the far end of the table found him dolloping butter onto a chunk of bread. When he looked toward her with a conspiratorial smile, he followed it with a wink. Bryce stared with a contemplative stare at the woman he seemed to be falling in love with.

Unless she missed her guess, the shared laughter between Tangle and Hannah stiffened Bryce's back and his jealousy was like a burr. The entire situation was fraught with multiple problems, the least being Tangle and the most dangerous… Lars.

Looking toward Zeke with his mouth full, he managed to nod at Rey's incessant questions. Good old Zeke was like a grandfather to the boy. The elder had taken the boy in hand and Lark marveled at Zeke's eyes, alight with pleasure. For the first time in a while, Zeke seemed content. The best part was how Rey was transforming into a congenial young man around the men, most especially Zeke.

Theresa walked into the kitchen from the back staircase and lifted the coffeepot with a towel. With practiced efficiency, she filled the mugs while the men talked of rounding up horses and looking for some bothersome coyotes and wolves. Lark found that odd. They'd had coyotes before. This was the first time they'd decided to take time to hunt them. She'd have to remember to ask Cort about that.

As though reading her mind, Cort said, "The boys and me will be leaving for a few days. Day after tomorrow," Cort announced.

That pronouncement surprised her. Turning toward him, she held her husband's gaze. The clatter of forks stilled. Both Hannah and she exchanged questioning looks. The men were up to something.

"Can I go, too?" Rey asked.

Rey's eyes centered on his father while Bryce's attention was fixed on Hannah's face. Lark returned her attention to clearing the platters of food and then paused at Bryce's response.

Bryce darted a glance at his son and ruffled his hair. "The next time."

"Why not this time?"

At Bryce's flustered expression, it was clear he didn't know what to say. Thankfully, his discomfiture eased with Zeke's timely response. The old man got to the meat of the bone and found solutions like nobody else could.

"It's like this. You ain't got a horse to ride," Zeke said matter-of-factly.

The older man sipped his coffee, his blue eyes on the rim of the cup. Lark was interested in how this was going to play out. And from the looks of all the other faces, she knew they were interested, as well.

At first, Rey seemed to consider that. "There's plenty of horses on this ranch. Can't I borrow one, Uncle Cort?"

When Bryce looked in the direction of his brother, Cort set down his fork full of food and frowned. "Your father is my new foreman. He makes that kind of decision. And besides, he's your father and knows what's best."

Rey's head swiveled back to look toward Bryce. Lark held her gasp at what the boy said next. "Just because he's my pa don't mean I have to do what he says."

Bryce tossed the linen napkin down and lowered his cup of coffee. The two of them glowered. In fact, so did Cort. Lark cleared her throat, hoping someone would come to Bryce's rescue. Then it happened when Zeke spoke like a prophet out of the Bible.

"Showing respect for your father is the first step in makin' you part of this family. You say you want to ride with the men. First thing. You need a good horse. And that takes time to figure out which one. You gotta get used to each other. I'm plannin' on havin' you pick one out from the herd. With me. And then we'll get the right saddle. Course, all that takes money. Your uncle ain't in the business of giving away horse-flesh and saddles. So, you stay here and do your job. Get your schooling. Then we'll work on getting a horse."

"I gotta do all that to get a horse so I can work?" he asked Zeke.

Lark watched the grin on Cort's face and the rare smile on Bryce's. There was disbelief on Rey's face as this boy might've met his match in crusty Zeke Waterson. Easing back in his seat, she caught Bryce's wink in Hannah's direction. It seemed that everyone had come out of this fight with Rey, mostly unscathed. Bryce, on the other hand, was certainly perturbed.

Zeke swallowed what he'd been chewing and added, "Heard Missus Van Stadt is a mighty fine teacher. She'll be here till we finish fixin' her broken porch and windows. You'll have plenty of time out on the range. I expect I'll be here with only a few men. Who do you think will keep watch over the ladies?" Zeke continued.

"You and me?"

"That's right."

Lark choked back her chuckle but Cort let loose with a guffaw, stifling it with her sharp glare. Zeke was good at this. Lark bent over the remaining dishes and helped Hannah carry them to the kitchen, returning to hear what would happen next. Beneath her breath, Theresa mumbled about how kids had to learn to hold their tongues around adults as she spun with the meat forks in hand.

"Yes. You and me. 'Bout time we got to know each other. Think you want to learn about ranching?" Zeke didn't give Rey time to answer. "Well. I got time to teach you. So, we best get to it tomorrow. Be up to my house at sunup or I'll come looking for you."

With a last look over her shoulder, Lark found Hannah brush a quick glance at Bryce. Tangle stood and thanked her for the fine supper. Cort excused himself, mumbling about paperwork and followed behind Tangle. Finally, Zeke stood and took charge of a baffled but contrite Rey. After Zeke stretched out his arms, he informed the boy they were about to commence their first lesson down by the corral. Only she, Bryce, and Hannah were still in the room, and he looked like a man who'd just been stranded out on the plains with a long walk ahead.

Lark left them but peeked from the kitchen doorway, watching Hannah lift the last of the plates. Standing to leave, Bryce pecked her on the cheek and walked into the hallway, whistling all the way out the door, leaving a grin on Hannah's pink face.

TEN

DECISIONS

D OG TIRED, BEDRAGGLED, and legs sore as hell from long days in the saddle, Bryce rode beside Tangle, Damon, and Mason toward the corral. The smell of coffee, pork, and fresh baked bread sure beat dried beef and thick, overboiled coffee he'd swilled the last four days. Luis still hadn't been found, which only added to his frustration. The varmint must have found a hole in the ground.

"You joinin' us for supper or you goin' to the big house later?" Tangle asked before he slipped from his saddle.

Running a hand through his dirt-caked hair, Bryce lifted his chin in the direction of the ranch house. "Be up there to see my boy."

"If you change your mind, we got a poker game tonight."

"Thanks. I'll pass."

"I'll take your horse."

"Obliged." After he stepped down, Bryce watched as Tangle led the two horses away without the usual teasing between them. Couldn't blame anyone for avoiding him. He was as mad as a peeled rattler after they'd come up dry on the hunt for Luis. This no-account was better than good at hiding his tracks and staying out of sight like the yellow dog he was.

Squinting, he took in the sprawling two-story ranch house. This was Cort's good fortune, paid and had been a high price in pride. Now that he had a chance to make a life here, he'd be satisfied with half as much. He planned to use his mettle and hard work for the chance to prove himself worthy.

Catching sight of Hannah in the distance, he tracked her poised strides in the direction of Zeke's house. She was wearing a pretty blue dress and a braid draped over one shoulder. One helluva pretty sight he'd missed out on the range, though he'd thought about her. She hadn't looked his way, and he gave thought to intercepting her until he caught the whiff of horse and sweat. What was he thinking? She'd made her position clear. His hands were tied by her vows, and he was about to burst at his seams with going around in a circle.

Kicking dirt with his boot, he turned toward the back of the cookhouse where they kept a big tin tub. After a soak and scrub with lye soap, he'd head up to the house and have a smoke and sip Cort's whiskey. Might improve his sour disposition before facing Mrs. Van Stadt. What would he do about that unreasonable, stubborn, *married* woman? Nothing of his reasoning seemed to put a dent in her thick head.

SMOOTHING HER HANDS over the skirt of her dress, Hannah kept glancing at the window. Zeke's office had become a schoolroom where she delivered lessons to Rey, ever since she'd left her broken house. The boy sat hunched over the slate, his bottom lip caught between his teeth while he worked on his sums. He always became contrary if she looked over his shoulder, so she pretended to be looking from the window or dusting a chair while he worked. Today, she didn't have need to pretend.

She could have sworn that Bryce was going to head this way. Instead, he'd hesitated and pivoted toward the cookhouse. Counting off every one of the four days he'd been gone, she grew more flustered with her preoccupation with this illicit attraction. Waiting for a response from Lars that might never come seemed pointless. Was he alive? How long should she wait?

"I'm finished, Missus Van Stadt."

With a last look toward the bunkhouse, she returned her attention to her student. One corner of his mouth raised when she leaned over the desk and examined his sums. Squeezing his shoulder to suggest her approval, she was always impressed with his flair for numbers and his neatness. However, she accepted that his reading lesson tomorrow would pose more of a struggle. Having lived in the wilds of Texas, he had missed quite a bit of learning.

She shuffled his hair. "Every problem is solved perfectly. You are very good with numbers."

"Ma said that, too. She taught me when she wasn't sick."

"You miss her, I know. I'm very sorry. Don't forget you have a family right here."

He shrugged. "I guess Pa is trying to be a father. But I still miss my mother. Maybe my father will find somebody else and marry. But I don't think I'd like it."

"Really? Why is that?"

"None would be as nice as you. But you can't get married 'cause you're already married."

"Yes. I am." And that fact kept playing over in her head. She needed no reminders of her dour predicament.

Hannah cleared her throat, finding herself looking toward the clock. Bryce had ridden in an hour ago. By now, he must have gone to the house. At that thought, the door swung open. Expecting Zeke, instead... there was Bryce, filling the doorway with his hat in hand. He wore clean clothes and fresh combed hair. He offered her a brief smile, then turned his attention to his son.

Dropping the chalk on the desk, Rey looked up to see his father. "I didn't know you were back, Pa."

"Got in maybe a few hours ago. Had to clean up before supper. Thought I'd find you and Missus Van Stadt here."

From behind Rey, he set his hat on the desk and leaned over the boy's shoulder, scrutinizing the work. When his face lifted, his eyes pinned hers. With his wink, her face flamed hot when she followed his eyes to where they skimmed the neck of her dress.

"What've you been up to while I've been away?" he asked Rey.

Lordy, she knew his question was equally directed to both when his heart-stopping gaze held hers for a short moment.

"Missus Van Stadt is teaching me sums today, then subtractions. I'm good at both."

"I see." And Bryce did see. Genuinely impressed with the lines of numbers that his son had worked out, he turned the oak chair beside the desk and straddled it, setting a firm hand on Rey's shoulder.

"Zeke worked it out. Said if I want that horse so I can ride with you and the men, I had to take care of my math and reading and muck stalls. But if I do a good job, he'd ask if I can start taking care of the horses with Alonzo and Adoeete."

"Sounds good. I'm proud of you, Rey. We can talk about the horse in a few days."

A wide smile lit the boy's face. With a sidelong glance toward Hannah, Bryce thought she was the prettiest schoolmarm he'd ever laid eyes on. But she was damned determined to fight him every step of the way.

Bryce stood and held her eyes. "Thanks, Missus Van Stadt." For now, she'd have it her way. Sooner or later, they'd have to settle what was between them.

"I enjoy teaching. And Rey's a quick learner."

"You're a fine teacher. Don't know where we'd be without your help."

"Can I go up to the ranch house? Theresa said she'd have some cookies ready if I finish," Rey interjected.

"Go ahead, son. Make sure to tell her to save a few for me."

Rey scrambled from his seat, neither of them missing the sound of his clomping boots on the steps outside. Now they were alone and neither moved, at first. She fidgeted with her dress and then laced her fingers in front of her. Looking away from him, she reached for the slate board and then Bryce stayed her hand. He had things to say once he managed to unglue his tongue from the roof of his mouth. When her blue eyes centered on his chest, he held back a chuckle.

"I've missed you."

"I…." she started.

"I... what?" He tilted his head and waited.

"All right. I admit it. I missed seeing you. Talking with you. But don't you see? There can't be anything else. Surely you understand that. I can be Rey's teacher and nothing more."

"At least you admit to missing me. That's a start."

"I wrote to Lars several weeks ago. I've still not received a reply. Maybe he *is* dead. I don't know if I'm married or a widow. I don't even know if my letter got to him. Or if someone got the letter and held it up."

Holding his breath, he released it on a sigh. Reaching for her, he pulled her close enough to feel her warmth. Her eyes glittered as they skimmed his face. What he wouldn't give to have the right to pick her up and carry her upstairs to one of Zeke's beds and forget the world. His skin against hers, without the barriers of clothes or damnable vows.

She stiffened and he recognized the war raging inside of her noble head. Being moral and upright was becoming a sore spot. Her body tensed when he closed his arms around her. Still, he rocked her against him, breathing in the scent of her, the pleasure of her.

"Bryce?"

"Hmm?"

"Before you returned, do you know what Rey was talking about?"

"Rey? He has a thousand different things on his mind. What was it this time?"

"He talked about missing his mother. He wondered if you would marry again. He wasn't too happy about that. And he also mentioned that you couldn't marry me because I'm already married."

Bryce tightened his hold on her and pressed a kiss against her hair. "Guess he picked you out as a possibility for me. He's smart." Chuckling, he slid one hand up and down her rigid back.

"This isn't funny."

"No. That's damn right. And I'm asking you again to file for a divorce. I'll go with you to a lawyer. And sooner or later, we may find Lars and make him sign the damned papers. If, in fact, he's alive. No one would find fault. He abandoned you. Let's see this through."

"He's in some Montana gold camp, I think. Maybe alive. Maybe dead.

But I'm left with a ranch to run and a marriage I'm struggling to honor. What if he comes walking back into my life? *Our* lives?"

She might as well have thrown scalding water on his head. He let her go and backed away. Her back was ramrod straight and her eyes sparkled with what might be either fury or unshed tears. Her chin lifted in defiance.

"Jesus, woman. I don't think I can take more of this. Let's leave here with Rey."

"My faith won't let me do that. I can't. This has to be solved."

"You mean you won't consider your own life. Or mine. Or Rey's future. We always circle back to your sham marriage."

"That's not fair. Don't you know how guilty I already feel? You must know I'm very fond of Rey. I want what's best for him."

She turned away from him and stared at the clapboard wall with her head tilted as though the answers were in the wood. Pinching the bridge of his nose, he waited, hating this constant circling around each other. Trying to think of something to say that would change her mind, nothing came to mind... except for a few cuss words.

"The ribbon cotillion is in town the end of this week. You should attend. Find someone suitable for a wife," she said flatly.

No words could have cut him more deeply. This was the last thing he expected from her mouth. So he said the first thing he thought. "Christ. How can you be this stubborn?"

Frustration boiled over and his temper flared. What the hell had gotten into her? He didn't want other women. He wanted *her*. Right now, it was all he could do not to shake sense into her.

She turned to face him, keeping her distance. With a withering look, she crossed her arms and he clamped down on his teeth. "I have no choice. Neither do you. I'm married. God knows. I wish I weren't. Neither of us can change the facts. You and Rey need both wife and mother."

"You refuse to do one thing to fix it. Well, if that's how it is, *Missus Van Stadt*. I think I'll just do what you suggest. Wouldn't hurt to find somebody to take as a wife. You're right. He needs a mother. And I need a woman to hold. To make love with. To have babies and build a ranch. You don't seem to want to fight for us. So, I guess you've made your decision. Since it seems it's what you want, I'll see about that dance and if I'm lucky, come back with her. Just maybe you'll finally have what you want. Which seems to be loneliness. See if your vows keep you warm at night."

Bryce could have sliced his own tongue for his spiteful words, but now too late to call them back. Every ounce of venomous anger poured from his hurt. When she ran from the room, he'd never felt more like a horse's ass. His jaw muscle twitched. So be it. He'd attend that dance. Maybe she was right. Still, he craved only one woman and she had just dropped him over a cliff.

ELEVEN

RASH DECISION

HANNAH SWIPED AT the tears welling in her eyes amid quick whispers bantered between Lark, Cort, and Zeke. From the constrained glances in her direction, she knew the main topic—the sudden disappearance of Bryce. .

At the sharp rap against the kitchen door, everyone looked up to find Mason scraping his boots and stepping inside. Sweeping off his Stetson, he paused and centered his hard glare on her. Hannah gripped the edge of the table and braced for the bad news she expected to hear. If only she could take back what she'd said to him. Now she'd have to live with her acerbic words, ones that she regretted.

"Well?" Cort snapped. "Do you know where my wayward brother got to? Spit it out."

"Yep. He rode into Ogallala."

"He was supposed to join us today on the coyote hunt. What the hell got into him?"

"Don't know what to tell you. We saw him ride out like the Devil was sticking him with a pitchfork. Looked pretty mad."

"What provoked him?" Cort asked.

Mason's eyes skittered over the women's faces before he answered. Hannah knew all too well what he was about to reveal.

"Told Alonzo and me he was going to that cotillion to find himself a bride."

The silence that followed that surprise announcement rolled through the room like a heavy fog. Hannah stood, feeling the floor sinking beneath her at the collective stares. She grabbed the back of a chair. He'd meant what he'd said, and it was her fault because she'd pushed him away. Her stomach threatened to heave, and she bent just as Lark grasped her arm.

"Hannah. Sit. I'll bring you some water. Take deep breaths. This can all be fixed."

Forcing a wan smile, Hannah could only nod while she folded her hands against the table. The room looked awfully dim. When she had enough courage, she looked up at Cort and Zeke. Their mouths were pursed but they said nothing. They didn't have to. Their smoldering glare was answer enough.

She recognized Rey's familiar bootsteps. With a quick glance over her shoulder, she found him standing behind her, his face drained of color. He shifted from one foot to another. "I don't want him to come back with some lady I don't know. Why can't he marry Hannah?"

His innocent question summed up what they must all be thinking, and she was to blame. Her heart broke when she realized Rey had heard what had been said. Guilt welled inside and when Lark pressed a glass to her hand, she ignored it. Instead, with her elbows resting against the table, she dropped her head into her hands. The trembling started in her lip, becoming a tide of shudders through her body. If only she could find a dark place to escape the accusing glares.

In his anger, he'd taken her advice. *Married.* Tomorrow he'd most likely be hitched to some woman. How would she ever be able to face him again? Or even look at his bride without crying with jealousy. A gentle hand touched her shoulder.

"It's all right, Hannah. He'll come to his senses before he does something so stupid. He might be a lot of things, but he isn't dumb. Just hotheaded," Lark said.

Hannah dropped her hands to the table. The truth was as bitter as willow bark tea. "He has every right to marry someone. It's his decision." She was fooling herself and miserable.

Reyes moved closer, his eyes drilling into hers. She hadn't given thought to how much this would hurt him. Teeth gritted, his wrinkled forehead portended the coming outburst of a riled and confused boy who needed a father in his life.

"He should marry you. You just won't. You're just being mean."

His words struck her like a hard slap.

"Reyes!" Cort barked. "That's enough."

Holding up her hand, she signaled Cort to let her explain. "Rey. I'm a married woman. Your father needs to find someone to help him get on with his life. You need a mother."

He balled his fists. "No. I don't have to like her, and I don't have to stay here. Once I get older, I'm leaving. Your husband isn't here. You *should* hate him. Tell him you want to marry my father."

"Rey," Cort repeated, this time grabbing for the boy.

She felt her heart nearly stop when Reyes escaped Cort's grasp then tramped to the door, slamming it behind him. Cort ran a hand through his hair with impatience as he started to follow. That's when Zeke stopped him.

"Leave him be, Cort. I'll go see to him. All of you need to cool down," Zeke chided.

She stared at her folded hands. The door squeaked closed. Looking up, she saw the backs of Mason and Cort as they followed Zeke from the same door. Moments ticked by on the clock. Lark kneeled beside the chair, and Hannah dropped her head against her friend's shoulder, the grief-filled sobs unstoppable.

"I'm a good listener, Hannah. Getting out our sorrows is better than keeping them in."

Lips juddering, Hannah leaned away and tried to smile... and failed. Their eyes held. She couldn't bring herself to ask the question aloud. How could she ever face Bryce again, or the woman he brought with him?

"I think we need to plan a welcome dinner," Lark said. "Can't have a dinner like this without cake."

That idea startled her. Didn't Lark understand how much a celebration would hurt?

"You can't expect *me* to welcome them."

"First of all, I'm betting he comes up dry. That will be call for a celebration. Then we'll have the opportunity to rub his nose in the mess he made by riding off without a word. Besides, it'll keep us busy until we find out what's what. This disagreement between you both won't live long. He'll come back to his senses. You'll see I'm right. That doesn't mean I won't enjoy watching him squirm. Right now, he's drunk and already staggering to a hotel bed. Tomorrow he'll have one pounding head—much deserved."

Nothing Lark could say would make her feel better. She didn't believe for a minute that he wouldn't do what he set out to do and she died a little inside.

"Believe me. I'm thinking he'll come back hungry as a bear and with a mighty big hangover, a stubbled face, and the stink of whiskey and tobacco on his clothes. It's clear to me you had words. Taking a bride is most likely the last thing he'll do with the feelings he has for you. The thing he should really worry about is facing Cort's wrath. He's furious."

"What if you're wrong?" Hannah ventured.

"Then he'll be in a world of trouble. He's smarter than that. The Enders men get themselves into trouble but always get back out. When he sees the wedding cake I've got for him, he'll be ashamed of himself."

WHILE FIDDLES AND piano music filled the room with a tune he vaguely remembered, Bryce pressed a sweet gal snug against him, moving with the changing tempo. She looked mighty fine in her green dress. But he had some qualms about the yellow ribbon around her neck. Just didn't seem right. Women should be courted properly.

Looking across the pretty woman's shoulder, he took note of the prune-faced, matronly woman sitting on the opposite side of the room. Her pinched-lipped expression warned him that she watched for improprieties. Hell. If he wanted to hold a girl close, he didn't give one damn thought about what that old buzzard considered proper. He'd paid his money, hadn't he? Besides, he wasn't the kind to take advantage of women.

Not that he thought less of this delicate sprite, but wearing the ribbon made it seem she was property to be bought and sold. That gnawed his gut while his fingers itched to pull it loose. But that would signal he'd chosen her and that wasn't the case. He understood some women's desperation that drove them to seek husbands, devaluing themselves with each pleading smile. Some would wind up being hurt in more ways than they knew. He wished he had feelings for this sweet smiling woman with light yellow hair, nearly the color of her ribbon. If for no other reason than to save her from a life of drudgery with a man who'd use her.

As soon as he'd taken her hand, he'd known there was only one woman he wanted in his arms. This wasn't the woman. Yet he wouldn't be so unkind as to set her aside right off.

Small hands drifted along the back of his neck, calling his attention to her deep blue eyes. In point of fact, he couldn't remember what this woman said her name was. Maybe she hadn't said, come to think about it.

"I cannot tell you why," she said, her face far nearer to his own than felt comfortable.

"Pardon?"

"I said. The name of this song is 'I Cannot Tell You Why.'"

"Thought I recognized it." In reality, he hadn't recalled this song. "By the way, you haven't told me your name."

"Augusta. Augusta Pearl Langford."

"Pretty name."

"You haven't told me yours."

Jesus Christ. He'd neglected basic civility. His throat nearly closed, he said, "Bryce Enders."

Her eyebrow lifted. "I've heard the name."

He leaned back from her and her eyes flickered across his, more interested in him than he wanted her to be. "Yeah. Well. Not surprised. My brother has a bit of a reputation."

"Everyone around here knows about the Enders Ranch."

That gave him more pause. Was this sweet thing looking for a man with money? The Double E was surely enticing. "Why are you here, Miss Augusta?"

"Mister Enders. *Bryce.* I'm sure you know that I'm trusting someone to claim me for a wife tonight and hoping it might be you."

Damn. She was straightforward. While Augusta might be intent on roping in the Enders brand, he had no interest in marrying her. While mulling how to extricate himself, he glanced at the wall clock. He didn't like being cornered.

The music ended and partners shuffled toward the punch bowl. Still, she clung to his arm until he gently pried her fingers away. Nodding his head, he managed a short grin.

"I'm not the right man for you, Augusta."

Her soft grin melted into a cold frown. Whether her disappointment was genuine or not, it didn't matter.

"Did I say something wrong? Have I offended you?"

"No. Just afraid my heart is already taken. I finally realized what I need to do."

She sighed while her toe tapped the floor to the music. She looked past his shoulder and fluttered her fingers at another approaching man who looked ready to claim her. Bryce shook his head as she turned from him, escorted on the arm of an older man without so much as a good-bye.

Wending his way toward the door, he drew in a deep breath of night air, clearing his muddled head. He ambled to the Saddle Tramp Saloon to find relief from his misery in a whiskey. Damned if he didn't feel like he'd just escaped an Indian attack.

The first swallow sent fire down his throat. The second reached into his soul where thoughts stirred of his new responsibility. *His* son. A boy he couldn't help but love. Sinking into a drink wouldn't solve anything. But it wouldn't hurt to numb his troubles for one night.

He had left his brother shorthanded and expected he'd be fired, unless Cort was willing to give him a second chance. As to Hannah. Scouring her from his mind was impossible. Still, she'd slammed the door on any second chance. Unless he figured a way to persuade her to trust him.

The twang of the piano mellowed into a passable melody. Barely taking notice of the cowpokes and drifters bellied up to the bar on either side of him, his spiteful words, spoken out of frustration, filled him with remorse. His stupid threat... unforgivable. The smell of men's sweat sent him back to thoughts of the gold camp. Did he want to go back there if Cort chose to fire him? He had a son to raise. That camp life was out of the question.

After a couple more gulps, the room chatter muted. He knew he was drunk. Just as he thought to stumble to the hotel to sleep it off, a hand clamped his arm. Darting his eyes to the buxom woman in a skimpy outfit, he knew what she wanted. Her full breasts spilled from the getup enough to make a man drool like a baby. She was an older woman with a bright smile and crooked teeth, framed between full red lips. Winking, she tugged his arm. He braced himself at the precipice of a stupid decision.

"Come with me, big man. I'll show you a good time upstairs. Look like you need it."

The voice of a crosscut saw and the smell of sweat weren't attracting him, but he followed anyhow, directly into trouble he didn't want. *No.* He didn't exactly follow. She led him up the stairs. On legs feeling like they were packed with wet sand, he wobbled into the room. Wincing at the slam of the door, a dim lamp cast shadows in the dingy room. Even while his vision blurred, the rumpled, dirty bed sickened his already riled gut and he'd seen cleaner barn floors.

While she slipped a lacy thing from her shoulders, he stood frozen, then considered bolting to the hallway. The door wasn't too far away. He'd come here to find out if he could put Hannah out of his mind and he was coming up woefully short.

While he allowed her fingers to pluck one button and another, sweat beaded his lip. At his third button, he grabbed her hand and jerked it away.

"What's the matter with you?" she hissed.

Shaking his head to clear it, he reached into his pants pocket and yanked out a greenback. Snatching it, she stuffed it between her breasts. "Maybe another time. You gotta name?" he asked.

"Alice."

"Alice. No offense to your talents. Seems another gal took root in my head."

"Well, sugar. You got that kinda look of a man already taken. If you need a place to sleep it off, you can bed here for the night."

He gave a second look at the bed and knew he'd crawl to the hotel before he'd sleep there. "Hotel will do. Thanks."

Just as his fingers closed around the door handle, he stopped. Even with his foggy mind, a thought hit him. Maybe this foray into town on a fit of anger wouldn't be a total waste of time. The tapping of Alice's toe told him she was a mite perturbed and anxious to have him gone.

"Change your mind, sugar?"

"No. But gotta question. You know a lawyer in this town?"

"Honey. I know one very well. One o' my best customers."

LARK LISTENED TO the slap of Theresa's rolling pin against the pie dough and figured the thing would snap before much longer. *Thwack. Thump. Thwack. Thump.* She frowned, lowering her stirring spoon. Looking over her shoulder, she found Theresa's eyes glowing like hot coals.

"I understand you're mad. Like you, I'm not in my best frame of mind, either. I'd like to use that rolling pin on Bryce's fool head if I didn't already think Cort would have something else in mind."

Theresa stopped what she was doing and pointed a finger in her direction. "That man is just plain crazy. Goin' off to marry somebody he don't know. Right in front of our noses. Breakin' that Hannah's heart."

"We can't talk about this in front of her. Let's try to make the best of whoever he brings back. I'm betting he doesn't. He most likely came to his senses."

"I don't have to like her."

"You liked me, didn't you? And Cort brought me back here."

Theresa harrumphed and Lark picked up the spoon again. Apparently, Theresa had been building up steam all morning. And if Bryce dared show his face, she didn't know if she'd contain the string of vile words she, herself, had in mind.

Theresa's hands stilled and then rolled the pin across the dough before replying. "No. Didn't like you running things in place of Missus Harris. Didn't seem right. 'Sides, after we cleared the air, I did like you. You showed your pluck."

"Mmm. Thanks for that. But Cort and I had a bit different situation. You know it."

"Her sick and all. Yes. But you loved that man, and he loved you. And Missus Harris was always a Harris. No matter."

"Yes. I'm thinking Hannah will come to her senses. No one thinks it's much of a marriage and Bryce will figure out what to do. Let's not make things worse by sticking our noses into their situation. Hannah has grit for putting up with her no-account husband for too long. Cort thinks Bryce will show up with a sheepish grin with only his horse to keep him warm. He best not expect a warm welcome at the bunkhouse after sneaking off."

Theresa snorted. "We can't hide this weddin' supper. Hannah's been upstairs all morning, her eyes all puffy and red. Said she has a headache. Rey's been stirred up something awful while the hands are keeping him busy."

"All I can say for sure is that I don't know if Cort is madder because Bryce took off without saying anything to him or that he's crosswised about the Lars situation. Either way, once Bryce walks in this door, the first thing that'll greet him is a wedding cake. Hopefully it'll be the slap he deserves."

A throat was cleared. Both women swung around to the sight of Hannah standing in the doorway, wearing her drab work dress. Her hair was pulled into an austere bun, emphasizing her pale face. Pink-rimmed eyes looked from her to Theresa.

"Can I help you before I leave?"

"Leave?" Lark set her hands on her hips and her lip twitched in consternation. "What in heaven's name do you mean? Where are you going?"

"Home. Alonzo is getting my wagon hitched. Said he'd bring my chickens and cow back soon as I got the coop fixed."

Theresa mumbled an ungodly word before leaving them alone. Lark lifted her chin. "The men have been working on your place, Hannah. But it's still not livable."

"I can't stay here. I'll make do. Please don't make this harder on me."

Recognizing that stubborn chin of hers, Lark accepted there'd be no convincing her to stay.

"Nothing to say except I'm a married woman. High time I acted like it and put Bryce out of my head."

Lark sighed and stated the obvious. "You love Bryce."

"Afraid so. Something I'll have to get over."

"That's right. *You* said vows. I'm sure you meant to keep them. Made promises to a man who broke every pledge and kindness owed to you in return. I don't see why your feelings should be set aside. They're real. Ask yourself what vow has Lars ever kept?"

"Words change nothing. Bryce with another woman will eat at me and I just can't do it."

"You've changed Reyes into a contented young man. Thanks to you, he and Bryce are communicating. They need you. Sooner or later, your husband will either be found dead or you'll find out where he is. It's long overdue."

"None of this can matter now."

When Hannah turned away, Lark chose that moment to stop her. "Bryce isn't that much of a mule's hind end to wed someone he hardly knows. He's flustered and so are you."

Without looking back, Hannah said, "I'll be glad to continue lessons with Rey, so long as it's at my house."

Lark tucked her chin and slapped her hand against the table. "Somehow this mess will uncoil," she murmured to no one. When the door closed, she added, "This is neck-wringing day and Bryce is first in line."

TWELVE

THE GOLD CAMPS

TODAY HIS HEAD hurt, and that was the least of his problems. Bryce judged that he was about to face a fierce storm of condemnation, which he deserved. Hell yes, he deserved it. Taking a punch wouldn't be the first or last time. Might as well get it over with.

Once he'd led his horse into the corral, Alonzo appeared but didn't acknowledge him. Instead, he muttered a string of swear words as he led Bryce's horse to the stable, without so much as a look over his shoulder. No doubt, he'd riled everyone when he didn't show up to lead the men on the so-called coyote and wolf hunt. Being an ass didn't feel very good.

Striding to the bunkhouse first, he stowed his rifle and saddlebag. The stove was cold, meaning no one had been here since early morning. Usually, Zeke strolled down to offer a greeting, but even he was nowhere to be seen. Worse, he expected Rey to bound out of the barn with his usual string of questions. Instead, he'd been met with silence.

Every step he took in the direction of the big house felt heavier. He'd shirked his duties, even as his brother made him foreman. Gritting his teeth, he expected to be fired—a just punishment. Then the thought struck him that someone might have come down sick. Lengthening his strides, he reached the back door and stomped his boots against the wood landing.

After a quick rap against the frame, he opened the door and met Theresa and Lark, their eyes offering only a brief, smoldering glance. They were slathering white frosting on a cake, their mouths pursed in concentration. Nita held the baby between her arms while little Bryce offered him a toothless, slobbery grin, with his five sugary fingers in his mouth. At least one person was glad to see him because he was invisible to everyone else.

Finally, the two women stepped back, admiring their handiwork before settling their blazing glares at him, effectively nailing his feet to the floor. Backing out seemed the coward's way, even if he had the gumption to move. Both women's backs stiffened, and just their sour expressions said *we dare you to move.* Lark set the spoon down and set her hands against her hips. Lifting his chin, he wondered which of them would take the first punch. Right now, he'd rather face three armed Comancheros.

If not for the baby gurgles and incessant ticking of the clock, he might as well have been standing in front of a firing squad. Doffing his hat, he twisted the brim between his fingers.

"Ladies. I've interrupted."

While he waited in the cross hairs of cold stares, it dawned on him that Hannah was missing from the room. If there was some kind of shindig, he'd think she would be in the middle of this kitchen. A cake and the smell of cooked beef seemed meant for a celebration. *A birthday? Had Lars returned? Was this a homecoming?*

"Where have you been?" Lark snapped. "Nita. Theresa. Would you please take the baby upstairs and clean him up? I have something to say to this man. In private."

"Yes. But I'd rather not miss this," Nita said.

Theresa *harrumphed.* "Don't want to stay in this room with *him.* I might be tempted to throw my iron pan at his head."

Bryce's eyes followed the women as they shuffled past with cold, lingering stares. The baby flapped his hands at him. Feeling like a schoolboy, waiting on the teacher's punishment, he cleared his throat. At least he was down to one. The most dangerous one.

"What's got everyone so riled? I know I left for Ogallala in a temper. I know I let Cort down because I wasn't here to do my job. I'm sorry for all of it. I'll make up for it by working longer hours. That is, if you're willing to give me a chance. Have I missed anything else in the list? Or is this about Lars returning?"

"Lars has nothing to do with this at the moment. As to running off, Cort will settle that. He was of a mind to fire you until he considered the upset that would cause your son. The one who cried thinking he'd been abandoned by you again. Zeke has him under his wing and they're out for a ride. On Rey's new horse, which appeased him for the time being."

Bryce sucked in a long breath, then released it slowly, wishing he'd be on the well-deserved receiving end of a right hook for having upset the son he'd come to love. "I've been a mule's hind end and promise to do whatever I need to make amends, starting with my son. Then with Hannah. Where is she, by the way?"

Lark leaned to one side, looking around him. He looked over his shoulder and shrugged. "What?"

"Where's your bride? Did you leave her outside? This is your wedding cake and supper for you and the lady you threatened to return with. Where is she?"

Dumb struck, he slapped his hat on his head. It didn't take more than two seconds to piece together the threads. So that was what this was about. The damned ribbon cotillion. "Christ," he muttered. A low-bellied snake couldn't feel as low as him. "Where's Hannah?"

"She left yesterday morning. Said she couldn't face you or your new bride. The one you told Mason you'd find at the ribbon cotillion. You broke her heart, Bryce."

Just as his stomach tightened, the front door slammed. Cort's long stride thudded with purpose, and he braced himself to meet either his brother's fist or a richly deserved tongue-lashing. When Cort appeared in the kitchen, his brother's hard face and slitted eyelids said what words couldn't.

"So. You slithered back. No bride with you, I see. Alonzo said you were alone."

"No. My mule head knew before I got there I couldn't and wouldn't consider a bride. This is between Hannah and me—a misunderstanding. Besides, there's more to it." And it wasn't their business.

Cort took the steps to stand in front of him. Lifting his chin, he waited for his brother's fist. Then he'd pick himself up and accept no pay for a month if that suited him. But if his brother expected him to discuss what transpired between him and Hannah, he had another think coming. Besides, right now he had to find her and Rey if he had any chance to repair the damage he'd inflicted.

His brother cocked an eyebrow. "Give you a few minutes to explain yourself so long as you understand I'm mighty pissed off."

"I'm sorry and willing to take on whatever job you offer. I'd like to stay on but if you tell me to leave, I will. Reyes comes with me. I sure as hell didn't mean to go off like I did. No excuses except my temper, something I usually control. I'm not proud of how I reacted. But I have no intention of talking about what happened between me and Hannah. If that's all, I need to find both of them and apologize."

"All right. Here it is from my standpoint. You're my brother. I gave you a home here and I'm not going back on it. First thing you do is to straighten things out with your son and then Hannah. Once you get back here, we've got work to do. You left us a bit shorthanded while the men crisscrossed Rocky Creek. She shouldn't be out there alone. You know how dangerous critters like *coyotes and wolves* can be."

Bryce got the veiled warning. "I'll talk with Rey and saddle a fresh mount. Heard he has his own horse. Thanks for that. Anything else?"

"No thanks necessary. He's my flesh and blood and this ranch will always hold a place for him. Same as you. But not if you pull this shit again. That's when we'll settle the matter another way. I hate to bloody that nose of yours, but I won't be so easy to get along with if you hurt that boy or that woman again."

He looked to where Lark busied herself with washing plates, her face flushed but not offering an opinion. "Unless either of you have something else, I'll be on my way."

"If you want to find Rey, I just saw him at the corral," Cort said.

"You look like you haven't slept much, Bryce. Hope you have a headache to go along with it."

"It might make you happy to know I feel like I was stomped by a herd of cows and then propped up against a wire fence." He looked toward the cake. "I take it the cake was meant for me and my so-called bride."

"Yes. Glad you came to your senses before we got to it," Cort added. "The men will feast on it when they get in."

Bryce pinched the bridge of his nose. "I'll regret this for the rest of my life."

"Guess I don't need to put a dent in your face today."

"If it comes to denting my face, I'd rather Hannah witnesses it."

Cort grinned. "Get going before I change my mind. My fingers are itchin'. Careful how you handle this, Bryce. You better hope Lars doesn't show up, or you'll know real pain. The kind I might not be able to fix."

"Lars isn't coming back. I'll go to Hell to keep him away from her. Just so you both know."

Bryce left by the back door, glad to be outside where he could think better and cussed beneath his breath. After stepping into a hornet's nest, he'd lived to tell the tale. From now on, he planned to put his son and Hannah ahead of his exasperation.

"SO HERE YOU are. Been looking for you, son."

Rey didn't look up from brushing his roan mare. The animal's ears swiveled at the sound of his voice. Only silence greeted him, and it seemed they'd come full circle. He cleared his throat, hoping for a reaction.

Rey scraped the brush across the animal's hide, avoiding looking toward him. Waiting him out wasn't going to work and at this juncture, being a father was as tough a job as he'd ever had.

"Can you put down the brush long enough so we can talk?"

Setting the brush on top of a barrel, the boy turned toward him. The eyes that stared back were dark blue and dispassionate. The air bristled with animosity.

"Where's your new wife?" Reyes prodded with an icy stare.

Bitterness dripped from each punctuated word. Bringing home a wife would have been the ultimate betrayal. Bryce understood what was eating him because he would've felt the same way at that age. Now, if only he could undo the damage because his son deserved better than to have to worry about being bounced from one adult to another.

"Got no wife."

"Mason said you was going to Ogallala to try and find one. I heard him talking to Uncle Cort."

"Mason should mind his own business."

At his son's wide-eyed surprise, he figured he might as well get on with an explanation while he held Rey's full attention. Clearing his throat, he continued. "I'm not perfect. None of us are. I went off half-cocked over something that had nothing to do with you. I danced with a woman in town. But that was it. I said things that I shouldn't have said to Hannah because I was mad. Never meant to cause you any upset."

"If you didn't bring back a new wife, why are Aunt Lark and Theresa putting together a wedding cake?"

"Because they thought the same as you and wanted to welcome a new woman here. Or maybe they wanted to make me feel worse when I didn't come back with a bride. Either way, I couldn't feel worse." *Lark wanted to rub my nose in the cake, and she succeeded.*

"Why're you tellin' me?"

What kind of question was that? Confounded, he yanked his hat from his head and hooked it over a post. "I'm trying to tell you that you're more important than anyone else. I won't ever abandon you. From now on, you'll be with me. At least till you're grown and set out on your own... if that's what you decide. But that's a long way off."

Rey's eyes stayed on his without any clear sign about just what he was thinking.

Bryce shrugged. "Can we shake hands? Or something?" He extended his hand. When it was ignored, he dropped it to his side.

"Still don't know why you're telling me."

He cleared his throat. "Because it seems like it's important to you.

I don't want you misunderstanding or misinterpreting what's between me and Hannah. Besides, I just about got everybody mad at me and it bothers me that you're putting me off. Don't want hard feelings between us. I'm apologizing."

Rey shrugged. "Guess I was pretty mad."

This time, his boy proffered his open hand, then when Bryce clutched it, he tugged the boy into his arms. Closing his eyes, he thought about Gabby. Rey had the same tilt of his head as his mother whenever she was perturbed.

"I thought you'd left me. That you didn't want to be stuck with a kid."

Bryce set him back, still grasping the boy's trembling shoulders. "Nope. Won't do that. I admit I'm scared to be a father. Never been around kids to know how to raise them. So, I guess I'll just have to make mistakes and fix 'em as I go along… with your help. And hope my father set a good enough example for me to follow."

Rey launched himself at his midsection, wrapping his thin arms around his waist. With shaking fingers, Bryce sifted his fingers through the boy's dark hair. Raising his eyes to the loft, he thanked God for this reprieve.

"I *love* you, Rey." *Jesus.* Did fathers say that aloud to eleven-year-olds? An indescribable feeling rushed through him at having the love of a son. Except to be born to a woman and man who'd never been able to marry then foolishly fallen in love when neither should have, his son was about as good as it got.

Rey pushed away and looked up before he asked, "Did you love my mother?" Bryce was struck with a question he hadn't expected and wasn't sure he knew how to answer.

Bryce's jaw tautened while Rey's serious eyes looked to him for an answer. This was a crucial moment and the answer he gave would make a big difference in their relationship.

"I loved her. Gabriella was beautiful, kind, and very smart. Have to admit that we were young and kinda dumb when it came to thinking before we acted. I loved her deeply. But that was long ago. And I'm a lot different than I was then."

Rey's shoulders hunched, seeming to give thought to his admission. But what his boy said next was a blade to his gut. "She cried a lot. Luis wasn't very good to her. They fought all the time."

"If I'd known, I would've come back. But your mother accepted that she was married to Luis, and it just wasn't right for me to stay. Besides, it just made me jealous to know she was married to someone else. So, I left for the goldfields. I didn't know she died. My heart is broken about that."

"She was a good ma. Luis didn't want me around after she died. Said I reminded him of why he hated her."

That son of a bitch. Gritting his teeth, the thought of killing Luis was now an obsession.

"You don't have to worry about him anymore. You're safe here. We'll build a life together. How would you feel about us building a small ranch near Uncle Cort?"

"Will you marry Hannah? I like her."

Bryce laughed. "Son, I'd like to marry her. But she's already married."

"Just like my mother."

Jesus, Reyes was perceptive for his age and had nailed the situation. "Yep. 'Fraid so."

"She's pretty and smart. Hannah. Err... I mean Missus Van Stadt is good with figures and I'm learning a lot from her. I can help Uncle Cort with cattle counts."

"Well. I'll just bet he's glad for the help. Still. Mind your manners around her. Ladies deserve respect. Especially mothers and teachers."

"Aww. I know. Lark... I mean... *Aunt* Lark already told me about my manners."

"Good. I make you a promise that I won't go running off like that again. If I do, you'll know where I got to and why. I'll always tell you and be honest about it."

"If you see Missus Van Stadt, could you ask if she still wants me to come out to her place? She's been teaching me, but she left here kinda upset. I think she got mad because you went off to marry somebody."

"That's another reason I wanted to see you. I'm sure I disappointed her. So I best get over to her place and set her straight about a few things. We had a misunderstanding that has nothing to do with you. I'll bet she can't wait to see you again. Any arguments between her and me have nothing to do with you. She cares an awful lot about you."

"When will you be leaving?"

"Just as soon as I get mounted. Speaking of which. You got some prime horseflesh in this roan of yours. Heard Zeke gave her to you."

"I thanked him. Swore I'd take good care of her and not run away."

Bryce couldn't swallow his chortle in time. Rey's face brightened and he expected his did, as well. They'd found common ground and that was all that mattered.

"As long as you don't run away, you'd make me a happy father. Do you have a name for your horse?"

"Zeke told me I could name her whatever I like. So I decided to name her Draco for the stars all bunched in the sky that look like a dragon. Least ways, that was what Missus Van Stadt told me."

"Draco." Running his fingers over the scruff of his chin, he pretended to give that name some deep consideration. With a light slap against Rey's back, he said, "Grows on you. I like it. We'll go riding together soon."

"Don't forget to ask Missus Van Stadt if she wants me to come by for my lessons. Maybe she'd ask her husband to change his mind and let her marry you."

Damn. All he had to do is convince *Missus Van Stadt*. Reaching down, he ruffled Rey's hair and gave him one last hug. A hug that started to feel natural.

THIRTEEN

STUCK AMID THORNS

NUDGING HIS HORSE along Rocky Creek, his eyes searched Hannah's cabin. At first, he'd been hell-bent to get here, until he gave thought to what he planned to say. Besides, he guessed she probably wasn't much in the mood for listening. The first thing he'd better settle with her is that he hadn't married. That rash threat was made out of pure frustration, even though it had been her suggestion. An apology was due and if she didn't accept it, he'd keep working at it.

With the cabin in view, he removed his hat and swiped his face with his sleeve as he studied the repairs that were well underway. Cort couldn't spare many men this time of year. Tangle and Alonzo had been here several times to right the porch and patch the barn roof, but more had been done here than they could have accomplished. Narrowing his eyes, he looked the place over and wondered if someone else had been helping her.

Returning his hat to his head, he urged his horse into a trot then reined up beside the corral, sending a meadowlark into flight from the tufts of buffalo grass. Aside from that, it was eerily quiet. His horse sidestepped nervously beneath him. Reaching for his revolver, he rested it across the pommel, keeping his eyes on the house. Chimney smoke drifted skyward, indicating she was here.

Suddenly, the screen door squeaked open and she appeared. The grin he'd plastered on his face at the sight of her melted away when he found himself looking straight into the barrel of Hannah's Henry rifle.

Their eyes held but neither spoke. Gulping what little spit he had, he watched and waited. From the look of her upraised chin and pinched mouth, he deliberated whether she was mad enough to shoot him in his miserable heart. Nudging his hat farther back on his head, he considered her stillness.

"Mind if I step down, Hannah?"

"You have the nerve to come here? Today, of all days? No. You may not. Get out and don't come back."

Before he considered his reply, she stepped off the porch and cocked the rifle. He had a hard time accepting she might blow him out of his saddle, but the threat was real. Her eyes and face were tired-looking, and she was edgy. Slowly, he shoved his revolver into his holster without taking his eyes from hers. One mistaken word could mean she'd get a shot off.

"What do you mean of all days?"

"You muleheaded, miserable excuse for a man. You don't even have the brains of a grasshopper. Did you forget this is your wedding celebration? Shouldn't you be with your new wife? Now go home. Or did you come here to rub my nose in it?"

So…. she *was* jealous. When she hefted the rifle higher and aimed at his chest, he decided she wasn't about to hear him out unless he took drastic action. Slamming his bootheels into his horse's flanks, he charged to her right. The deafening explosion was followed by the splintering of wood behind him. Jumping free of his rearing horse, he yanked the rifle from her hands and tossed it into the dead rosebush beside the porch. His throat closed as he held her arms firmly, giving her a gentle shake.

"What the hell has gotten into you? This isn't like you. Hear this. I'm not married to anyone."

Hannah looked away from him. But her body shook beneath his grip, her eyes fixed on some distant point. The vein in her neck pulsed then tears streaked from her eyes.

"All right, *I'll* do the talking." He tugged her close enough to feel her warmth against him. Her sobs tore his heart into pieces. Still shaking from nearly being shot, he could hardly draw breath. What had he done? He'd been a fool to make an empty threat—one he'd never carry out.

"First. Let's get something straight. I have no wife. Never have. I'm not married, though I found a nice spread of food at the Double E. A wedding celebration that Lark probably planned to rub my nose in. And it worked. You can bet my ears and pride are still stinging after I faced a furious Lark and temperamental brother. Just about took a fist to my jaw—well deserved, I might add. From the look in Theresa's eyes, I expected she'd beat me with a hot pan."

The tension in her arms relaxed beneath his hands. When she turned her face up, her red, tear-filled eyes unraveled him. He touched her wet cheek with his finger. "Is this what this is about? Me marrying somebody else?"

"Yes." She covered her face with a quaking hand. "I'm sorry. I just meant to scare you away," she murmured. When she dropped her hand away, he drew a long breath.

"I was jealous. I'm not proud of that. After all, you're free to marry anyone you like. But your words hurt, and I thought you meant them. God help me, I shouldn't have taunted you. When you stormed away, I almost ran after you."

"Christ, Hannah. I wish you had. I was frustrated, angry and hurt, as well. I hurt you back. What I said was unforgivable. Don't forget, though, you were insistent about Lars, a fact that runs through my head every damned day and I don't know what to do about it. Your husband is a burr that keeps getting bigger. My threat. Your cross words. None of it was the best way to handle this. We just proved one important thing. We can't hide our feelings anymore."

Pressing the palms of her hands against his chest, her eyes lowered and she sniffed. Given other circumstances, he'd take that as surrender, but Hannah was a different sort.

"I'm trapped by Christian beliefs to honor my marriage. I was raised that way. Maybe it's hard for you to understand."

"Maybe I've never felt strongly about religion, though I trust we can resolve this."

He wrapped his arms around her, then she nestled her head against his pounding heart. The softness of her hair against his splayed fingers had him draw in a satisfied breath. Glancing across her shoulder at the cabin, he considered how close they were to her bed. As though she'd read his thoughts, she leaned away and offered him a wan smile.

"You came here just to tell me you aren't married," she whispered. "But *I* am. And this is as far as we can go."

He shook his head. "I acted like a love-sick fool. Besides, I'm supposed to be a foreman and I let down my men and my brother. Went off to town, attending a dance I had no interest in. All because the woman I wanted in my arms was here and out of my reach."

"Did you dance?"

"I did. But she wasn't you. Pretty... but no one could take your place. Let's say, I extricated myself and found myself swilling whiskey at the saloon. Feeling a mite sorry for myself."

Throwing back her head, her musical laughter sent heat surging through him. That kissable mouth enticed him to toss caution to the wind, before he thought better of it.

With a coy smile, she asked, "Did you break her heart?"

"Plenty of others there took my place. Besides, I'd done enough damage for one day. Got drunk. Stayed at the hotel. *Alone.* In case you're wondering."

There was a solemn expression on her face, and he knew she was about to ask something. He pretty much guessed what it might be. "No." He tilted her chin up with one finger. "I did not sleep with any woman. There's only one I want. I've made that clear enough but she's not quite agreeable to the idea."

"What will we do, Bryce?"

"Eventually, I think I could break down your will. But I'm not keen on waiting. I want you legally. If you've got time, let's go inside. I have plans and need you to consider them. Hear me out. Maybe over coffee?"

"Plans?"

"Gave it some thought while I was in Ogallala. Let's go inside so I can explain."

"I guess. Now that you're here. I'll listen."

"Yep. That's what I want to hear."

"I'm sorry for shooting. I wouldn't have shot you."

He grinned and tapped her nose. "Just don't scare me like that again."

"We both learned a lesson."

"By the way, Reyes wanted me to ask you if he can still come by for his lessons. You sure have impressed him. So you know, I had a long talk with him. We got some things settled between us. Keep in mind, we come as a package."

"He's a great young man. Like his father. Even if you had married someone, I'd still want him to come for his lessons. That wouldn't change. Tell him I expect him. I wouldn't like you half as much if he wasn't included in the package."

"He figures you'd make a good mother. Like most kids, he doesn't understand the complexity of this situation. Given the chance, either me or him might consider shooting Lars. Go get that coffee ready while I see to my horse and saddlebag. I've brought something you need to see, and it could be the answer to the dilemma."

A tentative smile lit her face, and her tears gave brilliance to her blue eyes. This image of her would always stay with him. Having other babies and this woman beside him would be all he'd ever need, once they'd climbed the mountain of troubles.

"Bryce. If Lars doesn't return, I won't be able to hold on to this ranch much longer. I'd have to sell to Cort. I know that. If my husband shows up, I'll ask him for a divorce."

"Exactly. Now you're thinking." He sniffed the air. "Wait... Is that bread I smell?"

"Oh... my God! It'll be burnt. Come in when you're ready. I'll set out some supper."

Whirling, she lifted her skirt and bounded up the steps like a boy, forgetting about her rifle still poking out from the rosebushes. He couldn't help but admire her slender waist and round bottom. His fin-

gers ached to loosen her braid to set her hair free. Once she was out
of sight, he rubbed his chin, amazed at all the repairs he saw. Odd that
Cort's men had accomplished all of this.

The hairs rose on his arms as he led his horse into the corral. Something didn't sit right. His hand rested near his holster and his eyes narrowed on the tree line then turned to the barn loft. Nothing stirred, yet
he couldn't shake the feeling he was being watched. An eagle soared
high overhead. A breeze ruffled through his horse's mane. Refusing to
ruin a perfectly good meal with his woman, he set aside what might be
his imagination.

STEPPING INSIDE, HIS saddlebag draped across his shoulder, he rested her rifle in the wall rack. Clutching his rifle at his side, he started
toward the kitchen, admiring the colorful rag rug but the shiplap walls
were sorely in need of paint. When he'd charged in here during the tornado, there'd been precious little time to observe her personal things.

He hung his hat from the hook, then when he turned, he was pretty sure his mouth dropped wide open at the sight of three paintings
adorning one side of the hallway. Leaning his rifle against the wall and
dropping his saddlebag to the floor, he lifted one painting from where
it leaned against one wall. What he saw was a depiction of a familiar
grove of trees that was so beautiful, he swallowed against a lump in his
throat. *She'd* painted this. In fact, as he looked at the rest of the paintings, each elicited scenes of this ranch.

One in particular held his attention where it leaned against the opposite wall, unfinished but detailed. There was no doubt he was looking
at his buckskin horse, ground tied against the backdrop of a clouded
sky. The outline of a man without features, stood nearby. Him. Hannah
had been painting him. Returning the painting to the floor, curiosity
drew him into the small parlor.

Little light filtered in beneath the porch roof from the window. Pots
of paints and brushes rested on a table beside an easel. A small school

desk sat beside a larger one. On either side of a small stone fireplace, shelves were neatly stacked with books. No wonder his son wanted to be here for his lessons. He wondered if she were teaching him to paint, as well. This extraordinary woman surprised him at every turn.

Her talents went well beyond sewing and painting. From what Rey told him, she knew geography, reading, and ciphers. Rey hadn't exaggerated. More certain she didn't belong here with a man like Lars, he intended to press his case until he won.

Picking up one of the books, he flipped through the pages. Some fellow named Walt Whitman wrote *Leaves of Grass.* Skimming over the words, he found himself enjoying having a book in his hand again, though poems weren't his interest.

"Ah. Here you are. Sneaking around my parlor."

A skewer must have poked him right in the ass at the sudden sound of her voice. Dropping the book, he pivoted, facing her winsome smile. Being caught in the middle of discovering her secrets was irksome but he wasn't sorry. Her eyes dropped to the book on the floor at his feet.

"Are you familiar with Walt Whitman?"

He lifted the book and set it back on the shelf before answering her. "No. Looked like he was describing nature. Not something I'd likely read."

"Exactly what I expected you might say. Rey seems to like *his* poems. But he'd rather read Warren's *Common-School Geography* I borrowed from Cort's library. Reyes also enjoys calculations. Soon he'll be far beyond what I can teach him. In short, you have a quizzical and intelligent son."

"Thanks for what you're doing for him. He needs this. I don't think his mother and Luis were near a school."

"Someone taught him some reading."

"Had to have been Gabriella. There's a lot I'll never know."

"So now you go on from here. That's all any of us can do."

"Enough about me. How about you? These paintings are remarkable. You've kept this side of you a secret. Sure wish I'd taken notice of them before now."

"I dabble in painting because the winters are lonely. When Lars was still here, he wouldn't let me waste money on paper and paint. So I never hung some of them till after that storm. Just glad they weren't destroyed where I'd hidden them. Lars hated anything I did if it wasn't practical. Lark knows about my paintings. She has one hanging in her house. They aren't remarkable, just things I see."

He balled his fists at his sides, wishing he could bust her husband in the mouth. "This is more than dabbling. You have a gift. Your husband doesn't deserve to breathe the same air as you. Don't waste your talent, Hannah."

"When I can paint, I will."

Closing the little distance between them, he opened his arms and she walked into them, surprising him. He wasn't about to question her change in mood. Lowering his head, he kissed the tip of her nose, then lower until his mouth drifted over her parted lips. Her soft breath stirred him to beg for more. His long, lazy kiss invited her to stay. At the sound of her moan, he leaned away, enjoying the sight of the serene smile in his vision.

"Oh, God. What you do to me, woman."

In the silence, he said the first inane thing to cross his mind. "You painted my horse. It isn't finished."

"You don't mind?"

"Mind? Why would I mind?"

She shrugged. "Because... Lars considered it all a waste of time. I kept my unfinished work hidden in the barn loft. I wanted something of you."

"First. I'm not Lars. Don't ever forget that. I'm not offended at you painting me. I'm flattered. Why didn't you finish it?"

"I have to be careful about money. Paints and brushes are expensive. I'm almost out of paint. Maybe someday I'll start again."

Bryce tucked her hand in his and pressed a kiss against her palm. As he took in the sparse, worn furniture and then the paintings leaning against the wall, he made a mental note to see that she got the paint and paper she needed.

"I hope you're hungry. Supper's on the table and I've got apple pie from yesterday."

"You go ahead. I need to get something from my saddlebag that you need to see."

Her eyes widened. "Please don't tell me there's bad news."

"No. Not bad. Just important."

———————

SHE WAS FLUSTERED at serving him a meal on the old, scarred table. More, she felt ashamed at her chipped dishes, and scant living conditions that were worse since the storm. She fidgeted with the platters while from the corner of her eye, she saw Bryce studying the room. His fathomless eyes settled on her and she wondered if she compared this little kitchen to the one at the Double E. Of course, he did.

She'd done her best to nail together the table and two of the chairs. Still, there was little she could do about raw wood walls, hastily nailed to the logs, nor the newspaper used to plug the holes.

Smoothing her hands over her apron, she poured coffee into the cup in front of him. When he leaned his weight against the two back legs of the shaky chair, her tongue refused to cry out a warning. Pride was a sin, so she'd been taught. For now, she hoped he wasn't dumped to the floor.

"Hannah. Everything looks fine. The food smells good. I'm hungry enough to eat a whole chicken, feathers and all. Please sit down and stop looking so nervous."

"I hope the coffee is to your liking."

"I've had all kinds of coffee and I take to anything. I've eaten here before. Remember? This is the best I've had in a while. Now sit."

Just as she started toward the table, he lurched to his feet and pulled out her chair.

"I was raised with manners. Sometimes I forget to use them," he said.

Incredulous, she offered him a slow nod before thinking to say, "No need for formality. I'm not used to it. In fact, it makes me uncomfortable." After she was seated, he took his and sipped the coffee.

She wondered at his speculative grin and peculiar mood. In the quiet, they spooned vittles, simply enjoying the moments of contentment. She found pleasure in just watching him eat. Setting aside her spoon, she sipped her coffee and considered him over the brim of the cup. Attentive to his mannerisms, she didn't miss how he sopped gravy with his bread, sparing a moment to sip his coffee between chews. He rarely looked up, keeping his attention on the food as though in a hurry.

Taking note of his freshly trimmed hair and beard, she breathed in a whiff of bay rum. Pleasure rested between them like a comfortable old blanket. Her study of him was marred only by the gun and holster he wore most of the time. She'd heard of his skills as a marksman yet the idea of him killing seemed at odds with the congenial man who sat here. Which circled her back to shooting the corral post. Clearing her throat, she decided to get to her apology again.

"I'm sorry I shot at you. I had no intention of hurting you. Just wanted to scare you away."

Bryce lifted his head, still chewing. She saw him swallow. He said nothing. Instead, he stared and leaned back in the chair, shaking his head.

"I accept your apology. Besides, I never thought you'd really shoot me, although for a split second, you had me scared. Am I to conclude you missed me on purpose?"

"Maybe." She grinned. "Glad we're still friends. I did shoot over you."

When he arched his eyebrow, she suspected he still had something on his mind. Resting his hands on the table, he steepled his fingers. "Come on, Hannah. We can't be friends. This thing between us is more than that. You know it. Reyes knows it. Even Lark and Cort know it. We've gone beyond friends. I want more and so do you."

"There's nothing I can do unless I can find my husband and appeal to him. Unless I'm a widow, I'm a married woman."

"Want to hear my solution?"

She nodded and shoved her cup aside while he stood and retrieved papers from the bench where he'd dropped them. In fact, she'd been eyeing them with curiosity. Hardly able to contain her questions as he fanned out the documents against the table, she searched his eyes. She was afraid of what these might mean and more afraid to touch them.

Clearing her throat, she lifted the first page and skimmed the words. Looking up, she pinched her lip between her teeth. A building terror rose inside at the prospect of her freedom.

But at what cost?

"A divorce decree?"

"That's right. Yesterday, before I left Ogallala, I decided to pay Marcus Layton a call—the lawyer. We had quite a talk. Along with most folks around here, Marcus has no liking for your miserable husband. That alone should open your eyes. However, knowing this has to be done legally, he drew up the decree. All we need is your signature."

Following the course of his finger, she saw the line waiting for her signed name. Her stomach churned at the enormity of this decision. A divorce flew in the face of everything she'd been taught about the finality of marriage. But more, Lars would blame Bryce. She dare not forget her husband was a dangerous man. If Lars thought Bryce was behind this....

"Sign. For your own well-being and mine, Hannah. Please."

"I'd be free?"

"No. I still have to get Lars to sign on the next page."

"How? He isn't even here."

"I'll track him down. And he'll sign. I'm not allowing the woman I love to continue suffering."

Love. He'd said the word she still couldn't say. "Even if you find him, he won't agree. You don't know how powerfully built a man he is. Everyone is afraid to take him on in a fight. I won't have you getting badly hurt or killed over me."

"Sign and I'll worry about the rest."

Within the long silence between them, Hannah shivered. She couldn't move. Steel blue-gray eyes and a determined jaw faced her across the table. Panic set in and it overtook all sense of reason. When she didn't pick up the ink pen he slid her way, he scrubbed his hands across his face and then straight-armed from the chair. Marching away, he left her tremoring. Her body jerked with the slam of the door. His saddlebag still lay on the bench. Resting her face in her hands to smother her sobs, she felt the weight of this moment squeezing her sense of reason and her breath away.

FOURTEEN

REVELATIONS AND PERIL

B RYCE DIDN'T KNOW where he was going. Anger had a color because all he could see was red haze. Maybe if he shot that barn full of holes it might make him feel like he'd shot her husband. But it wouldn't change her stubbornness. Stopping beside the splintered fence post, he snapped it and tossed it aside. Finding himself mindlessly circling around the barn, his searching eyes had him suddenly pull up short. *Tracks.* Tracks that led into the barn. Hunkering, he studied them.

Not Hannah's horse, Pie. Somebody must have been stabling a horse inside. Double E hands wouldn't do that. The question was... who? Even more exasperated, he stood and kicked dirt with his boot toe, pivoted, and tramped toward the house, bound to find out. That was when he saw her sitting on the porch step, her mouth a thin line and her eyes watchful as he slowed his pace and halted, standing over her.

The papers were clutched neatly against her lap. Her eyes sparkled in the light while she bit her lip. Crouching in front of her, he was going to see this through. Lifting a hand to touch her, he thought better of it and then dropped it to his side.

"Sorry, Hannah. I thought I was helping you. Instead, I overstepped."

Damn. How he hated her predicament. Not many women would be as strong as this one, trapped between her convictions and her freedom. Wanting to hold her and kiss away every bad thing in her life, rattled by her distant stare, his memory circled back to the mistakes he'd made with Gabriella. Touching her right now was out of the question. This time, he had to get it right.

The thought of loving her, holding her beside him every night, kept him awake. But she wasn't ready for that next step. On an indrawn breath, he took a seat beside her. To his surprise, she dropped the decree onto his lap, her neat signature was plain as day.

"You've changed your mind." *Lordy, I might have become a believer.*

"I might regret this, Bryce. I don't want you hurt. Confronting him will mean trouble. He's heartless. He's bragged that he's killed with his bare hands. I believe him."

"Let me worry about him. Once I find him."

Reaching into the pocket of her apron, she proffered a worn and wrinkled letter.

"This might be of help. This came about a year ago and the last time I heard from him."

Taking the crinkled paper from her hand, he held it up to the light. The scribbled words were short and to the point. Most of it made little sense. Clearly, the man was hardly literate. Just to be sure he had the facts straight, Bryce read and reread the careless words.

Wife, got with group gone north to Montana way. Comanches in Areezoni too much for one man. Big gold here. Keep my ranch goin' girl. Stayin' here till rich. Near some place called Beaverhead R. Don't spend no money less I say. Got good cabin. Stake claim. Husband Lars

Bryce nearly crushed the letter in his palm. Shaking inside, the edge of irritation had returned with a vengeance. How little her husband cared about his wife or how she might be faring made it all the more imperative to find and kill him. With her agreement, he knew what he had to do. He had a good idea where Lars had gone because he'd mined the camps.

"Bryce. The furious look in your eyes… scares me. I shouldn't have given you the letter."

On a long shuddering breath, he dropped the letter onto her lap. Despite his promise to keep his hands to himself, he gently snugged her against his side while she rested her head comfortably in the crook of his neck. In the quiet, he collected his thoughts before speaking.

"You've been brave long enough. I know the mining camps. I lived in Alder Gulch for a long while. I have a good idea where your husband is, and I can easily mix in with the likes of those miners. Knowing how they think and act is to my advantage. I'm taking that decree with me and when I get back here, I'll have his signature. You'll be free."

"He won't sign. I just know it. And you'll have wasted your time."

"First of all, you are *not* a waste of time. He'll sign because I won't give him any choice. No matter what I have to do, I'm cutting your tie to that bastard."

At her juddering sigh, he pressed a soft kiss to her head.

She tilted her worried face up. "Is there any way I can convince you not to go? There are some Sioux and Arapaho still waging skirmishes. Please. Stay."

"First. I know how to keep out of their way. Besides, if I don't take care of this, neither of us will have a life. There's nothing you can do or say that will keep me from facing him and settling this."

"Reyes? He needs you as much as I do. More, in fact. Think about him. What if…." She didn't finish.

Hannah needn't remind him of his responsibility to his son. This decision weighed heavy on him when he said, "I'm counting on you, Lark, and Cort to look out for him while I'm gone. If I didn't have you and them, I wouldn't go."

Covering her face with shaking hands, he looked skyward, trying to decide how he might ease her worry. When she dropped her hands away, he grinned at the splotch of flour on her cheek and her sunburned, freckled nose. He'd never been more captivated. His fingers turned her face up to his and he kissed her deeply, leaving no room for doubts about his feelings.

He was staking his claim and this time, she didn't resist. The sound of her whimper brought him slowly back to the surface. Someplace inside of his wanting her, the thought of those tracks intruded. She must have felt him tense at the question in her eyes when he released her.

His head snapped sideways. His eyes searched the corral and the distant woods and creek. Something out there made him nervous. Was it this place? A ranch owned by her husband? Or an unseen enemy?

"What is it?"

"I'm not sure. Sometimes I get a feeling we're being watched. You see anyone, have your gun near."

"I've been doing that for a while now. I can take care of myself. When will you leave?"

"It's July. If I'm guessing right, I can be up to Bannack in about three or four weeks."

"You might get caught in an early snow by the time you start back. I'll be worried sick."

"I know how to find shelter. Besides, once I get south in Wyoming, I'll make my way to the U-P back to Ogallala. Should be home by end of September or early October. Course, I got to make sure Cort will hold a job for me here. Either way, I'm going."

Her hand slid over his and their fingers threaded.

"You haven't answered my question. When will you leave?" she asked.

"Soon as I clear this with Cort. While we're at it, I have a question. Saw some horse prints by your barn door. Someone's been stabling a horse here. And it isn't yours. I know the indentation on Pie's left front hoof. Which of our hands has been coming by?"

"None of them, lately. Most of the Double E is busy. Didn't want to be a bother to Cort or Tangle and the rest. Or you. I need the help with repairs, so I withdrew one hundred dollars from Lars's bank account in Ogallala. Told the clerk it was intended for repairs, and he approved it."

"You hired someone?" What the hell was she thinking? A lone woman hiring someone she didn't know. "Please tell me you know the man you hired."

"Yes and no. He comes by every once in a while, if he has time. I pay him when he finishes. He lives somewhere near Ogallala with his wife. Said he fell on hard times and was looking to make a little extra money. He fixed the barn door and even did some repairs on the corral and my roof."

"I don't like it. Alone with a man you hardly even know."

Standing, he crossed his arms and glared downward at her frown. Her reaction was predictable. She rose to meet his stare and then with a back as straight as an arrow and hands on her hips, her eyes warned him they were about to have another disagreement. Jesus Christ. They had just shared a kiss. Now she was hissing like a stepped-on cat.

"For your information, I have a gun and know how to use it. He keeps to himself and leaves by suppertime. Never asks for food. Brings his own vittles. Even brought me beef from town. I paid him, of course. Didn't really need it, but since he'd brought it, I didn't waste it. Escobar has been nothing but polite. Even takes his hat off whenever he speaks to me. Besides. I didn't know you until lately. Still gave you a chance, Bryce Enders."

"You may not have known me at first, but you knew my brother. That had to be factored in."

Stepping back from him, she tapped her boot toe, then crossed her arms while her beautiful eyes flashed.

Pressing his case, he said, "All right. Let's start again. Maybe he's what you say he is. Just a man lookin' for work. Why doesn't he look for work at our ranch? We'd pay more. Or in town? Did you think of that?"

"I take it he's needed most of the time on his small vegetable farm."

"And you've never seen him before?"

"No. But I don't go to Ogallala often. Besides, I don't know *everyone*."

"What's his name?"

"Why do you need to know?"

"I'll check his name out with Cort. He'd know. Or Lark would've heard of him and his wife. I need to know because something feels wrong."

Hannah pinched the bridge of her nose. He gripped her shoulders and waited while what he said sank into her head. "Hannah. Please tell me his name and what he looks like. It's important. Indulge me."

When her hands dropped away from her face, she chided. "You are the most stubborn man I've ever known…. next to Lars."

He rolled his eyes. "Don't go insulting me."

"Ha. If you must know, his name is Escobar Diaz. Black hair with streaks of gray. Rides a good-looking black mare. Those are the tracks you see. He likes to leave his horse inside the barn when he comes. I don't know why…."

When did recognition dawn for him? Before the description or at the mention of the Spanish name? Whatever else she rambled on about, his ears were ringing and her words died, replaced with the full force of panic.

He'd bet his next pay that Escobar Diaz was Luis Montez. The bastard was poking around and now had his sights on Hannah. Or he was using her to hide in plain sight. Maybe he was wrong. But too much was at stake if his guess was right. He hadn't seen Luis in a very long time. If his hunch was right, he had no intention of putting his son or Hannah in the middle. Then it hit him. Beef. He'd brought her beef. How did a man afford such a thing in town if he was down on his luck and needed money?

Unless he was the cow killer. And feeding her Enders meat.

As his thoughts tumbled, he slipped his arm around her and she rested her head against his fear-filled heart. "I want you to come back to the ranch with me. No arguments. Until I know for sure who this man is, I don't want you left here alone."

She stepped away and glared up at him. "I have to see to my garden. What about my only milk cow? Then there's the chickens. Alonzo just got them back here for me. I can't just leave. I'm lucky I still have some stock."

"I'll send one of the hands back."

"No."

Gritting his teeth, he thought about hauling her into his arms and plunking her onto his saddle, even kicking and screaming. How had he managed to fall in love with such a feisty, mulish woman? Couldn't he have found a complacent woman? One *without* a husband?

Shit. Of all the luck to have this happen right now. Oddly, he loved her for her grit and strong will... even as she tested his.

"Have it your way. Against my better judgment, I'm leaving you here. But I'll be back with Cort. I'm keeping my son at the ranch till I know what this Escobar might be up to. Then we'll decide what to do about him. Keep your gun with you, especially if he shows up. Don't let him get close to you. Don't let on you suspect anything."

"I doubt he'll be here today," she said.

Once he'd tightened his saddle cinch, he slapped his hat on his head and tucked the decree inside his saddlebag. Once mounted, he gave a last nod and then nudged Hunter toward the river. All the way to the ranch, he prayed he was wrong about Escobar. If he found out no one knew this man, he and Cort would charge back and wait for the bastard to show up. With every movement of his horse beneath him, he gave thought to turning back.

FIFTEEN

THE CONFRONTATION

H ANNAH SPENT THE rest of the afternoon pacing and peering from her window. Pondering Bryce's warnings, she recollected that Gabriella had been married to a Mexican man down in Texas. And from the few things Reyes had told her, the man was not much of a father or husband. In fact, Rey had looked shaken at the mere mention of his *father's* name.

Lately, Cort, Bryce, and Zeke seemed to be keeping something from the women. She and Lark had figured out that the coyote and wolf hunts were excuses for something else—something the men were doing their best to hide. Not even Lark could draw it out of Cort.

Maybe Escobar was what he said. Just a man down on his luck. Bryce made a point of questioning why he didn't seek work on the Enders' ranch. Why hadn't she considered that? Giving thought to Bryce's argument, she considered how a simple farmer owned such a magnificent horse? Worse, when she'd described Escobar, Bryce's eyes turned to ice and that cold, faraway look came over him like he'd seen a ghost. When he'd held her, the tense, brewing conflict was palpable. Now that she believed him, what would she do if Escobar returned?

Picking up her rifle, she closed the front door, effectively closing out most of the daylight. Ramming the bolt, she returned to the kitchen door and did the same. It had been a long while since she'd locked the house against the outside, and only when the coyotes yipped and the wolves howled. Or when Lars was drowning himself in whiskey out in the barn.

Laying her rifle across the table, she sat. Resting her elbows against the table, she propped her chin against the back of her folded hands, giving in to tears, waiting to the steady sound of the ticking clock. If Escobar showed up, she'd have to find some excuse to send him away. If he was the man Bryce hated, she didn't know if she could mask her wariness nor her anger. One thing for sure, Bryce had left her questioning her carelessness in trusting this man.

After scraping the plates and plunging them into the basin water, the sound of an approaching horse near the porch caught her attention. Escobar always went straight to the barn. Slipping from her apron, she picked up the Henry and walked to the parlor window. Standing to the side of the worn curtains, she peeked outside. Her heart nearly stopped.

Reyes sat atop his new horse, the animal decked out with a hand tooled saddle. At first, he looked around as if expecting her to appear. He hadn't worn a hat today, and his windblown, shaggy hair, reminded her of Bryce. When he called out, she was jolted into the question of what to do.

"Missus Van Stadt? You home?"

The chickens clucked and she saw them running toward the new henhouse. She stood rooted to the floor, forgetting to move, wishing he hadn't come today. What if Escobar and Luis were the same man? Remembering the locked door, she walked into the hallway. Rey usually tied his horse to the front post and came right in after knocking and announcing himself. If he found her door locked, he'd find it odd. There was no use in hiding.

"Missus Van Stadt?" he called out again.

By the time Hannah unbolted the door and opened it, Reyes stood on the porch with his satchel of books clutched in one hand. They stared at each other for a moment. Then his eyes widened at the Henry she gripped at her side. Pulling open the screened door, he stepped inside, peering around her shoulder as though he might discover something amiss. Trying to think of an excuse for the gun, she drew a blank.

"I'm glad you came for a lesson, Reyes. I just wasn't expecting you."

"Aunt Lark told me you wouldn't mind. So I decided to just come over. Figured Pa might be here."

"He left a short while ago. I guess you didn't see him."

"Sometimes I cut across the range and farther down the creek. Wanted to see how my horse would do at a gallop."

"She's a fine horse."

"Draco. Named her after the Dragon you told me about."

"Well. It's a mighty fine name." Pushing a strand of hair from her face, she forced a smile. Focusing on his small talk was wearing her nerves raw. "We don't need to stand here. Why don't you come into the parlor, and we'll get started."

Oh, God. What if Reyes were discovered by Escobar?

"Why do you have a gun in your hand? Did someone bother you?" he asked from behind her as he followed her into the parlor.

"No." Hating to outright lie, there was no use in worrying him needlessly. Instead, she came up with the best excuse she could pull out of her bonnet. She cleared her throat. "I heard some wolves howling last night and thought it best to keep the gun handy."

She leaned the gun against the inside parlor wall and said a prayer that Escobar didn't choose today to come by and adding a second prayer that Rey accepted her concocted excuse. Thankfully, he simply shrugged at her explanation. Taking a seat behind the smaller of the two desks, she waited while he dragged his books from his satchel.

Then, setting out the Robinson's mathematics book, she dismissed her qualms and gave him directions to open to page nineteen and compute the answers on his slate. That would give her time to figure out a plan of action should trouble arrive.

Taking a seat at her desk, her mind wandered back to her school days. Unlike Reyes, she often daydreamed while she listened to the ticking of the school clock. There were no clocks in this room. Even what little paper she had... was gone. Blessedly, she still kept her graphite pencils, some of the few things she'd been able to salvage when she left New York.

Watching Rey, his head bent over the book while he scrawled his numbers, the repetitive scraping of chalk against the slate jangled her nerves with every minute that went by. Dare she look from the window and alarm Rey? Her skin prickled and she was so fidgety she wanted to walk around in circles. *He'd come.* She felt it. With a side-long glance toward her rifle, she drew a calming breath. To protect Rey, she'd use it. Bryce would keep his word and return. A day of reckoning was upon them all.

After a time, the worst *did* happen. She recognized the sound of a single horse riding to the barn. Standing, she peered from the window. A sick feeling started in her stomach and made its way to her throat. *Escobar.* Feeling blood draining from her face, she leaned back against the wall to think. Another quick glance found the man looking toward the window, one bushy eyebrow raised.

He turned his horse and dismounted, looping the reins over a corral rail near the barn. His dark eyes trailed over the roan out front. This wasn't going to go well. *Pray God. This can't be Luis.* So deep in thought, she didn't hear Reyes drop his chalk and stand.

"What's wrong, Missus Van Stadt? You look scared. Your face looks white. Who is it?"

"You stay here. It's just the man from Ogallala whose been fixing the barn for me. Name's Escobar. Nothing to worry about."

"I thought Tangle and Alonzo did that."

"Sometimes. But they're busy right now." *Oh, Lord, please don't keep asking questions.*

Reyes moved closer to the window before she could stop him. Hannah wanted to reach for him, but she was too late. He leaned closer to the glass and then his eyes riveted on the man near the barn. His surprised expression turned to outrage, and his fists were balled at his sides. His mouth drew into a tight line. With an abruptness she hadn't calculated, he lurched for her rifle. God was on her side when she was able to wrest it from his grasp and then with a stern look, she pressed a finger against her lips, pleading with her eyes for him to stay quiet. His face flushed but he slowly nodded.

"That's Luis. I hate him. He's bad. How come you have him come here?" he whispered.

"I didn't know it was Luis until now," she hissed under her breath. "Your father was worried and rode back to the ranch to find out if there was such a man as Escobar Diaz in Ogallala. I didn't know this man lied about who he was."

Clanking spurs and thudding boots against the porch floor stopped them both. Hannah looked toward the boy, his furious glare fixed on the hallway. Once again, she pressed her fingers to her mouth. "Shh. Say nothing."

With sickening dread, she remembered not locking the big door. Luis would be free to walk in if he chose. And if he did, he'd discover Reyes. Rifle in hand, she mouthed, "Stay here. Don't let him see you."

To her relief, the boy nodded but his fury was unmistakable in his drawn face and red cheeks. Imagining that Reyes might be thinking his stepfather was here to find him, she just hoped he'd stay out of the way until she had time to encourage Luis to leave. Since Cort and Bryce weren't here yet, she wasn't going to let this man harm a hair on this boy's head.

A fist pounded against the door frame, forcing her into a decision.

"Missus Van Stadt? Are you there? It is Escobar."

Would holding the gun when she met him at the door be wise or foolish? If he suspected she'd figured out his identity, he might kill them both. One last glance in Rey's direction found him in a stiff-legged stance, his fists still at his side. She saw a twitch in his cheek, but he offered a sharp nod.

Leaving the rifle within reach near the parlor door, she smoothed her skirt and stepped into the hallway. Finding herself face to face with a liar and wife abuser, with only a screen separating them, she thought she might have made a mistake leaving the rifle on the other side of the wall. Heart pounding furiously, a rivulet of sweat ran along her neck. She forced a weak smile.

The man's flat, emotionless black eyes stared through the screen, reminding her of a snake. Today, he was not an innocent farmer, down on his luck. No doubt, there wasn't a poor wife. Thankfully, he hadn't made any attempt to open the door. At least not yet.

"I wasn't expecting you, Escobar."

"I told you I'd come whenever I had time."

Clearing her throat, she searched for the right words. When she hesitated, he looked over his shoulder toward Rey's horse. When he returned his half-lidded eyes to her, they raked her with an insolence.

"You have a guest."

"Yes. I teach painting to some of the children. We were so busy with our concentration, we didn't hear you ride up."

"Is he or she hiding in there?"

Luis's face was near the screen and his eyes searched hers and then the hallway beyond. Her hands itched to slam the door and bolt it. "Like I said. His parents pay good money for his lessons. Perhaps you'll come by another day?"

Biting her lip, she felt stupid for letting it slip that it was a boy because now he scrutinized her and then the windows of the parlor. He lifted a hand and pressed it against the frame as though to bar her escape. *He must suspect something.*

"I came a long way and hoped to make money."

Somehow, she had to allay his suspicion. The threatening tone of his voice left her no choice but to make a decision.

"Very well. One corral post needs repair. I accidentally shot it when I aimed at a varmint last night."

"A varmint?" His eyes narrowed, pinning her where she stood.

"Perhaps you could tend my horse. If you still have time, before you leave, you might round up stray, unbranded cows."

"I'll look after your horse and see if I find a post to repair the corral. Then I'll be back to collect the money before leaving. Maybe you have more work for me the next time."

"Maybe. Now, if you'll excuse me?"

She waited, her eyes staying on his sweat-stained back as he stepped from the porch. Relieved that he left the porch, she released her breath. Today, he'd left his horse tied near the far end of the barn door, something he hadn't done before.

At the sound of running horses and splashing water, Escobar lifted his head and ran for his horse. At the same time, he drew his revolver from his holster. Stunned at the turmoil erupting in front of her eyes, she watched dumbly when he slipped his rifle from his saddle scabbard.

Her eyes turned beyond him to see a line of mounted cowboys, led by Cort and Bryce, water spraying into the air while they crossed the creek. Momentarily distracted at the sight of the riders, she didn't notice that Luis had turned his rifle in her direction.

She froze at the sight of his face brimming with hostility—coal black eyes burning like the Devil. She dropped to the floor just as he fired again and again. Crawling on her hands and knees, she slammed the door closed. More shots splintered the wood above her head, and she screamed.

SIXTEEN

RAGE

REYES DOVE ONTO the floor beside her, the rifle gripped between his hands. Beads of sweat dotted his face as he rolled to his side. His eyes looked fiercely into hers. Taking the rifle from his hands, she warned him to stay flat. Now she had to decide if they should slither to the kitchen or flatten against the hallway wall. Clutching the Henry, she lifted her head and kept her eyes on the door. Deciding it was too risky to bolt it, she hand signaled Reyes to stay low.

A brief quiet followed the initial gunfire. There were no voices nor sounds of horses. Rolling onto her side, she tugged Rey's sleeve, pointing to the wall. Plastering themselves against the inside wall, they waited with only the sound of their rasping breaths. Her heart pounded in her ears. Maybe Cort and Bryce had killed the attacker. He deserved no less. But what if Luis were still out there. Looking toward the bolt, she gave thought to ramming it closed.

That hope died when the air exploded with volleys of gunfire. Bullets shattered the front window and a horse trumpeted. Rey's horse had most likely pulled loose and escaped. Sensing that Reyes was about to leap to his feet, she pressed him down with all her might. Her shoulder twisted against him as he struggled against her hold. She'd clearly miscalculated his strength.

"Stay *put.* Do you want to get shot? Or worse, have your father storm in here after you and get himself killed? Draco can be rounded up later," she snapped.

"Luis will try to kill my father. He hates him. I don't know all the reasons, but I guess it has to do with me."

"This has nothing to do with you. Luis has a crazy mind. Your father is good with guns and Luis is up against a better man. You mean the world to your father, and he wants the chance to prove it. Don't you want the same chance?"

Rey thumped his head against the wall and sobbed. He swiped snot and tears with his shirtsleeve and she wished she could find the right words to console him. Instead, she warily kept one eye on the door, afraid Luis might confront them.

"Yeah. I want him to be here for me. Like he said he would. I'm tired of being with folks who don't like me much."

Before she had time to think what to say, gunfire erupted from all directions. Through the blasts, she heard men's shouts.

"Luis! Come out of the barn or we'll burn it down around you!"

There was no mistaking Cort's angry yell during the pause in gunfire. Curious, she dragged herself along the floor and through the parlor, careful to avoid the glass shards. She beckoned Reyes to follow. Crawling along the floor behind her, he joined her in flattening against the wall beside the broken window and then she peered out. At least three horses were inside the corral, running in wide circles. She recognized Cort standing in the shadows of the trees beside her porch, his rifle aimed at the barn loft window. *Where was Bryce?*

"Missus Van Stadt. I don't see my pa."

She offered Rey a quick sidelong glance. He had positioned himself on the opposite side of the window and joined her in searching for Bryce.

"He's out there somewhere." Watching the boy, she saw in him a young version of his father. Bryce would be proud of how he'd brought the rifle to her in the middle of the shooting.

Reyes peeked out again. "Look. I see Tangle hiding at the corner of the barn. Mason and Alonzo on the other side of the trough."

"Lordy. I hope Luis surrenders."

"What will happen to him if he does?"

"Killing a man's cows is a serious offense. Cort might decide to send him to jail or hang him. I hope he considers using the law."

"I don't. He was mean to my mother. And she died because he didn't help her get well. He let her die."

Hannah's heart broke at the venomous words from someone so young. Yet, she understood how much he'd suffered because of Luis. To watch his mother die, not knowing how he could help her, would likely always stay with him. Reaching for his arm, she squeezed it, letting him know she was listening. Whatever happened, it was in the hands of the men outside and God upstairs. This was an inevitable confrontation, and no one would stop it.

Luis broke the lull, shouting, "Where are you, Bryce? This is between you and me. I figured I'd never find the bastard who *took* my wife. I was willing to ruin your rich brother and his fine ranch. Until this morning, when I saw *you.* Visiting the whore. Seems you found another woman to ruin. I had the chance to kill you and maybe her. Wanted to wait, instead. Make you suffer."

Silence.

"What does he mean, Missus Van Stadt?" Reyes questioned.

How did she explain such debasement coming from the mouth of a madman? Especially to a young boy. "Nothing. He's crazy. His words are meaningless," she blurted. His mouth curved into a thoughtful frown, and she hoped he wouldn't recall the words later.

It was Bryce who finally answered. "Come down and let's settle this between us. It will be my pleasure. If anyone deserves to die, you do... Luis. You had a wife willing to put up with despair and abuse all those years. She stayed with you... willingly. You treated her like a harlot. I'm about to pay you back for that, Luis!"

Hannah shivered at Bryce's fierce hatred, spewed like venom. Bryce's voice was loud, deep and fueled by inner rage. Worse, Reyes was witnessing what he shouldn't have to witness. There was nothing she could do.

The newly repaired barn door suddenly slapped open with a kick from inside. Luis shouted, "Everybody else drop your guns and step into the corral where I can see you."

Bryce's voice boomed. "Not a chance. I give my word that no one will shoot you. This is between you and me. Step out into the light and we'll see who outdraws the other. Face *me* unless you're the coward I know you to be."

Hannah pressed the back of her hand against her mouth, helpless to stop the madness, that is, unless she raised her rifle and shot Luis herself once he showed his face. What if she missed? Besides, Bryce would never forgive her for taking his right to avenge Gabriella's death. And on every level, she understood. While she watched the men outside, Rey's hand pressed against hers where he'd scooted beside her. With his face tilted toward the ceiling, he squeezed his eyes closed. "Please let my father live, God," he said.

Boots crunched against gravel with long, deliberate strides. Peering again from the window, Bryce stood in the middle of daylight, his hat shadowing his face and his gun hand hovering near his revolver. Luis marched toward him with his rifle still in hand.

"Drop your rifle or die," Cort called out. "You can use that revolver you got strapped on."

Her gaze stayed on Luis while he set his rifle down and ambled to a position about forty feet from where Bryce stood. Now both men watched each other with an intense focus, leaving her to hold her breath. Luis reached for his gun while Bryce's gun boomed, putting a hole through Luis. A red bloom soaked the man's shirt as he flew backward, slamming to the ground. One of his legs convulsed in spasms and she thought she heard him groan. Drawing in the breath she'd been holding, she leaned her head against the wall and thanked God that Bryce still stood.

"Did you see that, Missus Van Stadt?" Rey asked, his eyes wide and his voice filled with pride.

She couldn't manage to choke out a response. It was over, that's all she needed to know.

"Cort?" Bryce shouted.

"Yeah?"

"Check on Hannah and Rey."

She lifted her head, and her eyes took in Bryce's profile. His voice was strong. *He was alive.* But she couldn't bring herself to move. As limp as a rag, she slowly eased her grip on her rifle. Kneeling beside a shaking Reyes, she had to decide whether her legs would support her. She closed her eyes a moment before daring to look from the window. A mixture of men's shouts and the smell of sulfur hung in the air. She searched the men moving around outside, her mind in muddled haze. Bryce looked over his shoulder toward the shattered window where she and Rey had perched during the gunfight.

From where Cort moved on the porch, his frame partially blocked her view of Bryce. She couldn't have imagined the next blast of gunfire that sent Bryce tripping backward until he hit the ground. Everything happened so fast, Hannah didn't know who'd screamed. Her? Or Rey? With some presence of mind surfacing, she wrenched the rifle from the boy's hands where he'd lifted it, taking aim in defense of his father.

The sight of a bloody Luis, his smoking revolver gripped in his waving hand, sent her heart to her throat. Cort fired. Luis jolted, and the killer fell to his face. Tangle and Mason ran toward Bryce as Cort holstered his gun and followed them.

Hannah wouldn't have any recollection of stumbling to her feet and running, terrified that Bryce had been killed. On some level, she felt the need to protect Reyes and tuck him into her arms. On the other level, the man she loved lay bloodied and possibly dead.

Falling to her knees beside Bryce, she pressed her hand against the warm blood seeping from a hole in his shoulder, dangerously close to his heart. Cort kneeled beside her. A crying, struggling boy was clutched within the arms of Tangle. Men scurried around her, shouting indiscernible orders. Finally, the cloud in her head lifted and she focused all of her attention on Bryce's blood-soaked shirt, reminding her of the wounded soldiers she'd tended. Cort tore open Bryce's shirt and pressed his hands hard against the wound, trying to stay the bleeding.

"Mason, Alonzo, Billy, Damon! We got to get him to a bed. Jude. You and Dan ride those horses into the ground if you need to. Get the doctor. Take extra horses. No stopping. Just bring Collier back here," Cort shouted.

His deep, commanding voice snapped her out of a haze and now she needed to do something. She sniffed and ran her hand across Bryce's face, brushing his hair from his damp forehead. He was so still.

Looking up, she said, "I'll need hot water and my sewing kit. My bed is in the room to the left of the front door."

"Mason. Get what she needs while me and the rest carry him to that bed," Cort demanded.

"I'm staying with him. Let me go!" Rey's voice called out. "Nobody better get in my way," Reyes said as he squirmed free of Tangle's grip.

Hannah looked toward the wild-eyed boy, his dark hair nearly hanging over his eyes. "Tangle. Why don't you come along and bring Rey. I'll need his help. He can hold the lantern."

Thudding boots, jangling spurs, and scraping chairs mingled with long, pitiful groans from a half-conscious Bryce as she followed the men to the bed. Leaning over her patient, she needn't have looked up to feel Cort's blazing eyes watching both her and Bryce. His anguish was hers.

Someone set a basin of water and towel beside her. She pressed a damp cloth against Bryce's wound and then wrung out a second wadded towel into the basin, turning the water a deep pink. At the sound of a low growl, she turned to find Cort's head buried in his hands where he sat beside the bed. For now, she didn't have time for words of solace. None of them would matter.

As the hours wore on, bloody towels used to clean and stanch the bleeding were piling ever higher on the floor. Reaching beneath Bryce, Hannah felt his ragged flesh where the bullet had luckily passed. Thankfully, she wouldn't need to dig out the bullet.

"What do you think?" Cort asked hoarsely. Hannah looked up to see a man who'd weathered so many experiences... both good and bad. Tough and hardened were part of his character. With lips nearly chalk white and his expression bleak, she witnessed a scared man with his brother's life in the balance. The two of them were of the same mind where Bryce was concerned.

"The wound's in the shoulder but not real far from his heart. Still, I don't think anything vital was hit. That will be up to the doctor to figure out. I don't want to close it up till he gets here. For now, the bleeding has slowed. We just have to watch it."

She couldn't bring herself to admit it aloud. But she wasn't at all sure whether he'd bleed to death.

"What if it starts bleeding again?" Cort asked.

"We may have to cauterize it. He'll need some whiskey to ease the pain of that and something to clean the wound. Think you already know how much it'll hurt him if it comes to burning it. For now, I'm hoping we won't need to. I don't know how to do a fine enough stitch to stop this deep a wound. So much blood."

"Jesus," Cort moaned. "I should've been keeping an eye on Luis."

A whimper from the other side of the bed reminded her that Reyes's eyes were fixed on his father's face. So single-mindedly focused on Bryce, she'd forgotten the boy was standing on the other side of the bed. When Tangle took the lantern from Rey's shaking hands, he squeezed the boy's shoulder. She could have bitten her own tongue in half at alarming the boy.

Darting a glance at Cort, she found him with the heels of his hands pressed to his eyes. He dropped his hands and looked at her. "You got whiskey somewhere?"

"The cabinet beside the door. Lars always keeps whiskey around."

"Mason. Go get it. And get the fireplace stoked and the poker ready. In case we need it."

"Sure, boss."

Hannah returned her gaze to Bryce's pale face. He took that moment to open his eyes, groaning when he tried to move his head. She touched his face and forced a brief smile, hoping he didn't see how worried she was.

"Stay still, Bryce. Don't need to start up that bleeding."

"Where?" he whispered.

"In my cabin. In my bed. The doctor's on the way back from Ogallala."

"Ah."

One corner of his mouth lifted briefly. Was that a weak smile or grimace, she wondered. Her fingers brushed his forehead. His heavy eyelids were slits.

"Wanted to be here. Not this way."

There was no question that her face flamed when she deciphered his meaning. She dared not look up at the faces watching them. Mortified at his unabashed suggestion, she cupped his jaw and accepted it was the pain talking.

Someone cleared a throat. There were footsteps. A quick glance found Cort and Rey still standing on the other side of the bed while the rest were gone. Bryce slid his fingers along the sheet, found hers, and gripped her hand with surprising strength.

"Luis?"

"He's dead," Cort answered.

"Good. My boy all right?"

"I'm here, Pa. Beside the bed. Tangle told me you'll be all right."

"Glad not hurt. And Hannah. Do what Uncle Cort and Hannah say."

"I promise."

Hannah's heart broke at Rey's pursed mouth and how he was holding back a sob. There was no doubt the boy was as brave as the rest of the Enders. Bryce's eyes closed and so did hers for a moment. He was so weak. She simply was not going to allow him to die. When he next opened his eyes, they were sunken and vacant.

Cort took that moment to call out to Mason. "Bring that damned whiskey in here."

"Cort. You killed cow killer," Bryce slurred.

"That I did. Finished what you started, brother."

"Better shot."

"We'll find out once you get better. I think you're faster than I am."

Hannah reached for the bottle of Old Crow he handed her and she set it on the bedside table. Setting to work, she poured a liberal amount onto a clean towel.

"This will sting," she warned Bryce.

"Do it."

Pressing the whiskey-soaked cloth against the bloody hole, his piti-ful growl seemed to reverberate from deep in his lungs. He squeezed his eyes shut and his jaw clenched. She felt spasms in the damaged flesh beneath her hands and then his back arched.

"Bryce. I'm going to help you swallow some water. Then I'm going to drizzle whiskey into your mouth. Try to swallow. Do you hear me?"

"Hear you," he answered hoarsely.

Hannah tossed the whiskey towel aside. Cort lifted his brother's head, and she held a cup of water to his slack mouth. Much of it trickled over his chin. Pouring whiskey into the cup, she dripped it slowly. He managed to swallow and cough several times then licked his lips. After repeating the process several times, she nodded. Cort lowered his head against the sweat-soaked pillow.

Hannah leaned closer. "Bryce. I'll want you to take more whiskey."

At first there was silence. His eyes were closed. Had he fallen uncon-scious or drifted to sleep? She glanced up to see Cort's raised eyebrow and thinned mouth. But he said nothing. Cort's arms folded across his chest. She took solace in the steady rise and fall of his chest but still bit her lip with worry.

"Rey," Bryce said hoarsely.

Hannah thought she'd missed the slurred word until Reyes leaned over and gripped his father's limp hand. Her heart wrenched at the fear written in the boy's face.

"Pa, I'm here."

"Listen to Cort and Hannah," Bryce mumbled in a whisper.

"I will. Promise to get well."

"Try." Bryce lapsed into an uneasy sleep.

Hannah swiped away her welling tears. With Bryce's voice so weak, she feared his words cost him what was left of his strength. Cort turned away when Tangle tromped into the room. She looked up to where the cowhand waited for orders.

Cort looked over his shoulder. "How 'bout you and Reyes go help settle the horses for tonight. Get some bedding up in the loft and some can bed in the kitchen. Tell Alonzo to go back to the ranch and let Lark and Zeke know what's goin' on here. I'm not leaving."

"Will do. Come on, Rey. Let your father rest. Besides. I could use the help," Tangle said.

When Reyes hesitated, Hannah stood and walked to the other side of the bed and tucked him against her side. "Go on with Tangle. I'll let you know when we need more help in here."

Their gazes held. He nodded and followed Tangle into the hallway. In the silence that followed, Cort and Hannah stared at each other across Bryce's still form. The stark pain in Cort's eyes was surely reflected in her own.

Clearing her throat, she whispered, "Cort. If it starts to bleed again, I won't wait for the doctor. Don't think I can manage to stitch it enough."

"I know. The boys will hold him down. I'll be the one to do it."

"Let's hope the doctor gets here before it comes to that."

———————————

CORT DOZED IN the chair. Bowls of half-eaten stew sat on a tray. Neither of them had any appetite. Mason popped his head through the partly open door. Simply shaking her head, the door closed. Sometime later, Tangle poked his head inside and assured her that Reyes was fast asleep in the parlor. From the window, men milled around outside, smoking and swilling coffee.

Hannah kneeled beside the bed, fighting sleep, until finally slouching, resting her head against the bed beside Bryce. Sometime during the night, a hand brushed her cheek, jerking her awake. Bolting upright, she found Bryce smiling. But his eyes were too bright.

"Napping. Look sweet."

"I didn't want to sleep."

With a glance around the room, she found Cort missing. "How do you feel?"

"Hot. Chills. Weak."

She touched his head. Dear God. *Fever.* "I'm going to get Cort to sit with you while I brew willow bark tea. That'll bring down the fever." As she started to rise, he grasped her arm and held her firmly.

"Love you."

"Oh, Bryce. We can't talk about this now."

"Why? Maybe no more chance."

"Don't you *dare* talk like that. Once you get well, then we'll have time to figure out our feelings."

She watched one corner of his mouth lift. His face was pale beneath his thick scruff. "Nothin' to figure out. I know."

She leaned over him and pecked his cheek with a kiss. "Hold on. For me and Rey. Another thing. If you must know. I love you, too. Very much. Now that I said it, you best promise to get well."

He closed his eyes. "Got to burn it. Whiskey. Kill infection."

The sound of boots had her look over her shoulder. Cort filled the doorway, brushing his fingers through his sleep-tousled hair. Blinking, he studied his brother through his glazed eyes.

"Is it bleeding again?" he asked gruffly.

"Yes. More than I'd like to see. Has a fever, too. I'm going to get some willow bark tea into him."

Cort cast a look at the dawn light, now filtering through the window. She followed his stare. "Where the hell is that doctor?"

The decision to cauterize the wound might either save Bryce's life or kill him, and she recognized his indecision. She wasn't even sure it was the right thing to do.

The decision was made when Cort turned down the sheet. "Hurry with the tea. I'll hold off the poker till you get it down his gullet."

Hannah winced, knowing he'd come to a fateful decision. She leaned over Bryce and grazed his fevered face with her fingers, flinching when Cort ordered Mason to heat up the poker. Hannah didn't need to look up to where Cort stood over her to know the enormity of his verdict. Grief drifted through the room like a cold New England fog. Nodding, she hurried from the room.

SEVENTEEN

DO NO HARM

HANNAH GRIPPED BRYCE'S hand. Inside, she wondered whether he'd heard what she'd finally been able to say aloud. *I love you.* No, he'd already sunk into darkness. The untouched tea sat on the table beside the bed. If only he'd live, she'd swear her undying love, again and again. She'd worked in a New York hospital during the war, learning all she could from the nurses. Cauterizing infectious wounds sent some men to their doom while others simply fell into silence for days after thrashing against the pain.

For her, it was the smell of burning flesh that she'd always remember. Cauterizing nearly did her in, until some kindly old doctor handed her a damp cloth to cover her nose. After that, no one could convince her that you'd become accustomed to such suffering.

Looking up, she found Cort's stark expression and sunken eyes holding hers. When Mason arrived with the glowing poker, even he closed his eyes with this decision. But providence interceded while she pressed a cool cloth to Bryce's head. In that moment, he opened his eyes and they seemed focused. Did he recognize her or where he was? *Horses.* The sound of hooves hitting the dirt and men shouting stilled her hand. Cort and Mason left the side of the bed to look from the window while she strained her neck to see around them.

"Thank God. They're here. The doctor's riding beside Dan," Cort said.

Mason left the room, the poker in hand. Cort followed him. Hannah, glad for the doctor's arrival, leaned over Bryce and kissed his brow.

"If I'd known getting shot would change your mind...."

"Don't talk foolish. Doctor Collier is here, and he'll know better how to tend this wound."

"Stay."

She nodded with a level gaze. "I'm not leaving. Not even for Collier." Loud voices and tromping boots were followed by the gruff voice of the blessed physician.

"Where's the patient?" Alfred Collier's gruff, no-nonsense voice had her stand, to make room for the examination. His tall frame marched to the bed then slapped his medical bag onto the chair. Leaning over Bryce, his eyes traced the man's face. When the doctor sniffed the bloody bandage, Bryce's eyes opened and looked at the man towering over him.

"Well, now. I can tell you and Cort are brothers, and not just in looks. Both of you have a penchant for bullet holes where they shouldn't be. Let's have a look. Hannah. I'll need your help with two fresh basins of hot water, if you don't mind. One for the instruments. Cort, you get over here and hold the lantern above his chest so I can get a better look."

"You think it's infected," Cort said.

"I don't think. I know. The smell of it is enough."

Hannah's insides trembled at that news but did his bidding, only too glad to have the doctor give the necessary orders. On the way into the kitchen, she found Reyes pacing the hallway and Tangle leaning against the wall. The boy's drawn face and tired eyes were enough to give her pause. But right now, she had to center her attention on his father. Still, it would help if he felt included.

"Rey. I'll need help carrying the basins." The boy swiped his nose. Understanding how hard this was for him, she lifted her chin. "Come with me. We've got things to do. You need to draw on your courage."

WHILE CORT HELD the lantern high above his brother, sunlight glinted through the dusty window and shadows crisscrossed the room. Hannah stood beside the doctor where two bowls of hot water were setting on a table. Rolls of bandages had been cut into various lengths. Probes, clamps, sewing needles, silk thread, forceps, and scalpels and retractors were arrayed on a clean white towel. Beside those were a brown bottle filled with chloroform and another with carbolic acid.

"Ready?" Alfred Collier barked, with a quick glance in her direction.

Acquiescing with a quick nod, she winced at the sight of the gaping, bloody hole. Sweat dotted Bryce's face. She tore her eyes from his still form and watched while the doctor dripped chloroform onto a cotton swab. The window had been opened for both fresh air and to refresh the air of the heady, overpowering sweet scents of chloroform and the lightly pungent odor of carbolic acid, transporting her back to the New York hospital.

"Hannah. Do just as I told you. No more than two minutes. Thankfully, he's already in a deep sleep."

Her hand shook while she pressed the cloth over Bryce's nose, keeping her eyes fastened on the hands of the doctor's gold pocket watch. "One minute."

Bryce's mouth lay slack. His eyelids twitched.

"Two."

"That's enough," Dr. Collier said. "He's unconscious."

The lantern swayed slightly when Cort glanced away, and Hannah's stomach soured. When the doctor dabbed carbolic acid around the wound, Bryce's long, pitiful moan had her bend from the waist and press a hand to her stomach.

With a brief look toward her, Collier lifted his eyes. "You're made of sturdy stuff, Hannah. Take a deep breath."

Nodding, she handed him the probe and then the forceps. Mesmerized by the surgeon's quick hands and intense focus, Hannah envisioned the rows of patients in the New York hospital. This time, every move of this doctor's hands meant the difference between her past and future. This man she loved... *had* to live.

Blood splattered the surgeon's medical apron. Cort's face appeared ghostly in the lantern light. And from outside, she heard a wagon arrive. The familiar voices told her that Lark, Theresa, and Zeke were here. Tangle's yell of disapproval halted the approaching footsteps. Then all went quiet amid whispers.

With a final dabbing with carbolic acid, the doctor stuck the needle into loose flesh, tugging the boiled silk thread through his ragged skin. He repeated this until the hole was neatly closed. Hannah held Bryce's shoulders, keeping him in place. Still, he managed to lift an arm free, nearly swiping the doctor's steady hand away before Colt caught hold of his arms with a powerful grip.

A cry of pain cut the air at the last firm tug. Once the fresh bandages were snug around his shoulder and neck, she cried inside at his pitiful groans. Then Bryce sank into quiet stillness, motionless. The doctor listened to his chest and heart with his stethoscope, then turned toward her.

"Heart's strong. You did a fine job, Hannah. You'd make a fine nurse. As to you, Cort, you can put down the lantern. We've done all we can do. You look like you could use a sip of whiskey and I think I'll join you once Hannah and I get this mess cleaned up."

"I'll take care of this, doctor. Why don't you both see to some fresh air and then I'll join you once I finish," Hannah said.

With a hesitant nod, the doctor left the patient to her. Cort gripped her arm before following the doctor out of the room. His eyes were red with weariness and her body shook with emotion.

"You are one helluva good woman. Bryce needs you."

"And I need him. But we have a legal issue still between us. You know that."

He held her eyes without further comment. The tic in his jaw conveyed what he was thinking. "My wife's here. Once I give her a proper welcome, I'll send her in to help you. She's most likely chafing at the bit at having to wait so long to know what's going on."

ONCE THE DOOR closed, she bent over Bryce then smoothed the back of her hand across his warm forehead. Seeing the gentle rise and fall of his chest, she wondered what he thought about in that deep sleep.

She'd just begun to wipe down the doctor's instruments and bottles when the door opened. She lifted her head to find Lark coming toward her. Without preamble, she walked into a much needed embrace, allowing the dam of tears to fall against her friend's shoulder.

"I was about to give Cort a piece of my mind about not sending for me sooner and changed my mind when I saw his face. I was worried sick after the men told us. Seems I had good reason to be worried. Cort is shaken and so are you. I'm here to do whatever is needed. Brought Theresa along to help out."

They leaned away from each other. Hannah dropped onto the chair beside the bed, exhaustion setting into every bone in her body. "Look at him. The pain of the surgery must have been fierce for him to cry out. The doctor said the bullet went through but nicked his clavicle. Left a big hole. It was close range. Lost a lot of blood and he has an infection. The doctor thinks he was able to clean it out."

"Uh-huh. Alfred knows what he's doing. Bryce is tough. In a couple days, we'll move him to our house. In the meantime, we'll leave some hands here to do chores and watch out if you need anything. Cort will be by every day. Theresa will stay on and do the cooking. You'll have enough to do with tending Bryce."

Lark kneeled beside her while they both watched the steady rise and fall of his chest. "Thank you for coming," Hannah said. "Especially knowing about that baby you're carrying."

"I'm fine."

"I hope you told Cort."

"He's known for some time. How could I keep him from seeing my roundness. He's hovering and walking on the moon, both at the same time. And I'm just gloriously happy. No thanks necessary. You couldn't keep me away because Bryce is family. And we think of you the same. Now. *I'm* going to finish cleaning this mess while you eat a sandwich. Theresa packed more food than could feed every man here and the army. Then *you* get some sleep. Let us help you the rest of the way through this."

"You know the cow killer was Luis Montez."

"I know most of it. Alonzo had a good deal to say and Cort will fill me in on the rest. He's anxious to see Little Bryce. Nita will have her hands full because he's gotten used to being spoiled."

"I feel guilty and stupid. Lark, I had no idea about Luis. Escobar Diaz didn't exist. I was taken in, and we all could have died because of it. You should have seen Reyes's eyes when Luis rode up."

"Bryce came riding back to the ranch and recounted your story. He asked us both questions. Did we ever hear of a man and wife by the name of Diaz on a farm near Ogallala. Escobar Diaz. Not a man or woman on the ranch had ever seen nor heard of anyone by that name. I never saw so many men scramble for the corral and barn at once. Most important. You, Bryce, and Reyes will be fine. Luck was on our side. Don't you blame yourself."

———————

THE SMELL OF bread and chicken soup drifted to his nose from somewhere. Inhaling a long breath, he tried to pry open his sticky eyelids. The bright light piercing them was painful. A throbbing in his shoulder reminded him that he'd been shot. Running his fist over the sheets, he figured he was on a bed. But the question was... where?

Squinting through his curtain of eyelashes, he blinked to clear his vision. The far wall came into clarity, finding himself looking at a cracked mirror on the opposite wall. Beside it was a painting of a pasture. When he tried to lift his arm, a sharp pain knifed through his shoulder. Thinking better of moving, he ever so slowly rolled his head to face the glass window. The sky was obscured by the arching branches of the oaks. He was at Rocky Creek. In her bed.

At least his brain wasn't completely addled. Vague memories of shooting Luis Montez and then the searing pain that followed came back to him. He recalled sailing through the air and hitting his knees.

Then, just before everything sank into blackness, he'd heard another gunshot and shouting. A woman's voice cried out. Reyes had called for him. But he couldn't move.

Using his right arm, he lifted his hand and flexed it. At least his gun hand worked. Sliding his fingers against his chest, they met a bulging wad of bandage. When he tried to push onto his elbow, pain streaked through his upper body. Thinking better of that effort, he dropped back against the pillow. *Jesus.* He had to get out of here. Where was Cort? Cort would haul him back to the ranch.

Thirsty, licking his lips, his vision centered on the pitcher of water beside the bed. It looked mighty inviting, if only he could reach the half-filled glass. Maybe he should make a try for it until the thought of tumbling to the floor changed his mind.

While he contemplated a strategy to reach for it, the door handle turned, and Hannah appeared with a tray. His nose recognized the steaming chicken soup. What he wouldn't give for a steak and some of that bread of hers. Her pretty face almost made him forget how hungry he was. Her mouth curved into a sweet smile as she set the tray beside the bed.

"So. You're awake, at last. I was beginning to worry."

"I...." He paused. His throat felt like he'd swallowed ground glass. "Uh. Thirsty. You and Rey all right?" he croaked.

Without answering, she helped lift his head and pressed a glass of water to his mouth. Not wanting to be treated like an invalid, he took the glass from her and managed to hold it with the help of his good arm. He swallowed a few sips and looked toward her, offering a quick nod. Then she took the glass from his shaking hand.

"Nobody hurt. But you scared us nearly to death. Reyes and I... we stayed flat on the floor, terrified. I was afraid to move. Afraid Reyes would get in the line of fire."

"Luis. Dead. You're safe. All I need."

He crooked his finger, patting the bed beside him. She sat on the edge and primly arranged her skirt. "It's normal to have a dry throat after all you've been through. That will improve in a day or so."

His sore throat was the last thing he wanted to think about. Contented with her nearness, he studied her soft, golden-brown braid. It glimmered in the light. That same green dress with pretty little flowers on the collar made her look like an angel. But then his idle musings were ruined, thinking about this bed. Lars had lain with her in this bed and the thought made his skin crawl.

Drowning in her blue eyes, he couldn't help but feel her inner glow while she studied him. He'd rarely seen her when she wasn't angry or worried or determined to keep distance between them. She worked hard at it. Now, here she was beside him. She'd said she loved him. Unless he imagined them, which he refused to believe.

When her eyes trailed the length of him, he had no doubt she gave thought to his nakedness beneath this sheet. Their eyes met and held at her blush. She'd seen more than she'd ever admit. Maybe it was best not to remind her of his missing pants. Or their whereabouts. He'd take it up with Cort.

"Let me fix the pillow behind you and help you to sit up. If you'd like, I'll hold the water to your mouth."

Leaning on his good elbow, he was able to lift himself to a sitting position, even as every motion sent pain through his upper chest and along his arm. Where her fingers touched his skin, he tingled. Beads of sweat formed rivers converging in the hollow of his neck.

"Hannah. Got one good arm. I can hold that glass."

She handed it to him and just to prove it, he lifted it to his mouth. Gulping, he returned it to her with a smile on his mouth. And he figured he did a fair job of hiding the pain.

"Stop fussing."

Her smile was erased at his sharp order, but he hated not doing things for himself. Frustration compounded by the fact that he couldn't leave for the goldfields to find his intended target. Not to mention how the weather might change on him.

"Is that bowl for me?" he asked.

"Chicken broth. No solid food today. Doctor Collier's orders."

"Can I express my opinion of his orders?"

"No. The doctor saved you from bleeding to death. Cort and I were about to use a hot poker to seal that hole in your shoulder. Alfred got here and took over."

Leaning comfortably back against the pillow, he watched her fuss with his sheets and then with his pillow. "Can you stop and come sit here again? Please?" He pointed to the space beside him. Her head tilted as though considering it.

"You need to eat first."

"I'll eat that *stuff* after we talk."

"If you keep the conversation short."

"A deal. Now sit."

Once seated, she smoothed her skirt and folded her hands against her lap. With her chin tipped down, he pondered what ran through her sweet little head. No doubt, it had something to do with Lars. The same issue of her marriage was wearing thin.

"How long have I been here?"

"Four days."

"Jesus. I've been out cold all that time?"

"In and out. You had a bad fever the first few days after surgery. With Theresa's help, we were able to spoon willow bark tea down your throat. Your fever broke last night. You were sweating and delirious. Cort helped with getting you cooled down. Took us most of the night."

"Guessing you must feel awkward at having a naked man in this bed." There. He'd said it, enjoying her blush.

"I've witnessed naked men before. I keep my eyes averted, if that's what you mean."

Forgetting about his shoulder, he started to cross his arms and flinched. Regardless of his damnable shoulder, he still planned on leaving for the gold camps. For now, he couldn't resist teasing her.

"Really? Naked men? How many would you say?"

"Now you sound both jealous and ridiculous."

"I am." *And* he was.

"I worked in a hospital in New York during the war. Most soldiers were stripped of clothes. Though we tried to avoid seeing the obvious.

There were older women who'd take that responsibility. Men all have the same…."

He grinned and cocked his head. "That so? *What,* exactly?"

Plucking at the sheet, she averted her face, while he enjoyed her discomfiture. Which caused his teasing to turn serious. He stopped abruptly at her sharp glare. Figuring he'd gone as far as he dare, he cleared his throat, deciding it prudent to change direction.

"I'm sorry. Couldn't resist teasing."

"Be careful. I might put hot pepper in the soup."

He grinned. "I'll be more careful about teasing you in the future. Where's Rey?"

"Cort, Zeke, and Lark took him back to the ranch. They promised him they'd come back once they rounded up his new horse. Draco took off during the fracas."

"Grateful neither of you were hurt. When we rode up, Luis swung his rifle toward your cabin and blasted it. Think my heart stopped before I started shooting. The coward dove inside the barn. Must've thought he killed you. Did he know Reyes was in the house?"

"He knew someone was there. He saw the horse out by the trees. I said I had an art student with me. It was all I could do to keep Reyes quiet. If he'd had a gun in his hand, I'm sure he would've shot Luis."

He reached for her and she came willingly, curling beside him with her head nestled beneath his chin. Touching his mouth to her hair, he closed his eyes at her contented sigh while breathing in her sweet rose scent. He caught her face with his good hand, slanting his mouth over hers. Tracing the curve of her lips with the tip of his tongue, he felt her respond. Then she broke away.

"I'm not apologizing," he said.

"I love you," she whispered.

He shook his head. "Somewhere in the haze of my fever, I heard you admit that."

"You heard me right. In fact, you're right about my stubborn nature. And deep down, I know you're right about Lars. I just can't move forward until I'm certain Lars is no longer my husband."

"A kiss isn't going to make a difference to Lars."

"Please don't force me to go against what I believe is right and wrong."

"Have I told you how much I love you? For that reason, and many others, I have no intention of forcing this. But I'm not giving up, either. I'll do what I need to do to settle things."

"Yes. You were plain enough about it. And until I almost lost you, I accepted that you'd leave to find Lars. Now I love you too much to see you get killed. I don't want you to go."

"Lady. You don't know how determined I am. I'm planning to eat all that soup and more if it'll help me get on my feet sooner. I'm going to make sure he never touches you again. Now. Bring that soup over here. I'm so weak that I might need some help."

Hannah's musical laughter brought Theresa to the open door of the bedroom. The woman's scowl and crossed arms reminded him they were chaperoned. Not able to hide his grin, he winked at the scowling woman. She *harrumphed* and stomped away but not before the door slammed behind her, leaving Hannah with a surprised expression and a rosy face.

AFTER SUPPER, DISHES were cleared and Theresa retired to the attic loft above. Not for the first time, Hannah wished Lars had fixed up that dusty room. Dare she use more of her husband's money for needed repairs? Contemplating his vicious tirades, her body shivered. If he returned to find money missing, she'd suffer a beating or worse.

Creeping quietly past the bedroom door where Bryce slept, she started for the parlor where she'd been spending the nights. The old floorboards creaked beneath her bare feet. Stopping, she listened and waited, hoping she hadn't awakened Bryce. Hearing shuffling footfalls from the other side of the door, she guessed he'd gotten out of bed. She tiptoed close to the door and tilted her head, listening for any more sounds.

"Hannah. I hear you. Come in, please."

Hesitating, she took a soft step forward. It wouldn't be proper to be with him in her nightdress. But if he needed something, she'd attend to it. She rapped softly and then opened the door.

The sight of a shirtless Bryce standing beside the bed took her breath away. Muscular arms and a taut, firm stomach told much of how hard he worked. She followed the trail of dark hair that disappeared into his waistband. Pants. Somehow, he'd managed to shrug into them, even as weak as he seemed. A saucer-sized splotch of dry blood on the bandage gave her pause.

"Are you going to stand there gaping with your mouth open, or are you planning to come sit with me?"

Closing the door, she said a silent prayer that Theresa wouldn't hear them. Now that she was here, she'd help him back into the bed and leave. "You shouldn't be out of bed."

"Hannah. My legs are just fine. My shoulder is sore as a son of a bitch but I'll get weaker if I don't start getting out of that bed. Cort will be here tomorrow. This might be the last time we're alone for some time. Granted, I'm almost as crusty as Zeke right now. But I'd like you to stay. Talk with me."

The effort of walking had cost him as evidenced by the beads of sweat on his face. When he sank to the edge of the bed, she wanted to help him lift his legs. That was something he didn't like—help.

"You'll need to stay in bed or a chair until that shoulder heals. Doctor Collier warned against riding a horse anytime soon," she added.

He darted a glance at her, and his frown was answer enough. "I can ride a horse as long as I have one free arm. I'll keep bandaged until the thing heals up. Now. Sit down. Things need sayin' before tomorrow."

She walked closer but chose not to sit. Even as his penetrating eyes fixed on hers, she wouldn't waver. "I don't see how talking will change my marital status. I'm expecting he might return any day. Where will that leave us?"

With surprising strength, his good arm caught her and tugged. She tumbled forward between his outstretched legs, and he wasn't letting her go. There was no time to voice her protest before he pressed his advantage, finding herself seated across his lap and his mouth near her ear. Her heart raced.

"As a matter of fact, maybe I'm tired of talking around that worthless piece of paper you seem intent on honoring."

When he twisted his body, she found herself lying across the bed, stretched beside him. Face to face, she was mesmerized by his beseeching, deepest of blue eyes. One hand cupped her face. When she averted her face, he pressed his mouth against her jaw then kissed her with a gentleness of spring rain while his fingers traced her neck.

Their breath mingled and even as she made a last, feeble attempt to look away, his fingers held her prisoner. When she pressed her hand to his chest, she felt the wild beat of his heart—a heart that had almost been stilled by a bullet. A vision of Lars appeared in her mind, striking fear in her very soul.

Each button of her shift fell away. His eyes were unrelenting as they beheld her skin, and she shook with the power he held over her. She whimpered, wanting him to stop. Not wanting him to stop. Once freed, his fingers roamed across her with gentle reverence. She was so warm. His mouth moved along the length of her neck, and she arched, then whispered his name.

He returned to her mouth, swallowing anything she thought to say. This man loved her, that was all that mattered. His fingers trailed over her skin, sending tremors through her wherever they touched. *My husband must be dead. How else will I find happiness?*

Lifting her arms, her body shivered at his sweet, reverent smile. Then the voices of warning whispered—infidelity is sinful, vows are sacred. His sweet, audacious eyes glimmered with love, and she shivered with need. Then a voice called to her. *You've promised fidelity.* With a soulful cry, she grasped his arm and stared through him.

Bryce released her and her eyes read his agony. Jaw taut, he rolled away from her then swung his legs over the edge of the mattress, keeping his back to her. Shoulders hunched, Bryce leaned forward, dropping his head into his hands. "Dammit, woman. This isn't going to work as long as he has a hold on you."

Pressing her hand across her trembling mouth, she lowered her eyes. She lifted her eyes at the sound of rustling clothes. Standing, he shrugged into his shirt, his back still to her. Regret stabbed her as he refused to turn toward her.

She wrenched her gaze from the rise and fall of his back, then stared at the wall. With a sorrow-filled sigh, he shifted his stance and looked over his shoulder. The lines at the corners of his eyes were prominent as he watched her. He'd given her the chance to decide. And now she had.

Standing, she came around him. Her eyes were drawn to the blood-stained bandage and his face was marked with the creases of emotional and physical pain because of her—the first man to show her real love.

His voice was hoarse. "You wanted this. For the first time, I felt the passion inside you. Let go of *him.*"

Shaking her head, she closed her eyes against his disappointment and perhaps, surrender. "I can't. Not yet." She started to reach for her clothes, strewn on the foot of the bed.

He caught her arm. "Don't turn away from me. This situation is driving me crazy and worse, driving a wedge between us. Let me say what I need to say. Then it'll be up to you from now on."

When she looked downward at her feet, his fingers lifted her face. Divining what he was thinking, she wanted to shrink into a ball and hide from him and her foolish demons. Instead, she stood before him, letting him have his say. She reached to touch his face, but he jerked away from her. "Don't," he hissed. "Not unless you're willing to have me. All of me."

He sighed. "You can't have this both ways. I love you. And because of that, I'd die for you. The one thing I can't do is live with you and your misplaced sense of loyalty and those demons that plague you."

"You know I want *you,* Bryce. The time isn't right until I'm free to promise my life. Give me that."

Reaching around her, he snatched her nightdress from where she dropped it and then tossed it to her. "Get dressed."

Sitting, he slumped forward and rested his elbows against his knees. He dropped his face and ran a hand through his hair while she hurriedly slipped into her nightdress and padded on bare feet to the door. "Before I leave, I'll need to change that bandage."

"No. Forget the damned blood. I don't want a nurse. I want you. I wish I could understand what goes on in that head of yours. I'll always respect your wishes because I love you. Make no mistake. You are my personal fight and I intend to win. This isn't the end."

"You'll regret finding Lars… if he's alive."

He lifted his head. "Doubt I'll regret finding him. But I regret a lot of other things. Get some sleep. Cort will be here tomorrow to take me back to the ranch. At least you'll have your bed back."

She closed the door behind her and lay awake on the parlor settee most of the night, thinking she'd never know such tenderness again. Turning onto her side, she cried at her failure to show him how much she loved him. She cried for the lost moment tonight. Then she closed her tear-filled eyes at the thought he was no match for Lars.

EIGHTEEN

PERILOUS PLANS

T HE NEXT DAY, Hannah paced the hallway and Lark circled the parlor, both trying to wear off their tension. Cort arrived that morning with the wagon, Reyes riding alongside. The brothers were secreted behind the bedroom door, discussing whatever seemed to be on their minds. Reyes stood sentinel, hoping the door would open soon. There was no doubt in Hannah's mind they were making plans for a dangerous mission to the gold camps.

"When are they going to come out? I want to talk with my father," Reyes blurted.

Hannah looked over his freshly trimmed hair, curling slightly around his ears. Not able to resist touching his head, she smoothed the wayward locks only to have him present his best scowl, reminding her that she had much to learn about being a mother. If she were ever free of Lars.

When Lark walked into the hallway, she leveled her eyes on Reyes. "Your uncle and father are talking business. Once they're done, we'll have something to eat. How about if you go get his horse and saddle from the corral and bring them up to the wagon then tie him off?"

"All right. But if they get done talkin', I want to see him, anyway."

Lark darted a glance at her before answering, "You can talk his ear completely off his head when we get back to the ranch. Or all the way back, if you decide to ride beside us in the wagon."

"All right. I'll get his horse. Don't forget me."

"We won't forget you," Lark said. "We like having you around."

Just as he made it to the door, he stopped. He looked over his shoulder in her direction. "Thanks for taking care of my father, Missus Van Stadt."

"Your father is a very good man," Hannah replied. "I'm glad I was of help."

"Yeah. And I wanted to know if I can come back soon for lessons."

"As soon as you're ready." Hannah smiled. It felt mighty good to feel cheerful about something. "I'll be right here."

"After my father is well."

The door slammed behind him before Hannah could think of anything else to say. Lark came up beside her. "Why don't you and I see about getting the sandwiches out. Bet more than a few are hungry. We're just wearing out the floor," Lark suggested.

When Hannah glanced again at the closed door, her grin faded. Something felt wrong. From Lark's wry expression, the woman knew more than she was letting on. They'd hardly spoken and whenever they'd crossed paths, his exasperation was palpable. Lying awake in the parlor each night, she'd imagined herself as Bryce's wife—a sweet fantasy. The silent yawning days ahead left her with a sense of isolation. She'd ticked off the chores in her head, knowing that tending her garden and the stock would mask her loneliness. But the lingering scent of him would be gone once she'd washed the bedding. Holding this ranch together seemed to be her only real purpose, something she'd grown accustomed to doing.

Early August

BRYCE PACED THE room and waited for Dr. Collier's verdict, not that it would matter either way. Finally, he snapped his medical bag closed. No matter what the man said, he'd had enough wounds to keep his own counsel. He was damned tired of being lectured about eating, resting, not riding, changing the bandage and *avoiding alcohol.*

Sure as hell, he wasn't about to admit he and Cort got so drunk last night, probably neither of them would have hit the floor with their hats if given three tries. Maybe Cort wasn't as drunk, else Lark would've kicked him out of bed. And then Cort would've been in a sour mood by now, or just maybe he was.

"I would advise keeping a fresh bandage on that incision for at least a few more days. Then use the salve I left. Help heal it. That shoulder will be hurting for quite a while. Weeks. Riding a horse isn't a good idea, though I doubt you'll listen to my advice."

"I'm listening, Doc. I just don't always follow advice very well."

"Suit yourself. Don't think I need to come out anytime soon unless you get shot again."

"Thanks for all you did for me."

"Had help from a mighty fine nurse. I'll see myself out."

Bryce shook the man's hand then the doctor nodded before leaving. The house was quiet. Reyes most likely shadowed Zeke, who'd become a surrogate grandfather. The one thing still missing in his boy's life was a mother. Lark and Hannah had filled in, but it wasn't permanent. And more and more it gnawed that he didn't have his own homestead.

Finding himself wandering the empty house, he started past Cort's office. The door stood partially open. Not missing the smell of tobacco and whiskey wafting from the room, he tapped the door and waited.

"Come in," Cort called out in a gruff voice.

Inside the office, his gaze skimmed the massive shelves lined with hundreds of leather-bound books, then his eyes settled on his brother. Cort sat behind his mahogany desk, puffing a cigar clamped between his teeth. He leaned back and waved him to take a seat. If he knew one thing, his brother rarely wasted time getting to the point.

"Figured you'd be down once the doctor left. We need to settle a few things."

Bryce dropped onto the leather chair and stretched his legs out, crossing them at the ankles. "All right. What do you need to talk about?"

"Cigarette or cigar?" Cort slid a lidded box in his direction.

"Some other time."

"I can guess what the doctor told you. You won't be staying put like he suggested. Getting to know how you think. Happens I wouldn't sit still for long, either, if that's any consolation."

Bryce grinned because Cort had hit the nail on the head. Steepling his fingers against his stomach, Bryce nodded. "Maybe we're more alike given our history."

"Huh. Figure you're going to look for that piece of cow dung named Lars Van Stadt."

"Yep. Like I already said. We talked about it, and I know how you feel. About time I set Hannah free," Bryce declared.

"I'd like to tell you to forget her and find somebody else, but I'd be wasting my breath. Just so you know, both me and Lark already see how you look at each other. Right from the start. What exactly is your plan? Do you know where he is?"

Bryce skimmed his finger along the back of one ear. "Yeah. Got a fair idea. But I'll still need to do some searching. There's gold camps scattered all over the hills. Lived there, myself."

"Heard he went down to Arizona. Right smack in the middle of the Comanches. You can't be stupid enough to go there."

"Agreed. First of all, Hannah showed me the last letter from Lars. Apparently, the sonofabitch decided against Arizona and went north. Somewhere around Grasshopper Creek and Beaver Creek in Montana, the way I figure it. Crowded with placer mining up in those hills. I'm heading there as long as you and Lark are willing to look after Reyes while I'm gone. And if I don't come back...."

Cort dropped his cigar into a bucket on one corner of his desk. Leather creaked as he leaned forward. With a wrinkled forehead and clenched fists, he waited for his younger brother to start in on a lecture.

"Do you know what time of year this is?" Cort snapped.

"Last I checked, it's August fourth. And it's 1878."

"Which means snow will begin in those mountains before you get the hell out. A man can die up there, freezing to death. Dangerous even when it isn't snowing."

"I'm takin' the U-P as far as Green River, along with my horse, gear, and packhorse. Then trek north into Montana from there."

"Cheyenne giving the army trouble here and there. How do you propose to keep your scalp?" Cort challenged.

The vision of Indians—women, children, and old men—being forcibly rounded up and marched across the plains, sickened him. He recalled nearly retching at the sight of them crowded into cattle cars. Sympathy for the Indians was as popular as sheepherders showing up in town for a celebration. Thankfully, he and Cort held the same principles with regard to Indian treatment.

"One man alone, is how I'll evade them. I know how to track and stay out of their way. Besides, they aren't interested in one man, usually. They're more interested in stealing as many cows and horses as they can get away with. Any other questions?"

"All right. See you made up your mind. Crazy as it is, I guess I did pretty much the same thing when Lark was threatened. Stood up to a demented killer and his gang. I don't figure I'll change your mind."

"Nope."

"We'll need packhorses and provisions."

"We?" A spasm started in his cheek before he set the flat of his palms against the desk.

"No. You got family to consider. And one on the way."

Cort's eyes narrowed on him. "I've finally found my brother. You're family. I'm not about to let you go up against Lars without help. You'll need to have an extra gun along. I'm going even if I have to trail behind you every step of the way. Besides, Zeke and Tangle can keep things under control while I'm gone. Lark has plenty of help."

"What if Lark needs you? If one of us goes, it's going to be me. Alone. My final decision."

"Do you know how much a train ticket will cost? With all the gear you'll need?"

"Got a fair idea, seeing as how I worked for the Union Pacific for a while."

"I'm in the financial position to get us on the train with provisions and horses. Not to mention ammunition and guns."

"I've got gold put away in a bank in Virginia City."

"You willin' to wait? I got the money now."

He scrubbed his hands across his face, giving thought to his brother's proposition. Cort was right. Accepting these terms was the only way. No use arguing because weather wasn't on his side. Besides, Cort knew Lars and that alone would make it a hell of a lot easier to identify the bastard.

"You, brother, are holding the aces. I guess it's the two of us. If you get shot, I'm not going to be able to face Lark again. Or Hannah."

"Don't plan to get shot. Just make sure you don't, either. One hole in that shoulder almost did you in."

"You win. Pack whiskey. Never know when it'll come in handy. And... Cort?"

"Yeah?"

"Don't shave that face of yours. Miners are distrustful. Best way to fit in is look like them and make sure you let me do most of the talking. They'd just as soon shoot us as dandy claim jumpers or lawmen if we ride into Bannack looking like we're hunting down one of their own. Lawmen and claim jumpers aren't welcome. Could easily be treated to a quick bullet in the head. Guilty or not."

"I'll follow your lead. Figure I've looked a lot worse than a miner a time or two."

Bryce laughed. A lot weighed on his mind and most of it centered on his son and Hannah. If he failed to set her free... well that was too painful to contemplate. There would be no room for distractions where they were heading. From the time they reached Montana, they'd appear to be on the hunt for gold because that's where Lars would be found.

———————

TIGHTENING THE CINCH, Bryce squinted across his saddle toward the porch. Lark was in Cort's embrace. Their lips met and parted. Cort touched her face and stroked her back before taking her mouth again. Unabashed, even while seven cowhands sat atop their horses, some gazing at them and a few focusing on their boot toes. Zeke stood outside of the corral with an arm draped around Rey's shoulders.

Alonzo and Adoeete stood outside of the main barn, heads bent, looking at the dirt and smoking. Both darted looks in his direction, their eyes unfathomable. He'd bet there were several loyal hands wanting to wring his neck for leading Cort along with him into the wilds of Montana. Tangle and Mason led horses from inside the barn and mounted. They'd decided to ride along to see them off in Ogallala.

With one last hard tug on the cinch, Hunter was ready to go. Two packhorses stood slack-legged, loaded with food, guns, and ammunition enough to get them where they were going. They even had pans and a pick along, hoping to convince folks they were looking to stake a claim. That might or might not get them into the hills without too much trouble. At least they wouldn't be mistaken for lawmen.

"Well. This is it, Hunter. You ready?" he mumbled to his horse.

His horse snorted. When he turned, Cort ambled toward his waiting horse with Lark walking beside him. Bryce led his horse to where Mason and Tangle sat their mounts, clutching the leads of the packhorses. Zeke and Reyes walked to where he waited for Cort. Taking in his son, he could hardly believe how much the boy had changed since he'd come here. Still a bit thin and gangly, his shoulders had broadened. There was a maturity about him in his expression and the way he worked his tail off. No longer was his son a stranger.

Reyes managed to fit into the family he had once resented. He'd just turned twelve, and Bryce couldn't be prouder of how he was turning out, for which he owed Zeke a debt. Grinning, he looked skyward and silently thanked Gabriella for gifting him this boy. His flesh and blood.

"Pa. Can't I come with you?"

Jesus. He'd already had this talk with Reyes. His boy looked like it was all he could do not to break down and cry in front of the men.

Facing each other, he searched for how to answer. All he could think of was... the truth.

"Reyes. Where I'm going, your uncle and me would look mighty suspicious with a kid in tow."

"I'm big enough to hold a gun and ride a horse."

"I know. But not this time. Besides. You've got to get schooled with MissusVan Stadt. Make sure you help with the ranch chores while we're gone. Zeke and Tangle need you helping to round up cattle for the drive to Omaha in September. There's a lot to do to get ready for winter."

Swiping at the tears in his eyes, Reyes said, "I don't want you to go. What if you don't come back?"

"I already told you. I'll come back. I promise. This is home. Don't forget that."

"Zeke said I can sleep in his house if I want."

Bryce glanced to where Zeke listened from a few feet away, the man's expression fathomless.

"That'd be fine. Don't forget your own room in the big house. Stay close to Zeke and Tangle. Take care of Aunt Lark and make sure Hannah... Missus Van Stadt don't need anything."

The boy bobbed his head before wrapping his arms around Bryce's waist. Holding his boy against him, he breathed in his scent of soap, hay, and hint of licorice. While running his hand across Rey's bony back, he thought about everything the boy had suffered, all because his mother and father had made a mistake. Loving his son with all of his heart was easy. Learning to be his father was the hard part.

Beating hooves in the distance had him look beyond Rey's shoulder. From beneath the brim of his Stetson, his eyes narrowed at the sight of Hannah riding toward them, her hair in a long plait that bounced with the rhythm of her horse.

Reaching the corral, she reined in and dropped from the saddle and then looked toward him with her typical hard, unreadable stare. Wearing her boy's blue pants and a white shirt, she managed a smile. And he had to smile right back when he took in the blue ribbon fastened in her braid.

He'd missed her more than she'd ever know over the last few days they'd been separated. What with their disagreement and getting their gear together, he'd kept away from her. Besides, he'd made staying away his mission. His eyes perused every detail of her face while she strode toward him, waving to the cowhands as she marched his way. Aware that eyes were following them, he did his best to keep his hands at his sides, even as he itched to feel her against him.

Darting a glance at his son, he said, "Reyes. Why don't you go say good-bye to Cort while I speak with Hannah?" The boy nodded, then trudged toward the house.

"You're leaving. You weren't going to tell me," she said breathlessly.

Back straight, her voice soft, her admonishment was clear enough, making him grin. From the corner of his eye, he watched the hands adjusting saddles while Cort and Lark were talking. It seemed everyone was giving them space. He poked his hat back on his head. "Didn't see any point in telling you anything about my plans. Especially since it wouldn't make any difference. I'm going. It has to be done. That's that."

Her blue eyes flitted across his face as though memorizing him, just as he was committing every detail of her. The rugged ride ahead would be tiring but he'd have the vision of her in his head to keep him company. Her fingers were laced in front of her. Careful to keep his distance with so many eyes casting glances, he should mount his horse to put an end to this dreary good-bye. Her smile enticed him, keeping his boots planted against the dirt.

"Guess there's nothing left to say, Bryce. Except. Please be careful. You don't know how dangerous he is. Lars enjoys fighting."

"Size isn't always an advantage, Hannah."

"He's killed before. Boxing matches back East."

"I'll keep it in mind."

Dammit. His determination to keep his distance crumbled. Reaching for her hand, he lifted it to his mouth, then pressing a kiss against her palm, he hardly wanted to let her go. But he did. Those trembling lips of hers tempted him to do much more. Stepping away, he tugged his brim low, shadowing his eyes from her view.

"Remember to watch out around Lars," she murmured.

He poked his boot in the stirrup and threw his leg over the saddle. He looked down at her. "I've got a man with me who killed Will Cardin and lived to tell the tale. A fist is no match for a bullet, darlin'."

Her eyes squeezed closed for a moment. He imagined everything she was thinking and when her lower lip twitched, he knew how scared she was.

"I'll miss you, Bryce. Make sure you take care of that shoulder. Change the bandage."

He grinned. "You don't know how much I'll miss you. Best plan that wedding for when I get back."

"When will you be back?"

"Hoping end of September or early October. Depending on how long it takes to round up Lars." He tapped two fingers to his brim and turned his horse, following the others toward Ogallala.

NINETEEN

TO THE MINER'S CAMPS

ORT'S HEAD LOLLED to one side of the seat as the train rattled across the plains. Bryce stared from the window at the massive buttes dotted with sagebrush and juniper. He knew this land. After all, he'd spent years digging gold out of it. Now he just hoped his experience led him to Lars.

Glancing again at his brother, he couldn't resist studying him while he slept. How did he manage to sleep with the banging and lurching of the train? *He* sure couldn't. Everything inside was too coiled to find solace in sleep. Taking in his brother's slack mouth, he listened to his soft snore. Then his thoughts meandered to how Lark and Cort had met. It sure seemed they'd started out with a few challenges, and they'd overcome them. He hoped to do the same.

When his musings circled to the scar at Cort's hairline, he gave thought to the mention of his brother's time in prison, surmising maybe it happened there. Or had the scar been the result of a saloon brawl? One thing for sure, Cort kept a tight lid on his personal business. Just as he, himself had done. Until it had confronted him, head on.

Guessing they'd be at Green River by three or four o'clock, maybe he'd try for some shut-eye at the hotel, if they found a room. The next day, they'd set out for South Pass City. While the train passed the barren hills and mountains, Montana's rough terrain spread out in every direction. Those hills could get a man in a world of trouble. Which brought him back to his sleeping younger brother. He'd tried to look out for Cort when they were young, until the War separated them. If something happened to his brother, he'd never recover from guilt.

He shook his head. He'd make sure he had Cort's back. Six days of empty, rough land in the wilds of Montana, where danger lurked at every bend—that's what they were facing. Tugging his hat brim lower, he'd just sunk into a nap when his brother groaned. He darted a glance in Cort's direction to see him scrubbing his hands across his bearded face.

"You asleep?" Cort asked.

He lifted one eyebrow. "My eyes are open, aren't they?"

Cort dropped his hands to his lap. "So you're awake and peevish."

"Peevish? Just thinking about how much I'll miss Lark's cooking."

"You figuring to make me jealous or are you just thinking about what you really mean—Hannah."

"Neither. We'll soon get into Green River. Last I saw it, there was a decent hotel. The Overland passes through. Expect we might find ourselves camped out if it's full up."

"No matter. We got provisions, if need be."

"Planning to get to South Pass City in two or three days. Once there, I'll ask around about Lars. Betting he'd be remembered. Heard Bannack is playing out. So he might've moved on."

Cort leaned forward. "Make no mistake, Bryce. Lars isn't smart. He makes up for it in brawn. He can break you in half with one hand. Don't tangle with him unless you got a gun. You'd be no match in a fistfight."

"If I have to kill him, so be it. Any way I can."

Cort's mouth thinned at the suggestion he was willing to kill Lars by any means possible. They were of the same mind when it came to the man, but for different reasons. When the train slowed, Cort reached for his Spencer from beneath the seat, then Bryce did likewise. They settled their hats and checked their revolvers. The hunters were more than ready. From now on, much of civilization would be left behind.

Having seen to their horses and provisions at the livery, they walked to the nearest hotel. Once paid up, they crossed the bustling main street to the closest saloon.

"Quite a place. Didn't expect all these buildings," Cort muttered.

"It started as a rail stop and then everything changed when Bryan got hit with drought. Forced folks to set up back here."

"Surprised there's so many folks here. Right now, my stomach is about to gnaw my backbone, so I'm for a beer and then vittles at the restaurant," Cort said. "Over supper, it'll give you a chance to tell me about your mining operation."

"Not much to tell. Eat hearty, little brother. In two or three days we'll reach South Pass City. That's the last we'll find half-decent food and passable beer before we reach Grasshopper Creek."

By morning, drizzle and cool temperatures found them ascending into mountains. Tucking his chin against the pelting rain, he and Cort left the flats of Green River behind and made their way into the high buttes, stopping only long enough to rest the animals and choke down jerky and soda crackers while rain poured over their slickers.

"Think we'll get into snow," Cort said.

"Possible." Bryce snugged his wet slicker higher around his neck. "I've worked the camps and the railroad for years. Only saw big snow once or twice this time of year. Don't think our luck will hold coming back down if Lars turns out hard to find."

"Bet Lars is holed up in a ramshackle cabin."

Bryce swiped the water from his face. Damn both this weather and her so-called husband. What he hoped was to find Lars already buried. That was wishful thinking because the man was probably too ornery to die—unless he cheated at cards and someone did them a favor.

Three Days Later

BRYCE REINED HIS horse and yanked his packhorse close, waiting for Cort to catch up to him with his balky pack animal. Once alongside, Bryce pointed out the town below. Cort tipped his Stetson back on his head, his eyes taking in the view of the town spread before them.

Rubbing the itchy, thick scruff on his face, Cort muttered, "South Pass City, huh? Looks abandoned."

"That's South Pass City," he replied. "Most folks are gone. Still got a bit of a store, one saloon, and some residents living off the land. The Sweetwater used to be full of gold and then when it played out, folks left for easier digs. Still got a few hearty miners around, though. Almost settled here till I decided to move on to Alder Gulch."

"Let's wet our whistles and rest these horses. Got to readjust the packs. She's been bitchy ever since we got into the hills," Cort spat. "I'd leave her here if I thought I'd get a fair price."

"Mine isn't much better. This is the last of any kind of civilization till Bannack. Best look for a place to bed down for tonight. Somewhere dry because from the looks of the sky, it's gonna rain."

"Don't look probable we'll find a boardinghouse. Course, that schoolhouse looks vacant," Cort remarked.

Bryce followed the direction of his brother's jutting chin to where the dilapidated building stood. Their horses plodded down the main street where they turned into the livery corral. A short, gray-haired man limped toward them. When he got close, he spat tobacco then one-eyed them.

"What can I do for ye, gents?"

Bryce said, "Stable these horses and gear."

"Depends."

"On what?"

"If'n you got money."

Turning toward his brother, Cort tucked his jacket behind his holster, putting his revolver in plain view. "We got enough."

"That'll be ten dollars for the night. Water and feed them."

Bryce poked his tongue into the pocket of his cheek. The price was steep, but they were at a disadvantage. These were hard times and gold wasn't flowing anymore. Besides, they didn't have many options. Before he had the chance to question the cost, Cort peeled out greenbacks and slapped them onto the man's outstretched hand.

"There's extra for good care, including our provisions. Keep in mind. I got a bad temper," Cort grumbled. "Don't take kindly to stealing."

"I can watch out. If'n you're lookin' for a drink, saloon is open. Not many in town. Nobody to bother you."

Lifting an eyebrow, Bryce shifted in the saddle and dismounted. His brother had telegraphed the wrong message when he'd shown his wad of cash. Word was already out and knowing that, he lifted his rifle from the boot. Pain seized him like he'd taken a bullet. Leaning against his saddle, his jaw tautened while he waited the agony to ease. Wincing, he looked over his shoulder to where the liveryman stood.

"You got a place we can stay? Bryce asked.

"Restaurant got stew. Rooms are hard to come by. Ask Priscilla at the saloon. From the looks of you, wonder if you're sick. Don't need sick folks comin' to town."

"Nothin' you can catch." Bryce clamped down on the pain, knowing he'd pushed his tender shoulder too far. As he walked ahead, Cort followed behind.

"You don't look all right, Bryce," Cort said when he caught up to him.

"I'll be fine. That liveryman is as crooked as a willow branch. Check everything before we leave."

"Already planned on that."

Just as they crossed the street, Cort stopped. Bryce followed his brother's intense focus to where a buckskin-clad man sat atop a big Appaloosa, guiding the animal at a walk along the center of the street. Bryce guessed he was a hunter by trade, given those buckskin clothes and fancy buffalo rifle tucked in a boot, and the broad-shouldered man rested a Spencer across his lap. Long black hair and dark eyes gave him the look of an Indian. The way he sat the horse and his firmly set jaw commanded respect. By his size and manner, it would be best to have him on your side.

"You know him?" Bryce blurted.

Cort gave no reply. Instead, he strode toward the rider and Bryce followed behind, both baffled and suspicious.

Cort called out, "Gus! My eyes must be acting up again."

Stone-faced, the man's unreadable eyes turned toward Cort. He nudged his horse into a trot, closing the distance. Dark eyebrows rose when he recognized his brother. "Cort Enders. Nothin' wrong with your eyes. What the hell brings you so far from that pretty wife?"

"Business trip. Why're you here? Lookin' for another stake?"

"Not here for gold. Just helped track some Cheyenne. Soldiers took 'em south. I'm heading for the train in Green River then back home to my horses."

Bryce studied the broad-chested man. From his vantage, he appeared as quietly dangerous as any frontiersman he'd ever come across. The knife scabbard at his waist was well used and when he turned his black eyes to him, one corner of his mouth turned up in what might be either a grin or a grimace.

"This must be your long lost brother," Gus said. "Look too much alike not to be."

"Yep. Meet my brother, Bryce. Bryce, this is Gus Quaid. The man who helped me kill Will Cardin. I owe him my life."

Extending his hand, he wasn't surprised at the man's powerful grip, sure that Gus packed a formidable punch. Judging from his rough palm, he'd done his share of hard work. Gus's eyes trailed over the revolver at his hip then returned his attention to Cort, leaving him to take in everything. Gus and Cort were longtime friends and he was finding himself more curious.

"Shit. That little problem wasn't nothing. That coward outlaw and the prison sentence wasn't your fault. Least I could do is get you out of the mess you got into. Had a fine time doing it. Lark wasn't hard to look at and is one strong lady. Too bad she was in love with your ugly hide, or I'd have run off with her. How's she?"

"Doing well. We got ourselves a baby boy. Another on the way. Just so you know, I'd have tracked you down if you thought of running off with her. Friend or not."

"Maybe you would've. Maybe not. Besides, Lark would never leave you for nobody. Either way, I should be kicking your ass home.

Surprised you're up this way and leavin' that wife all alone with a yung'n on that big ranch."

"My ranch is well-armed and manned. Right now, we're looking for somebody my brother needs to have a serious talk with."

"That so? Who might that be and where you heading?" Gus queried.

"We're looking for Lars Van Stadt. Placer mining on the Grasshopper," Cort answered. "Or the Beaver River. You ever hear of him?"

Bryce had been watching and listening, his attention turning from one to the other. He and Cort were clearly good friends. Better still, there was a chance Gus had come across Lars, and if not, this mountain man would make added insurance, if he cared to tag along. That would be a stroke of good luck. Gus scratched the back of his ear in thought, then looked toward him. The blank expression on the man's face was answer enough.

"Haven't heard of no Lars. If you're headin' for Bannack, it's no place to mess with. Got serious miners there and they're not welcoming strangers," Gus remarked. "If you need an extra gun I won't mind stringing along."

"What about your place at Belle Fourche?" Cort countered.

"Still there. Last I saw. Nobody to go back to. Got two hired hands watching my horses."

Tilting his head back, Gus stared skyward as though he were communing with someone. Bryce sensed a deep sadness in Gus. Something profound must've occurred to turn him into a drifter, of sorts.

"How 'bout it?" Gus said, "I'd be glad to help. Could use an adventure, so count me in."

His brother's eyes held his. "What do you say, Bryce?" Cort asked.

"Can't see why not. It'd be good to have an extra pair of eyes and an extra gun."

"Settled, then. You and Cort can tell me what's goin' on over a beer. Let me tie off my horse and we can get inside that hole of a saloon."

Gus dismounted and led his horse to a hitching rail. Bryce figured Gus would be worth his weight in gold once they came up against Lars. Burly, no-nonsense, and as muscular a man as he'd ever run across.

Over several beers, the three of them sat at a corner table. Bryce filled Gus in on the woman Lars had left floundering against odds and then Cort filled him in on Lars's callous disposition. All the while, Gus listened intently, his jaw hard at hearing Hannah's story.

That night, the three of them bedded down inside the abandoned school. A large slate board still hung on the wall. Pages from old readers were strewn among the mice droppings.

Two upturned student desks and a rusted potbellied stove set him to thinking about Hannah and Reyes. In the darkness, scurrying mice and Cort's snores were all that broke the silence. Bryce ran his hand over his sore shoulder, softening the pain as he imagined her scent and gentle touch.

"Bryce?" Gus's deep voice wasn't one you could ignore.

"Yep?"

"Figured you were awake. This Lars. He ever hurt the woman?"

"Expect he did. Left her alone on his ranch for almost two years, fending for herself. She fears his retribution. Not a man to mess with nor a husband worth spit."

"Don't hold with men like that. If it comes to a fight, I'm the one who can whup him. Saw you rubbing that shoulder. Best let me do the fighting if it comes to that. Can remember your brother losing his sight back in Kansas. Only took a thud to the head."

Bryce rolled to sitting. This was the first he'd heard of Cort losing his eyesight. He squinted into the moonlight from the window and made out Gus, stretched out on his blanket beneath the window.

"He lost his sight?"

Cort's voice snapped through the dark like a bullwhip. "Stop talking about that, Gus. Dredging that story gives me jitters. You two are gabbier than two old women at a sewing party. Might as well have brought Nita and Theresa along."

Clearing his throat, Bryce settled back against the floor. A rustling of a blanket told him Gus's palavering was over. Turning his head, he studied the big moon framed in the arched window. Someday, he'd hear the story from his brother. Once things were settled here.

_____

EARLY MORNING FOUND them filled up on coffee, bacon, and eggs. Bellies full and mindful of thieves, they checked their provisions and then mounted up. Riding away from town, they held their rifles in full view of the five residents who'd come to see them off. Twisting in his saddle, Bryce kept a wary eye on the townsfolk as their horses climbed a long, narrow trail. Now all they had to do is keep from getting shot as claim jumpers. Or worse, lawmen. From here on out, they'd be watched.

Bryce glanced over his shoulder to find Gus bringing up the rear behind Cort. The man's eyes searched the trees and rocks. There was no need to warn either of them of the dangers ahead. They already knew that from now on, they were dependent on no one but themselves.

TWENTY

REGRETS

HANNAH KNEELED IN the dirt of her freshly raked garden. The late August heat had her swiping the sleeve of her shirt across her sweat-glazed face and then swatting flies from her head. She sat back and studied the wilting vines and wondered if they'd return to life. Looking over her shoulder at her forlorn cabin, the shade of her porch beckoned. The air hot was still—not even the brown leaves of the oaks were moving in the stagnant air.

Tossing aside a clump of weeds, she stood and pressed her hand against her aching back. Once she reached the porch chair, she plunked down and reached for the ladle from the water bucket. Sipping from it, she recalled that it was just this kind of day when a tornado tore through. Oddly, that thought compounded her loneliness. *He'd been here.*

At night, she'd lain awake, listening to the sounds from the darkness. An occasional coyote yipped, blending with the bawling of cows. Flies fluttered and buzzed in the blackness that cloaked her each night. She hated the empty room and loathed the very fact she hadn't been courageous enough to beg him to stay. What if he didn't return? She already knew the answer. She'd spend her life living with bitter regrets.

After he'd left here, she'd clutched his sweat-stained pillow and tattered shirt against her nose. His smell, his bloody shirt, his son, were among the countless reminders of the man she dreamed about. Yesterday, Reyes rode up to the cabin with his books. She'd found joy in being near Bryce's son. Teaching him. Listening to his chatter and rambling stories about ranch life while relating tales about Zeke and his encounters with Indians roaming the ranch in years gone by. Most of all, his admission that he missed his father ripped through her heart because they had that in common.

Even as Reyes confessed that he'd asked Tangle and Zeke to help him search for Bryce, she bit her lip at having given it thought, herself. If only she were daring enough or smart enough to avoid the dangers. Becoming lost or killed would only make everything worse. Given another chance, she would have agreed to leave here with him. But that wouldn't have been fair to Bryce or Reyes when they had a real chance of making a good life here.

Chickens clucked and picked at the seeds in front of her, bringing her back to the here and now. Her horse stomped in the corral. Dust lifted on a soft breeze. A hawk sailed overhead. This was a contented familiarity but no longer enough.

Looking toward the creek, she gave thought to Lark's invitation to stay at the Double E. Mason had offered to come by and check her place, feed the chickens, then lead her milk cow to the Enders's barn. Mind made up, she stood then turned toward the cabin. Plans. Gathering books and papers, she set them beside the door. In the kitchen, she filled a basket with bread and apple pie. Stuffing her clothes into a valise, she gave a last look around. Her paintings were stacked on the floor in the parlor, some shot full of holes, others unfinished.

Oh, God. Divorce or not, Lars was already part of her ugly past. Tears blurred her vision at the sight of the unfinished painting in the shadowed corner of the room. His horse as clear as if the animal were standing in front of her. The man... an outline. Stepping closer, she stooped to hold it out in front of her.

Unfinished.

LARK LOOKED UP from her wilted flower garden, shook dirt from her skirt, and offered a welcoming smile. Hannah sat stiff-backed, her eyes tracing Lark's smile. In that moment, she considered turning this wagon around and heading home. She had no business bringing melancholy to this cheerful place. Yet, she couldn't face another day alone. Shading her eyes with one hand, she watched tall, willowy Lark stroll closer to the wagon. Hauling back on her horse, she brought the wagon to a stop. Lark's smile faded, turning to a deep frown while she sat motionless and straight as a fence post. Her dearest friend motioned for her to step down while she wondered why she'd come.

"Why don't you step down? You look like you could use some woman talk," Lark said. "Never saw a sadder face."

Hannah jolted at the sound of her voice as though she were emerging from a trance. Lark was standing beside the wagon, her hands on her hips, waiting for a reply. How had Lark known she needed exactly that? She wrapped the reins around the brake handle.

"I brought my satchel and some books to work with Rey. If you don't mind my staying on a few days."

"Of course not. You're more than welcome. Nita and Theresa aren't much for conversation. I'd enjoy having your company. Reyes is off on his horse. No doubt he's following the men around while they check on the water. Lordy, this heat has everything parched."

Nodding, Hannah stepped down, joining Lark in unloading her valise, basket, and books before starting toward the porch stairs. Adoeete appeared from around the corner of the house and Lark asked him to tend the wagon and horse.

Nodding, he heaved himself up onto the wagon seat with the ease of youth, then sent the horse into an even trot to the barn. Once they were inside, Hannah breathed in cooler air, then she dropped her satchel near the main stairway before following Lark into the kitchen. Once they'd set aside the bag of books and basket of food, they took seats across from each other.

The conversation centered around the workings of the ranch, the weather, and wisps of local gossip. Lark chattered while her muzzy mind tried to keep up. Her thoughts weren't on everyday things. In fact, she could hardly put into words where her head had drifted. Theresa joined them and fussed with the pie and bread. Cool tea was set in front of her while the baby gurgled indecipherable words where he played on the floor with wooden spoons.

"Looks like he's beginning to sprout some teeth," Hannah said, reaching down to tickle the baby. He slobbered and broke into wide-mouthed giggles.

"Yes. He keeps me up with his fussing. I didn't think anything could wake my husband when he was asleep until little Bryce came along."

With a sniff, Theresa lifted the baby. "Time I see this one got some clean pants and leave you women to your talking. I'll see you have a fresh bed, Miss Hannah."

"Thank you, Theresa. But don't go to extra work for me. I'm not used to fancy beds."

"More reason," Theresa muttered before leaving them, the baby looking over the woman's shoulder.

Lowering her chin, she wondered if she'd made a mistake coming here, dragging her woes along with her. A soft hand squeezed hers. Lordy, she hadn't meant to stir up Lark's pity. Or maybe she needed honest chiding.

"Now. Tell me. What's going on? I haven't seen you look so melancholy since that tornado blew by your house."

"Truthfully. I'm not sure. I'm just lonely. And worried. Never felt so helpless."

"You love and miss Bryce," Lark stated matter-of-factly.

For a moment, her eyes held the hazel eyes staring back. There was no use in looking away. Besides, she wasn't good at outright lies and Lark was too smart for them.

She sighed. "Yes. With all my heart. Tried not to. Then tried to hide it. But it doesn't matter. It's inside me and I don't want to let go."

"Oh, but it does matter. I hope you know that we don't judge either of you. We're a little biased. Still…. we think that you and Bryce make a wonderful couple. Lord knows, you both need some joy in your lives.

They *will* find some way to extricate you from a mistake of a marriage. You will have a life together."

"I've committed to a brute of a man. And Bryce has gone after him. I won't ever forgive myself if Bryce is hurt…. or worse. You know what Lars is capable of."

"Ahh. First thing's first. Cort is a crack shot and so is Bryce. Cort isn't about to let Lars kill his brother. Knowing your husband, he won't be easy to convince. But I have a good feeling you'll be a free woman once they get back here."

"I hope you're right. You know he wasn't healed enough to go."

"Enders men are tough. Besides, nothing neither of us could say would've stopped them. Remember how Cort made an untenable decision between chasing me or living up to his obligation to his dying wife. Bryce has made his decision where you're concerned. I believe it was the right one."

"Why do you suppose they aren't back? It's been three weeks."

"Hannah, listen to me. It'll take at least two or three weeks just to get into the gold camps and then, God willing, find Lars. Your miserable husband probably left a trail of enemies along the way. Count on Bryce to sniff out that varmint. Weather and rough trails will slow them. But they won't stop until they do. Just maybe they'll find out that Lars was shot by another no-account. That's what I think happened."

"I wish I could shake a premonition I keep having."

"Hannah. I've been through hell and back. I'll wear this scar for the rest of my life because of a man far crueler than Lars. When Cort decided to go up against him, I tried to protect Cort by running away. Cort wasn't one to give up. Neither will Bryce. You can't think the worst or Rey will sense it."

"You're a wise woman. And I'm fortunate to have you as a friend."

Lark patted her hand and stood. Then, Hannah couldn't have been more surprised at Lark's next words. "You and me have things to do. Starting tonight. No more moping around here."

"What do you have in mind?"

"First, there's supper. Then we'll plan out tomorrow. Reyes needs work on calculations and reading while you're here. Got some vegetables for jarring. Hope you're ready to roll up those sleeves because we're going to keep busy, that's what. Nothing like it for worries."

She followed Lark's finger. "Starting with the bowl of potatoes. You peel and I'll fry ham," Lark ordered.

Hannah rose from her seat, managing a quick grin. "Don't forget dresses. We've got sewing to do."

Lark clapped her hands and laughed. "Now, that's what I want to hear. I was thinking the deep blue satin would make a beautiful wedding dress for you. Bryce will be on his knees begging for your hand when he gets back. A real big shindig, as Sienna Harris, would say."

Somewhere along the way, the work *did* ease the dread. Potatoes were fried and ham sizzled in the skillet. Fresh bread was sliced and the coffeepot was set on the table when there was a quick rap against the kitchen door. Startled, they both lifted their heads at the same time, staring at the door as though it were a wild bear. Hannah opened the door to find Mason standing on the other side of the screen, doffing his hat.

Lark's mouth formed a shaky smile, as she stared in his direction. When color drained from her face, Hannah understood why. Since the cowhands rarely came up to the house, unless something was wrong, Mason's appearance struck them with fear. Had he brought bad news? After stomping his dirty boots, Mason stepped inside.

"What is it?" Lark asked, her chin raised.

"Sorry to get here late. Zeke sent me into town four days ago to check on an order of nails. Brought back the mail. Sorry if I interrupted your supper."

"Not at all. Is there a letter from Cort?" Lark asked.

"Nah. Don't appear so. But Bryce's order got in. Seeing as how Missus Van Stadt is here, thought I might as well bring it in. Quite a large bundle of things for her. Adoeete is outside waiting. Mind if we unload the wagon and bring them in?"

Hannah shot Lark a quizzical glance. *What order from Bryce?* Whatever it was, from the beaming expression on Lark's face, her friend was privy to it.

"Please. Bring them in. Set some in here and anything too large can go to the parlor."

Hannah couldn't believe what she was seeing. One after another, a parade of boxes and brown-paper-wrapped squares marched past her. A large string-tied parcel rested against the leg of the table and she ran her hand across the wrapped rectangle, itching find out what was beneath the paper. Just as she thought there couldn't be more, Mason looked toward her with a broad grin.

"There's more," Mason said with a wink.

Mason and Adoeete hoisted a crate and carried it into the kitchen with Lark leading them into the parlor. Too stunned to follow, she stood planted where she was. Adoeete tipped his hat and left. Mason brushed his hands, and said, "Special order, according to Harry at the post depot."

"Thank you both," Lark said.

Once the men left, Hannah kneeled on the kitchen floor and stared at the parcels. Dazed and shaken, her head spun with the notion that these were for her. What had Bryce done? She looked up at the sight of Theresa closing the door after the men. Lark leaned against the wall, a knowing smile lighting her face.

Theresa broke the spell. "Well. You gonna stare at them things or open them? I'm gettin' all jittery wonderin' what's under that paper and in that crate."

Hannah looked to Lark. "Are you sure these are for me?"

"Very. Told us he ordered them. Came from Omaha."

"If you don't open them, I will," Theresa prodded. "Never did have any patience."

Nodding, she carefully untied the strings and peeled back the brown paper. Beneath were large squares of thick white paper. She dumped a burlap sack, spilling brushes and an array of paint jars beside her. Pressing her fingers against her mouth, she tried to still her trembling lips. Over the next few minutes, Theresa and Lark joined her in tearing, tugging, and ripping open the wrappers. A sense of Christmas filled the room on this tenth day of September. She'd never had so many presents. In fact, she couldn't remember the last time she'd received a gift of any sort.

"There's five rolls of canvas. These things cost far too much money," Hannah whispered.

With an iron-pan grip, Theresa pried open another of the largest packages. Hannah's eyes widened and she gasped at the sight. "Lordy, he bought a pine stretcher board." Lark's hand squeezed her shoulder but she couldn't bring herself to look upward, else she might bawl like a sick cow.

Lark smiled from ear to ear. "These gifts couldn't have arrived at a better time. I don't think Bryce worried about the money. Besides, something tells me he has a good amount put aside, seeing as how he didn't have much to spend his gold on up there in Alder Gulch."

"So many colors I won't know where to begin. These are the finest sable-hair brushes I've ever seen. Never owned one." Feathering the bristles with her fingers, her body quivered with the enormity of this gift, both in kindness and cost. "They're so expensive. This paper is like touching white satin."

Theresa lowered her hefty body onto a chair beside her. "Miss Hannah. Now don't start that rain spout and ruin them eyes. You know what? I'd like to see that dimpled smile of yours more often. That man wants you to paint your heart out. That would make him happy."

Lark added, "Theresa's right. Let's take some of this upstairs and then have us a celebration over our meal. Might even help ourselves to a special cider I've been saving," Lark suggested.

"I'd like that. I'd like it just fine." Looking around the room at the piles of paper and string, she wondered aloud, "I wonder what Bryce and Cort are eating. Where do you think they are?"

Theresa harrumphed. "Ha! Those men is eatin' and sippin' some mighty strong whiskey beside a fire. Most likely talkin' men talk. Give Cort time to brag about the next baby on the way. Now let's get started before I starve to death. I'll bring little Bryce down here. Nothin' breaks up the sorrows like a baby."

THE LOW BURNING fire crackled, sending enough light in all directions to see the outlines of the horses, tethered beneath the cottonwoods. The sound of the creek slapping lazily along the gravel bank reminded Bryce of Rocky Creek. He'd lain awake, camped near that creek many a night, wanting her in his arms. Instead, he'd kept company with her cows.

"You awake?" Gus called.

"How'd you know?"

Bryce heard rustling from where Gus bedded down. Rolling to his side, he made out the man sitting cross-legged, his eyes glittering in the firelight. Deciding to join him, he got to his feet and walked to the fire, then poured some overboiled coffee into his cup. Then, taking a seat on a log, he sipped, watching Gus over the rim. "Coffee strong enough to put a hole in a man's gut."

"That so? I know coffee ain't what's on your mind. Camped like this, you get to know another man by the sound of his breathing and how restless he is. Want to talk about what's bothering you? Besides finding Lars," Gus asked.

Bryce shrugged. "Might's well. Can't sleep, anyhow. It'll be my turn to take watch once Cort gets back. Besides, I've got some questions for you."

"Fair enough. What do ya need to know?"

"How do you know Cort?"

"Met in Texas. He was as wild as hell and bent on gettin' himself into trouble. If trouble didn't find him, he found *it*. Escorted him and others in an Army wagon to a Texas prison. When he got out, we ran into each other and rode together till he went his own way. Seemed like he learned some lessons the hard way."

"I should've been there to look out for him. Just a kid. Damn the war. Kills me to know my kid brother went through that. Getting into that kind of trouble wasn't how we were raised."

"Can't fault yourself. Even kids get to make mistakes. He turned out fine. Maybe thanks to Lark."

"I figured, from what little my brother told me, they met as a result of the first owners of the ranch. Harris."

"That arrangement nearly snapped him in half. I'll leave him to tell the rest."

"Cort filled me in on some of that. What Cardin did. Didn't know he was blind. How'd it happen?" Bryce asked.

"That's another story he'll have to tell you." Gus cleared his throat. "How'd you get involved with the married woman? Hannah."

"Met her when she was struggling to keep the broken-down place together. Cort and Lark help her, but her damned husband abandoned her for the goldfields. He was abusive and he left her with nothing to live on. Hasn't cared to return. Nor send her word of his whereabouts."

"Don't like the sound of that. At the same time, she's married and you got no say in it."

Heat roared inside of him like a furnace, ready to bust open whenever he gave thought to her so-called husband. The longer they rode into Montana, the more rage pulsed in his veins.

"She doesn't want to be married to him. He left her alone to take care of his broken ranch. Lars went placer mining. All while she keeps the ranch going on her own. Cort's men round up her strays, brand them or add them into their count. Then he pays her a cut. Splits up the money fairly.

"Course, my brother never says anything about the extra burden of hauling hay to those cows she pens up. Sure doesn't hurt that Lark and Hannah are friends but Cort's got a weak spot for women in trouble."

"So once you find him, how will you convince him to set her free?"

"Got a legal divorce decree. All he has to do is sign it."

"And if he doesn't?"

"Then I'll look for another way to set her free."

Silence weighed heavy between them, and Bryce guessed his meaning was clear enough. Stretching his legs, he looked skyward at the stars. Gus's indrawn breath and deep voice cut into his thoughts.

"You said she was abused. Sums up all I need to know."

"You ever married, Gus?"

Gus rolled to his feet and leaned back against a nearby tree, then stared into the darkness with his arms wrapped around his waist. "I'll always have her with me. Brulé took her. I chased them until I had no horse under me. Her screams still wake me."

Bryce heaved himself to his feet. The pain in the man's voice was enough to make a grown man cry. "Jesus Christ. I'm sorry, Gus."

"You can bet I made renegades pay over the years. Always hope I'll find her among them. You ever love a woman like that? Besides Hannah?"

"Thought I did. A nurse during the war. Followed her to Texas. Stayed on. Until Gabriella's husband came back from the war. We both figured he'd been killed. After all that time away, you'd think he'd want to return. When he showed up, I left for the mining camps."

"What then?"

"Found my brother's ranch by accident. By chance, Gabriella's brother-in-law showed up a few weeks later, in part because of my brother's notoriety glorified in the newspapers. The stories were like a beacon, a compass. Anyway, they brought my son up from Texas to find the boy's uncle but surprising them, I was there... his father. I didn't know him. If I'd known about him, things might be different. Reyes just turned twelve."

"Ain't that just a kick in the ass. At least you have something of the woman you thought you loved."

"I loved her. Just not with the kind of love that would last longer than snow in June. Hannah's the woman I want for my wife."

"I'm figuring on getting you back home in one piece."

Gus's footsteps faded into the darkness, without so much as a good-night. Bryce dumped his coffee and dropped onto his bedroll, arms folded beneath his head. There'd been certainty in Gus's husky voice. Staring at the stars, a cloud drifted across the sliver of the moon. With Gus along, Lars was going to be outsmarted, outgunned, and out of luck once they found him.

PUFFS OF STEAM rose from boiling pots of vegetables. Hannah peered through the vapor to find Lark's pink face looking back.

"Critters must be gorging on my vegetables about now," Hannah uttered. "Not much I can do about it."

"Most vegetables grew like weeds before this drought. I tend mine and they're still not looking healthy."

She watched Lark ladle cooked carrots and potatoes into a waiting bowl and gave thought to what she'd do for food this winter. It might mean taking money from her husband's account to buy necessities. "I almost lost everything in the storm. If it weren't for Bryce putting up a fence to keep out varmints and stray cattle, I'd have nothing."

"Some will recover. If not, we've got enough to share. Should be able to finish this up before supper. Tomorrow, dresses."

Looking up, she saw Lark swiping the steam from her face. The prospect of sewing was far more pleasant than cooking in this heat. "Good thing I brought an extra dress. I feel like I'm wearing a wet rag."

When the door squeaked open, both turned to see Theresa's head poking into the room. "You women done here? I got to get that pork fried up. Go on to the porch and sit. Both of you look done in. Besides, it's cooler out there than in here. I'll bring out some cool tea."

"Sounds divine. Besides, my son hasn't seen me most of the morning," Lark declared. "I'll go upstairs to check on him, then join Hannah out on the porch."

Hannah couldn't agree more as she hooked her apron on the wall and started toward the porch. Lark's footsteps faded along the upstairs hallway. Stepping outside, she breathed in the soft, warm air scent laden with the smell of tallgrass and sage. Red coneflowers poked their bright heads between the stalks. A light breeze lifted her damp tendrils. But her attention was drawn to the dust plumes rising in the distance.

Odd that it didn't settle. Instead, the spirals grew larger. Before she had time to wonder more about it, she saw the outline of riders breaking from the swirling dust kicked up beneath horse's hooves. Darting from the porch, she cupped a hand over her brow. Something had to be wrong. Men didn't run horses in this heat. Unless….

When Zeke's white horse crested the rise between Tangle and Jude's mounts, her eyes fixed on another horse trailing behind Jude. Her eyes widened at the sight while she pressed her hand against her mouth to smother a scream. Draco, Rey's riderless mare, galloped with them.

With her heart thrumming in her ears, she ran, half stumbling through the high, orange-yellow grass. As they grew close, her eyes froze on the slumped boy in front of Zeke. The horses slowed. She swallowed her agony. Standing beside his snorting horse, she looked up, witnessing Zeke's grief-stricken expression. Cheeks red, his jaw clenched, his tear-filled eyes were about to spill over his cheeks.

The screen door squeaked open and quick bootsteps stopped somewhere behind her. From far away, she heard Lark's voice shout. With a glance over her shoulder, she found Theresa hugging the baby to her shoulder. Mason appeared beside her and reached up for Reyes's limp body, waking her from her shock.

Wanting to hold him herself, she shouted Rey's name. There was no response. Face pale and his eyes closed, she wasn't sure he breathed. Her heart was in her throat as she latched on to her fading courage.

"Just lead us to a bed," Mason ordered, snapping her from her trance.

"Follow me," Lark hollered. "Did anyone go for the doctor?"

"Sent Billy and Dan with spare horses. Told 'em not to stop for nothin'," Zeke replied, from where he tromped behind them.

At the top of the stairs, Mason carried Rey's wilted frame to the bed where Hannah bent over him, brushing her hand across his face. "What happened to him?" Dizzy with panic, Hannah drew herself upright because she had to. There was no time for simpering because this bloody cut had to be dealt with.

Lark filled a basin with water as Hannah looked toward Tangle's drawn face. Lark handed her the damp towel and she pressed it against Rey's head.

"What happened to him?" she asked again, this time more sharply.

"We found him lying on the ground, his horse standing nearby. We figure his horse spooked and threw him. Didn't have time to figure out what. But he sure got a good jolt to his head," Zeke mumbled.

Sucking in her breath, she thought if she had her way, he'd never sit that horse again. If this boy died, she and Bryce wouldn't be able to live with the awful loss.

"Hannah. Never mind why it happened. We've got to clean this cut and keep his head cool. Alfred Collier will know what to do."

Nodding at Lark's firm rebuke, she admitted that Lark was right. Blaming these men was outright unfair. She looked over her shoulder at Tangle. "I'll need my medicine bag from my house. In the kitchen. Black leather. Please get it."

"That'll take a good amount of time. Almost two hours there."

"Please get there and back as fast as you can. My herbs are in the bag."

Tangle left the room without another word. Zeke groaned and ran his fingers through his long mop of white hair and then dropped onto the chair beside the boy's bed. "I love the boy. He's like my own flesh and blood. If he don't wake up, my heart ain't goin' to make it," Zeke murmured. "Shouldn't have let him go off on his own."

"It'll be all right, Zeke," Hannah said. "All of us have taken falls and we're still here. We all accept this as part of ranching." That was the best consolation she could come up with. Because deep inside, she blamed him and herself. The truth was, she couldn't be sure he'd be all right. Bryce had expected her to look after Rey and she'd failed. They all had. Smoothing her hand over Rey's head, she felt for the lump. "Do we have ice?" she asked, turning to Lark.

Lark looked up from yanking Rey's boots from his feet. "I'll see if there's some left in the spring house so late in summer. I'm not sure there's any."

Hannah's full attention turned to his still form. "Reyes Enders? Can you hear me? Wake up, sweetheart." Her pleading brought no response. She clutched his hand between her trembling fingers and whispered, "We've got lessons to do. Your father will want to see you up and around soon as he comes home."

In the silence, she darted a glance at Zeke. He leaned forward on his elbows, his face buried in his hands. Rey's eyelids fluttered and his eyes peered from beneath his lashes.

"Head hurts," he mumbled.

Hannah touched his shoulder. "Try to stay awake. Please try to open your eyes."

When his eyes closed, Zeke grumbled something indiscernible. She smoothed Rey's hair, and to her surprise, he whispered, "Draco." Then he murmured, "Find."

"Draco is in the corral. In a while, I'm going to give you some medicine. We'll get that bump to go down. Do you hear me?" she asked.

"Want Pa."

"I know. You'll see him soon," her voice crooned. And silently prayed she was right.

Zeke stood. She nearly cried at his shaking hands when he squeezed the drowsy boy's shoulder. Neither she nor Zeke could take their eyes from the boy while Lark pressed another cool cloth against the boy's head.

"Theresa is seeing about ice," Lark said.

Hannah worried her lip between her teeth, thinking. *Think, Hannah. What medicines do you use for the swelling?* She wasn't about to wait for the doctor.

TWENTY-ONE

SALTY'S CAMP

THE FIRST SIGN of trouble, as they climbed ever higher into the mountains, happened so quick that Bryce had just enough time to call himself a fool. A glint of sunlight from the rocks above was followed by one powerful gun blast. Horses reared and whirled. From the corner of his eye he saw one of the packhorses kicking his brother's horse, sending Cort into a wild spin. The commotion was enough to divide his attention between the confusion and the attacker.

That was long enough for a reload. A second boom rent the air, sending Gus's Appaloosa bucking while barely clinging to the saddle. Gus and Cort's cusses joined the commotion. His own horse fought the bit. They raised their rifles and at the same time, gained control of their wild-eyed mounts.

By the time Bryce steadied his sight on the probable location of the shooter, he guessed the attacker was gone, or changed position. Bryce knew miners. This one decided to make a statement with two powerful explosions from a buffalo gun, meant to scare the hair off trespasser's chests. If this attacker wanted them dead, they'd be dead.

These isolated men were territorial. He'd been one of them and for certain, he'd never hung out the welcome sign. Whoever shot at them was waiting to see if they'd turned tail. While he scanned the rocks, Cort called out.

"Guess we ain't welcome. Is there another way around this bluff? Nearly killed us."

"Probably have lookouts no matter which way we go. You two stay here. I'm going to head into that gorge and see if I can talk him out of hiding. Don't shoot."

"If he starts shooting again, we're damn well going to shoot back," Cort retorted.

Bryce regarded his brother's piercing glare and the quiet fury in his taut jaw. He touched his heels to his horse, urging him forward, keeping his rifle rested across his lap. Echoes of his mount's hooves bounced off the narrow, rock-walled canyon—an eerie reminder that the attacker would know he was there. His skin crawled, knowing he was in the man's sights. Miner or miscreant, if he was crazy enough, Bryce knew he'd be dead in a few minutes. Abruptly, a small boulder tumbled from the ledge, and Hunter danced sideways.

"All right. I know you're up there. Can I ask a few questions? Before we move on," Bryce shouted.

"Turn 'round and stay pointin' south," called a craggy voice.

The voice came from somewhere above him. "We're looking to stake our own claim farther along. Around Grasshopper Creek. We aren't claim jumpers. We'll keep movin'. Give my word."

Bryce was met with the sound of the wind. "You still listening?"

"Behind ya."

Shit. Bryce twisted in his saddle and brought his horse around, now facing a hunched old man wearing worn overalls and suspenders over a stained red shirt, and on the business end of a Sharps Big Fifty pointed at his chest. The man's face was buried beneath a white beard. A floppy, moth-eaten hat shadowed the man's eyes, so there wasn't much chance of reading his intent.

"Good-lookin' buffalo rifle. Appears to be a Sharps."

"That it is. Get on with what ya got to say. I got work to do. Don't mind leavin' your body to the buzzards."

"Could you point it away from me while we talk?" The man lowered it slightly and he judged that the old miner was willing to listen. "My name's Bryce Enders."

"Don't know ya. I'm Len Paris. Some call me Salty."

"Well, Salty. My friends failed to find gold near Green River. Heard better diggin's up here."

"Most good places taken. Best ya move toward Bannack. Heard they still got claims for the takin'."

"Might do that. Mind if I have my brother and friend come through the gorge with me?"

"Long as ya keep movin'. Else I'll drop all of you and keep them horses for myself."

"Thanks. We'll just do that."

Bryce waved Cort and Gus forward and all three faced the old miner. "This here's my brother, Cort, and the other is Gus Quaid."

"Heard tell o' Gus Quaid."

"How'd you know me?" Gus asked.

"You gotta reputation in these parts. Clearin' out renegades with the Army. Guess the miners can give ya a pass. Think a man like you is trustworthy."

"No one ever called me a liar or thief," Gus replied.

Bryce cleared his throat, thinking Gus was their ticket. "We're lookin' for a man while we're here. Maybe you heard of him."

Salty lowered the Sharps to his side and shifted his weight from one foot to the other. Thankfully, Gus's name had impressed the man enough to hold his attention. "What's the name?"

"Lookin' for Lars Van Stadt."

At first, Salty's stare turned hard as nails, then his mouth dropped open. Once he clapped it closed, he gave a last chew to his wad and spit.

"You say he's a friend of yourn?"

That was a cautious question requiring a careful answer. The outcome depended upon the right one. Glancing toward Cort and Gus, he found their eyes had narrowed. Cort shrugged. They were leaving this decision to him.

"No. We got something to settle between us."

Salty yanked his hat from his head. Now Bryce was able to see the mean-looking scar running from Salty's right eye to disappear into his hair-covered cheek. Penetrating blue eyes glared back at them.

"No meaner son of a bitch than Lars. No lie. He'd kill his own mother if she had one nickel. Never met a man could break a man's neck with one hand. Saw him do it with my own eyes. Come through here... mebee year or more ago. Tried to steal old Tarrow's claim right out from him. Lars shot him to death afore the man had a chance to say howdy. His wife run off screamin'.

"By the time any of us got up to his place, Lars was packed and gone. Guess he didn't find enough gold. When I run into him in a saloon up in Bannack last winter, we traded words. I lost the fight. He let me live."

"Last you saw, he was in Bannack?" Bryce asked. At least now he knew where Salty might've gotten that slice to his face.

"Heard he mines up on Grasshopper Creek where it comes into Beaver. If you run across him, ya better shoot and save your questions after."

Tipping his hat, Bryce figured it best to keep his intentions and particulars to himself. "Thanks, Salty. We'll move on. You don't need to worry we'll double back."

"Gettin' near sundown. Might as well come up to my camp. Gotta small cabin. Place to sleep and eat for the night. Least I can do for ya now I know you're lookin' for that bastard. 'Sides. Could use company."

With a sidelong glance at Gus and Cort, he asked, "What do you both want to do?"

"Sounds good. Horses need rest," Gus replied.

"Jesus Christ. Thought the cat got your tongues. Begun to think the two others didn't talk at all." Salty one-eyed them and muttered, "Follow me."

Trailing Salty farther into the gorge along a narrow, steep trail in single file proved to be nearly impossible. Bryce figured the man was touched and leading them on a merry chase when they eventually lost sight of him. The man's cackling laughter echoed from the rocks.

The ledge trail opened into a wide clearing where a slant-roofed cabin sat beside a rushing creek. Smoke drifted skyward from a chimney. For tonight, they'd bed down with a roof over their heads and maybe some half-decent vittles... in the company of a contrary, lonely old coot. Best of all, they were like-minded in their hatred of Lars. For once, luck was on his side at sniffing out her husband quicker than he figured he would—thanks to Salty.

"I WANT HIM sitting up with pillows behind him for part of the day. Make sure you keep him awake as much as possible," Dr. Collier said as he bent over the drowsy boy.

Alfred Collier's prognosis wasn't as ominous as she'd expected. Hannah breathed a sigh of relief as Lark, standing on the other side of Rey's bed, murmured a quiet thanks. She'd stationed herself beside the business-like, respected doctor. Zeke hadn't moved from the room in five days. Zeke's unshaven and pale face had Hannah worried as much about the elder man as she did about Reyes. For herself, she was wrung out with worry. Lark didn't look much better. But Zeke's state of mind was worrisome.

"Can we give him anything for the pain?" Hannah asked.

"You did just right. The ice you scrounged up helped with the swelling. That oil of sage you used looks to be working, Hannah. Appreciate you thought to use it. Hadn't thought about that stuff for a while."

"What else can we do?" Zeke asked. "That boy means the world to us."

"I've seen worse bumps. Make sure he wakes and takes in clean water and broth. Keep watch on that lump. If the bruise spreads, tell me immediately. I'm heading for the bunkhouse to check on Dan's sore hand. Rode all the way to Ogallala and back with a big blister. Got to tend it before it's infected. Then I'll stop back to check on the boy."

The doctor stuffed his stethoscope into his medical bag and snapped it shut. At that sound, Rey's eyes opened. Zeke lurched to his feet and she stepped aside, making room for Doc Collier to bend over the boy, studying Rey's eyes.

"Hey, there, Reyes. I'm Doctor Collier. Glad to see you're awake."

"My head hurts. I don't want a doctor."

"Well. I'm here anyway. You got a lot of worried family sitting here. Good if you stay awake a while."

"Where's Zeke?"

"I'm here, sonny. I'm not leavin' till you get out of that bed."

"Where's my horse?"

"Safe and sound in the corral," Zeke muttered.

"Don't be mad. Wasn't his fault. A bobcat ran across the trail and Draco got scared. I should'a held on better."

"That's part of learnin' to ride. Just don't scare us like that again," Zeke admonished.

"Doctor? How long before he can get out of bed?" Lark ventured.

"Keep the swelling down with cool cloths. No leaving the bed for at least a week. Light food. Should be as good as new."

"Thanks. I'll have some coffee and pie set out before you leave," Lark offered.

"Sounds good. By the way, where's Cort and Bryce? Figured they'd be camped on the floor."

"They had business up north."

Hannah tipped her chin, knowing how gossip spread. They'd agreed to keep this to themselves and hoped the men did the same. With a nod, the doctor didn't ask more. Once the door closed behind him, Hannah joined the others in hearing Rey recounting his adventure. Bryce would be jarred if he knew this happened. For some time now, she felt like a mother to Reyes. Now, with all her heart, she hoped it would become official. For now, all she could do was pray for their safe return.

LEADING CORT AND Gus down the main street of Bannack, Bryce's first thought was how much the town had dwindled. Once the territorial capital moved from here to Helena, decline was expected. The saloons and hotels didn't look as busy as they once were. The mercantile still held displays of kitchen goods and clothes but there was a scarcity of folks along the boardwalk, many homes they'd past boarded up. Passing the Silver Slipper Saloon, he cringed at the number of times he'd spent upstairs.

Being stared at never set well, and there were plenty of gawkers while they rode down the street. The curious, suspicious, and sometimes malevolent glares set his nerves on edge. Around here, vigilantes and road agents were the rule of the law. The three of them rode past the new Methodist Church that had been erected as a kind of fortress against Indian attacks. Only last year, he'd heard that the Nez Perce had been pushed this way, sending panic across this part of Montana Territory.

Guiding their horses to the livery, they dismounted. Just as they yanked their rifles from the saddle boots, a heavyset man, wearing a flapping leather apron, limped toward them.

"You fellows got tired-lookin' mounts. Gonna cost prime money to feed 'em."

"It'll have to do, Sim," Bryce retorted.

The liveryman's eyes widened. "Hell and blazes. Bryce Enders showin' up is about as unexpected as a fifth ace in the hand. Thought you'd been killed. Never forgot the big ruckus at the saloon."

Lifting a hand, Bryce halted the liveryman's recounting of that incident—one he wanted to forget. "Those days are over, Sim. Just passing through."

"Who be these two?"

"Gus Quaid. A friend. The scowling man is my brother, Cort."

"That so. See ya got pans. Most claims been picked over. Better not figure on staking 'round here. Find yourself dead. Nobody wants to share."

Cort replied before Bryce had the chance to think of a reasonable response. "Like we said, we'll move on. Wet our whistles at the saloon. Any more questions?" The edge in Cort's voice was warning enough. The liveryman lifted an eyebrow, and his brother eased his stance.

Sim's beady eyes darted from Cort's face back to him. "Sure. Whatever you say. Looks like it'll take twenty dollars."

Cort reached into his pocket and slapped a Liberty onto the man's outstretched palm. "Take care of these horses. And our gear."

Bryce had seen a change in his brother over the last days. Ever since they'd been shot at, he'd gotten downright prickly. Looking toward Gus, he found him eyeballing the windows and doors along the street. Knowing Gus, he'd already figured that their arrival spread like wildfire and if the wrong people were of a mind to take whatever they had, they'd have a fight on their hands. All he wanted to do is step through the batwing doors and get down to the business they'd come here for. Lars.

The saloon was quiet when they ambled inside. The thin, dark-haired bartender, standing beside the back door, swiped his hands against his apron and walked toward them. Two gals sporting thin, black lace froufrous and wearing prudish mouths, surveyed them from their perches on the divans.

The older-looking woman puffed a cigarillo, clenched between her teeth. She eyed them with mild interest. "You men ain't here to make trouble, are you?"

Bryce darted a look at the bartender, ignoring the woman. The bartender leveled his big brown eyes at Gus before turning his attention back to him. "Here for a drink. Be on our way," Bryce said, deadpan. *Besides, what if we were here for trouble? What the hell would you do about it?*

"Beers if you got 'em," Cort added.

Bryce pivoted, resting his elbows back against the bar, appraising the patrons. His brother's eyes were scanning the staircase while Gus trained his attention on the gambling table where three men sat, the table piled high with chips and cards. From the looks of these patrons, he'd bet most of their faces were on a poster. From his vantage, their white hands hadn't seen a day's work. In short, these weren't miners.

When his attention was drawn to the lone, dark-suited dandy sitting alone at a corner table, something about him niggled. Bryce watched him flip cards, a bottle of whiskey beside him nearly full. Apparently sensing the perusal, the dandy offered an almost imperceptible nod in his direction, setting his teeth on edge. After the silent exchange, he stood and left, the bottle in his hand. Trouble was brewing and his bones didn't lie. Which meant he had more than one bad apple to worry about.

"Barkeep. You gotta name?" Gus asked.

The bartender looked up from wiping down the bar.

"Ed. Who are you fellows?"

"I'm Gus. These two are Cort and Bryce."

"You ain't miners. Don't look like."

"Well. Don't rightly know what they're supposed to look like. We're lookin' to stake a claim up higher above Grasshopper Creek," Gus said matter-of-factly.

"Good luck, gents. Most been taken. You got here five years too late."

Now that Gus had opened the door, Bryce intended to dig in for all it was worth. "Figure we might talk to a man we know from down South. You might know him," Bryce interjected.

"Lots of men come through here. Especially Saturday night. Come down from the hills like thirsty ants."

Bryce kept a poker-straight face. From the corner of his eye, he saw Cort set down his beer, his jaw taut. This was the moment of truth. If Lars were around here, Ed would know about it. This was the chance he had to take. "Name's Lars." It didn't take more than a minute for re-action. The flicker across the bartender's eyes and mouth looked like he sucked a lemon. One thing was certain—he'd struck pay dirt.

"Shit. You got rocks for brains if you're friends with him. Never met a meaner son of a bitch," he said in a lowered voice.

Bryce released the breath he hadn't known he held, feeling like he'd just won a bag of gold. "Can you give us an idea where his digs are?"

He raised an eyebrow and a corner of his mouth. "You're lookin' to get shot full of holes. But that's your lookout. Maybe you'll get lucky and get out in one piece. Best watch out for Ruby. She don't take to strangers less they're payin' customers."

"Ruby?" Bryce lowered the beer in his hand before he'd had a chance to swallow any. Christ. Lars was even worse than he thought. Damned if he'd ever let on to Hannah that her husband holed up with a woman.

Not just a woman. A prostitute. Those are the kind that clung to the miners. To think all this time, Hannah had been faithful to her worthless, two-timing husband made him both sick and enraged. Gulping against the knot in his throat, he imagined wrapping his hands around Lars's throat and squeezing the life out of him. Killing was too good for the varmint.

TWENTY-TWO

FOUND

A FTER TWO DAYS of jolting rock trails, following a rushing river where they couldn't hear their own breathing, they found themselves wending in and out of sparse trees. Bryce began to think they'd gone the wrong way. They'd passed one abandoned cabin after another with no sign of miners.

Finally, from the vantage of a flat bluff, they saw a roughhewn log cabin situated beside a calm pool, deep in the shadows of a small stand of box elders and cottonwoods. No one worked the sluice box at the creek. Smoke drifted skyward from a stovepipe chimney.

Bryce turned in his saddle. "Gus, you stay back here. If this is Lars's cabin, I don't want him to know there's three of us."

"I'll be ready. If he twitches wrong, I'll send him to Perdition."

"Counting on you."

"What do we do about the woman? *If* she's there," Cort asked.

Glancing toward his brother, he nudged his horse down the steep slope. "I don't give a damn about his woman. All I want is his signature on the divorce decree."

Cort barked, "That smug bastard won't give an inch. He doesn't know you. He knows me. Best I lead in and face him and start off making him an offer on his ranch. See where it goes."

Bryce twisted in his saddle with a grimace. "You tried that before."

"Maybe lucky this time. Selling might make him consider releasing his hold on Hannah while he's at it."

Bryce tugged the brim of his hat lower over his eyes. "All right. You do the talking."

"Don't bring up Hannah right off."

"I already said I'll follow your lead. Let's get to it." Every nerve unraveled inside, one at a time. Clenching his back teeth, he hoped this would be easy. From all accounts, he knew better.

Clutching their rifles, they came within thirty feet of the cabin and stopped. No one appeared and there were no signs of horses or mules. The sluice sat idle, which might mean Lars was working farther up in the hills at another site. Or he'd left the territory.

"You in the house!" Cort shouted.

There was silence except for the moving water and buzzing flies. As they waited, the door creaked open, and a rifle barrel poked from the darkness. Cort returned aim while he dismounted, keeping his rifle leveled at the door.

"Who are you?" a man's coarse voice called. "I kill claim jumpers on sight. Start talkin'. Fast."

"Lars, it's Cort Enders."

The door flew open and Lars's broad frame filled the doorway. Gray-streaked hair hung in wet straggles around his broad, flat face. Wide-eyed, he looked from Cort to Bryce. Dirty gray overalls hung below his stomach. His stained blue shirt hung open, revealing a sun-darkened and pock-marked chest, suggesting he'd been peppered with buckshot. Those muscled arms of his were as thick as fence posts. Now he understood why Cort warned him.

"Cort? You got to be lyin'."

Swaying, Lars moved closer to them and squinted in Cort's direction. He still held his gun trained on them, setting Bryce's jaw twitching, both at the man's unsteadiness, and his unpredictability.

"Why would I lie? Came to find you. I'm still offering a good price for your place. Why not take it?"

"'Cause it ain't for sale, that's why. Hannah's job is to keep it runnin'. She's *my* woman and her job is keepin' my place goin'. Don't get no ideas."

Bryce caught the almost imperceptible nod from his brother. So much for leaving Hannah out of this.

"Hannah's struggling to hold your ranch together. Leaving her alone wasn't very gentlemanly. I'm still offering a good price for your place. Then you'd be free to stay here."

"Not interested. Best git. I'm keepin' what's mine."

The muscle contracted in Bryce's jaw. Now his hackles were up, and his finger itched to pull the trigger. But it would feel better to ram the butt of his rifle down the varmint's throat.

"Come out here, Ruby. Got company." Lars lowered his rifle.

Gritting his teeth when Cort lowered his rifle, he kept his gripped... not trusting what could happen next. A buxom woman stepped outside, wearing a threadbare blouse that outlined her fullness. No doubt, she was game for playing. Wild red hair was piled in straggled disarray and her unevenly painted lips said all he needed to know. Barefoot, her long legs disappeared beneath a tattered blue skirt. Deep-set brown eyes darted from one man to the other. There was a proud smirk around her mouth. He had the distinct impression they'd just enjoyed each other in ways he didn't want to visualize.

"Ruby. Say hello. They come all the way from near my ranch in Nebraska. All for nothin'. Dumb suckers."

She licked her lips. When her eyes returned to Cort, they trailed him from his boots to his face. For the moment, all their attention was drawn to his brother.

"You need her company? She's good. If you got money."

"No, Lars. We're not here for that," Cort retorted.

"Aw, hell." Lars spat on the ground then glared. "Guess you get enough at home. You come a long way to buy my ranch. Could'a saved you a trip."

Bryce figured his brother's plea was about over. Cort remained stoic then remounted.

"You're stubborn," Cort snapped, once he'd settled back on his saddle.

"I like it when I get your goat. *Big* deal rancher. *Rich* son of a bitch. How does it feel not to git what you want?"

That was the limit of Bryce's patience. Now it was his turn, even at the cautioning glance from his brother. "I got business with you, Lars."

"What business might that be? I don't know you."

"I know your kind. No matter. I have something for you. Call it a gift."

Ignoring his brother's look of warning, he used his free hand to unbuckle his saddlebag, then turned with the divorce papers clutched in one hand.

"Bryce... this isn't the time," Cort muttered.

"Hell it isn't."

Lars took some staggering steps closer. "Time for what?"

At least he'd gotten the varmint's curiosity. "Your wife wants a divorce. Sign the papers and set her free. You don't want her. Seems you like what you got... right here."

Bryce's demand couldn't have been more direct nor stark. Lars's depraved, sadistic bark of laughter cut the air sending to flight some roosting sparrows. Just as suddenly, his laugh ended. Their eyes stayed on each other, like two bucks ready to do battle.

"You in her bed?"

"You're a degenerate, immoral louse. How can you call yourself a husband? Or even a man?"

Bryce knew he'd laid his cards on the table and now risked it all. And from the expression on Lars's red face, the man was mad enough to eat the Devil with his horns on at the challenge. Contemplating killing the man, Cort dismounted then moved between them.

"You didn't tell me you was married, you horse's ass," Ruby shouted.

Stunned at Ruby's sudden outburst, Bryce watched as she rounded on Lars. Abruptly, her hand sliced the air with a wild swing, cracking across Lars's drawn face. Roaring, he knuckle-punched her, knocking her to the ground where she scrambled away from his boot kick.

"Get back inside," he yelled. "I'll deal with them before I fix you."

Ruby held her bloody nose, shoved to her feet, and scampered inside the cabin, slamming the door. *Christ.* Bryce hadn't expected to deal with both him and a woman. Right now, he only wanted one thing. Determined to get this man's mark or signature, he dangled the paper in front of Lars's face.

"Sign the papers. Then you'll be free of the woman you don't want," Bryce ordered.

Lars jutted his wide chin. "No. And if you been takin' her, you owe me money."

Bryce folded the document, tucked it into his jacket pocket, then slipped his rifle into the boot of his saddle. Turning, he charged toward Lars's midsection, only to be spun around in Cort's grip.

"Calm down. We won't get anywhere this way," Cort hissed.

Shrugging from his brother's grip, and with one last glance at his opponent's smirk, he mounted his horse. By the time he looked toward Lars again, the man's rifle was leveled at him.

"You shoot my brother and I'll kill you where you stand. And take your ranch," Cort warned, his voice deadly calm.

"Both you git. Don't come back else I'll shoot you both dead," Lars shouted. "Ask anybody. I don't think twice about killin' them I don't like."

"We'll be around Bannack. Let me know if you want the money for the ranch. Looks like you need it," Cort said.

Bryce clenched his teeth, almost choking with rage. They'd lost this round. The grip on his reins kept him from reaching for his revolver. There'd be no signing. Not today. Pursing his mouth, he turned his horse.

While they nudged their horses away, he heard the click of the rifle hammer from behind. Dammit. If his brother hadn't stopped him, he'd have shot Lars with no more feeling than killing a rattlesnake.

Gus was expressionless, standing beside his horse with his rifle at his side. "Didn't take long. Had a bead on Lars. Could tell things were edgy. Saw the woman. Don't need to tell me how it went."

Bryce pinched the bridge of his nose and sighed. "Christ. He's worse than I thought."

Cort slapped his hat against his leg. "Best ride back to Bannack and come up with a new plan. Bryce, if he refuses to sign those papers, we'll have to draw him into a fight. With witnesses."

Deep in thought, Bryce nodded. He'd fight to free Hannah any way he could.

———————

THE OWNER OF the hotel made room for them. Broken furniture, stained bedding, and cracked walls offered little hints of the former heyday, before the gold started petering out. The restaurant offered either stew or salt pork and potatoes. Both choices turned out passable if you washed it down with decent coffee. Shoveling food into his mouth, Bryce kept his eyes on the same dark-suited man from the saloon.

Sitting at a corner table, the man brushed them with a quick glance, then sipped his coffee. Easing forward in his seat, he muttered, "Gus. You get a feeling about that dark suit in the corner? Something about him has me on edge."

"Yeah. Got the same feelin' in the saloon."

Cort set his cup down hard. "Only one thing for us to do. Introduce ourselves."

"Hey." Grasping his brother's arm, he stayed Cort when he started to rise from his seat. "No. Don't want to start one fight before we settle the other."

"Bryce is right. Let's finish up so's we can see if he follows us, then settle it in private," Gus said.

Trouble was coming from two directions. Lars was as variable as a storm and thorny as a bale of barbed wire. The stranger in a dark suit was watching them. He'd given thought to forging the signature. Then, how would he ever look her straight in the eyes? Even if he pulled it off, if Lars returned, she'd never forgive the deception.

They left the table, finding another in the adjoining saloon. Three dirt-covered miners swigged beer at the bar. The gambling tables were empty except for one. Four men puffed cigars, studying cards. Turning his attention to the banter between Cort and Gus, his eyes settled on a newspaper article tacked to the wall beside them. Tearing it from the nail, he spread it in front of him. As he read, his back stiffened. Grinning, he wanted to shout hallelujah. There in bold print was the solution to the problem of Lars. When he looked up, his companions were watching him as though he'd lost his mind.

"What the hell is it?" Cort asked. "You look like a cat who just found a bowl of milk."

Bryce slid the paper across the table. Cort read it and lifted his eyebrows nearly to his hairline. *Saturday, September 14. Prizefight.*

Gus grabbed the worn paper then held it into the light of the window. When he grinned, Bryce figured he was thinking the same thing.

"Yep. You read right." Bryce waved one of the fancy women over to their table. Leaning beside him, she made certain her full bosom pressed against his shoulder. He figured she was about to ask who'd go first, from this table.

"Gotta question for you, honey?"

"I can do you upstairs. Four bits for the first time. After that, more like ten."

He winced while his comrades looked amused. "Not tonight. What do you know about this prizefight?"

"Cost you."

Poking his hat back on his head, he glared. *Christ.* Reaching into his pocket, he tossed two coins onto the table. Grabbing them into her palm, she tucked them into the purse tucked between her bosoms. With a creased mouth, she appeared to be considering.

"Well?" he snapped.

"Every other month, miners come down for the fight. Except winter. A lot of broken noses and arms once it's over. Also keeps the undertaker busy—calls himself a doctor. Gold flows from loose pockets while the drunks fill the rooms upstairs. Nobody ever beats Lars, but they keep comin' back. Got forty dollars to put down, then you get to fight."

"You mean fight Lars?"

"That's right. Saw him beat one till you couldn't see his face no more. Lost an eye. Lars would've taken the other eye out if that man hadn't got to his knees and begged. Turned his claim over to him to save it."

"Forty dollars gets you into the fight?" Bryce wanted to be sure.

"What I said. The bartender holds the money. Takes his fat cut. You got too nice a face to get into a fight with that man. He'll mess you up good. Or kill you."

"Thanks for the information."

"Sure, honey. Anything else you need? 'Cause I ain't sayin' anything else without more money."

"Not for now." He'd already returned his eyes to the newspaper.

Her chortle followed her. When he glanced up, she'd sashayed to the bar where she'd curled her ample frame against a grubby miner. A quick look at his brother's hard stare and Gus's clenched jaw told him they'd already figured what he planned to do. They were right. He was already enjoying the feel of landing his first punch.

"You can't be so stupid to fight him," Cort spat, slapping his open palm against the newspaper. "Besides, that's two month's wages you'd lose. Not to mention your life."

"If I win, I'll have the leverage I need. Better yet, I'll kill him with my bare hands and have witnesses of a fair fight. Either way, this is an opportunity I'm not turning down."

Cort's piercing stare didn't waver. "I'm not going to let you do this. We'll figure out another way."

"It's my decision to make."

Gus grinned when he read the ad.

"What say you, Gus? It seems you like it better than my brother."

Gus whipped his hat off his head and slapped it atop the newsprint. "Yep. I grinned because I'm doin' the fightin'. You won't live long enough to finish any fight with that brick-headed varmint. You saw his size. You ain't no match for him. But I am. Put up your money, gents. I'll take him on. And *win*."

A HARD-RIDING horse had Hannah lift her head to see Zeke riding to the end of her corral. Waiting as he slowly dismounted then straighten his arthritic legs, her heart ached at what he must endure. Everyone recognized his condition was worsening. Dropping her rake, she met him as he hobbled toward her, his mouth grimacing.

"Good to see you, Zeke. What brings you out here? It isn't Reyes, is it?"

"Boy is doing fine. But Lark got a telegram. Dan happened to be in town for supplies when he was handed a message. Macon had been holdin' it for almost two weeks. Figured one of us would be in town, sooner or later."

Reaching into his pocket, he withdrew the folded paper and handed it to her. She did her best to keep her hand from shaking as she held it. Her blue eyes held his unfathomable stare.

"You know what it says?"

"I know."

She skimmed the words. The date sent was August 20 from South Pass City. They were on their way north and had a good idea where to find Lars. Seemed they were now in the company of Gus Quaid. She'd heard of him and knew him to be a legend for his scouting with the Army.

"Nothin' bad, Hannah. Those men know how to take care of themselves. Nobody is fool enough to take on Cort in a gunfight. Nobody shoots straighter than Bryce. And Gus is a man you'd be glad to have on your side in any kind of fight. Bigger and faster than Lars. Best of all, he can track better than the Indians."

Relieved, she folded the missive and returned it to him. *Nothing bad.* Still, they hadn't faced Lars yet. Her anguish grew each day. "South Pass City?" she asked.

"Gold town. Looks like they're on the trail of that husband of yours."

"I'm truly sorry for all this trouble, Zeke."

"The trouble isn't you. It's that man you had the bad luck to marry. There's been enough mistakes all 'round and time they got fixed."

Releasing her breath, she took consolation in the fact that no one was hurt. As far as she knew. "Can you stay for coffee and pie?"

"Now I ain't never been able to turn down pie. I'll be up to the porch once I loosen the cinches."

"Zeke?" He stopped and pivoted. "Uh-oh. From that look on your face, I don't think I'm goin' to like your question. Go on."

She bit her lip. "I've been thinking I might take the train. Maybe find out where Lars is. He might listen."

Zeke snapped his hat from his head and whacked it hard against his leg, looking downright cross at her suggestion. "Little lady. You do that and you'll make things worse. I can't spare men to go out lookin' for you. Got nobody can escort you. Bryce and Cort would have my head if I let you do a fool thing like that. Not to mention all those women at the house. Don't need my head dented with a fry pan. Men got their pride. No man wants his lady coming to his rescue. So, hell no. Get that notion out of your head."

His spurs jangled against the hard packed dirt. He was right. It was a fool idea. But the idea stayed in her head because she didn't know what to do... except to worry.

———————

BANNACK. ONCE A booming gold town of thousands had now dwindled to about a hundred folks. Until the Saturday fight. That's when men of every shape and color roamed the streets. He found it hard to believe there could be so many miners left along Grasshopper and Beaver Creeks. They'd come from almost everywhere, looking for a good time gambling, whoring, and making money on the blood of those who fell under the blows from Lars. Men arrived in wagons and on horseback.

Tinny piano music likely awakened the dead and gave the town a macabre circus appearance, spreading in every direction of the main street. With a clear view of stiff corpses, displayed out front of the local undertaker, Bryce took note of the sign placards above the caskets, identifying the proprietor as doctor, barber, and undertaker.

Turning toward the rope-cordoned, makeshift arena beside the livery corral, he was itching to get on with it. Boards had been slapped over the dirt. Indeed, the town had taken on a festival atmosphere, minus the clowns and elephants. No doubt he and Lars would be center stage. Especially when he'd fight with every ounce of his strength before surrendering.

From what he could tell, there were five fighters. Christ. How did Lars take such a beating every other month, unless he was made of steel. Not for the first time, he thought about the money Lars must be hoarding. The sick man kept his new woman yet hardly provided for his own wife. Before tomorrow was over, Bryce aimed to make sure Hannah finally got her share of his proceeds... as well as her freedom. She deserved every ounce of gold and every cent of money Lars had stashed.

"Bryce," Cort called out.

When he turned, his perturbed looking brother strode to his side, kneading his scruffy face.

"What did you find out?"

"Lars shows up on the day of the fight. Stays away from saloons till after he pounds his opponents into mush."

"Figures. Where's Gus?"

"He's around."

Huh. He knew Cort and Gus well enough to know the two of them were concocting something. "I already told Gus. And you. I fight my own battles. I've been in fights before and did pretty well for myself."

"I didn't say anything." Cort folded his arms across his chest, a smirk on his mouth.

Pushing back his hat on his head, he raised an eyebrow. "You don't have to. Whatever you two cooked up, forget it. This is *my* fight."

"Not a chance we'll let you get killed. Lars is built like a mountain and twice as hard. You wouldn't last more than a round against him. Worse, you're scheduled for the number-two spot. Lars won't even be winded by then, so I've heard."

Jutting his chin, he said, "Cort. If you try to stop me, you'll piss me off. You wouldn't want me in *your* fight. Stay out of *mine*."

"Think about this *really* careful. Don't let your pride get you killed. I don't want to be the one left to tell Hannah that Lars broke you in half. Don't you know what that'd do to her? Knowing Hannah, she's most likely agonizing over what might be happening. Not to mention, Lark.

"Besides, Reyes needs his father. That boy can't take another loss. As for me, in your place, I'd want to squeeze the life out of Lars's fat head. But that's pride and a lot of other things that have no place here."

"I've already given it thought. It's settled. Now, where's Gus?"

"Eating a big steak. The restaurant opened for business with an improved menu."

Bryce's laugh died when he saw the black-suited man with three cowboys trailing behind him. "Son of a bitch. The black suit and his cohorts just walked into the saloon. Wish I knew what they were up to. The hair stands up on my arms when they're nearby."

"Let's worry about Lars. Don't get yourself distracted. I'll nose around about that dandy. Probably just an ordinary gambler."

Bryce leaned closer and muttered, "That's just it. Once I win the fight, I'm not leaving without getting his gold and money from that cabin. We'll be targets. They look like that's what their waiting for."

"We'll worry about them once this thing is over," Cort said.

"Cort. Ruby is another consideration. She won't let loose of his money or gold, even if Lars isn't around."

"She will if she's faced with armed men."

The thought of defending himself against a woman made him queasy. He'd never shot a woman and hoped it didn't come down to that. Because he was taking what belonged to Hannah if he had to walk through Hell to do it.

THE DAY ARRIVED under azure skies. Puffy clouds raced over the buildings when Bryce stepped out onto the iron-railed balcony of his hotel room to study the activity below. Sun beat down on the dusty streets and milling crowds. The spectacle of music, shooting contests, and horse racing filled Bannack with noise. Women in feathered hats lifted their skirts and picked their way over the ruts, careful to circle around the unwashed men who'd come down from the hills.

Piles of horse droppings drew flies in the unusual heat of fight day.

Sporadic shooting erupted, sending up shouts from farther down the street. Women in froufrous of silk and satin leaned from the windows of the two saloons facing the hotel. Wagonloads of miners clutched bottles of whiskey, hooting and hollering.

At the loud rap on his door, he turned, slipping his revolver from his holster. Standing to one side of the bolted door, he called, "Who is it?"

"Gus."

"I'm not changing my mind," he grumbled.

"Open up."

Bryce shoved his revolver into his holster and unlocked the door thinking he might as well get this over with. The door swung open. The buckskin-clad mountain man barged past him, slamming the door with the heel of his boot. They faced each other, neither smiling.

"Guess you're here to either convince me or drive me crazy with talk. Or were you planning a quick fist?"

"You're already crazy. If I wanted to stop you with my fist, I would've done it by now. Cort and me decided there was no use reasoning."

"Appreciate what you're trying to do. This is my fight."

"All right."

"Huh. No arguing?" Bryce raised an incredulous eyebrow.

"Yep. But there's some things you'll need to know. He fights dirty. No rules. Knee him hard if he tries to get you in the midsection. That seems to be what he does... from what I hear. He'll be twice as mean when he knows he's fightin' you. He'll goad you. You'll need to keep your lungs filled or you'll go down faster. Back off and get your breath."

When it seemed Gus was finished with the lecture, he relaxed. Until Gus added one more warning.

"Another thing. If things aren't goin' good, Cort and me will put a stop to it. We'll stay out of it as long as we can."

"That's your concession?"

"Uh-huh. Don't think I won't break Lars in half if you get in trouble. I'm not interested in your pride."

TWENTY-THREE

FIGHT DAY

SHIRTLESS, LARS'S BROAD, muscled arms gleamed and rippled as he faced his first opponent. Cort winced as the first man went down in fewer than two minutes, struggled to his feet, swayed, and went down again under his opponent's powerful punch to his chin, snapping his neck back. He watched Gus unbutton his shirt, slip out of it, and then hook it over a rail. Confidence in Bryce's ability to hold off this brick-hard man waned.

Lars stood over his unconscious challenger and nudged the man hard with his boot. Two men jumped the rope, dragging the bloodied man from the ring. Guzzling from a canteen, Lars dumped the rest over his head and shook off the water like a rain-soaked dog. With his eyes on Lars, Cort sidled closer to Gus. "If you take Bryce's place, he'll be mad as a poked rattler. But I don't give a damn. Be careful, Gus."

"Your brother is no match for this bastard. I am. That is a plain fact."

He watched Bryce step into the ring and then confer with the bartender. The bandage that had covered his jagged scar was gone, exposing the dark red scar. Bare to the waist, Bryce flexed his arms, readying himself to engage Lars. Cort checked his revolver, keeping his own option near his hand.

Looking toward the ring, Cort saw his brother's two-finger tap-of-the-temple greeting, taunting Lars. Then from the corner of his eye, he found a bare-chested Gus positioning himself to enter the ring. Amid hoots and hollers, the fight was on. With only five feet separating them, they circled each other. Lars muttered something and Bryce's face tightened with killing rage. There was nothing Cort could do but listen to their gibes and watch his brother get bloodied, expecting himself to cringe after each savage punch.

"Yeah. I'm the one who'll take you down, bastard. Remember who I am. *Bryce Enders.*"

"Well, now. This'll be a pleasure. Wife stealer. I'm about to put you six feet under."

"Welcome to try."

Cort watched and listened to the two of them deriding each other. When they were given a nod from the side, Lars circled and spit. Bryce remained still, his eyes following Lars. Never flinching. Just watching.

"He might do all right," Cort said to no one in particular, wincing at the blood on Bryce's shoulder from the bullet wound. "Christ," he mumbled between his gritted teeth.

Cort clamped down hard on his back teeth when Lars struck first. Helpless, he watched as Lars rammed his left fist into Bryce's jaw and then used his right to center a gut punch. Bryce fell backward against the rope, gasping and blinking. Cort released a held breath when Bryce straightened and landed his own punch into his opponent's midsection, then hooked a right into his opponent's jutting chin. When Lars's head snapped backward, Cort felt a moment of relief.

Looking stunned, Lars swiped his bloody nose and circled around Bryce. But Bryce didn't wait. Lowering his head, he charged, sending the bigger man backstepping. When Bryce's leg went out from under him, Lars caught him in his side with a hard blow from his boot. Cort's fists balled at his sides when he heard his brother's groan.

He moved closer to Gus. "I should step in," Gus said.

"No. Give him a little longer."

Scrambling onto his knees, his brother panted. Before Cort had a chance to shout a warning, Lars lifted his booted foot. Bryce must have seen it coming because he rolled to his side, then struggled back to his feet. Blood dripped from a slice on Bryce's head.

Before Cort gave thought to whether his brother could see clearly, Gus had already hurled himself over the rope and into the ring. There were collective jeers from the crowd, both fighters seemingly oblivious to the uproar. Whistling and catcalls egged on the fighters. They circled, eyes blazing like torches.

Cort swallowed against the lump in his throat. He had to make a decision here and now. Drawing his revolver, he watched and waited while Gus moved in closer to Lars's left side, trying to draw Lars away from Bryce. Lars wasn't having it and landed a powerful punch, snapping Bryce's head backward.

Dropping onto one bent knee, his brother swayed, sucked in a breath, then swiped his face. Cort cocked his revolver, even as his brother somehow found the willpower to stand. Swaying, Bryce lifted his bloodied fists while Gus edged along the rope, taking a step forward to block Lars's next move.

Incredibly, Bryce found the energy to stand and land several hard blows to the face and gut of his opponent, sending the man backward several steps. Blood ran from his brother's nose but his eyes were filled with rage—the only thing keeping him standing.

Engrossed in the fight and still gripping his revolver, Cort shifted his eyes in time to see a woman sitting atop a black horse. She wore a tattered straw hat, and her wild red hair was draped over the shoulder of her torn blouse. *Ruby.*

Before he supposed what she was about to do, she lifted a revolver and aimed. The blast sent onlookers ducking and cussing. Bryce turned his head just as she pointed the gun again. Gus slammed into Bryce, taking him down hard to the floor.

The second shot opened another hole in Lars's chest. Blood spurted from the wound in his head and the second bloomed across his sweat-slick chest. Cort wouldn't soon forget the surprised expression in the dying man's eyes nor his blood-smeared hand as he sank to his knees, a surprised look on his face. Then he flopped to his back in a bloody heap.

All the while, Cort kept his gun trained on the woman, her cold stare on the man she'd shot.

"Ruby," Lars mumbled.

That was his last word, whispered from a slack mouth. Cort still held his gun on the woman, ready to fire if she decided to turn her gun on his brother. Instead, she dismounted and dropped the gun from her hand. The quiet crowd slowly rose as one, looking at the spectacle of the man who'd never lost a fight.

"One of you pick up her gun so she doesn't do anyone else harm," Cort called out.

Several men scrambled, grabbing up the gun. Another took hold of the sobbing woman. Gus leaned over Bryce and helped him to his feet. Stepping over the rope, Cort shoved his gun into his holster then crouched beside the bloody body. Pressing a hand against Lars's neck, he found no pulse.

He looked up at his brother's bloodied face. "Dead."

"Not sorry," Bryce slurred.

Cort and Gus supported Bryce between them, expecting him to collapse—bruised, battered, and bleeding, but alive. Before they had time to help him to the nearest doctor, the bartender faced them.

"Got no money comin'. Ruby did him in. Bets off."

"Fine," Cort said. "We got what we wanted."

"Best leave soon as you can. Lots of folks ain't happy about losin' money on bets."

Cort shook his head and jerked his chin toward the limp woman, tripping along in the grip of a few men, leading her away. "You see to her?"

"See she gets to the marshal in Virginia City. Knew this would happen. Ruby was plumb crazy."

"Well, so was Lars."

"Can't argue that."

"You gotta doc around?" Cort asked.

"Yep. The undertaker. Good enough to clean up his bloody nose and set a bone, if needed."

By the time Gus pulled on his shirt and gathered up his weapons, most of the crowd had moved to the saloons. The only thing left to do was get Bryce patched and home in one piece. The body of Lars lay in the sun while a few townsfolk walked near for a closer look.

TIRED, BATTERED, AND in excruciating pain, Bryce rode between Gus and Cort, following the creek to Lars's abandoned cabin. Every muscle in his arms shot pain through to his neck and down his arms. He flexed his sore and swollen hands while gripping the reins. No matter, he'd pry up the loose floorboards with his bare hands to find the money and gold Hannah deserved. The windfall belonged to her for all her hardships.

After they'd dismounted, it didn't take more than an hour to find the stashed gold and greenbacks. Even if he had the disposition to grin about Lars's death, it would pain his jaw thanks to the man's powerful punches. Just now, he was pleased to be back in the saddle for the long ride home, looking forward to reaching South Pass for a much-needed hot bath to ease his bones and bruises.

Once they'd tied down the panniers on the pack animals, they led their mounts up the trail. Bryce twisted around in the saddle with the warning he'd been thinking about. "I want something understood. No telling Hannah or Lark about Ruby. So we have the story straight, Lars was killed by a gunman who had it in for him. I won't have her knowing her husband took up with a whore."

"How you gonna explain the cuts and bruises?" Gus asked.

"A fight with Lars. She knew him well enough to know he'd be disagreeable. While we're at it. Appreciate what you were willing to do for me, Gus. I didn't like you taking my place but I would've done the same in your shoes."

Gus laughed. "Sure woulda liked to get my hands on that son of a bitch. Got to say, you sure got a good right hook and held your own."

"Let's get out of here. We might make South Pass City in a week if we push hard and these packs don't slow us," Bryce said. With each motion of his horse, pain shot through him. Pain must be written on his face but his two companions kept to the grueling pace he set, knowing his best chance to recover lay ahead of them.

Ten Days Later

LOOKING UP FROM her desk, Hannah found Reyes gazing out of the window instead of working on his writing assignment.

"What has you daydreaming?"

"Wish he was back. Zeke said he can take care of himself."

"Zeke is right. Still, I understand how you miss him. I miss him, too."

"Are you and my father getting married?"

Hannah stood, cleared her throat, and paced a few steps to consider her answer. Turning, she looked toward him. "Your father and I talked about it. How would that be with you?"

"I like you. You're as nice as my real mother. Saw you kiss my father one time."

Heat creeped along her cheeks. Nervously, she smoothed her skirt and brushed a nervous hand across her face. "You do know it's rude to spy on adults, right?"

"Yeah. Sorry."

"But if he asks me when he comes back, I'd surely like to be his wife and your mother. How would that be? Not that I'd ever want you to forget your real mother."

He shrugged. "All right with me."

She smiled at his tepid response. Sensing he still had something else on his mind when he averted his face. She waited, her hands resting on her hips. "What else did you want to tell me?"

"I want to look for them. Zeke said there's another man with them. Maybe I could help."

"Yes. Gus Quaid. I've seen him here at the ranch. Been some time ago. A good friend of your uncle and aunt. Think he was an Army scout. I'd bet he's leading them home right now."

"Can we go meet them at the train?"

"As soon as we hear they're coming. In the meantime, finish the writing and I'll pack cookies to take back to the ranch. It's getting late."

Once she left for the kitchen, she stood beside the window, staring out at the range, her mind lost in a fog of worry. Drawing in a long breath, her lip twitched as it always did when something felt wrong. *October and they aren't back.*

North of South Pass City

SADDLE SORE, TIRED, and sullen, the three of them kept their tongues from wagging and their horses from stumbling. His bruises and shoulder had begun to heal, but every wrong move was punishing.

They'd left the Wind River behind and crossed the Big Sandy toward an escarpment where a stand of tall pines and willows offered shade. Stark, windswept plains spread out ahead of them. Following an old Indian trail through the mountains, their progress had been slowed by the extra horses. Getting home before the first snow was going to be tricky.

Gus pointed ahead of them. "Let's put up a camp in those trees. Need to give these horses a breather."

"I'm hungry enough to eat a steer, hide and all," Bryce agreed. "But I'd be satisfied with hot coffee."

The sound was akin to a sizzling fry pan then was followed by high-pitched zings. The bullets flew over their heads. More shots were fired, sending dirt into the air. Bryce kicked his horse into a run, leaving the packhorse to her own lookout. Cort rode wide of him and into the trees while Gus disappeared within the cover of outcroppings close behind.

Dismounting, they yanked rifles from saddle boots, positioning themselves for a good vantage.

"Dammit. Figured it would've happened sooner," Gus shouted. "Had a feelin' way back."

"What and who?" Bryce shouted.

"I been twitchy since we left Bannack. Sneakin' sonofabitches. The black suit must lead a band of road agents. Must've figured we got our hands on Lars's gold and followed us till we weren't paying attention," Gus hollered.

"Let's position ourselves so we can pick them off one at a time. Thin them out. Bunched up makes us easier targets," Bryce called.

Crouching low along a rock ledge, Bryce studied the tree line. Cort was somewhere in those shadows. Gus shimmied between rocks above him. Suddenly, shots came from every direction, splintering rocks around them.

Bryce fired at two men on the ledge to the right of Gus, sending them screaming to the boulder pile below. Rifle shots fired from the trees took down three horsemen charging from the river. Gus's rifle poked from the rocks, firing repeatedly at a target behind him higher up.

Bryce trained his attention on the trees. A fog of sulfur and gunpowder hung in the air. Twisting onto his side for a better vantage, a sudden splitting sharp pain blossomed in his back, like he'd been branded. Blinking against the sunlight, the sounds around him faded like clouds floating over the sun. Reaching for the edge of the rock where he rolled face down, he had the sensation of slipping from the ledge. He groaned and grabbed at air while hearing muffled voices and thudding boots. Her face was in his vision, then gone.

SUNLIGHT BURNED HIS eyes. The air was cold. Blinking, he tried to clear his vision. Pain rippled through his back with every jolt. He recognized the sound of plodding hooves. With each movement, he tensed his body and trembled with the exertion and stabbing pain. He moved his hand across a blanket.

The motion stopped. Gus's bearded face leaned over him. Their gazes held. In his muzzy brain, he failed to think what to ask. A canteen was tipped to his lips while his head was lifted. Water drizzled over his chin. He swallowed then licked his dry lips.

"What happened?" he croaked.

"You took a bullet in the back. Got you on a travois. Be in South Pass City by morning. They might still have a doctor."

"Cort?"

"He's just ahead. Takin' it slow as we can."

"Gus."

"You'll be all right."

"Numb. Can't feel my legs."

"You got a bullet in there. Doctor will pick it out."

"Don't want to live like this."

"Don't talk like that. Had to pull that brother out of his addled head once. No more talkin' about dyin'.'"

With every breath, he gulped against the sharp pain in his back. Then closed his eyes, focused on making his legs move. They didn't. When he tried to wiggle his toes, he felt nothing. Numb. *Dammit.* What would he do if he didn't walk? His son? The jouncing resumed and forced him to grasp the edge of the travois while he rethought life with Hannah. He wouldn't saddle her with an invalid. No matter that he'd love her for the rest of his life. Self-pity was filling him, but he was at a loss to stop it.

If he didn't have his boy to consider, he'd use his revolver to put an end to this. But he couldn't do that to Reyes. Or Cort. Not now. Not *yet.* Until he knew for sure.

TWENTY-FOUR

THE INVALID

C ORT PACED THE surgeon's parlor, stopping to pick up a dusty book from a shelf then slapping it down without opening it. At the sound of bootheels striding across the porch, he turned. The door opened to a cold gust of wind and a haggard Gus who ducked inside.

Poking his chin toward the closed surgery door, Gus asked, "Any word from Doc Merrick?"

"No word. Did you send those telegrams?"

"One to Doctor Collier. Asked him to meet us in Green River. Briefly told him about Bryce. The other to Lark. Gave her the news as easy as I could."

"Thanks. Guess we just wait. Last I saw him... he looked bad." His gut clenched at recollecting the sight of his brother's ghostly face and wrenching pain. "Doc has him on his stomach—partly conscious and groaning. Makes me sick to see him like that, much less hear his pain."

"He's tough. Already survived that gunfight a while back. He givin' him laudanum?"

"What little he has."

Both looked up when the surgery door swung open. The gray-haired doctor swiped a hand across his red, tired eyes, then pinched the bridge of his nose. After a few moments, he steadied his gaze on both of them.

Sucking in his breath, Cort expected the worst. It was all he could do not to shove the doctor out of the way and find out for himself if Bryce were still breathing.

"Thought I heard voices. Good you're both here. He's bruised badly. Think his ribs took a pounding, maybe one broken. Bandaged his middle snug. An old gun wound in his shoulder got torn open a bit. Bleeding is stopped. Applied some stitches and ointment."

Cort ground out, "What about the bullet in his back? Said he's numb and can't move his legs."

"Expect so. Got some laudanum down him to ease the pain and get him to sleep. Gave me a chance to probe. That bullet is sitting too near his spine. I'm not as versed in this kind of thing. Can't get it out without doing more damage. Best hospital for this is in Philadelphia. Since you have Alfred Collier on your side, he's your next best chance. He's younger. Had more surgical experience back East. I hope you convinced him to come here."

"Christ. We got to move him to Green River to meet Collier. Can he be moved?"

"Normally, I'd say no. But I can't do anything for him without Alfred's hands and scalpel. Need to fix up a wagon with plenty of bedding and some way to keep him still. With luck, if we leave today, we can get him there in a few days. The cold weather is setting in. That's why we need to move sooner rather than later. Of course, I'll go along that far and do what I can to be of help. Not much need for me here these days."

"You heard him. Can you get a wagon together? Whatever it costs."

"I'll see to it," Gus replied. "And Cort. He's tough like all the Enders."

When the door closed behind him, Cort took that moment to ask the doctor to lay out the truth. "What are his chances? Don't sugarcoat it."

The deep-creased frown of the physician's face was answer enough.

"Collier is the best at this. Knowing him, he'll do the surgery right away. That's the best I can say."

Cort pressed his linked fingers at the back of his neck and paced. While not a direct answer, it was the answer he expected.

"All right." Dropping his hands to his sides, he looked toward the doctor's stoic expression. "Got no choice. Let's get him ready."

The first thing he saw was his brother's bare back, bathed in sunlight from the window. Moving beside the bed, he studied the bloody bandage across his back. Bryce's cheek rested against a pillow. There was a steady rise and fall of his back. Pulling up a chair, he straddled it. And waited.

"I'm awake," Bryce mumbled.

Cort leaned over his brother's still form. "How you feeling?"

"Like hit by train then kicked by a mule."

If the circumstances weren't so serious, Cort would be inclined to chuckle. "The bullet in your back is near your spine. Doc Collier is meeting us at Green River to get it out."

"Merrick said can't do it."

"Collier will patch you up. Then we'll get you home. Course, we got to take you in a wagon for a couple uncomfortable days. Try to go easy."

"Do what you have to."

Cort stood but Bryce stopped him. "Did you kill them?"

"We figure there were about seven of them. Must've trailed us for some time. Maybe met up with the others. Killed all but two. Think I winged them. Didn't take time to go after them."

"Thanks, Cort."

"You can thank me by getting well."

"If I don't make it. Reyes."

"He won't be going anywhere. But you'll by damned make it. Hannah would kill me if I let you die."

When there was no response, he crouched beside the bed. His brother's eyes were squeezed closed. But he knew he was still awake. "You'll make it, Bryce."

His brother's face was taut with emotion. There was no reply.

HANNAH RODE UP to her barn after looking for strays. The sound of a rattling wagon caught her attention just as she dismounted. Looking over her shoulder, she saw Tangle guiding a team and wagon across the creek. At the sight of Theresa and Lark seated beside him, her heart stopped. Zeke rode beside the wagon, his face drawn taut.

Something was very wrong. It was the same feeling she'd had every night. By the time she'd loosened the cinches and closed the gate, the wagon drew up.

Not one of them smiled in greeting.

Bracing for bad news, she straightened her back and lifted her chin, but her knees threatened to sink. Tugging her coat around her, she shaded her eyes against the late fall sun then darted a questioning look at Lark. Tangle averted his usual animated face. Theresa tucked her chin and closed her eyes. Zeke sat atop his horse and leaned forward... looking lost for words.

"One of you tell me. Now. Whatever it is, I've got to hear it," Hannah snapped.

Tangle jumped down and helped Lark and Theresa to the ground while Zeke remained mounted, his shoulders hunched inside his wool coat. Lark's golden-eyed gaze held hers.

"No good way to bring bad news. Cort sent a telegram. Came a couple days ago. So no telling how long they've been in trouble."

"Go on." Hannah swallowed and tamped down the wail that waited to erupt.

"It seems that Cort, Gus, and Bryce were on their way home from Bannack. Almost to South Pass City, we think. They were bushwhacked. Bryce took a bullet in the back. Alfred Collier is already on the U-P to Green River to meet them."

"How bad is it?"

"Figure bad enough. Didn't say much in the telegram. You need to know. There was mention that he can't move his legs."

"*No.*" She grasped at air, dizzy as her heart pounded in her ears. Looking up from where she slumped to the ground, she drew in a breath of the chilly air. Zeke kneeled beside her. Her head rested against

Lark's lap while fireflies circled above her. She'd done what she swore she'd never do—fainted.

Zeke's hoarse voice said, "You've got more backbone than almost anybody. You need to pull on that strength because Bryce will need you. So, if you've a mind to go to Green River with us…. you need to get your things together. Can't sit here with a job that needs doin'."

She pushed onto her elbows with Lark's help. Tangle grasped her arms, lifting her to her feet. She drew in several deep breaths. "I'm going. You're right, Zeke. Give me a moment to pack. Will you be coming, Lark?"

"I would if not for the baby and the one I'm carrying. Theresa, Tangle, and Zeke are going with you. Mason and Alonzo will tend your place."

With a last look at her friends, she said, "I'll just need my valise and medical bag. I assure you, I'm not usually the fainting kind."

Not waiting to hear their response, she demanded her head to clear as she marched to the house. Tossing whatever she thought she'd need into her satchel, she tugged on her gray dress and waistcoat. Giving the room a final inspection, she picked up her medical bag, valise, and reticule and then strode to the waiting wagon. For only the briefest moment, she considered Lars. Then he was erased forever.

SWEAT SOAKED THE pillow beneath his cheek. Pain shot through his back with every jolt. They'd resorted to giving him sips of whiskey, but the stuff wasn't potent enough. After the next big lurch, there was no hope of biting back his yowl. It felt like he'd been ripped apart with a dull hatchet. When the wagon stopped abruptly, he heaved the whiskey he'd just swallowed. From the corner of his eye, he saw the old doctor leaning over him. He swiped his sweating brow and dabbed the vomit from his mouth.

"Sorry. Not much we can do about the wagon ruts."

"How far?" Bryce mumbled.

From his other side, Gus said, "No more'n an hour. Hang on."

The sour spit in his mouth kept him from letting loose a string of cuss words. Drifting into blessed darkness where pain stayed at the edge of consciousness wasn't what he wanted. He'd always clawed his way out.

This time, he didn't have the energy. So he let go.

The next time he opened his eyes, he lay on his stomach against a soft mattress that wasn't moving. A basin and piles of towels and bandages sat near him, blocking his view of the wall. Hearing muffled voices from somewhere on the other side of where he lay, splitting pain in his ribs stopped him from rolling over. Each time he'd tried, it nearly sent him sinking into pain-filled darkness. His neck was stiff and cramped. Warm drool pooled beneath his chin. Weepy with helplessness, he scrubbed his fist across his itchy nose.

"Cort?" he called out.

"I'm here." There were footsteps and his brother's glazed, red-rimmed eyes peered at him from where he crouched.

"You drunk?"

"Not yet. Sure would like to be. Why?"

"Eyes red. Where are we?"

"You're in what serves as the surgeon's office in Green River. Train arrived. Gus went to get Collier. Doc Merrick is here, too. He got together what might be needed for the surgery."

"Might not make it."

"You say that again and we'll settle with fists once this is over."

"If I stand."

"You *will*. Got no time to argue. Hear Collier's voice. I better go find out what he's got to say. Besides, I'm not much of a nurse. Just so you know, my eyes are red because I need some sleep. Sooner you get better the better I'll be."

"Tell them hurry."

"I will. Hannah would make a better nurse."

"Don't tell her."

"What if she already knows?"

"Keep her away." Clenching his teeth against the pain, he used his arms to lift his upper body from the bed but dropped back down with a groan. "Don't tell."

"Ahem. Sorry to interrupt but I need to examine my patient. Mind if I take your place?"

His brother rose, making room for the stern-faced Alfred Collier. Standing aside out of his sight, the doctor flipped the sheet and blanket out of the way. From where he lay, he couldn't see the surgeon's eyes.

"Hello, Bryce. We've met a few times. You're sure as hell banged up from the look of the bruises and cuts. Seems like you brothers must be competing for the most bullet holes and bruises. Just so you know, this will hurt for a few minutes while I probe. Do you want some more laudanum?"

"No."

There was a sensation of something cold lower in his back. He clenched his teeth and tensed at the sudden burning pain threading along his spine, reaching north into his shoulder. Try as he might, he couldn't squelch the bellow hurdling from deep inside his chest, sending him to sweet darkness.

"HE'S OUT COLD. But I've seen enough."

The resigned expression of both doctors' faces said it all. Cort looked from Alfred Collier to Doctor Merrick. There would be no promises. "Can you get that bullet out or not?" Cort demanded.

"The long and short answer is I don't know. Took plenty of bullets out of soldiers during the war, and since then. But seldom saw any this close to the spine. If he were near Philadelphia, there'd be a good chance. As it is, I might do more damage. Doing nothing would leave him in awful pain for whatever time he had left before an infection racks his body. Got to go in there. No other choice. Unless you want me to give him something and wait for the end. If I do what I can, the worst... he'll die. Or not walk again. But he also might come out all right. I'll do my best. That's all I can promise."

Swiping his hand across his beard, Cort studied his boots. "I don't know. This decision should be his."

"He's in no condition to make a reasonable decision. I will tell you that Omaha has a new hospital. They got some younger and impressive doctors. But I just don't know if he'd survive getting there. The more he's moved, the more chance he'll never walk. Or worse. This is up to you."

"Christ." Cort sighed. "Okay, I'll have to live with it. *Do it.* When will you start?"

"As soon as early morning. Merrick will assist me. Brought everything medically I think I'll need. I'll give him some chloroform to knock him out for the surgery. It's getting late in the day. Best we start when the sun comes up, after I've had some sleep."

"Gus and I can take turns watching him."

"From the looks of you and Gus, you could both use sleep. Better eat and take turns."

"After this is over, I'll sleep."

"Suit yourselves. See you here early."

TWENTY-FIVE

THE NURSE

TANGLE AND ZEKE dozed, slouched against the seats where they sat across from the women. Theresa's head lolled with the sway of the train. From Hannah's view from the window, the land was flat, dotted with endless sagebrush and juniper. Imagining what it had been like for Bryce out there, searching those camps and eating by campfires, she hoped that same fortitude would get him through this.

When she glanced again toward the men, Zeke's eyes were open and studying her. He winked and she offered a quick smile. Looking away from her, he shook Tangle awake. Grumbling, Tangle opened his eyes.

"We get there?" Tangle croaked.

"Looks like we're there. See the tops of buildings from this side."

Theresa opened her eyes, smoothed her skirt, and spluttered, "'Bout time we got there."

For her part, Hannah could hardly keep from jumping up from her seat at the sight of buildings ahead. Too jittery to sleep, she'd managed to swallow some of a sandwich from the basket Lark sent along. All she wanted and needed was to see him. With her deepening sense of guilt, she was on the edge of madness, believing she'd brought this down on him. She'd never forgive herself if the worst happened. He'd sacrificed too much to save her from Lars. A man she hated and not worth her thought. Thinking back, she'd had the power to stop Bryce with a word. If only she'd agreed to accept the truth of what Lars was.

The train bumped forward, the whistle blasted once and then again, and the engine slid back, vibrating to a shuddering stop. Hannah waited while Zeke and Tangle stood, leading the women from the train car. They found Gus waiting beside a wagon, waving them forward, his expression rigid.

Once they'd closed the distance, Gus didn't mince words. "Glad you're here, Hannah. Theresa. Before we get to the physician's surgery, you should know how things stand."

Hannah brushed past him. She needed to see for herself. Tired and fueled with impatience, she'd do her own assessment. Gus grasped her arm, bringing her up short.

"Ma'am. You have to hear what I've got to tell you."

"Take us there immediately," she insisted. "I won't be put off. Whatever's wrong, I'll face it."

"He's in surgery. The doctor has been workin' on him for hours. Might be best you wait at the hotel and rest. Nothin' you can do."

She lifted her chin. "Zeke, Tangle, and Theresa are free to settle at the hotel. I'm going straight there. I need to be there when he wakes up."

Gus shrugged and assisted her to the wagon seat, setting her carpetbag in back. The others climbed in and settled against the blankets. Once the gear and bags were stowed, Gus set the team of horses in motion. No one spoke. She gave cursory interest to the cattle pens, houses, saloons, and the impressive brick courthouse.

Gus brought the wagon to a halt in front of what appeared to be a private white clapboard house. Tangle and Zeke helped the women step down. Hannah marched up to the door, leaving the others trailing behind. Stepping inside, she was assailed by smells of carbolic acid, whiskey, and a hint of laudanum. Someone had thought to open a window where a soft breeze lifted the worn curtains.

A heavily bearded man leaned forward on his elbows, his face cradled in his hands. When he dropped his hands from his haggard face and looked toward her, she gasped. She hardly recognized Cort. His shirt was splattered with blood. Sunken, bloodshot eyes stared at hers as though not seeing.

"Cort." His agonized expression nearly made her cry. She swallowed, searching for what to say. Those deep blue-gray eyes were darker and sunken. Wanting to avert her eyes at his pain, she held his pitiful gaze... mirroring his agony.

"Imagine I'm not much to look at. Haven't had much time for cleaning up. How's Lark?"

"She stayed behind with the baby. She's safe. But worried."

"Glad she stayed home. No use in all of us wringing our hands."

Moving closer, she kneeled in front of him. "Tell me how he is. The *truth*, please."

"They've worked on him for the last three hours. Heard him howl a few times. Must've knocked him out again with chloroform. God, Hannah. He's been in pain for too long. Maybe a week or more. Lost track."

"Will they let me see him?"

"Once they finish. I've already been threatened with death for opening that door."

"How did this happen?"

"We left Bannack and were riding north of South Pass City. Maybe a week out, we should've realized we'd been followed. The same bunch who'd watched us in Bannack. Got too relaxed. That was when all hell broke loose. Ambushed us. Took cover best we could. Bryce caught a bullet in his lower back."

"But the doctor can remove it and he'll be fine." That was what she kept telling herself.

Stillness settled between them. He dropped his chin and gazed at the floor. She pressed her hand against her stomach and felt an urge to retch. At the same time, she wanted to touch his sullen face.

"What did the doctor tell you?"

"Said he can get the bullet out. No promises about walking again. And no promise he'll live through this because it's too close to his spine.

Bryce said he couldn't feel his legs. I'm worried about his frame of mind. He's not the kind who'd want to be an invalid."

"He'll walk after they get it out. I'm not leaving his side."

Cort's mouth thinned at her pronouncement. "Not sure it's a good idea, Hannah. He loves you. But he asked me not to tell you about this. He won't be happy you're here. Figures he'll be useless, and he doesn't want you saddled with him."

The others took seats and listened without speaking. Rising to her feet, she met each one of their drawn faces. "I'm not giving up hope. And none of you better, either."

Zeke's eyes pinned hers. Theresa walked into a back room with her face averted. The others stared at the wall rather than at her—all of them grim.

"He will walk. Not one word otherwise." In the silence that followed, her heart crumbled because she divined what they were all thinking. She pivoted and pressed her head against the wall and cried.

———————

GUS HEAVED A sack of potatoes and beans from the wagon and Tangle shouldered the flour through the back door. The kitchen smelled of coffee and bread. Zeke and Theresa had found ways to busy themselves, setting out sandwiches. At the least, the scent of blood and chloroform seemed purged. Even so, there didn't seem much interest in eating. Just keeping busy kept the weight of worry easier to chew.

Crowded around the small table, Theresa admonished them about how whiffy they'd all become. Something about sheepherder's socks. Stirring her coffee, Hannah managed a few nibbles of a sandwich, not sure if she tasted anything. There was a pall over the room as the parlor clock ticked off the minutes.

When the gaunt-looking doctors appeared, Cort lurched from his seat. Hannah jerked her head up and took her place beside him. They waited like statues as Dr. Collier plowed his fingers through his tousled gray-brown hair. He looked from Cort and then back to her.

"Did everything we could. He's sleeping for now. When he wakes, he'll be in considerable pain. Give him a half spoon of laudanum every four hours. No more. We'll be at the hotel if you need us. Need to sleep and then get food. He'll be out for some time. From the looks of you, I advise you to follow our example."

"We got some food set out. You're welcome to it," Theresa said.

Alfred glanced down at his blood splattered clothes. "Best we both head to the hotel. Thanks for the offer."

"Before you go. How about the bullet? His legs?" Cort asked.

"We won't know anything till he wakes and we can find out. Even then, he might not have feeling for a long while. In the worst case, as I've told you, he might not use those legs again. I got the bullet out clean. Had to do some sewing and repairs but don't know if it'll be enough. He's heavily bandaged. Giving him another day, then we'll roll him to his back. In the meantime, see if you can spoon water and broth into him. Won't be easy."

"When can he travel back to the ranch?" Hannah asked.

"I'd wait four or five days. He'll need to be flat on a stretcher for the trip. Make arrangements with the rail conductor."

"I'll go sit with him. In case he wakes."

"That'd be a good idea. Maybe you can work out a schedule. He'll need sips of water as often as you can, once he wakes. Watch for fever. Don't move him till I see him tomorrow. Then maybe we can get him more comfortable."

Hannah pressed her hand against the doctor's arm. "Bless you both for everything. We are in your debt."

The elder doctor's ruddy face favored her with a wan grin. Dr. Collier's jaw tautened, and he nodded. "Get some rest. All of you."

Once they left, she didn't know how long she stood there, listening to her heart pounding in her ears. The others sat in quiet thought. She had to make her legs move.

Cort was the only one to speak. "Go on. I'm too raw to go in yet. It'll be good when he wakes to see you. No matter what he says."

From the doorway of the surgery room, she was met with Bryce's still form beneath a mound of sheets. Laying on his stomach, she studied the steady rise and fall of his back. His head rested against his left cheek and his thick dark hair fanned his forehead. He looked peaceful. Coming closer, she found his eyes closed and his mouth slack.

Her fingers smoothed his hair from his forehead. He was too warm. Then her eyes stilled on the sight of the bruises and crusting cuts on this side of his face. Her fingers touched the yellow streaks. One eye was somewhat swollen. It was clear as day from his puffy nose and bruises, he'd been pummeled. *Lars.* Her hand withdrew and formed a balled fist. How she *hated* Lars.

"Oh, Bryce. What happened?" *Had it been Lars?*

She squeezed her eyes closed. There was certainty that Lars was responsible. If it were possible to despise Lars any more, she would. Beneath Cort's unkempt beard were signs of crusted blood. Looking across her shoulder at the sound of the door, she found Cort filling the threshold, his eyes fixed on his brother.

"Guess he'll sleep for a while," he whispered.

"When he wakes, I'll try to get him to swallow water, and hope he doesn't choke. On his stomach for so long can't be comfortable."

"After the jostling getting him here, it's a wonder he made it at all. That bullet, where it was. I didn't want to move him. Doctor Merrick wasn't willing to try getting it out. Thank God we had Collier here."

"Cort?"

"Hmm?"

"The bruises. Cuts. What happened in Bannack?" God help her. She needed to know.

"That's for him to tell. I promised him."

"Can you tell me if I'm still married to Lars?"

"Lars is no longer your husband."

Closing her eyes, she thought of the cost to set her free. It had been too high. Indebted and filled with abiding love for Bryce, she couldn't imagine living without him.

Cort cleared his throat. "The others went to the hotel. I'll start arranging for his train ride home by the end of the week. Take turns watching over him. Guarantee he won't be easy to get along with while he's healing."

"Thank you for everything, Cort."

Taking in the room, her gaze settled on the probes, scalpels, and a bloody bullet resting in a basin. The doctor's bag sat on the floor beside the bed. A brown bottle of laudanum sat on the table. The goat-smell of carbolic acid lifted on the breeze from the partly opened window.

"I'll take that bowl and the doc's instruments and see they get cleaned," Cort offered.

She hardly remembered Cort moving around the room and leaving. When she finally settled into a chair beside the bed, she dropped her face into her trembling hands. Leaning her head back against the chair cushion, she fell into a restless sleep.

A groan jerked her awake. She shoved strands of hair from her face, not knowing how long she'd slept. The light from the window was dim. A blanket draped her lap. When she looked toward Bryce's face, his eyes were open and he was staring.

"Can't be you," he slurred.

Tossing the blanket aside, she knelt on the floor and touched his head. He was still too warm.

Blinking, he said, "It *is* you."

"I'm here. I'm not *you*. I'm Hannah."

One corner of his mouth curved in what she surmised was a half-smile. "Bullet out?"

"Yes. Are you in pain?"

"Hell, yes. Thirsty, too."

She stood and poured water from the pitcher into a glass. As she knelt again, she realized the dilemma. He twisted his body to accommodate her but grimaced at his feeble attempt.

"Can't move legs."

"That will come in time. I'll get help to roll you enough to drink."

"No. Stay. Talk first."

Returning the glass to the table, she offered her full attention. He moved his hand, and she grasped it. "Hannah. You should know. Lars."

"He signed the divorce papers."

"No. Dead."

Relief not sadness. Satisfaction not disapproval. Contentment not loneliness. Guilt and solace. All these emotions washed through her. What kind of wife felt nothing with the news of her husband's demise? Drawing a breath, she said, "The bruising is because of Lars. Isn't it?"

"Yes. Killed by someone else. Wasn't me."

Sighing, she stroked a shaking finger across his scruff. "You've suffered so much for me."

"Gold. Money. Cort has it. Start new life."

"*We'll* start a new life."

The color of his eyes deepened to steel. The door opened and she welcomed Cort's intrusion. His arrival had averted cross words between them over this misguided surrender. Bryce's eyes turned from hers to center on his brother.

"Figured you'd be waking up by now. Theresa will be in with broth. Once the doc gets here in the morning, we'll roll you over. Gonna hurt like hell's own fire."

"Getting used to it."

Clearing his throat, Cort said, "Hannah. Would you tell Gus he's needed here? You eat something while I tend to Bryce for a bit. Personal things."

Dismissed. Damn the bullet that might very well still kill the man she loved one piece at a time, and maybe destroy the life they'd planned to share. She would fight for him. And for Reyes. Both of them needed this man... whether he walked or not.

TWENTY-SIX

REJECTION

"WAY I SEE it, we have two options. Keep him lying on his stomach to avoid any worse pain… starving him to death in the meantime. Or make it quick and get him onto his back so we get water and broth down his throat," Alfred Collier explained.

Bryce couldn't find enough spit to swear. Everybody talked around him like he had no damn say at all. Cort darted him a glance but gave his own opinion.

"That isn't much choice. Gus, Tangle, and me will move him so quick he won't have time to yelp. Zeke's out helping the women fix some food. That should keep them from charging in here like the Billies on Gettysburg."

"Do it. Tired of bein' on stomach," Bryce grumbled.

Someone plugged his mouth with a leather belt. Biting down, he discovered his brother was right. He didn't have time to yell when the thunderbolt struck his back with fury. Clenching his jaw, sweat rolled over his eyes and the room dimmed. He figured he was near the other side of sanity. Squeezing his eyes tight, he prayed for the pain to ease.

Hands grasped his arms and tugged him. A pillow was stuffed behind him. Unclenching his jaw, the strap dropped away and he swallowed air like a man who'd almost drowned. Someone dabbed his brow with a damp towel.

"Bryce. Lean your head back. Try to sip this water." Cort held a glass to his mouth.

The edge of the cup tilted against his parched mouth, leaving time for water to slip down his dry throat. There was a pause before he managed a second sip. Through slitted eyelids, he saw *her*. An angel on the other side of the room. Watching. The next gulp was bitter.

"Don't need *that,*" he said. "Don't want to be drugged."

"Bryce. It'll help you sleep a while. Just a little. Hear me?"

It was the doctor's voice coaxing him. But he didn't want to hear *his* voice. He wanted to hear *hers*. Most of all, he didn't want to feel numb.

Fighting the drowsiness, he struggled to find Hannah in his vision. Clawing against the ledge where he'd been shot, he gave into slumber against his will. But her rose scent followed him.

Morning Light

OPENING HIS EYES, he found himself half propped against pillows. There was a dull throbbing in his back and a sting in his shoulder. The doctor walked into the room, carrying a glass. He hesitated.

"See you're awake. Think you can handle the glass on your own?" the doctor asked.

Bryce looked up at the tall surgeon, determined to prove he could manage. Even as his hand shook with the effort, he swallowed.

"Looks like you're coming back to life, brother." Bryce's eyes swiveled to find Cort seated in the shadowed corner.

"Depends. When will I be able to move my legs?"

"Talk like that will only make you crazy, brother. It'll come in time," Cort muttered.

The doctor had already pressed his stethoscope against his chest but hadn't yet corroborated his brother's assessment.

"Strong heart. Lungs sound good. Now for the truth, from you,

Bryce. If you lie to your doctor, it gets you into more trouble than lying to your wife. Got you sitting up. That hurting your lower back?"

"Hurts some. Not like it did when I was in that wagon."

The doctor straightened without comment and retrieved something from his bag. "Good sign. I'm going to try something with your legs. Let me know if you feel anything."

Keeping his eyes on the doctor's movements, the sheet was lifted. "You feel that?"

"Nope. What was I supposed to feel?"

"I stuck your foot and leg with a needle."

"They're numb. If I didn't see them for myself, I'd swear they weren't there. Will I get them back?" He figured if he repeated the question enough times, he'd get a straight answer.

Bryce glanced at Cort who then looked toward the doctor. During the silence, the doctor covered his legs and snapped his bag closed. Collier's mouth narrowed, seeming to consider an answer.

"Maybe. I've seen cases like this where a man gets feeling back over time. While I think there's a good chance, I can't give you the promise you want. All we can do is give your back time to heal. End of the week, we'll have you in a special bed for the ride back to Ogallala. Then… just have to give it time and see. The men at the ranch can take care of seeing your legs get moved. Otherwise, you'll lose muscle."

"Thanks for the honesty. Helps me with my decisions."

"You'll get through this, Bryce," Cort interjected.

"Neither of you is in my place."

Clearing his throat, the doctor added, "I'll leave you two to discuss this. I've got a train to catch. Meet you back in Ogallala. I've left instructions with Cort and Hannah."

As soon as the door closed, his brother's face hardened. Cort turned a chair around and straddled it. Bryce held up his hand attempting to stay whatever argument Cort had in mind.

"Before you start the lecture, let me ask you this. What if you couldn't walk again? Protect Lark. Handle roundups and trail drives. Ride beside your men."

Cort retorted, "What if I lost my eyesight and never saw Lark again or rode a horse and couldn't even find my food on my damn plate?"

"Gus let that piece of information slip while we were still in Montana. He didn't elaborate. Now seems like a good time."

"You're about to hear how Gus saved my ass from something worse than blindness. It was plain self-pity. I almost lost the woman I love because of it. Sitting helpless in a prison cell, that gave me time to think."

Bryce flinched at the picture his brother painted. Staring fixedly, he nodded. "All right. I'm listening. That doesn't mean I'll change my mind about anything."

———————

WITHIN THE DIMNESS of the room, Bryce closed his eyes, reliving the shootout. What he should've done different. Then he replayed all that had befallen Cort, considering whether his brother's situation paralleled his own. Sightless, behind bars where human voices were vague and distant, those were part of his brother's tormented past. Knowing that he hadn't been there to help—ate at him. But none of that changed his own situation. Besides, Cort married Lark before he'd lost his sight. Damned if he'd saddle Hannah with a helpless husband. Setting her free was kinder.

Deep in thought, he lifted one eyelid at the sharp rap on the door. It had to be Hannah. Opening both eyes, he shoved himself up on his elbows and settled against the pillows. Deciding to get this discussion over with once and for all, he called out. "Come in."

The door swung open. Hannah gripped a tray while Theresa eyed him from over her shoulder. Prepared for what he would say to Hannah, he braced his emotions and crooked his finger in invitation. Her mouth was pursed as she set the tray down. "I'm not going to bite. Smells good, whatever it is."

Beautiful in a blue dress, when she faced him, he drank in her delicate face and sweet freckles on her nose. He could almost believe that everything would work out. Until he tried to move his legs, reminding him how useless he was and might always be.

"It's chicken soup and fresh bread. Time to get your strength back," she said cheerily.

"It'll do. Thanks."

Leaning over him, she tucked the sheet around his waist, which afforded him time to fasten his attention on her profile. The scent of fresh soap and hint of lilacs were enticing as she moved around the bed, tucking the sheet.

"Do you think you can feed yourself or do you want my help?"

Now that he needed to get said what needed to be said, his disposition took a turn. He didn't want to be an invalid. Nor did he want to be treated as one. Her fussing reminded him of how helpless he was. And how tied down she'd be. "I can manage," he snapped. Even to himself, his voice had turned frosty.

Her hands stilled as she folded the blanket, dropping it at the end of the bed. Then she straightened, annoyance written on her face when she came to the side of the bed.

He looked up at her. "Hannah?" Without warning, he gripped her wrist and patted the bed beside him. "Stop fussing and sit. Let's at least talk this out."

At her hesitation, he added, "Please."

She sat, smoothing the skirt of her dress with her usual primness. He folded her hand in his where it rested beside him. When she sat back beside him, she leaned her head against his good shoulder then sighed. Her sweet scent and the soft touch of her silky hair made him feel alive. For a moment, he imagined they had nothing but a good life ahead. Until he cast his eyes at his motionless legs.

"We leave tomorrow. Home," she murmured.

Curling an arm around her protectively, his mind ordered his legs to move. When they wouldn't, reason warred with his pride. He couldn't provide for her. Not without his legs. The only solution was to make that clear. On an indrawn breath, he found enough courage to sever his heart.

"Move on with your life. Without me in it."

Lifting her head, her eyes flitted across his face. She drew away from him as though she'd been burned. The distress written on her face would forever stay with him. The blue of her eyes deepened, and he felt like he'd kicked a puppy.

"I'll do no such thing. You asked me to marry you. I'm holding you to it. You said Lars was killed."

God. He'd never tell her how he died. That would go to his grave. "Hannah. Just in case you hadn't noticed, there's a good chance I won't walk again. If we married and decided to start a ranch or have more babies, how in hell do you think I could run the place or provide for you? I can't live off my brother's charity. Particularly when he has both a wife and son with more to come. Besides, I don't even know if I'm able to... do the things a man does with his wife."

At the sight of her sullen, tear-filled eyes he considered slamming his skull against the headboard. He'd come this far. It was time to finish what he'd started.

"What I don't want is a wife fussing over me, trying to keep my spirits up day after day while I sit in a chair. It will be bad enough for Reyes. I won't have you tending my personal requirements—emptying my bedpan and bathing me like I was a child. Cort can be a father to Rey. But a broken husband is not what I want for you. Lars's money will build you another ranch house. Better yet, a dress shop in town."

"Are you quite finished? Because you've certainly made quite a few decisions for me."

"Not *quite*. The doctor told Cort that I need to have somebody massage my legs every day. I won't have you do that. Who'll dress me and shave me?"

"Now are you finished?"

"Isn't that enough? I'm sure you'll fight me on this decision."

"Like a wildcat. You don't know for sure that you'll never walk. The doctor said you might. He never said never. Besides, even if you don't walk, I love you and Reyes. You're my family. I'm not letting go that easily."

"If I refuse to see you when we get back? Then what?"

"So you plan to close yourself off. Let me ask you some questions, then. What if one of the hands at the ranch decided to court me? How would you feel if I married someone else? And what if you walked again? And in the meantime, I'd moved on?"

"I'd be jealous. Can't deny that. You're free to make that choice. I won't interfere. Not exactly like I can land a punch to any of your suitors."

"You are a stubborn man, Bryce Enders. Since you're so determined to be contrary, you don't need me to sit here chattering on like a fool with a fool. Tangle will be back to work those legs."

Stubborn, aggravating woman. What did he have to do to convince her that he couldn't be a husband? Before he knew what she was about, she stood and bent over him. Swallowing at the look of temper in her eyes, he expected a slap. Instead, she closed the distance until they were nose-to-nose and kissed him. Fool that he was, he returned the kiss. One hand cupped her face, and he was twice the fool when he deepened the kiss.

Damn the woman. He swam to the surface and slid his hands along her arms, setting her back. That darned, tantalizing smile irked him. She'd proven a point, but he wouldn't let it happen again.

"Well. You confirmed you still want my kiss. Don't fret. I'm not giving up. Neither will I let you give up. Finish the soup. I'll be back in a short while for the tray, at which time, we won't need to speak."

The door closed and he eyed the soup. That bowl of soup and chunk of bread challenged him. Reaching, he lifted the bowl to his mouth then sipped from the tilted rim, ignoring the spoon. Once finished, he stuffed a chunk of bread into his mouth and chewed, glaring at his useless legs. Dropping the empty bowl on the tray, he sank against the pillow and stared at the ceiling. He wanted to get out of this bed on his own two feet. He dozed until he heard her pick up the tray. Opening one eye, he found her back turned. She'd kept to her word. He kept his. The less they said to each other the easier this would be.

Tangle and Zeke filled the void left in her wake, offering their best snake-eyed glares. They were as sociable as ulcerated back teeth. Zeke bit off a plug of tobacco and said nothing. Tangle manipulated his lifeless legs like he was working a pump handle, also without a word. If he could reach his revolver, he might consider shooting holes in the ceiling just to get their attention. Least they could do is offer to get his pants on him and say howdy.

"All right. Spit it out before you either break my legs or freeze me into a chunk of ice."

Tangle snorted. "Got nothin' to say you'd want to hear. Except we're leavin' tomorrow."

Tangle left without saying more. Bryce tipped his head and pinched the bridge of his nose, knowing full well Zeke's eyes flayed him. "You got something to add? Or did you want to crack my head with the pitcher?"

"Yep. Thought did occur. No sense in breakin' a good pitcher. Gus said he'd see you off at the train. Got to get back to his place before the snow hits. Said he'd make sure he took care of that business in Virginia City when he could. Didn't ask what he meant."

That was some relief. The gold he'd stashed in a bank in Virginia City would see to taking care of his son and Hannah—if she needed it—and enough to see to his care over time. Sure didn't want to burden Lark. The thought of the years ahead filled him with a cold emptiness and he questioned whether he could live like that.

He looked up at the sound of a scraping chair. Zeke stood to leave but he paused at the door. Bryce found himself looking at the old man's hunched back. "Got little time for somebody as long-headed as a mule. Still. Hope somebody kicks sense into your head before that boy of yours sees your prickly side. Self-pity can ruin a man."

When the door slammed closed, he winced. His useless toes peeked from the blanket, mocking him. He willed them to move but there was nothing. *Nothing.*

TWENTY-SEVEN

HOME

November 1

H IS BEDROOM AT the ranch became a cross-trail of visitors...
at first. Sullen, he'd finally managed to drive away even cantankerous Zeke and sweet Lark, a feat he wasn't proud of.
Reyes was there often enough until he'd finally given up trying to find
anything to talk about. For a boy of twelve, Rey had found his niche
with the ranch hands and horses. On one hand, Bryce was relieved. On
the other, he was envious.

Thinking alone always circled him back to himself, finding he was
lousy company. Zeke had made it clear that he'd much rather be around a
castrated bull than a sick man feeling sorry for himself. Alonzo was given
the task of moving his numb legs... both without result or conversation.

Dan and Jude surprised him with a wooden wheeled chair. That was
the same day he sank into the bitter recluse he'd become. When they'd
carried him downstairs the first time and left him beside the front parlor window, his hand had itched to throw a vase across the room.

Watching the men ride out without him, he sat as useless as a four-
card flush. After a week of that, he insisted on staying to himself, in
seclusion. Even so, the sounds of horses and rolling wagons from outside his window, rattled his every nerve. Only at Cort's insistence did
he agree to be shaved.

Lark always held a bright smile for him, despite his contrariness. Cort stopped in to visit, sitting beside the bed while he ate breakfast, then again at night and over time, finding little to say. At first, they'd talked about buying more cattle. The beef prices. The antics at the bunkhouse. Reyes learning to rope. Until one day, he realized that sitting here wasn't the same as living. At least not for him. When he'd sunk to the bottom of despair, even Cort avoided him. Begging for a bottle of whiskey, he was outright refused.

Hannah visited less frequently when their arguments became more hostile. No matter how much he thwarted her, she returned—until their last confrontation. That was when she'd walked out four long days ago, slamming the door. Four days of torment, wondering what she was doing and if she were courted by someone else. After all, she was a pretty widow. Wasn't he the one who'd encouraged her to do just that? *Find someone else.*

"Hey, Pa?"

Bryce looked up from his chair to see Reyes's eyes peeking through the partly open door. He crooked a finger, inviting his son to come closer. Reyes kneeled beside him, and he ruffled the boy's hair. "Thought you were going to Miss Hannah's today?"

"Nah. Gotta go tomorrow. She told me that Mason had to finish connecting the new heat stove in her bedroom before the snow starts. Zeke said he can smell snow comin'. I never smelled it. Did you?"

Laughing, Bryce said, "Yep. When you smell that stuff, better take cover. It comes down hard in this country. Can get stuck for days." *Mason, huh? In her bedroom. That just tears it.*

"Well, Aunt Lark said she's got a sleigh from somebody who used to own this place. Just in case the birthing came sooner. They'd have to go get Miss Hannah to help."

"Seems like a good idea." He tried to think of something else to say, but his mind kept circling back to Hannah, alone in that house. With a bunch of randy cowhands willing to be at her beck and call.

Reyes scrambled to his feet and wrapped his arms around his neck. "Hope you get well soon. I miss you."

"Don't stay away. I like having your company."

As quick as the blink of a star, his boy was out the door. From the sound of it, his boots took the stairs two at a time, leaving him to stew over Mason. What in hell was he mad about? After all, Mason was a good man. He'd never hurt her. And he had two good legs.

Rolling his chair closer to the window casement, he spied his unsaddled buckskin standing slack-legged in the corral. Alonzo appeared and led Hunter into the barn as snowflakes fell in front of the glass. Winter... and his legs still had no feeling. Three months had passed since Montana, and he'd lost any shred of hope he'd walk again.

Reaching for the ranch ledger, he figured it couldn't hurt to look over the numbers. Columns of cattle counts and costs were becoming familiar. He marked places where he had questions. *Invalid.* This was all an invalid would be able to do. Slamming the ledger book closed, he smacked it against his knees and glared at his lifeless legs. Then it began. A tingling. After a time, needles pricked his legs in a thousand places, even into his feet.

Frozen, he counted off the seconds. Tossing the book to the bed, he scrubbed his hands across his thighs. Concentrating his attention, he ordered his legs to move. Nothing. With intense focus, he watched his socked feet. When his big toe waggled, he clenched his teeth and willed more.

Son of a bitch.

Nothing more. No matter how much he wished it. Sweat beaded his face and he swiped at it.

"Lord Almighty. You took a fever?" Theresa blurted from beside him.

Jolting at the sound of a woman's voice, he looked up to find Theresa holding a tray and wearing a scowl. His tongue was tied in a knot while he thought how to answer her. Since her head was cocked, he'd better come up with something.

"No. I...."

"Then what is it? I'll send for Cort. You look like you're sick."

"No. Don't. I'm not sick. I'd appreciate that coffee, though."

After she set the tray down, she poured the coffee and handed it to him, studying him like he was a bug, her eyes still raking over him. "Might be a big storm. Alonzo came in with milk and said the cows is startin' to give icicles."

He hoped his brief smile appeased her enough to send her on her way.

"You're scarin' me, Bryce. First you got the sweats and now smiling. I haven't seen you smile since, before."

"I'm fine. In fact, tell Cort I'll have supper with the rest tonight. If he doesn't mind helping me down the stairs."

"We was plannin' that anyhow."

"That so?"

"Why... don't you know December *one* is your birthday?"

With a look of disapproval, she left the room. Her chortle evolved into a howl of laughter in the hallway, but he wasn't amused. Instead, he was confounded about what had happened and a heap more confident. The wood chair creaked as he rested his head back. Jude and Dan built the invalid chair according to an ad from the Sanderson Mercantile. The idea of it unnerved him. But now this. He was afraid to hope.

While he sipped his coffee, spasms began again in his legs. Swallowing a shout of celebration, he set his cup aside and closed his eyes as the sensations eased and died.

"You all right?" His brother's deep voice caught him by surprise.

He opened his eyes and pulled himself up straighter in the chair. Cort hunkered beside him, watching him. No doubt, Theresa was behind this visit.

"Depends on what you mean by all right."

"Theresa said you looked sickly. Should I send for the doctor?"

"No. I'm fine. Do I look sickly?"

"As a matter of fact. *Maybe.* Hard to tell. Ready to go down for supper? Tangle and Mason are waiting."

"Sounds good." He rather enjoyed the bewildered expression on his brother's face. "You look surprised. Can't miss my own birthday."

"Huh. Well. Didn't expect you to be agreeable. Mason brought Hannah back for supper. She wanted you to have a gift."

Bryce followed the direction of his brother's pointed finger. Turning his head, his eyes settled on a painting, leaned against the wall. Squinting, he recognized a hillside where he stood beside his horse. It was the unfinished painting of his horse, now finished. Except that he was beside his horse, *standing.* He'd almost forgotten about ordering paints, brushes, and paper. He squeezed his eyes closed at the painful things he'd said in an effort to turn her away. *Dammit.* His life was empty without her in it. That was plain fact.

Giving thought to facing her at the table was agonizing to contemplate. "Maybe it would be best if I stayed here. We've had differences."

"It took a lot of convincing to get her here. Pretty sure she's given up hope you'll ever come to your senses. You lost more than just your legs. She loves you and I'm not even sure she should."

"Dammit, we've been over all this. I'm doing what's best for her."

"Big talk. From where I stand, you're feeling mighty sorry for yourself. No matter anyhow because Mason seems smitten."

Gnashing his teeth, his knuckles were white where he gripped the chair. Before he had time to protest, Cort wheeled him from the room but not before his right foot twitched. Without time to order his brother to turn the chair around, he was being carried down the stairs. At the bottom, he was greeted by his cheerful son.

"Pa. Wait till you see the cake Aunt Lark made. And Miss Hannah is staying for dinner. She brought me a book she found in one of her old boxes. She's sleeping in my room and I'm staying with Zeke."

"Hold up there, boy. Did she give you permission to address her as Miss Hannah?"

"Yep."

The truth was, his son was equally besotted with the woman he loved. Once in the dining room, Zeke took a seat beside Reyes. Cort slid the wheeled chair up to the table, directly across from Hannah. Lark sat to his right. But his attention centered on Mason's sappy grin as he leaned in, close to Hannah. There was no hope for it. He was damn jealous and angry. So far, she'd kept her eyes and attention on Mason, hardly sparing him a glance. Then her face flushed at something Mason whispered to her, setting his blood boiling.

"Happy birthday, Bryce," Cort said, slapping his back. "We've missed a lot of birthdays. Too bad Gus isn't here to celebrate."

"Yeah. Thanks to him and all the rest of you, I'm still breathing. I've been a lot of trouble. Hope you know I appreciate what you all did."

"Nonsense," Lark said. "Everybody has bad luck once in a while."

"Sure got that right," Zeke said.

Zeke's eyes shot him with a pointed look that would douse a candle flame. Bryce cleared his throat. The sooner he ate the sooner he could return to his solitude. Anywhere but here. He decided to buck up and face the challenges of the table. Dismissing his personal angst, he turned his attention to the food. "Roasted beef and potatoes. Smelled them all the way upstairs. Forgot about birthdays a long while back."

"Glad I didn't. Like to rub in the fact that you're older," Cort teased.

He grinned at Hannah's musical chortle while Theresa flitted around, refilling coffee cups. Nita entered the room with little Bryce in her arms prompting the passing of the baby from one to the other.

Family. What he'd always wanted. The thought returned him to his brooding melancholy, doing his best to avert his eyes away from Hannah, failing miserably. Little Bryce wound up on Cort's lap, his fingers stuffing pieces of bread into his slobbery mouth. Looking toward Reyes, he was reminded of the years he'd lost.

Sensing Hannah watching him, he held her gaze, allowing himself the pleasure of her winsome smile. When Mason's hand patted hers, drawing her attention away, he nearly bent the fork in half. If only he could pitch himself from this chair, he'd wipe that satisfied beam from Mason's face.

———————

THE HOUSE WAS quiet. Hannah would be leaving in the morning and he'd spent hours awake, flustered with his self-imposed exile. Within the glow of the lantern, he studied the painting. Besides being beautiful, she was enormously talented. Moreover, she had both endurance and a capacity for kindness. Why couldn't he let her go?

He knew the answer to that.

Staring at the ceiling, his arms folded beneath his head, he thought over and over again about that bullet. He'd survived a considerable beating only to be careless, taken down by a band of robbers. The painting mocked him. A man standing beside his horse.

Soft footsteps from the hallway caught his attention and when they paused outside his door, he held his breath and waited. At the soft tap, he cleared his throat. Somehow, he suspected she'd come to him, if for no other reason than to say good-bye.

"Come in," he called hoarsely.

The door opened then closed behind her. She stood in the shadows then padded toward him as moonlight turned her nightdress into a confection of silver. Her shawl wrapped her shoulders. When she stopped beside his bed, he slowly uncrossed his arms.

"Thank you for that painting, Hannah. I'll cherish it." Balling his fists against the bed, he hoped to keep from reaching for her. There was the chance he might not let her go if he touched her.

"You're welcome. I came to thank you for the paints, brushes, and paper. They are the finest I've ever seen. They must've cost you more than whatever your pay is."

On a raw throat, he choked back the words he wanted to say. That he'd give her the moon if he could. "You deserved all of that and more. The paintings exhibit your God-given talent. Glad you finished it."

Her fingers were laced together, pressed against her stomach. Her loose hair spilled over her shoulders, and he imagined running his hands through those silky tresses. Patting the space beside him, he invited her to sit. At her hesitation, he said "Please." Oh, God. What was he doing?

Lifting his palm, he knew he was doomed. She took his hand, and he closed his fingers around the warmth of it. She surrendered, stretching her legs beside his, she then nestled her head against his shoulder. Pleasure poured through him like warm honey while he pretended what it would be like with her.

When her face turned toward his, he cupped her face between his hands and lowered his mouth until it was inches from her lips, their breaths mingling. Her lips formed a soft smile of invitation. There was no resistance when his mouth slanted across hers, sipping her warmth then deepening the kiss.

At the sound of her soft whimper, his fingers trailed along the wild pulse in her neck. Nudging her lips apart, he coaxed her to sink with him, groaning with the pleasure. When he tried to move against her, his legs reminded him he was an invalid.

Abruptly, he tore his mouth from hers and dropped his hands away. Her shattered, withering expression shredded his heart as he dug his fingers into the bed. Righting herself, he saw the flash of anger in her eyes before she stood, her back to him.

"You have to decide, Bryce. I require a lifetime. A kiss here and a smile there aren't enough. We can't live like that. Secreting how we feel until we're both old. Fantasizing."

Dropping his head back, he frowned at the ceiling then sighed. "You deserve more than an invalid who can't attend his personals. Or make love."

"You've made that clear. I'm hurt that you think I'm so shallow that I'd only love you if you were perfect. The man I painted on canvas isn't the man in this room. I've made my decision to sell to Cort. After that, I plan to leave. That's something else I came to tell you."

His eyes turned, taking in the rigid profile of her face. The suddenness of this news was a punch to his gut. Even knowing there was an erratic sensation in his legs, he couldn't be sure it meant anything. He couldn't object. Not until his legs moved. If ever.

"If I could be your husband, I would. You've got to know that."

"You are an obstinate man. I'll still love you no matter where I go."

"I'll need to know where you decide to settle."

"No."

Heart pounding in his ears, he felt like he'd been gut punched again. What right did he have to ask it? He'd done what he'd set out to do— driven her away. When she scampered from the room, her hands were pressed to her face. In the wake of the closing door and dark stillness, he envisioned long, dismal days.

Restless sleep took him under. Then sometime in the fog of dreams, his mother's voice called him.

"Get up, Bryce. Soldiers are coming. You and Cort go and hide our cow as far in the woods as you can. Be quick. And take Nora with you."

Throwing his legs over the side of the bed, he wobbled unsteadily to his feet. Leaning sideways, he grasped the bedpost. Searching the darkness from the window, he shook his head to clear the cloudy realization that there were no soldiers. This wasn't his room. Shirtless and in cotton pants, he sure wasn't a boy. Painful spasms coursed his legs sending him hobbling to his chair. Dropping down hard, he rubbed his hands across his thighs, trying to ease the ache. He'd walked.

Christ. His legs had moved.

Stretching first one leg and then the other, he crossed his ankles. They responded. If he tried to stand again, would he fall and wake up the house? Sure as hell, he most likely didn't deserve this good luck but he'd take it just the same, praying to God it wasn't temporary.

He straight-armed from the chair and managed a few tentative, stiff-legged steps. Something told him to keep moving else he'd lose this gift. Unsteady, he managed one unbending leg in front of the other until he leaned against the casement, breathing hard from exertion. Light snow clung to the glass.

Tonight he'd keep pushing his legs. Then again tomorrow and whenever he could, until he'd walk straight to her and show her how much he loved her. If she would forgive him, he wouldn't ask for anything more. *Please don't sell out to my brother until... I can be a husband.*

TWENTY-EIGHT

WINTER SECRET

A S THE DAYS wore on, Bryce kept to himself, realizing small improvements. The tingling came and went while feeling returned by slow degrees. Keeping the secret became harder. Masking this miracle compiled his guilt over his deceit. With more certainty he'd walk, he'd finally decided it was time to reveal the secret. Lying awake each night, he wondered about Hannah. No one spoke of her.

He looked out from the office window and studied the frosted hills. Smoke rose from the bunkhouse chimney and a leaden sky promised more snow to come. Limping to his brother's big desk, he plunked down on the leather chair then glanced at the ledgers and maps spread out in front of him. Kneading his shoulder, he stared at the closed door. There was a soft knock, signaling the time for truth was here. He swallowed hard.

"Bryce? You all right?" Lark called. "Why is the door locked?"

"I'm fine, Lark. Can you tell Cort I need to see him?" He listened to her soft, rapid footfalls as they faded. Then he rose from the seat and unbolted the door, plunking onto the chair behind the desk, the map of Enders' holdings spread out before him.

Boots stomped inside of the front door followed by long strides. When the door swung open, he faced his brother's piercing eyes.

Wearing a sheepskin coat, high boots, and a deep frown beneath his winter beard, Bryce followed the direction of Cort's perusal of the empty wheeled chair.

Cort doffed his snow-dusted hat, dropping it to the floor, then he closed the distance between them. The hard stare and impassive twist at the corner of Cort's mouth signaled the secret was over. Lark and Theresa had taken up posts in the open doorway, each peeking around Cort's large frame.

"Had my suspicions for a while. What's going on? Explain how you got from that chair to this one. Don't lie and don't tell me you crawled," Cort said.

"Nope." To make his point, he pushed himself to standing. Cort backed a step... one brow raised and eyeing him. Bryce looked around his brother's frame to see Theresa's arm tucked around Lark's shoulders, both women wide-eyed, swiping their eyes.

"How long have you been hiding this?" Cort asked. "And why?"

"Not exactly hiding. I just wasn't sure the pains meant anything. Once I moved my legs, I wanted to be certain. The spasms came and went. I kept working them when no one was around. They're still plenty weak. Now I'm fairly certain I'm mending. Today I figured it was time to let you in on it."

"Christ!" Cort shouted. "I'm not sure whether to smash your nose or lift you in a bear hug. Damn." Cort swiped his eyes with his sleeve.

"Neither... I hope. A handshake will do. A hug from the ladies."

Cort started around the desk only to have Lark shove her husband out of her way. Rounding the desk, she cried out, "Hallelujah!" When she launched herself at his midsection, he nearly toppled over the chair. She snugged him against her rounded belly while he watched his brother, still with a look of shock, his boots nailed to the floor.

"Lordy. Thank you, Jesus," Theresa murmured. Then she dashed from the room, crying like a branding iron landed on her foot.

Once they'd settled at the table, the men sipped whiskey and the women with tea, each taking turns with questions. By the time things calmed, he circled back to his particular inquiries.

"Cort. Have you signed the papers with Hannah yet?"

"They're being drawn up with Marcus Layton. No telling when I'll get there to pick them up. This why you had the map out?"

"Yep. I'm asking you to hold off. Just one more thing. I'd like to buy another three thousand acres off you. Gus is bringing my account from Virginia City come spring. Figure you wouldn't mind having a neighboring rancher. Thinking we could run our herds together, if you'd like... that is, if you can trust me for the money. I can give you a down payment then the rest over time, with interest. I can stretch it out with a bank loan."

His brother scratched his beard. Bryce figured what Cort's next question would be. "You planning to take a wife along with that run-down ranch of hers?"

"If she'll still have me."

"Maybe she's already moved on."

His gut clenched. Was he too late? "Where'd she go?"

Lark sighed. "Cort. You're torturing the man. She's still at her ranch, Bryce. But it's my opinion that you have a lot of backtracking to do."

"Soon as I mount a horse, I plan to do just that. If she were here, she would've been the first I told."

"Better make it quick, if you intend to make her a bride because I'm sending Billy for the preacher. Happen to know he's at the Evanston farm. Stopped by here yesterday," Lark said.

"That's my plan. First thing I'm doing is *walking* to the barn to have a talk with my son. He's usually hanging around there. Zeke and all the rest will know soon enough. After my son, I'm heading for Rocky Creek." On stiff legs, he rose from his chair.

"You sure you're able to sit a horse?" Cort asked.

"My future depends on it. I have something to prove... to both of us."

THERE WAS A quiet wariness between Mason and him. Bryce figured he'd be first to apologize to the man who leaned against one of the stalls.

He cleared his throat. "Thanks for saddling my horse. Also, I owe you a debt for helping out around here and at Hannah's place. You've been a better friend than I deserve."

"Figured I never had a chance with her. Hope you don't hold it against me for trying."

Without a word, Bryce extended his hand. Without hesitation, Mason gripped it. "I still have to find out if she can forgive me. I haven't been easy to get along with."

"Don't know if the rest of us could've handled your situation any better. Just glad it turned out."

"Me, too."

"Sure you're up to riding?"

"That's something I'm about to find out."

"Got a sleigh ready. We fixed it up in case we had to retrieve Hannah for the new babe. Snow coming."

"Hunter can handle this weather. Besides, I need to find out if I can ride again."

Slipping his boot into the stirrup, he gave a hop with his right leg but failed to swing his weak leg over the saddle. Gritting his teeth, he tried again, this time seating himself. Tucking his collar beneath his chin, he tugged his fur hat over his ears then slipped his hands into heavy buckskin gloves.

Once he left the barn, a light, blowing snow clung to his face. All he'd packed were his apologies, though he wasn't above begging.

THE AFTERNOON GREW late. Shivering, she looked skyward from inside the open barn door. Offering her cow and horse a withering look, she tied her wool scarf beneath her chin and snugged her neck beneath the wool collar of her coat. She slid the barn door closed then trudged to the kitchen door, looking forward to warming beside her Sterling stove. Soon enough this place would belong to Cort, the two thousand acres and lock, stock, and barrel.

Her nose and lips numb, she stepped into the warm kitchen. Sniffling, she shrugged from her coat, gloves, and scarf, dropping them in a heap beside the stove. She rubbed her hands together over the heat then sat on the bench, tugging her frozen feet from her boots.

Just as she gave thought to heating some food, there was a thud at the front of the house. She lurched to her feet and reached for her rifle. Standing to one side of the front door, she called out. "Anybody out there?" When no one answered, she turned away, only to be brought up short by a deep, familiar voice.

"Open up, Hannah. I'm frozen to the bone. It's me. Bryce."

Her heart stopped. How could it be him? It had to be a trick. Still gripping the rifle in one hand, she slid the bolt and stepped back, the memory of Luis still vivid.

"It's unbolted. Open the door. I'll have a loaded gun pointed at your belly if you're not who you say."

The door swung wide, and a tall man filled her vision. Wearing a snow-dusted sheepskin coat and fur hat, his scruffy beard looked shot through with beads of ice. One corner of his full mouth lifted at her perusal. Did he notice she held her breath at the sight of him?

He grinned. "May I come in? Have to admit, never thought I'd face down your gun again."

Stunned, she couldn't find a word that would make sense. Instead, she nodded while he turned then closed the door. Those gray-blue eyes couldn't be mistaken. His eyes roamed from her head to her socks. Blinking, her vision settled on his legs and lodged there.

"You planning to use that rifle?" he quipped.

"Bryce?"

"You can close your mouth. Yes. Bryce. Without the wheeled chair."

She snapped her mouth shut. "How long have you...?"

Forgetting she still held her rifle, he took it from her hand then set it against the wall. Yanking free of his gloves, he tugged his hat from his head, hanging it on the hook while she stood in bewilderment. "You're walking. I think I'm going to faint. Maybe I already have."

With her eyes still skimming his legs, he took hold of her arms. She hardly remembered him guiding her to the bench by the stove. Still in disbelief, she followed his motion as he tossed his coat and gloves to the floor beside hers. Squeezing her eyes closed, she slowly opened them, thinking he could be a phantom. Then he crouched before her, a boyish grin on his mouth. Her trembling fingers brushed his snow-encrusted stubble. *So cold.*

Yet he was *real.*

She pressed a hand to her heart. "I can't believe you're here. I can hardly draw a breath."

"I'm here. All I want to do is fill my eyes with you. You kept to your promise to stay away, and I was damned miserable."

"It's what you said you wanted."

He sighed then stood. Unbuckling his gun belt, he draped it over a chair. There was a prominent limp as he walked to the stove to warm his hands. Even in the dim light, she hadn't missed the thinness of his face.

He looked over his shoulder with a faint smile. "I can always tell when you're about to hurl questions at me by that little twitch in your lip."

"The obvious question first. How long have you walked? Four weeks ago you were still in that...." She lowered her face at the reference to the invalid chair.

"Invalid chair. I won't bite if you say it. Still, I'd rather forget the months I spent in it."

"When did you know?"

Turning, he stood before her, arms crossed. "Prickling in my legs started after the last we saw each other. Just didn't know what it meant and didn't want to get anyone's hopes up, least of all, mine. Over the weeks that followed, I could hardly keep the secret. I practiced standing. Then a few stumbling steps. Then more. This morning, I came to the decision it was time to tell Cort and the others."

He cleared his throat. "You should've been first. I needed to be the one to tell you, as fast as I could get to you. I'm limping, but it's a helluva lot better than the other."

"So now you've come to explain this. In a snowstorm." She kept her expression stony while inside, she bubbled with joy.

"That's about it."

His upsetting declaration still ran deep. As did her love for him. Wouldn't hurt to let him squirm.

"I've come to tell you I'm sorry for being prickly and hardheaded. You didn't deserve any of it. I'll do anything to make things right between us if you're willing to give me the chance. What I'm not willing to do is watch you leave me without a fight."

Piteous, pleading eyes held hers in the lamplight. "I'm more than happy you can walk. But you still have to do better explaining why you're here, beside asking forgiveness. You risked a lot in this weather. You've acted like a mule's hind end. While I can get beyond those things, I need you to say what's important."

"Huh. Didn't expect you to make this easy. In case you forgot... I love you. Never, not for one minute, did I ever stop loving you. Even when a bullet sucked out my life. Even when I faced off with Lars and took his punches. Know that I'd do it again to have you."

She'd heard all she needed. Stumbling to her feet, she ran into his open arms where he wrapped her against him. His heartbeat throbbed against her cheek. "I love you, Bryce Enders. No other man would've sacrificed so much and gotten so little. I've been stubborn—and worse—I didn't think how much my principles would cost. Seeing you fight for your life... please forgive me."

"Look at me."

Tilting her face up, his mouth took hers in a breathtaking kiss while brushing her hands over the slightest bit of stubble. Against her lips, he whispered, "Marry me."

He raised his head while his hands held her face between his palms. "Well?"

"In case you didn't know, it has always been yes."

When he lifted her hand to his mouth, his featherlight kiss reached to her soul. Touching the faded yellow bruises, she thanked God for this miracle of a man.

"Your bed looks mighty inviting. We never finished what we started. No one between us now."

It was a heady feeling to think of herself as free from the burden of Lars Van Stadt and she needed Bryce Enders.

"If you'd rather wait…." he said. "Got it on good authority that Preacher Jeffers is on his way to the Double E. Should be there in a few days, lookin' for a wedding."

"The weather isn't in our favor, but I think I can make an exception," she teased.

"Then it's settled. Did I ever tell you I love it when you blush?" Before she thought of a response, he lifted her into his arms as she looped her arms around his neck. Even with an unsteady gait, he carried her into the bedroom, murmuring love words into her ear.

HE HUNKERED BEFORE her, drowning in her teasing grin where she sat against the edge of the bed. Plucking the buttons of her shirt, one by one, she slipped the garment from her arms then dropped it to the floor. Swallowing at the sight of her lacy camisole, he tugged the bow loose, drifting his fingers across her creamy skin, his heart pounding in his ears.

"Very pretty."

"Glad you approve," she teased.

There was a slumberous, sexy look in her eyes that stretched every nerve in his body. Hell, he more than approved. But point in fact, he was damned anxious to get her out of all these clothes. Turning his attention to her boy britches, she must have read his conundrum. Standing before him, she slid her legs from her pants, dropping them to the floor. When she reclined against the bed, he tugged her socks from her cold feet, then rubbed her soles between his hands while watching her eyes turn sleepy with pleasure. When he joined her on the bed, he studied her contentment, her eyes closed while his fingers brushed her skin and drawing out a moan of gratification. Every effort would be to erase bitter memories of Lars.

His attention turned to her frilly drawers. Eyebrow raised, he hesitated. When her musical laughter brought his attention back to her, he lifted a brow in question.

"Bryce. I won't break like glass," she said with soft whisper.

"Haven't had much practice with lacy things," he added. Pulling the ribbons loose, she stayed his hand, slipping from them, leaving him to gape. He wrenched his gaze to her sweet smile. Facing each other, his eyes were held hostage at the sight of her pure beauty. There was something to be said for savoring a moment, but this moment had been too long in coming. He was no longer a patient man.

Leaving her, he yanked free of his boots, then shucked from the rest. He turned his all-consuming eyes to hers, wanting her with every ragged breath he took. Her eyes watched him with a trace of wariness he aimed to remove in short order.

Easing alongside of her, he took her face between his hands and tasted her rosebud lips with gentle reverence. Deepening the kiss, she sighed, while her hand outlined his jaw. Sensing her relax, he settled beside her, breathing in her scent, planting delicate kisses to her chin and corners of her mouth. Cupping her face, he held her watchful gaze, silently cursing Lars for the son of a bitch he'd been.

Taking her curled fingers in his hand, he lifted them to his mouth, kissing each finger in turn. Shifting his body, he skimmed his fingers along her neck. When his hand traced her hip, her body tensed and her eyes squeezed closed.

"Look at me, Hannah. I am not him. He's gone. I'm here. The man who loves you with every ounce of my being. Let me prove it to you."

He waited. She didn't move. Her hands were fists between them. Sighing, he reached for her, settling her head against his shoulder, stroking the soft, damp skin of her arm, sensing her quiet dread. His heart pounded but he stilled. After a while, she nuzzled him. His eyes met girlish innocence. He needed her like he needed air to breathe. Minutes ticked by. He waited. And he'd wait forever or as long as it took. She lifted his hand to her mouth, her warm breath against his palm.

"Hannah. It's me. Bryce. The man who loves you."

"Can't you hear my heart?" she whispered.

With those words, they drowned in lover's rapture, only to resurface as one, with wordless promise to never lose each other again. Her flirtatious hands skimmed his stomach while he reflexively tautened beneath her touch. He studied her lazy perusal as she stretched beside him like a satisfied cat, drugging him with languid contentment. He'd won her trust, something he didn't take lightly.

Lifting, he slanted his mouth against hers, whispering love words against her mouth. They shared one kiss then another until fevered, they danced to the soundless music only lovers knew. Contented, they settled into serene sleep.

Without knowing how long they'd slept, Bryce awoke at the touch of her fingers feathering his chest. He turned his head to gaze at this woman beside him, her mouth well-loved and her eyes soft.

"Thank you for being you," he said.

"Mmm."

"Say my name."

"Bryce Enders. The man I love and trust."

He leaned in and pecked her nose with a kiss.

"Bryce," she murmured.

"Hmm." Her hair lay across his shoulder and he nuzzled her ear. "I'm an ordinary man in love with an extraordinary woman."

"You, sir, kept your promise."

"There will be many. Each better than the last."

"I think I have a lot to learn."

"When do you want to start?"

"Now."

"Why, madam. Are you seducing me?" Bryce teased.

"Maybe."

WAKING SUDDENLY WITH her damp body curled against his, he gave into the pleasure of listening to her soft breathing. At some point, he must have mounded a quilt around them. When he moved his legs, her foot stroked sensually along his calf, reminding him again at how fortunate he was. The simple act of moving his legs was something he'd never take for granted for the rest of his days. She turned, grinning up at him, her eyes flitting across his face.

"Now what's so amusing?" he grumbled. "For a minute, I thought you were sound asleep."

"Your whiskers tickled."

"Ahh. Something I'll tend to before we say our vows. As much as I'd like to stay here like this, do I need to remind you of a wedding?"

She jackknifed and looked toward the window before snatching the edge of the quilt to cover her body. Amused at her discomfiture, he couldn't help but chuckle when she pressed a hand against her mouth.

"Bryce. There's nothing funny about *this*. Why didn't you wake me sooner? I have to make some breakfast before we leave. What time is it? What will they think of us?"

He wanted to laugh again at her discomposure but thought better of it. "Hannah, I'm pretty sure they have a good idea what's what. Too late to worry about it, in any event. Of course, the women won't speak of it. At least not where most will hear. The men will keep it to themselves if they know what's good for them."

"What will we say?"

"Nothing. Except our vows."

With a quick kiss, he rolled from the bed, sensing her eyes drilling into his back, wishing she'd climb out from those covers before he finished dressing because he surely wouldn't mind the view. Pouring water into the basin, he washed, then pulled on his union suit and trousers. Looking over his shoulder, she still sat on the edge of the bed, quilt pulled to her neck. Those puffy pink lips were pursed. He picked up his shirt, wanting the wedding ceremony over with.

"Best heat some water to wash. Then get your valise packed with whatever froufrou you'll need for our wedding. I'll see to the horses then be back to help with the vittles."

"What will I do about my animals?"

Bryce had just finished shrugging into his clothes and turned to face her. "I'll send someone for them once the weather allows. In the mean-time, I'll see they're fed enough to keep them for a day or two." The window was frosted. A glance outside told him they'd never manage a wagon. They'd have to ride the saddle horses.

He shoved a chunk of wood into the new heater, then looked up to find her dragging the quilt from the bed. Bending, she grasped her pants from the floor and scurried to the basin. He poked his tongue into the pocket of his cheek, thinking he wasn't sure he'd get used to her in pants. But he wouldn't mind getting them off her.

TWENTY-NINE

WINTER VOWS

WEARING HEAVY COATS, gloves, hats, and anything else they could put together, they rode side by side through the half foot of snow. After finding a place to safely cross their mounts, he made a silent promise to build their house on the other side of Rocky Creek.

With a sidelong glance, his pink-nosed angel looked out from her woolen scarf. Her gloved hands gripped the reins, but she looked frozen to the saddle. He gave thought to turning back.

"Let's stop and I'll lead your horse. You ride with me."

She nudged her horse closer beside his. "I'll be all right. How much farther? I don't recognize anything."

Just like her not to admit to hardships. She was as independent a woman as he'd ever known. "We have the wagon road beneath us. We should be warming by a fire in another thirty minutes."

He couldn't know for sure whether those narrowed eyes meant she was worried or relieved. Just as he made the decision to plunk her in front of him for warmth, despite her stubborn refusal, the sound of bells caught his attention. Her head tilted in question. Raising his hand to signal silence, he squinted against the gleaming white landscape. A sleigh appeared, looking like a ship plowing a stormy sea. Bundled in wool and fur, his brother slapped the reins, sending the conveyance near enough to spook their horses into sidestepping. Jude followed close behind the sleigh.

"Bryce. I can't believe what I'm seeing," Hannah called.

Neither could he. Hannah appeared mesmerized by this horse-drawn contraption, her eyes wide where they peeked above the scarf.

"Jesus. The Harris sleigh," Bryce muttered under his breath.

Cort lowered his scarf from his face. "What the hell are you two doing out here? Got everybody worried."

"I might ask the same about you. Told you I'd bring her back."

"That so. Well, Lark insisted I find out what was keeping you. I kept my opinion to myself."

"Did you think we planned to miss our wedding?"

"On that point, best we discuss it later. Jude can lead your horses back. Get in and warm up with the blankets. And hang on to the seat. I'm in a hurry to get out of this cold."

Dismounting, he helped Hannah onto the seat, then dropped her two valises to the floor at her boots. Once he'd taken the seat beside her, he snugged the blanket around them and Cort turned the horse, sending the sleigh home. Hannah leaned against his side. One thing was for sure. She was his now and he was a happy man. No words from any preacher would change that.

———————

THE DINING ROOM glowed beneath the chandelier. The cowhands, wearing their best duds, helped themselves to the dried beef sandwiches, relish, and potatoes. Of course, the large Harris punch bowl was at the center of the side table where most of the men had congregated. He heard Theresa fussing with the men who'd been caught spilling more than a few drops of whiskey into their cups.

From the smell of the punch, Bryce guessed the bowl was thoroughly spiked, and from the look of Zeke's shifting eyes, he was most likely the culprit. They exchanged jovial winks, both joined in the conspiracy. Lost in thought, he didn't sense his brother behind him until the slap on his back nearly sent his drink into the cake.

"So. You're about to be a married man, brother. How does it feel?"

Zeke joined them and Bryce looked from one to the other. "I'm not bolting, if that's what you're driving at."

"Didn't think so. Of course, then you'd be a fool and I'd have to disown you," Cort said in his deadpan manner.

"Huh. Think you'll find I'm no fool. At least not today. Looks like the men are enjoying the food. Hope they leave something."

"You got the jitters," Zeke mumbled. "Eatin' before you say the vows might not be a good idea. You look a little peaked."

Saluting Zeke with his cup, Bryce replied, "This punch is helping."

"Zeke never has a wedding without his special brew. Theresa gave up keeping an eye on him. Lark is too busy upstairs with Hannah to care," Cort retorted.

Tugging at his stiff shirt collar, he looked toward the stairs. He sipped the punch, shifted from one foot to the other, and hoped the stuff would help relieve his shakes. "What's takin' so long? The preacher is pacing like a caged wildcat and my son has asked me at least twenty times when he can have cake. When I tell him no, he goes up those stairs. Figure he's getting a more satisfactory answer."

"I'll go check on that boy," Zeke said. "Maybe the rest of the boys, too. Some with beards."

Zeke made his way into the kitchen leaving Bryce and Cort, both men quiet. Bryce darted a glance at his brother and found a raised eyebrow.

"You're not making it easy on me. I'm just not used to standing around doing nothing. Don't make too much of it. Nervous enough, as it is."

"Big brother, you're about as nervous as a drunk in church. Women, no matter how tough they are, can't give up a pure feminine side. Looking pretty on the wedding day is a ritual you'll just have to accept if you want a warm bed tonight. Silks and satins will be swishing down the steps any minute. Seems your legs are still holding you up. Counting that as something to celebrate."

The preacher stepped from the parlor as if on cue, and thumping his cane, he brought the chatter to a halt. Expectant gazes fell to the man with the Bible. At the same time, a firm palm pressed him forward on his stiff legs. Suddenly she was there, taking his breath away as she descended the stairs.

It was a shimmery blue silk or satin but it made no difference. She was the most exquisite woman he'd ever laid eyes on. Her gold-brown hair was pinned back, and a cascade of long curls rested across one shoulder. He was already planning out how long it would take him to loosen those tresses. Standing beside him, her eyes looked up into his. He winked. Glorious blue eyes swallowed him with a hint of merriment. Her blush was endearing.

Rey moved closer beside him to one side. He looked down at his son, favoring him with a wink and squeeze of the shoulder. His attention was drawn back to the preacher as the man cleared his throat. In a booming voice, Micah Jeffers announced the names of the intended. A few chuckles and one loud guffaw were squelched at the preacher's blazing glare, which now turned to him.

"Bryce Cairn Enders and Hannah May Wells van Stadt are about to enter into sacred matrimony. For those still wearing your hats, please remove them."

Bryce was tempted to look over his shoulder, but a hand knuckled his back. He turned his head to look at his bride's profile. Her lips twitched. He offered his hand, and she slipped her fingers between his. Verses from the Bible droned and he lost himself in the feel of her small, quaking hand while words were just words. Someone poked his shoulder and he looked up. A clearing of a throat prompted him to say "I will" with the hope he hadn't misspoke.

Hannah's soft pronouncement of the same promise was accompanied by an assuring squeeze of her fingers with his. Slipping a ring onto her finger at the preacher's prodding brought a round of cheers, abruptly ended with the preacher's stern frown. The Micah Jeffers hard-as-nails stare stayed on him as he said, "It is my honor to pronounce you husband and wife…. and you may now kiss your bride Mister Enders."

No prods nor clearing of throats were necessary. He took her mouth in a prolonged kiss while the room erupted in hoots. When there was a tug on his borrowed dress jacket, he reluctantly broke the kiss to find Rey looking up with a serious expression on his face.

"Pa, it's time to eat."

"Don't you have something to say to Miss Hannah?"

"Yeah. Congratulations. Glad you married my father. Should I call you Ma from now on? Even if you're my teacher?"

Most of the guests had begun to file back into the dining room and kitchen to pick up the celebration, leaving him wondering how she would respond to Rey's question.

Hannah smiled and cupped both of Rey's cheeks between her palms. "That would make me happy. And yes. Even a teacher can be a mother. At least in this case."

Zeke grasped the boy's arm, mumbled quick congratulations, and headed the boy toward the kitchen. The preacher took Rey's place and offered his hearty felicitations before following the others from the parlor. Alone and facing each other, he said, "You're glowing. Not to mention beautiful."

"Thank you. I've married a most handsome man."

"Handsome. Huh. Now that I've shaved, guess I'm passable. Seems the bruises have almost healed. Cort took scissors to my hair while you were primping."

"Shall we circulate with our guests?" she asked.

He tugged his collar. "Rather we get up to that bedroom."

"Shh. Someone might hear. I'm already ashamed that everyone probably guesses we spent the night together."

"Honey. If you think for one minute any of them wouldn't do the same, you better think again. Now. If you insist, let's face those guests. No place we can hide."

He offered his arm and waited. She looped her arm with his.

"From now on, we face things together," she whispered.

———————

THE PULSE IN his neck threatened to break a blood vessel while he waited outside of their bedroom door. Shrugging, he figured he'd given her enough time to primp. Dim lamplight met him when he stepped inside. Darting his eyes toward the bed, he found her sitting cross-legged, her hair spilling in waves across her shoulders. A book sat in the cradle of her lap and her white nightdress revealed peeks of her skin. Setting the book on the night table, she grinned while he stood rooted to the floor. He hoped she didn't notice how nervous he was.

"I've been waiting."

He limped to the bed and lifted her hand in his. "Imagine that? I've been waiting for the last of our guests to leave. Cort, Tangle, Mason, and Alonzo required several toasts of bourbon. I gave thought to telling them to leave. That wouldn't have moved Cort any faster. Besides, it's his house."

She squinted. "Are you drunk?"

"Do I seem drunk?"

"Not sure. I guess not."

Still, she wrinkled her nose when he drew closer to her. He guessed that drinking spirits might always trigger thoughts of Lars. Determined to obliterate that past, he pressed a longing kiss against her mouth and felt her smile against his lips.

"Peppermint."

"Yep. Cort had a stock of them. The past is gone, Hannah. Didn't we agree?"

"Mostly. Yes."

"Good."

"Is Reyes with Zeke?" she asked.

"Sure is. That old man has been claimed as a grandfather. Most likely, he'll have our son playing poker before long."

"He means well."

"I know." He sat on the edge of the bed. Once he yanked his boots free, he looked over his shoulder. She watched him. He had to admit he enjoyed her watching while he divested himself of his clothes, one slow piece at a time.

"You won't be needing that frilly nightdress, Missus *Enders.*"

Grinning, she said, *"Hannah May Enders.* I like saying the name."

"And I've wanted to hear it. The name suits you."

Easing closer beside her, he tugged the gown from her shoulders and pressed a kiss against her neck, her chin, and then her cheek. Folding her into his open arms, he applied kisses to her eyes and lips while her fingers splayed against his bared chest. Her touches elicited shudders that rippled through him. Every muscle tensed when her fingers traced circles across his stomach. When her fingers spread across the rough scars along his shoulder, he clenched his teeth. Her hand stilled.

"Don't stop, Hannah. They don't hurt anymore."

"I'll never forget your sacrifice."

"I'll never forget how brave a woman I'm married to."

His fingers threaded in her hair while he drowned in her glittering, trusting eyes. Breathless, they fell into a haze of loving devotion. And then, sometime later, they awoke within each other's arms.

"I love you, Bryce. Have I told you?"

"Yes. Still, I like hearing it."

Holding her tucked against him, he silently promised that he'd make her happy with every ounce of his strength and with every moment he drew breath.

She turned in his arms and sighed. "I still can't help but worry about what our guests will remember. Alone and not married."

Sated and thinking of loving her again, he dropped onto his back and rolled his eyes. With a sidelong glance, he said, "They thought nothing. Now. Give me a few minutes to plan my next advance and I'll make you forget your confounded worries."

EPILOGUE

March, 1879

CORT WALKED INTO his office and came up short at the sight of his brother standing in front of the tall window, deep in thought, staring out toward the hills. A place where he, himself, often stood. Not believing and even questioning his remarkable luck and incredible past, he was grateful to have survived. He understood he'd interrupted his brother's private thoughts and was well aware of Bryce's aspirations.

"Never loses its beauty. Not even in winter," Cort remarked.

He caught sight of the corner table where maps had been spread. Now he knew for sure what his brother had on his mind. They'd talked about plans for the future. No mistaking there would be problems and rewards.

Bryce turned and crossed his arms and true to his fashion, got right to the point. "I want to build a house on this side of the Blue River and Rocky Creek. On that knoll we talked about."

Cort dropped onto his desk chair and slapped his hat down. He'd known for a while the matter of ranching together was coming up. When his brother hadn't moved, he pointed to a chair. "Have a seat. No time like now to talk."

While he waited for Bryce to sit, he picked up a document from his desk and skimmed the lawyer's words he'd already discussed with Lark. A legal document that would sell three thousand acres of his expansive land to his brother. The decision weighed heavy. Together, the Enders would have the largest ranch in Nebraska and retain generational water rights for years to come. As long as beef prices and weather were in their favor, they'd do well.

Or they'd all fail.

"Well?" Bryce urged. "Have you decided?"

"Is the price agreeable? I've been fortunate and we can't see why family shouldn't have the same chance. It'll take you a while to pay it off, all the same."

"No favors. I'll get it paid. If you're willing to wait for Gus to get back here with gold and cash from Virginia City, I can give you half now. The rest over time and cattle sales. Need to hold back enough to build my herd and a house. Not to mention hire on."

"Stretching yourselves a bit thin."

"We'll make it."

"I won't take no for an answer about the house, Bryce. Our wedding present is help with building it. And materials. We can afford it and the boys want to use their spare time to help with labor. Should be up by June. Before cattle roundup and arrival of the herd from Oklahoma."

"I sure won't turn it down. Hannah deserves a house. Plan to burn down the other place."

"I'll help you. Be a pleasure. Well, guess we've got a deal."

Cort shook his brother's proffered hand, sealing the agreement with a firm handshake. "Before I break out my best bourbon, I'm curious about what you were thinking as you looked out there."

"How I won't ever take my legs for granted. Pacing out the new house. Mounting my horse. Dancing with my wife. Trailing beside my son after he ropes his first steer and working a place that's mine. Christ, I could've lost it all."

"But you didn't. I know exactly how you feel. Had the same appreciation for my sight after losing it. Seems we had a lot to learn, didn't we?

Luck played a big part for both of us. Now Lark is about to give birth. Can't wait to see our new baby. Girl or boy. I don't care."

At Bryce's lopsided grin, he guessed what his brother was about to disclose. "About that. Seems like the Enders clan is getting even bigger."

"Huh. That so? Not surprised with the way you two look at each other. Congratulations."

"Said it might happen in late August or early September. I missed Rey's birth. I'm never going to get over that. Somehow he turned out all right, despite losing his mother and having to live with Luis. All thanks to you and Lark, Zeke, and Hannah. My son, Rey, was there when I needed him the most."

"You turned out to be a good father. This massive ranch will outlive us, Bryce. Just like Sienna and Wade wanted from the start. Seems like they got their wish."

"Guess so. For right now, how 'bout I show you again where we're building? Then we'll come back and have that drink to celebrate."

Clomping of boots echoed in the hall when they left by the main door.

After it slammed behind them, neither Cort nor Bryce were there to witness the soft flutter of maps against the table of the empty office.

SUSANNA LANE lives with her husband in rural northern Georgia, having lived most of her life in southern New Jersey. Together, they have two successful sons and daughters-in-law, as well as four adorable grandchildren, the gems of her life. Besides reading and writing, Susanna loves to travel the backroads of the Old West, and at one time, on horseback in the Rockies. Awestruck by the mountains at her first sighting, she finds nothing more intriguing than exploring and envisioning the pioneer experience and uncovering their stories. Retired from teaching, Susanna has the time now to write and walk beside her characters, figuring out what they'd say and how they'd say it. The underpinnings of her writing are both characterization and the alluring history of the Old West. She's a proud member of both Women Writing the West and Western Writers of America, having had the fortune to be awarded both the WWA Spur and the Will Rogers Silver Medallion in 2022 for her first novel, *Imperfect Promise.*